Readers love Amy Lane

Chase in Shadow

"…a beautifully moving story of forgiveness, acceptance and love."

—Smexy Books Romance Reviews

Gambling Men

"…a great friends-to-lovers story about changing up the rules and reinventing the game midstream."

—The Novel Approach

Super Sock Man

"This is a sweet confection of a story, filled with lovely characters happily finding their way to love."

—Joyfully Jay

The Talker Collection

"The growth of these two characters is wonderful to behold and when we see that final chapter between these beloved characters…well, let's just say tears were flowing and a smile was on my face."

—Love Romances and More

Living Promises

"Ms. Lane is not a pleasant afternoon curl-up read. She grabs her readers and never lets them go. Her writing is definitely in your face. *Living Promises* is painful and beautiful and so real."

—Black Raven's Reviews

By Amy Lane

Novels
Chase in Shadow
Clear Water
Dex in Blue
Gambling Men: The Novel
The Locker Room
Mourning Heaven
Sidecar
A Solid Core of Alpha
The Talker Collection (anthology)
Three Fates (anthology)

The Keeping Promise Rock Series
Keeping Promise Rock • Making Promises • Living Promises

Novellas
Bewitched by Bella's Brother
Christmas with Danny Fit
Hammer and Air
If I Must
It's Not Shakespeare
Puppy, Car, and Snow
Super Sock Man
Truth in the Dark
The Winter Courtship Rituals of Fur-Bearing Critters

Green's Hill
Guarding the Vampire's Ghost • I Love You, Asshole! • Litha's Constant Whim

Talker Series
Talker • Talker's Redemption • Talker's Graduation

Published by Dreamspinner Press
http://www.dreamspinnerpress.com

DEX IN BLUE

AMY LANE

Published by
Dreamspinner Press
5032 Capital Circle SW
Ste 2, PMB# 279
Tallahassee, FL 32305-7886
USA
http://www.dreamspinnerpress.com/

Cover Art by Reese Dante
http://www.reesedante.com

ISBN: 978-1-62380-010-9

Printed in the United States of America
First Edition
October 2012

eBook edition available
eBook ISBN: 978-1-62380-011-6

This is for Mate, as always, because all young men face a stalling point where they could remain young men forever, and the really good ones choose to step up and become really awesome adults. Mate, I've always been "tangled up in you."

This is also for Mary, because she loves it with so very much of her formidable, generous soul. Dex and Kane have become our touchstones, and we often think in their dialogue as much as we think in our own thoughts. Mary, you have been such a wonderful friend these past years—it makes me so proud to know I can give you Dex and Kane and you will love them and love them and hold them and call them George. They live to be adored by you.

ALL PATHS LEAD TO JOHNNIES

(David) Dex

"IT WAS okay, right?"

David Worral had to laugh. He'd never seen Dex Williams look so uncertain. They were driving down an empty stretch of Highway 87, right outside of Forsyth, Montana. They were in Dex's dad's old Chevy pickup truck, a big old beater, which they'd nicknamed "Shrek" because it had been beat to shit in its long life and had the green primer spots to prove it. The thing was too old for air-conditioning, so they had the windows rolled down and were talking over the wind as Dex drove seventy miles an hour down the straightaway.

"Yeah," David said, smiling shyly. "It was fine." He had to grimace for a moment. "Unexpected," he admitted, adjusting himself more comfortably, "but fine." His cock had begun to swell just from talking about it. Maybe fine was an understatement.

He fiddled with the ring on his finger—a plain titanium class ring that looked just like the one he'd gotten right after high school. But that ring was on Dex's finger now, and this one? This one said Dex Williams on the inside of it. It was secret, right? And just thinking about that secret made him uncomfortable again, so he struggled with the seat belt to make room for his hips and wiggled again. The seat belts were a late addition to the bench seat in the big truck, and they'd mostly been added because Dex's dad had been busted on the interstate for driving without them. Dex didn't see the point in them either, but then, Dex had always been the risk taker.

He'd certainly been the risk taker today. It was thirty miles to Forsyth from David's farm, which was, in turn, ten miles from Dex's. The boys had ridden a bus to school, and all during school, they'd sat next to each other for twelve years on account of their names being so close. But today… today had been different.

There was a rest stop between David's farm and Forsyth, stocked with sodas and chips and set back in some shade trees, which were watered by an open irrigation ditch that ran behind the stop. They'd stopped there on the way back from picking up supplies for Dex's mom in Forsyth, taken a whizz, bought some more chips, and tried really hard to avoid the fact that David was slated to go off to Montana State in September, and Dex—who'd never been great at school anyway—was going to stay home to help his dad grow potatoes and cows.

They didn't know what they were going to do without each other.

So there they were: David was leaning against a tree and taking a swig of soda, rubbing his taut stomach under his T-shirt because that's just what he did, when Dex walked up to him real serious like, getting closer than strictly necessary in an obvious effort to make sure he had David's attention.

David didn't mind. He'd wanted to touch Dex that way since they were in sixth grade. You didn't talk about that in Montana, though, so he'd started dating Sandra in high school, and Dex had dated Alyssa, because that's just what you did, right? You didn't make a move on your best friend, because then you wouldn't have a best friend, right?

But here was Dex, standing too close and smelling like sweat, and David was mesmerized by his ordinary brown eyes and sandy-brown hair.

"You gonna miss me?" Dex said softly, and David tried to swallow through a throat that was positively arid.

"Like I have an option," he said, and for this hushed, windless moment under the oak trees, he let some of his yearning shine through. Dex's hands on his hips were as natural as David's own, and the sun shining through his longish dark hair glittered off the almost impossibly long dark eyelashes. They were standing eye-to-eye, and David noted the straight nose, the square chin, the almost puffy lips. Dex had stubble and a broad chest and tightly strung abs, and he could in no way be confused with Sandra. David swallowed and took a risk, dropping his soda on the ground and putting his hands on Dex's lean hips in return.

Dex's look never strayed from that serious intensity, even when he thrust his hips forward so their groins met. David gasped—oh damn. It… it just felt so *good.* The ridge of Dex's erection pressing against the placket of David's jeans… it was hard and rough and….

Dex reached back and seized David's corn-yellow hair, angled David's head, and dove in for a kiss.

At the touch of those soft lips moving firm and possessively over his own, David melted and exploded both at the same time.

His bones softened and he became pliant, willing to do whatever Dex wanted, however he wanted it. His skin flared to life, craving, demanding, needing, and he shoved shaking hands up under Dex's T-shirt, starving for the feel of that smooth skin under his palms.

He must have made a sound, a whimper, something, because Dex's fingers tightened and he pulled David back. "I've been dreaming of this," he said. His face—which was the kind with the sweet apple cheeks when he smiled—was suddenly hard and intent and commanding. "There's a spot in those trees," he said, his dark eyes insistent. "Go there and take off your clothes. I'll be right there with a blanket from the truck."

David opened his mouth for a moment, sudden fear of being caught in the trees naked clearing up some of the sun dazzle in his brain.

"Hey," Dex said gently, "it's me. Trust me. Trust me. I ain't never let you down."

David nodded and smiled shyly. "Okay, Dex. I'll trust you."

So he went to the small clearing surrounded by blackberry bushes and oak trees, down by the irrigation ditch, and took off his boots and his jeans and briefs and his T-shirt, folded them neatly, and put them in a little pile. It was hot and humid in Montana in August, so he was comfortable naked, standing there, waiting, and anticipation made his skin buzz. He closed his eyes for a moment and wrapped his hand around his cock, then moved it smoothly up and over, oiling the head with the little bit of fluid leaking out. He moved his other hand to his nipples and gave them an experimental pinch, grunting when that turned out to be just where he wanted to be touched today.

He heard a rustling in the underbrush, and his eyes flew open to see Dex standing in the clearing with a blanket tucked under one arm. Dex had that hard, hungry look on his face again.

"Don't stop!"

David nodded and kept moving his hand on his cock, squeezing, oiling, pumping, while the little clearing was filled with the sounds of Dex's harsh breathing as he laid the blanket out at David's feet and took off his own boots and clothes.

David's cock was swollen tight, more sensitized by his own hand and the passing breeze than it ever had been when Sandra had played with it, and his breathing hitched harder. He made a whimper and clenched his stomach muscles, saying, "Dex, I'm gonna—"

"*Stop!*" Dex commanded, and David did. He stood there, trembling, and Dex came up to him, naked, and smoothed his palms down David's chest. "Don't come yet," Dex whispered.

David whimpered and Dex bent a little and took David's nipple in his mouth, playing with the end. David brought his hands up to thread through Dex's thick hair and tried to keep his knees from buckling. God. Just his nipples… he was going to come just from having his nipples sucked!

"Dex, I'm gonna—"

"No!" Dex pulled back and looked at him sternly. "I've been reading, Davy, and there's shit I want to do to you… stuff you're gonna like, I swear. But it'll hurt if you come first… you gotta hold off."

David closed his eyes and felt a shivering wave of want crash on him. He clung to Dex's shoulders and let it sweep through him, leaving him trembling, on the verge, but at the same time content to let Dex take control.

"You did homework?" he asked, and Dex smiled at him, so close that the quick warmth of his mouth was not a surprise.

"Yeah," Dex whispered. "I've been thinking about this a *lot.*"

David smiled back, and Dex whispered in his ear. "That smile, right there?"

"Yeah?"

"I've known you my entire life. You only smile like that for me."

Their bodies were nude and smooth against each other, and when Dex's arms came around his shoulders, David couldn't get enough of the feeling of their naked skin rubbing together. He started to thrust his hips then, frotting up against the crease of Dex's thigh and needing so badly that he was almost weeping with it.

Dex loved him.

"Shhh…," Dex whispered. "Here," he said, grabbing David's hair again and pushing him down. "Suck on it. Watch your teeth. Be gentle."

Oh God *yes!*

David sank to his knees on the little blanket and looked at it first, taking it in his hand, squeezing. Dex was probably like a lot of guys—six inches, maybe a little longer—but he was perfectly shaped, perfectly proportioned. It was every dick drawn in a notebook or on a comic (yes, David had seen them, done his own research furtively on the nights Sandra hadn't been able to hook up), and David licked across the head, almost surprised to find that it tasted like sweaty skin.

Shouldn't it taste like something more spectacular? Candy or bourbon or even the salty-bitter taste of David's own come when he'd licked it from his hand? Dex groaned and his fingers tightened in David's hair and he spurted a little. David shuddered, because *now* it tasted spectacular, and he wanted more.

Dex's fingers in his hair pulled him back, and David went unwillingly, sucking until the cockhead escaped his mouth with a pop. Dex angled his head up and looked down at him, cupping his cheek in the other hand.

"I want to come in your mouth," he whispered. "But that means we can't do that other thing unless we're late home. Is that okay?"

David moaned. "Yeah," he said mindlessly. "We can be late." (Nobody was *ever* late to his mother's table.) "God… please, Dex, can

I come too?" he begged, and Dex sank to his knees and kissed him, pushing him on his back on top of the blanket and continuing the hot, wet assault of mouth and tongue until David was bucking his hips frantically against Dex's thigh. Dex moved quickly then—he and David had been in football in high school, and David had been the wide receiver, but Dex had been the quarterback, and he was muscular and not too big and scary fast. Suddenly his cock was hanging in David's face like fruit, and David moaned as he pulled it into his mouth. While his mouth was full, he almost screamed when Dex did the same thing to him.

He wanted to howl, he wanted to gibber, he wanted to plead, but he couldn't do anything, because Dex was thrusting his cock into David's mouth while he fisted and sucked on David's cock in return. David was helpless, he was frantic, he was…

Tearing his face away from David and begging, "I'm coming… oh God… Dex, *please*…."

"I'll let you come," Dex promised, his breath panting out harshly against David's cockhead. "Just don't stop sucking."

David sucked him in hard and tight, and Dex gave one last squeeze and suck, his other hand going to David's balls. Oh geez, oh geez, oh geez! David made a desperate sound around Dex's cock.

Dex groaned and started to spurt down David's throat and pulled away long enough to say, "*Now, David!*" and David's world exploded into pleasure, amazing pleasure, give and take, fireworks, bright lights, and come.

Dex pumped forever into his mouth, too long for David to swallow it all, even though he tried, and David just lay there, convulsing, clutching Dex's hips to him, until Dex shook him off. With a grunt, he turned around, and pillowed his head on David's shoulder with a self-satisfied grin.

David looked at him adoringly, and Dex wiped at his cheek with a careless thumb. David turned his head and sucked the leftover come off of Dex's thumb with a smile, and Dex grinned some more.

"Good, huh?" he asked, and David shook his head, still breathless.

Dex's expression sobered. "Worth coming back for?" he asked wistfully, and David nodded and grinned some more. Silently, Dex pulled the class ring off his finger. They'd gotten matching ones because they'd gone through school together joined at the hip, and in spite of tradition, neither one of them had given their ring to their girlfriends. Dex grabbed David's hand and switched rings, and David slid Dex's ring on his own finger, where it fit just like it should. Not a word was said then about forever, or about ditching their girlfriends, or about coming out to their parents with the big scary scene and the "g" word. There was just the simple promise that David would come back, and they would do this again.

In the end they decided they had to come back in order to do it again anyway. It really was too late for them to try that other thing Dex wanted to do, so they cleaned themselves off in the restrooms and climbed back into the truck.

When Dex asked David if it was okay, David had no choice but to nod. Oh yes, oh yes, it had been more than okay, it had been something he'd dreamed about for *years.*

"It was real good," David said softly, trying to find words, and Dex turned his head.

"What was that? Speak up!"

And David looked away from those intent brown eyes and saw the buck crossing the road. He yelled, "Watch out!" but it was too late.

HE WOKE up in the hospital the next day, with a concussion from hitting his head on the dashboard as well as a broken arm and a whole lot of bruising and various stitches and cuts. He was disoriented at first, and then he saw his dad and mom, sitting in the far corner of the room, whispering.

"Dex?" he mumbled, wanting reassurance, because what he could remember had been horrific, and there seemed to have been a lot of blood, and he couldn't hear Dex's voice in his head, like he'd heard it since kindergarten and maybe before.

His mom and dad stood up then and looked at each other, that wordless communication that people have when they've been together for a lot of good years.

"David?" his mom said, and David closed his eyes at what he saw there.

"I'm sorry we were late for dinner, Mom," he said a little desperately. "I'm sorry, the supplies must have been all over the road—"

"David."

David looked up and met her eyes and started shaking all over. "No."

Then his dad spoke in that voice that nobody ever crossed. "Son."

"No," he said again, his voice louder.

"Son, he didn't—"

"*No*!" he shouted. "*No, no, no, no, no, no, no*…." And he must have yelled it for too long, because they sedated him, which was fine, because sleep was the best hope he had.

HE WAS actually a little more fucked-up than he'd first assumed when he woke up. He spent a month in the hospital mourning Dex, wondering what to do with his life. He missed the beginning of school in Montana, which sucked, and spent a lot of his time in recovery with a laptop, looking for another school that would take him.

He wanted some place that would not require him to visit home, even during Christmas break.

It was terrible of him. He had an older brother, who was working the farm, and three younger brothers and a younger sister, and he loved them, very much so. They visited him in the hospital each and every day. He listened to his eight-year-old brother read, and his eleven-year-old brother talk about sports. His thirteen-year-old sister would complain about her brothers, and his fifteen-year-old brother wanted to talk about girls. His twenty-year-old brother complained about how none of the other kids was working enough and…

And he wanted to scream at them, howl, because Dex was gone, and they hadn't just been friends, hadn't just been brothers, they'd been…

Oops. Nope. Couldn't think of that word. Couldn't.

Because Sandra was coming by every day to make sure he was okay and talk about their plans to go to Montana State and bring him stuff that she'd cooked with his mom because he didn't seem to be eating right.

Because Dex's girlfriend, Alyssa, was in genuine, true-love-forever mourning, and how could he fuck that up for her? How could he say to himself, "I loved him more than I loved Sandra, and he loved me like he couldn't love you, Alyssa, and we were just figuring this out, it was just new, when it all came to an end on Highway 87," when that truth would destroy people who had already been destroyed?

Running away to Sacramento wasn't the bravest thing he'd ever done, but it wasn't the stupidest, either. Sacramento may have been the capital of the state, but it was still a small place in comparison with places like San Francisco and Los Angeles. There was enough farmland nearby for him to feel comfortable, and there were enough exotic locales—like the Sierra Nevada and the ocean and even Southern California and Disneyland—within driving distance for him to feel like it was someplace new.

And it was far enough away from Montana that he could pretend that the interlude, that sweet, amazing, wonderful, perfect moment with Dex, had never happened. Maybe it was far enough away for him to mourn his friend however he could, instead of the way other people expected him to. Maybe it was far enough away to leave the hurt behind.

He called the dean of admissions when he saw that the startup date was a week later than MSU and explained the situation—and was admitted, much to his parents' chagrin. The tuition was considerably higher than it had been at MSU, as was the housing, and David promised he'd find a way to pay for it out of his own pocket.

After that one moment when he'd needed sedation, he'd been almost frighteningly calm in the hospital. Looking back, he thought that he might have scared his parents enough that they would have agreed to *anything*, as long as he was talking about the future, and he was grateful.

He went home for a week and looked around the battered, noisy farmhouse with new eyes. It seemed small and crowded, but it was also the home of his childhood. Every mark on the walls, every dent in the doorframe or scuff on the floor, had been made by somebody he loved. A lot of them were even from Dex.

Dex was buried on his folks' property, and although their driveways were ten miles apart, because of the way the properties lay, it was only a two-mile walk from David's doorstep. His second-to-last day home, he exhausted himself walking out there to look at the shiny new headstone with all of the flowers on it. He crouched down and rubbed his hand on the polished granite and sighed.

"You know," he said conversationally, "I can't even blame you. I wouldn't have been looking for the fucking deer either." The plot was watered and the grass was soft, so he sank down at the edge of it and tried to put things in perspective, but he couldn't.

"Twelve years," he said softly. "My whole life, I thought you and me were the same person. That last day, we even became sort of the same person, and that's what was so great about it. The being together so tight, we didn't know where the other one left off. Remember…." He had to smile at the memory. "Remember when you got the idea to build a sail scooter and take it across the stubble fields?" David laughed, remembering that. They'd worked on it for weeks, using big fat tires from an old bicycle and making sure they were oiled and suspended just right. David had learned how to use his mom's sewing machine, and they had cannibalized old tarps and waited for one of those days when the wind sweeping out of the mountains had just seemed to level anything its path. Then they'd both hopped on the platform and….

"God, Dex. It was flying. We ended up halfway to Forsyth and then had to take the sail down and walk back, but it was worth it."

They'd done that in the seventh grade and told the story all through high school. Usually when they told that story, Dex was the one who talked about ending up halfway to Forsyth, because the truth was, they'd barely cleared Dex's property before one of the tires blew. But Dex's story had so much more power, and David hopped on board that story in the same way he'd hopped on board that sailboard. Dex had always been able to help him fly.

"I… I'm not brave. I'm not a leader. I'm… you were strong, and you were the leader, and… and now I'm just going to be left, wondering how to live my life like you were there with the good ideas."

And for the first time since that panicked moment in the hospital, he felt the void of his best friend, his brother, his—and he could say it out here, with no one to listen to his head—his lover, and he felt it as real.

He didn't scream hysterically or stand up and kick the headstone or any of that. He put his face on his knees and listened as the wind from the mountains mercilessly leveled everything in its path. He remembered the person who had helped him fly with the wind instead of being beaten down by it, and he cried quietly into his knees, finally knowing how the big of the sky could make a person feel as alone as a heartbeat in space.

BY THE end of the year, his parents were out of money, and David didn't want to go home. He'd broken up with Sandra before he left—she'd understood, and he'd been relieved—so he had a new girlfriend now. She was a wide-hipped, uninhibited girl named Kelly who would do things in bed on a whim that David used to have to spend weeks with flowers, chocolate, and sweet talk to get Sandra to do even reluctantly, and (even better) Kelly would be the one to come up with those things.

"You could always do porn," Kelly said one night after a particular bit of holy-hell-orgasmathoning in her dorm. She was laughing as she said it, but he found that his cock started to get hard again just thinking about it.

"Porn?" He managed some skepticism. Of course, every boy liked to think he had the stuff of a porn star, if not too much class.

"Naw," Kelly laughed and shook her head. "Naw! I couldn't share you with another girl, sweetie." She pinched his cheek and wiggled her wide hips. "You are just too cute—and too good in the sack! No. But…." Her eyes, bright blue with wickedly arched eyebrows, grew even brighter.

"What?" he asked, because that was the look she'd had when she'd first had him go through the back door, and he'd loved that, so he was starting to enjoy the hell out of that arch of her eyebrows and twist to her plump red mouth.

"There's always gay-for-pay," she said, laughing, and for a minute, David got mad.

"I ain't gay!" he snapped, sitting up in bed and glaring. Dex had been dead less than a year, and sometimes it seemed that his time in Sacramento had been a dream, all of it suspended between that breathless hush between the two of them, looking at each other after making love on a hot windless day.

But Kelly didn't get mad. Not much made her mad, actually, and David both liked that about her and didn't. It was a great quality in a girl, but it meant that he was never sure if he had pleased her truly or if she just liked everything, and not just in bed, either. Clothes, perfume, jewelry, books—she was happy with it all, and he didn't trust it. Dex had been so specific….

David shook that thought off and concentrated on what she was saying now.

"You don't have to be gay, sweetie! That's the point."

David had looked at her blankly, and she rolled her eyes.

"Here, wait a sec," she said. She sat up and pulled her phone from the dresser, then started texting madly. She got a reply almost immediately, and David squinted.

"Who are you texting?"

"My roommate," she said briefly, then put the phone down.

"Isn't she in the next room?" David asked, seriously confused. He'd been pretty sure Andrea was with her boyfriend. That's what she and Kelly did on their weekends—had their boyfriends over and fucked like lemmings.

"Ignore that for a second," Kelly laughed. "Just close your eyes," she said, and he did. "Okay, now, I'm gonna touch you places. Don't worry, you'll like it."

He felt a gentle touch on the inside of his arm then and tried not to giggle like a kid. Her fingers weren't soft. She played the guitar and rode horses and went rock climbing in the gym, and generally didn't hang back and pamper her wide-hipped bosomy body like it looked like, so he knew those fingers were hers.

"Okay," she said quietly, tracing a firm path down from the inside of his arm to his waist to his thighs.

With his eyes closed, he found the touch stunningly erotic, and he became lost in it, lost in the touch and touch alone. His erection started to return, and he felt those rough fingers trace his length, then wrap around him, then stroke. He smiled a little.

"Kelly," he said breathlessly, "if this is the way to convince me I'm not going to notice it's a guy, this isn't the way to do it."

Kelly's body shifted on the bed, and she put her lips close to his ear. "Trust me, Davy. You're totally going to change your mind in a minute."

He was concentrating on her voice, and although he heard some rustling in the background, her voice was soft and her lips were soft against his ear, and the smell of their sex was in the air, and he wasn't going to be distracted from the swelling in his cock for all of the noises in the world.

"Okay, baby," she whispered. "Now I'm gonna stroke your cock just the way you like it, okay?"

Her hand was hard and firm, and he moaned, willing to play her game because she was so good at this. She moved around next to him, and suddenly he could feel her mouth on him and her hair brushing his legs, and he was well on his way to a second orgasm when she pulled her head up and a man's voice said, "Come for me."

He startled—and did. He was so surprised his hands splayed out and his body shook and he let out a pained grunt before spurting all over the hand on his cock, and then he opened his eyes in outrage and saw—Kelly. His girlfriend. Looking at him wickedly, without another person in sight.

He glared at her and sat up, grabbing the covers and pulling them around his waist, sputtering with complete bafflement.

"What in the *fuck!*"

She shook her head, her auburn hair falling over her face as she licked her hand. She looked like one of those girls in the porn videos. "Keep your panties on. I just had the guy stick his head in here and say something. It's nerve endings and perception, sweetie. If you think it's a girl touching you, it feels good. If you think it's a boy touching you, you *tell* yourself it doesn't, but it all feels the same. Human touch is human touch." She smiled evilly through the come on her face. "Do you want to see what else feels good to be touched?"

David shook his head no, although he was suddenly gripped by this idea. It wasn't like he was too ugly to be on camera, right? He had blond hair and blue eyes, a small nose, a long square jaw (but not too long), and girls had been telling him he had a nice smile since he was a baby. A part of him pinged sadly: Dex had especially loved David's smile.

And that's what decided him. "How would you even go into gay for pay?" he asked, pitching his voice just right, and Kelly laughed.

"Baby, there's a place right here in town."

And that's where David found out about *Johnnies*.

LATER, John would be doing everything on computer and not just sell the porn there, and he'd have an office suite outfitted to look like different locales, complete with a courtyard with a gazebo and a hot tub. When David applied, however, all he had was a nice respectable little house in a respectable little neighborhood, with a heavily enclosed backyard and a small pool.

It was May, and the sun was bright and hot, so after a phone interview and a downloaded picture, John took David inside and had a little chat.

John seemed nice enough, if a little young—barely older than David, actually. He had longish auburn hair and green eyes; he dressed super trendy and used all of that tacky slang that was about five minutes out of date, even by Sacramento standards, and they were still using words like "hella" and "yanno" pretty much to fucking death. He asked a series of questions printed on a clipboard in front of him like he was trying to be official, but the questions seemed to make John as uncomfortable as David—and most of them were sexual: Have you ever beat off with another boy? Have you ever touched another boy's cock? Have you ever had sex with a boy? Has your girlfriend ever anally penetrated you? Finally, David lost patience.

"Oh my God! It's like the questions are worse than having sex on camera!" he said with only half a laugh. "I've got a stiffie and I'm not sure whether to pull my pants down and prove it to you or run into the bathroom and beat off!"

John burst into giggles and grabbed the sheet off the clipboard, crumpled it up, and tossed it in the trashcan at the end of his desk. He shook his head. "I'm sorry. Seriously. I started this business about three months ago, right? And I just really don't want it to be sleazy. I mean yeah, everybody's having sex on camera, and it's porn, but…."

John turned to look at him intently, almost like a new acquaintance would, and he ran a hand through his carefully maintained red hair. "Look, I know you're straight, and you've probably figured I'm gay, but the thing is, do you remember the first time you saw porn?"

David blushed. It had been about two months ago, when he'd first started having sex with Kelly.

"Yeah," he said, laughing uncomfortably. Oddly enough, he found it wasn't John's sexuality that was making him uncomfortable.

In fact, it was the thought of having sex with girls when he was in this perfectly nice gay man's house.

"So, what'd you think?"

David blushed some more. "It was...." He looked around and couldn't seem to spot an escape hatch anywhere, so he soldiered on. "It was sort of nasty. I mean, it was girls, but they just looked so... I don't know... like they were trying to make it dirty and...." Oh God. Most uncomfortable conversation ever. "I just wanted to get hard, right? I didn't need the props or the costumes or the stupid dialog and they didn't need to make it dirty, like she was bad and needed a spanking or, you know!" Geez, this was hard to put into words. "I just wanted to see people getting it on so I could get it up. Is that so damned wrong?"

John was guffawing now, giggling so hard that he had to put his hand over his mouth. "Oh my God. That's it. That's *exactly* it! I'm so tired of sex and sexuality being dirty! Why can't it just be... I don't know, *good*? *Fun*. I mean, yeah, good sex can be really raunchy, but it can also just be, I don't know. Physical activity. You just need human contact, right? I mean...." John sobered a little and finished his thought. "People who don't like each other fuck all the time. I want people who like each other to fuck—and I don't want the 'Do they really swing that way?' thing to get in the way. I just want it to look good, and be happy, and make people happy to watch. Seriously."

"So the questions?" David asked curiously, and John nodded.

"Yeah. I can't figure out how, but I want to find guys who can think of it the same way. I want it to be fun, and hell, *lucrative*, right? But I want the guys to talk to each other and have human connection, even if they wouldn't date each other outside the office, you know?"

David thought about it for a moment and remembered that moment, him and Dex, eye to eye. There hadn't been any words for it, but he thought it was probably love. He didn't expect to ever have a moment like that again in his life, but if he couldn't? Why couldn't it be fun? Why couldn't it be friendly? Why couldn't it be just a good place to work?

"Maybe just talk to us," he said, thinking about it. "Get a feel for us, see if we've got the attitude or if we seem too needy or too weird about it. You know, we're your employees, right? Maybe just see if you'd like to work with us, and think about it that way."

John looked at him in surprise. "That's a real good idea, David. I think I'd like very much to work with you. Would you want to beat off on camera for me today?"

David chuckled and then sobered. "Yeah. If you can pay me, I think I could have a lot of fun doing that."

John allowed some residual laughter to float up between them. "Okay. I've got some employee forms all official and everything, and I'll have you sign those so we can pay you, and you're going to need a name."

"A name?"

"You don't really think some mother named her son Brett Sausagestuffer, do you?"

David laughed. "Gotcha. A porn name."

"Yeah. Make it something you can recognize in a crowded room, okay?"

David didn't even blink. "Dex," he said, nodding. "I always wanted to be a Dex."

(Carlos) Kane

Six Years Later

HE KNEW it wouldn't last forever. Hell, it was *never* forever. But the next day at school, the same girl who'd drooled all over his cock the night before was holding hands with her boyfriend and making limpid eyes at him, and when Carlos walked by, she turned up her nose.

Carlos stopped right where he'd been walking on his way to science, the one class he didn't fucking hate, and turned around.

"You're gonna look at me like that?" he asked, and he knew he had a reputation for being a player, but the girls who were begging him to fuck them usually were at least a little *grateful*, right?

"I'm not lookin' at you," she said, her tiny little nose turned up, her plump brown mouth pulled up over her dainty white front teeth. "I don't look at trash."

Carlos pulled up his own sneer, and he knew it wasn't pretty. "That's not what you said last night when I was cleanin' your chute," he said, and he knew he *had* it coming, but he still didn't *see* it coming when her boyfriend, Tomas, who was actually a decent guy and didn't deserve to be two-timed like that, leveled a haymaker at him from the side.

His science teacher, Ms. Darcy, saw the whole thing, so Tomas got suspended. Carlos heard the news sitting in the nurse's office with an ice pack on his cheek while Ms. Darcy looked at him skeptically.

"So, I know he's the one who swung first," she said dryly, giving him a gimlet eye. She was in her late fifties, graying and hatchet-faced, but she was also hella fuckin' funny when she was pretty sure nobody like the weaselly little vice principal everybody hated, the one who curled her hair in her office while she was getting drunk, wasn't listening in.

"Yeah," Carlos said, his eyes wide. "He just up and hit me outta nowhere, I swear, Ms. Darcy—"

"Cut the shit, Carlos. What'd you say to him?"

Carlos kept his eyes (which were normally a little narrow and devilish looking, if he said so himself) as wide as possible. "I didn't say shit to him, Ms. Darcy"—but he must have put too much emphasis on "him" and not enough on "didn't say shit," because she raised both eyebrows.

"What'd you say to her?"

Carlos blushed. He'd actually been raised better than to talk trash to a girl, but she'd made him so mad. Geez, this girl had chased *him.* He'd been checking out the lizards under the F wing when she'd followed him between the fence and the portable building, taken him between the two portables, dropped his pants, and sucked his dick. She hadn't even *said* anything. And hell, it's not like you just turned down that sort of shit, right? Carlos had been working out since the seventh grade, and carrying condoms in his pocket since the eighth grade because he wasn't stupid. Girls just fuckin' *gave* that shit away sometimes, and what kind of fool turned that down?

"I…." Some of his innocence slipped and his halo crashed to his feet. Ms. Darcy was cool. He hoped. "It just made me so mad, you know? There she was goin'…." He cut his eyes sideways and pulled up his teacher speak. "She's, uhm, goin' all… *personal* on me yesterday, right? And today? She just turns away like I'm trash, you know? And I didn't expect hearts and flowers, but fuck, it would just be nice if she said hello, you feel me?"

Ms. Darcy did that thing with her lips that old people did when they felt sorry for you but knew they couldn't explain why. "Well, Carlos," she said after some consideration. He noticed he didn't even make her blush.

"Well what?"

She sighed and took the ice pack off his cheek, checked the bruise forming there, and then put the ice pack back. "You know in the old days, when it used to be the boys chasing the girls?"

Carlos grimaced. "That was like, sixth grade, right? That wasn't so long ago."

She smiled then and put a hand on his shoulder. "Yeah, well, they used to tell girls stupid things like 'Why buy the cow when you can have the milk for free' and 'Only trashy girls give it away'—you've heard that?"

Carlos nodded glumly. "Yeah, well, everyone does that, won't nobody get some."

Ms. Darcy laughed then and looked around furtively before going to the little cooler that only the nurse was supposed to get into. She opened a big bottle of Motrin and pulled out two tabs and brought it over to him with a bottle of water that had been in the fridge too. "Here, Carlos. Don't tell anyone I gave them to you, okay? The nurse is supposed to call your parents and all sorts of bullshit, but she's at the other high school today, all right?"

Carlos took the medicine glumly, and when he was done swallowing, Ms. Darcy started talking again.

"Look, my dear, all I'm trying to say is that other people won't value you if *you* don't value you. You're a good-looking kid, and you know it, and you've got girls chasing you all over the planet, and that's fun, right?"

He nodded vigorously, and she laughed.

"Well, if that's what you want, that's what you're going to get. But if you want it to mean more, it's got to be something that doesn't just happen. You've got to make it important, you understand? Give it value—just don't give it away for free."

Carlos grinned, thinking of something funny. "Yeah, well, it's not like people are gonna pay me to do that, right?"

Ms. Darcy rolled her eyes. "That's not a career we want you to aspire to, no. What I'm saying is, you don't have to marry everybody you bang, but they're going to think you're trashy if you let them treat you that way."

Carlos kept the ice on his jaw and shook his head. "Ms. Darcy, I know you're trying to tell me something important, but all I can think of is that if I got paid to have sex, I'd be hella rich right now."

Ms. Darcy covered her eyes with her hands and let out a long sigh, the kind that told Carlos he was being stupid even when he wasn't trying to be.

"Or," she said with another sigh, "you could do that. Either way, baby, you'd probably better not talk trash to the girls you sleep with, or your pretty face is gonna get way broken, okay?"

Carlos had been born with a cleft palate. He'd needed operations—several of them—before his palate had been completely closed and his upper lip was repaired with only marginal scarring. He'd been lucky—the operations had happened when his family still lived in Mexico, because some charity doctor had taken care of all of that and his parents hadn't had to pay a dime. If he'd been born here in the

States, odds were he probably would have had that big disfiguring gap all the way up to his nose like he'd had when he'd been three or four, before the operations. He had pictures.

So even though he knew his face was pleasing—he had high cheekbones and those almond-shaped eyes and Spanish pale skin and a nice square jaw—he didn't take it for granted that someone thought he was pretty. Even if it was an old teacher lady, she was cool and he liked her, so he took the compliment seriously.

"I'll be more careful with my face," he said, nodding to show he meant it. "It's all I got, right?"

Ms. Darcy closed her eyes. "You got so much more, Carlos. You know that, right?"

Carlos held the ice pack tight to his cheekbone and risked a look in the mirror. "Yeah," he said without irony. "Like now I know I got a black eye."

BUT Carlos did take something away from that conversation, even if it wasn't all that Ms. Darcy probably wanted. For one thing, he stopped having random sex with girls. He stopped looking for a girlfriend too, because his reputation in that school was too widespread anyway. He was graduating in a month, so it was no big loss, but he kept thinking about that whole money thing.

His sister's husband, Hector, wanted him to work in his machine shop, but Carlos didn't really want to. It wasn't that he minded working hard, and he'd love to be a gardener or something—especially because he liked bugs and he thought he'd get to see a lot of them—but Hector was a prick, and Carlos thought Fabiola might be getting smacked around a little by him, and Carlos didn't want to see that. Especially since there was the baby around. Carlos got so mad thinking about Fabiola letting Frances see that bullshit. But their parents were back in Mexico because sometimes it was a damned sight better than California, and it was just Carlos and Lola, and he wasn't going to ditch her either. But God. He sure as hell didn't want to work in the machine shop!

He got on his sister's laptop and Googled *Porn + Sacramento* and was disappointed to get nothing but some hits on a former porn star who'd been born in North Highlands and some dirty old pervs getting busted for kiddie porn. Oh, hey, there were sex toy shops, and that was something he'd bookmark for later, but in the meantime, how about something he could do for money?

Finally, after hunting a little, he found a listing for a place called *Johnnies.* When he realized it was guy on guy, it hardly fazed him. After all, like Ms. Darcy said, at least he wouldn't be giving it away anymore.

THEY were ripping up the courtyard in the middle of the office suite when he went in for his interview and his audition. A blond guy wearing a pair of jeans, a football jersey, and some flip-flops greeted him at the door. He had a narrow, almost delicately pretty face for a boy, and he grimaced at the noise.

"We're not filming here until this is done," he said apologetically. "If you want, you can follow me to—wait. Where's your car?"

Carlos shrugged. "I took a bus," he said, because Lola needed the car to take the baby to a doctor's appointment. Since Carlos's graduation, that baby—well, she was not quite eighteen months old—had gotten more and more sickly, and Carlos was glad Hector finally said they could go to the doctor's. He loved the way she smiled when he bounced her on his knee, and he wanted to see that again.

"Okay, then," the guy said, "I can take you to John's, and if you pass the interview, we'll use his backyard for your introduction video." He grimaced and ran a hand through his hair. Carlos saw that he still had his class ring on his finger, and the idea that he still had one made him seem not so much older than Carlos himself. "John would rather have it here, because he likes the idea of professional and all, but I sort of like his backyard. It's real nice."

Carlos cocked his head. "Where you from?"

The boy had skin so fair it was milk-colored, and it pinked up a little. "Montana. Why, do I sound like it?"

"Yeah. Why'd you come here?"

The guy smiled and looked down, and for a moment, he looked almost shy. Carlos liked that, liked the way he looked shy. Carlos was pretty sure he was a porn star—wait, *model*—and he thought that maybe if this pretty boy could smile like that, then maybe he wouldn't be going to hell for fucking for money. Nobody could send that smile to hell. It was against every rule of hell Carlos knew.

"I came for the school," he said, shooting a look toward Carlos. "I sort of stayed for the porn. I'm Dex, by the way."

Carlos shook his offered hand, enjoying how his palm was long and his fingers were narrow. "Carlos Ramirez."

"Not for long," Dex said seriously, and Carlos blinked.

"Yeah?"

"Yeah. You pass the audition, and you're going to have to choose a name. Those things sort of stick."

Carlos felt sort of cheated. "So Dex ain't your real name?"

That yellow-gold hair was cut short, and it didn't hardly move when Dex shook his head. "No. My real name is David, but don't call me that, okay? The only one who knows it is John."

Oh! That was an honor. "Then why'd you tell me?"

Dex kind of grimaced. "Because I've been doing this for nearly six years, and unless my mother calls me, I forget sometimes." Dex turned to him with big eyes. "Man, whatever your porn name is, make sure it's something you don't hate."

"You hate 'Dex'?"

Dex shook his head, but he was thinking seriously about the question. "No," he said after a moment. "Not anymore. Here. You're not doing a scene with another person. Want to stop and get something to eat on the way? I'll take you to John's and then take you home if you want. How's that sound?"

Carlos grinned. "I don't never say no to food."

Dex sighed. "You're going to have to, you know. If you make it in." And then he proceeded to tell Carlos shit Carlos didn't even want to *know* about fiber and shit, honest to God *shit*, and what you don't ever want to do when you're getting your ass reamed by some other guy's tool.

It helped, though. When they got to John's, Dex walked in the front door without knocking and said, "He passed the interview!" and a guy with red hair stuck his head out of a small office and looked him over.

"He's damned pretty. What'd he say that convinced you?"

Dex grinned. "He got the fiber speech and it didn't scare him off."

John laughed. "Aces, Dex. I should have you screen guys more often."

"Or at least give the speech," Carlos said, nodding fervently. Dex had been more than nice—he'd been fun and downright human. Carlos didn't know if it was a blond thing (there weren't that many blond guys at Carlos's school. Hell, there weren't that many *white* guys at Carlos's school) or a Montana thing or just a Dex thing, but Carlos suddenly felt better about dropping his pants and jacking off on camera for a bunch of gay guys than he did about all those girls he'd nailed through school.

His audition went pretty good too.

He talked to Dex while John held the camera, and Dex asked fun stuff, like what his favorite part of sex was and where was the weirdest place he'd ever done it. He'd admitted that the couch in the drama wing of his high school got a good workout, and Dex cracked up, and the next thing Carlos knew, he'd dropped his cargo shorts and had his cock in his hand. Dex gasped softly when it was out.

"Damn, that's big!" he said, and Carlos looked up and grinned.

"Yeah, and I still got a turtleneck!" He'd been born out of the country, so he was uncircumcised, and he'd learned from the girls he'd been with that this was a rare thing.

Dex laughed, but his blue eyes were focused on Carlos's thick cock. Carlos grinned at him, feeling proud, and squeezed at the base and stroked. Oh God, it felt good, and he had a moment of panic. It felt *too* good. Sometimes when he was *this* swollen, *this* aroused, he had trouble getting off. He kept stroking though, kept fondling, let his noises amp up a notch because Dex and John seemed to get such a kick out of it, and he felt himself starting to soar. Oh God. This was good. These men thought he looked good, and they liked his cock, and suddenly what had felt trashy with all those girls felt classy on the rich green lawn of this guy's backyard.

But he wasn't going to come, and oh, fuck, he was so close when all of a sudden—

There was Dex's hand on his cock, and that feeling of someone else's fingers, that's what did it. It didn't matter if they were male or female, they were *someone*, and oh, oh no, oh *hell* there he went, spurting over Dex's hand and arm, and Carlos's knees got wobbly and he was afraid he was just going to collapse into the grass when he felt an arm around his waist.

He looked up and Dex was smiling kindly at him. "Easy, big guy. Gotcha."

Carlos smiled weakly, remembering the way girls kissed and wishing he had a little of that now. Dex's smile grew even gentler and he leaned in and kissed him and pressed that arm around his waist up over his shoulders in comfort. Carlos kissed him back without self-consciousness, because everyone needed to be held after they came with another person. That was just human, right?

Dex looked up where John was with the camera and winked. "I think he passed the audition," he said, and John said, "Oh *hell* yeah!" and then they all laughed.

That laugh, that was the best part of all.

Dex took him to the bathroom and let him wash up in private, and then Carlos signed some more papers and made an appointment for a blood test. John said that once the blood test came back clear, that would be that.

"So," Dex said as he was filling out the last of the papers, "what's your name going to be?"

"Who's that guy from the Bible who killed his brother?" Carlos asked, and Dex looked at him funny.

"Cain," he said and started to write it down with a *C*.

"Spell it with a *K*—it looks cooler," Carlos said sincerely, and Dex laughed and did just that.

"So, are you planning to kill a brother? Do we need to know where to hide the bodies?"

"Not my brother," Carlos admitted, "but I think this job would really stick it to my brother-in-law, and he's a major prick!"

Dex laughed and wrote "Kane" with a *K*, and Kane was born in John's nice little living room with the corduroy couches and the plush olive-colored throw rug. Kane thought there were worse places to be.

THAT night Dex fed him again as he took his sweet red BMW through the line at Adalberto's and told him when his next shoot was. Then Dex dropped him off at his sister's house, where he had the little back room because he'd given up the bigger room so Frances could have all the toys she needed.

When he walked in, Fabiola started whining at him about how Hector said he needed to start paying rent and Hector was going to kick him out if he didn't start working at the machine shop, but Kane was still high from the shoot, so it didn't bother him none.

"Don't worry, chica," he said, kissing his sister on a wan cheek. "I don't need Hector's charity. I got myself a *job.*"

Fabiola looked at him dubiously. "Jeez, Carlos. I hope it's legal."

He smiled back at her wickedly. "I'm eighteen, aren't I?" And before he could spill the beans about what he was doing, he poured himself a big glass of milk in the kitchen and then went to the living room to pull Frances out of the playpen. He hated those fucking things, and he wanted his niece to have better.

SOMEONE ELSE'S PAIN

Dex

AFTER eight years in the business, he'd stopped pretending that he wasn't gay, stopped pretending that the first guy he'd fallen for since his first male lover died actually loved him back, and stopped remembering that his real name was David.

But he'd still always thought of himself as a moral man, a moral *person,* until right about this moment.

Dex sat on one of the ultra-comfy couches in front of the giant plasma screen at John's office suite with the keyboard in his lap so he could edit the footage. He was watching the rushes of the threesome with Kane, Ethan, and Chance while he chewed the inside of his cheek. After all this time with John as a model, a camera man/editor, an accountant (because he had most of a business degree under his belt), and an advisor and friend, he hadn't ever seen anything like this particular film.

"It's disturbing, isn't it?" John asked quietly. He was sitting on the couch across from Dex—this room was never used for anything other than editing and business, so the furniture was clean, bright (John really liked the color green for some reason), and comfortably worn. But neither of the men felt comfortable watching the sex on the screen.

Dex nodded in response to John's question, but his eyes never left the action. Chance was stunningly beautiful—blond, blue eyed, an intense, high-cheekboned, almost narrow face—and he had this look, this lost little boy look, when he didn't know anyone was watching him. When he knew you were looking, he got this practiced openmouthed expression like every dumb jock you'd ever met—and suddenly, he was that guy too. So he was pretty incendiary on the screen, with the dumb jock and the hidden innocence, and the footage was hot, there was no question about it. But then, touching Chance (everyone knew his name was Chase because Tango was not exactly discreet about throwing his "secret" identity around. But then, Tango had a good reason for wanting Chase to come out of the closet) had always been like touching a magnesium road flare of sex and longing.

Need just oozed from the guy's skin.

And ever since Chase's breakup with Tango, there had been a whole other dimension of intensity and crazy added to his look, his touch, the horrible cauldron of something scary that Dex had always sensed under his "I'm just a dumb jock" exterior. Never more so than when he watched this last scene.

"Right there," he said quietly, looking at the beginning. Kane was there, beautiful, dark hair spiked a little because that's how he liked it, his soul patch groomed because yeah, there was a little bit of vanity working there, but mostly, just a nice kid. When Kane started a scene, he'd get rough, manhandle a guy, throw him around a little, dominate him—even when Kane was on the bottom, he was telling the guy how to move. He was a bossy fucker, that was for certain, but when he was off the set?

He'd brought Dex a coffee or a Jamba Juice pretty much every time they'd worked together. He texted dumb jokes, bought a new video game every *week* and invited people out shopping or to the water slides to play, and filled in whenever somebody needed help. That included off camera, when one of the guys was moving, or when the receptionist was overwhelmed and just needed a hand.

He might have liked to put his hand on your back and nail you to the bed when he topped (and he'd done this to Dex on set—it was one of Dex's favorite memories of *Johnnies*, actually), but during every other frickin' moment of the day?

He could be the sweetest mammal since Labrador puppies had been invented. And he would be horrified to realize that the guy he'd been fucking in that threesome hadn't been completely consenting because apparently he was losing his fucking mind.

Dex and John watched the film from the very beginning to see what had gone wrong at the end. There was the preliminary stuff, kissing, a little bit of joking, and then right there, Kane had kissed him and Ethan—a big burly Italian guy with a smile that would melt a grandmother's heart—engulfed Chase's cock in his mouth and….

"Oh Jesus," John said, a little bit horrified. "I think that's a real scream."

Dex swallowed. He'd gotten to know Chase, had watched him and Tango do a painful, delicate dance around each other because Chase refused to admit he was gay, refused to break up with a girlfriend that he adored but didn't love—not like he loved Tango. Anyone could see that.

Dex and Tommy, known as Tango, had worked together for nearly four years. Tommy was as good a friend as the real Dex, if nothing at all like him, and Dex had *never* seen Tommy as wrecked as when Chase had broken up with him in the name of doing the right thing.

And Dex couldn't even blame Chase. Chase was trying to be a stand-up guy, not to keep Tommy on a string when he couldn't find a way to let his girlfriend go.

Dex watched him on screen now. He was in a sixty-nine with Kane, sucking Kane's hugely wide seven-inch cock down his throat like he didn't need to breathe. Ethan came up behind him and entered him with his own nine-inch wonder (God, shooting scenes with Ethan sucked sometimes, even when the guy was being exquisitely gentle), and Dex and John both winced from the sound that came from Chase's throat. Then he threw back his head and screamed, "*Fucking more!*" and Kane had bottomed out on Chase's erection until the sounds coming out of Chase's mouth weren't real words.

The thing was, this whole scene would have been incredibly hot—just scalding, get-a-boner-thinking-about-it Grade A porn—if they didn't know that at the end of it, Chase had just convulsed on the bed, still coming, half out of his mind—

And weeping for Tommy.

Dex had been the one to call Tommy, and only because John had actually said, "Should we get an ambulance?" and Dex thought that Chase would have hated that. Chase didn't talk about his feelings. He liked to pretend he didn't have any. But Dex had been there when Chase had gone in to clean up Tommy's house. Tommy had made himself sick to cover up the misery that had been watching Chase with someone else.

Dex had seen Chase sitting in the middle of a pile of CDs, trying to excise every part of himself from Tommy's life while crying soundlessly over an old brown cat.

Dex knew that Chase's feelings, whatever they were, would probably make Dex's stomach cramp, and he couldn't stand to think of that much vulnerability all alone. So he'd called Tommy, and Tommy had taken Chase into the showers, and then they'd all left the two of them the hell alone until Chase had snuck out of the set and the office altogether, probably in the name of trying to be a good guy.

Tommy had followed Chase home with Dex in the passenger seat, and then they'd gone to Tommy's house, where Tommy had proceeded to beat a dinette chair against the kitchen floor until it disintegrated into splinters, and then Dex had held him as he'd cried.

So now, watching Chase come unglued in the guise of having sex, Dex was pretty damned fucking uncomfortable.

"Oh God," he muttered. "John, have you called him?"

John grunted. "I sent him the rushes this afternoon and told him to text back when he got them. Should I do something else?"

Dex shook his head and took out his cell phone to text Tommy. *Have you heard from him?*

The reply was immediate. *No, why?*

Dex took a deep breath. He didn't want to worry Tommy but…. *Watching scene. It's not good.*

Fuck fuck fuck fuck... he's not answering my texts, the fucking dick.

Dex leaned his head on his hand and watched as Chase started to convulse, coming helplessly, without any control over his body or the sounds coming out of his mouth or….

Let me know if you hear something. Take care of yourself, okay.

Dex, he's so fucking lost.

I know. We'll keep our fingers crossed.

Dex signed out and watched the screen again—the part they'd cut, where Chase wouldn't stop convulsing and Ethan was looking at him in confusion, and Kane?

Kane dragged him into his arms and just held him, rocking him back and forth and stroking his sweaty hair back from his face like an infant. Dex could almost swear he was singing.

"God," Dex said, "we can't…."

"Can't what?" John asked, his voice sharp. "Ethan and Kane are counting on that check—and I'm pretty sure Chase is going to be as well."

"If Ethan and Kane agreed not to post it…?"

John nodded. "Yeah, let me ask Chase." John pulled his phone out and it buzzed in his hand. He looked at it and closed his eyes. "He okayed it."

Dex said, "He texted you?" feeling almost excited, and John shook his head.

"It says 'OK'," John muttered. "Nothing about this is okay, dammit, but he okayed the paperwork, and…." John sat down and scrubbed his hands over his face.

He'd been dealing with shit, Dex knew. Besides the regular running of the business, there'd been stuff about his location houses, and he'd been planning to send some guys down to Puerto Vallarta on business, and then the stuff he thought he could leave to Dex had just become a major pain in the ass.

Chase was on his side now, and Kane was just stroking his back, leaning down, naked, covered in the aftermath of a threesome and not seeming to care in the least.

Dex had set the camera down long before—he'd called Tango by now and sent Ethan off to the showers, but he'd forgotten to turn the camera off. He appeared in the frame now with a blanket, and together he and Kane managed to wrap Chase up so he wasn't so naked. Dex looked at Kane and said, "Hit the showers, brother. I'll watch him," and Kane shook his head.

"You called Tango?"

"Yeah."

"We can stay with him until Tango gets here."

Dex had to smile, watching Kane's concern. You so wouldn't think it, but Kane? Wild-haired, wicked-eyed, intense, fuck-'em-into-the-mattress Kane was really good people.

Dex sighed. And Kane needed money. "We'll edit it again—as much as we can with Ethan and Kane, as little as we can with Chance. How's that?"

John scrubbed his face. "I'll be back in a minute," he muttered, and Dex grunted.

"John, man—"

"Yeah, I know. It's bad for me and it makes me a shitty person. But if I've gotta watch that fucking tape again, I'm gonna need a bump of coke."

Dex sighed and scrubbed his face too. God. He hated it. John was a friend by now—they worked late nights and watched pretty boys and cracked jokes and shared beers. Never a bed, although Dex suspected that John might have had a crush on him for a while there, but they'd been friends. Dex had sort of taken on a role as second-in-command, because John's business really *had* been in the nascent stages when Dex signed on, and it had tripled since then. He'd hired a receptionist and cameramen and other things, but Dex? Dex was his guy Friday. Dex was the one who knew every part of the business from the phone system to the speech to give the new guys to how much they should spend on getting guys to Puerto-fucking-Vallarta. He was John's twelfth model and the first one to stay in the picture for longer than a year. The stuff he learned in school—he was only a semester way from his business degree—helped, and so did that basic hard work sensibility he'd learned at home.

He just didn't think his parents would approve of *anything* he was doing with it.

It was, he had to admit, one of the reasons he hadn't been too keen to press his degree just yet. Once he had it, he'd have to tell his parents he'd found a job or tell them he did more than do accounting for an entertainment firm. His "real" life would begin in the eyes of his family, and he'd have to grow up, get married.

And, of course, stop being a part of *Johnnies*. No one here—not even John or Tango—knew the story of Dex and David, two boys coming home from their first time together, but that was okay. Even if they did know, they'd understand.

He was happy here. He'd mostly stopped shooting scenes, and that was a relief, because he was starting to want a relationship and the scenes just muddled that shit up, but still. He got to stay here, and be with the guys, and take care of them or be a part of their lives.

So *Johnnies* was important to Dex. He hated to watch its founder threaten to flush it down the toilet with his cocaine habit.

It wasn't every day or even every week, but every time John went to his back bathroom and came out with a tissue, snorting in little delicate, ladylike sniffs, Dex wanted to throw up. He *so* didn't believe in drugs. He knew some of the guys used them—in fact, they'd watched as more than one guy had sort of spiraled off the map because of a habit. Even something like poppers, which some of the guys said made sex outstanding, could fuck up a scene because it took away some of the choice or the personableness or the… the… *unselfishness* that it took to be a good lover on camera.

And let's face it, no one wanted to watch someone just lie there and take it because the drugs were doing all the work.

So yeah. Dex pulled his granny panties on and frowned whenever John went to the back room and indulged in his nasty little habit, but tonight? Tonight Dex wished *he* had something to cope with the total fucking helplessness of watching a friend self-destruct in front of his eyes, and feeling like he couldn't do fuck-all about it.

He started editing on autopilot, wondering if he shouldn't wait for John because his eyes were starting to burn and his eyelids were starting to droop. It had been a pretty stressful couple of days. He was on the third minute of what looked to be a thirty-minute video when

John came back doing that Victorian woman's sniff again, and his phone buzzed.

Dex looked at the number and the text and groaned.

"Fuck," he muttered, and John's dilated eyes were sympathetic. God, how could John be decent even when he was stoned but Scott, the guy on the phone, apparently couldn't be decent in church, even if he went.

Dex shuddered. How could he have been so wrong? He looked at the text again and squared up his jaw.

She's working late. Want to come over?

And that right there was the problem with dating someone on a porn set. You both start out necking at a location shot because you figure, "Hey, we both have girlfriends, we're in Florida. What the hell. It's not like our girlfriends don't know what we do for a living, right? What's one more guy?"

Except for Dex, "one more guy" was that breathless moment when they were done making love and *not* just having sex, and Scott smiled, and Dex suddenly felt like… like *David* again, and like Scott might be the lost Dex of his childhood. Except Scott really wasn't like Dex at all. Scott was a guy who liked getting laid but who was planning to marry his girlfriend anyway, because he figured he was still a straight guy having sex with other straight guys, and wanting one guy over all the others and touching him softly and thinking about him, the sound of his voice, the shape of his eyes, those things didn't make him gay at *all.*

Dex fought the temptation to chuck his phone through the plasma television. He texted instead.

We broke up three months ago, asshole. Lose my number.

David, don't be like that.

And forget that name.

C'mon. It's not like you didn't know what you were in for at the very beginning!

That doesn't mean I can't end it. Go away.

You can say what you want. I'll be at your house in five.

I'm not there.

I'll wait for you.

I'll call the cops.

Don't be stupid. You want it too.

Dex snarled at his phone and tossed it on the couch next to him, then started to rub his chest through his hooded sweatshirt.

"John," he said, squinting at his phone like he could change the shape of it as it sat on the couch.

"Yeah?" John had picked up his keyboard and was editing like a madman. Dex almost hated to break his rhythm.

"Does coke really make you more aggressive? Like you're a god and can do anything?"

John grinned at him, his eyes bright and alive. "Man, you'll feel like you can walk through the fuckin' walls."

Dex sighed. He hated himself on so many levels tonight. What was one more fucking thing going to matter? "So, can I have a bump of coke? I need to break up with an asshole permanent like."

John nodded. "You drive?"

"No," Dex said, thinking about his little house about three blocks from John's office suite. "Walked."

"Excellent. There's some on the mirror in my bathroom. Knock yourself out."

Dex stood and walked resolutely to the bathroom, ignoring the buzzing of his phone on the couch behind him. For nine years he'd been telling the world he was really someone else. Well, tonight he was going to *be* someone else. He was going to be reckless and assertive, just like the real Dex, and he was going to tell Scott to take his booty-call relationship and his "I'm not gay" bullshit and shove it up his ass.

Fuck it. Proof that feeling shit too deeply was a bad thing could be seen screaming in orgasm on the screens behind him. He was through with that shit for good.

Kane

KANE knew it was a dick-mobile—he knew it was gaudy and arrogant and so big it looked like he was compensating for something—but geez. It was *such* a sweet ride. The big black Lincoln Navigator was even dated as a dick-mobile, but he couldn't help it. It was what every guy in his high school had considered the hallmark of success, and now he got to drive it. And he had leather bucket seats and a cherry sound system and gold flashing rims and trim and tinted windows! He loved this fucking car.

But all things considered, he was ready to get out of it.

For one thing, he was parked on a nice little residential street, and if it hadn't been ten o'clock, there would be nice mamas outside with their kids, watching them play, and he felt like some kind of stalker sitting outside of Dex's comfortable blue house, finishing his carne asada burrito and churros and trying not to get sugar and cinnamon on the car.

But he couldn't really go back to his new house in Natomas, could he, now? And he probably could have checked into a motel, but dammit, he just really needed a friend right now, and he was only a little embarrassed to admit it.

And then he saw Scott drive up, and he narrowed his eyes. Not this prick again. Seriously—what did Dex have to do to tell this loser to blow town?

They'd watched—they'd all watched—as Dex had gotten involved with the guy who had the girlfriend and the acid tongue, the guy who was so vain he got pissed if you came on the tattoo on his ribs during a scene. It just hadn't seemed fair.

Dex was… he was the hub of *Johnnies.* He made sure you ate when you were on location and made sure your favorite lube was on hand during a scene, but it was more than that. He made you feel comfortable when you were in front of the camera, and checked in periodically with *all* the guys and sounded them out and made sure they were okay with what they were doing. Kane had actually *heard* Dex tell guys—good-looking guys hung like fucking *bears*—not to shoot a scene. "You're not going to be comfortable here—and that's fine. But you don't want to do something you won't be proud of later. Every guy here, gay or straight, feels some sort of pride in what he's doing. If that's not going to be you, we don't want you to hurt yourself."

And the thing is, that last part about hurting yourself? He meant it! Those guys could have made *Johnnies* a lot of money, Kane was sure of it—but Dex… Dex knew what hurt. He didn't want the guys hurt.

That's what had driven Kane to hang around and hold onto Chase when he was losing his fucking mind in bed. Chase was a friend, and he was hurt! And Dex was there, and when Dex was there, Kane felt compelled to do the right thing.

So Scott, who routinely referred to Dex as his "strange on the side" when Dex couldn't hear him, did not deserve Dex, not in a year or a hundred of them.

Dex deserved better.

Kane was done with his churro and about to get out of the Navigator and go kick Scott's ass the hell away from Dex's front door when Dex came hauling ass down the street in a way not Dex-like at all. Dex was a country boy. He walked like that—slouchy, easy, like he had time. Except not now. Now, Dex's shoulders were straight and he was practically running with a sort of manic energy Kane had never seen in him.

And then he started *yelling*, which was something else Kane had never seen.

"I said not to come over," he snapped, and Scott, who apparently did not have the sense God gave a cockroach, stood up off of Dex's porch steps and tried one of those smiles that most people seemed to think worked really good at getting other people into bed but Kane had always thought of as sleazy.

"Yeah, but Dex, you never mean it—"

"I mean it. I meant it every time." Dex shouldered his way past Scott, and then, much to Kane's surprise—and gratification—he slammed the door in Scott's face. Excellent! *Finally* that asshole was getting what he deserved! The door opened again, and for a moment, Kane was totally disappointed. Dammit! When was Dex gonna learn that some people weren't worth his—

And that's when the first CD case came sailing out the front door and nailed Scott on his high forehead with the corner.

Scott yelped like the dog he was and picked up the CD with one hand while he was rubbing his forehead with the other. "Death Cab for Cutie? Dex, you *love* this band!"

"I do!" Dex yelled, and it wasn't Kane's imagination, he was talking damned loudly for a guy who'd never raised his voice. "I *do!* And I love Coldplay and The Killers and Arcade Fire and"—each band was punctuated by another airborne CD—"Adele and Florence and the fucking Machine too!"

"But—" Scott ducked Coldplay. "Baby, I bought those because you—" A quick right saved him from The Killers. "Loved them! Oolf!" And he wasn't quick enough and Arcade Fire caught his cheek, cutting a little and leaving a small trail of blood tracking down his face. He was so shocked that he just stood and took Adele and Florence and the fucking Machine in the chest as the cases clattered to his feet and shattered on the concrete walkway.

"I *do* love them!" Dex shouted, still too loud for Dex. "I love them, but I don't love you, not anymore, and I'd rather pay for my own goddamned CDs than be your fucking booty call!"

Dex was standing in the doorway, panting, and his voice trembled and cracked on that last sentence. Kane, who didn't pick up on subtleties often, thought that might be a good place to enter the scene. He got out of his beloved SUV quietly and walked with as much stealth as he could manage to the shadows beyond Dex's porch light.

"You know it's not like that—"

"Are you leaving her?"

"No! We're getting married in February! You know that!"

"Do you even *want* to leave her? Chance broke up with Tango, you know that? I think it very well may fucking kill him. I'm not sure he's even right in his own head. But he didn't want to hurt Tango anymore, so he did it. What have you done to not hurt me, Scott? You name one thing you ever done to not fucking hurt me, and I'll get on my knees and blow you right here."

Scott swallowed, and for a moment, Kane almost thought he looked sorry. "You knew what we were doing," he said with a trace of defensiveness, and Kane thought that yes, yes, it was definitely time to say some lines.

"I know what you're doing now," Kane said pleasantly, taking some joy from the way Scott jerked, his arms going out like a startled baby's.

"Yeah, what's that?" Scott snapped.

Kane smiled. He didn't know why, but for some reason, when he smiled his regular, ordinary smile when he was mad at someone, it made them shut up and get all skittish like. The same thing happened to Scott, and Kane liked the effect so much he put more teeth into the smile.

"You're leaving, because Dex shouldn't have to tell you more than six, eight times."

"Yeah," Scott sneered. "You need that much babysitting, don't you, Kane?"

Kane shrugged. "I ain't smart, but Dex is. It's why I'd listen to him if I were you. What have you done to not hurt him? Have you protected him once? And I ain't talkin' 'bout rubbers, 'cause that shit's just fuckin' courtesy. He asked you to name something you've done to not hurt him. Do it."

Scott shrugged. "You're saying that like it was a relationship or something? Jesus, are you just too stupid to know a fuckbuddy when you see—"

Kane hit him. He'd been in enough fights to do the job right too—put his shoulder behind it, caught the bulk of the punch in that line from his knuckles through his wrist—and he was pretty gratified when Scott went down in one blow, just like the bad guys in the movies.

"Holy shit!" Dex said. He still sounded goofy, but now he was a little hazy, like he was having trouble focusing. "Kane, I can't hardly believe you did that!"

"Kane, you fucking psycho!" Scott was trying to yell, but Kane had nailed him in that pretty-boy mouth, so his lips would be all swollen, and he had to admit he'd done it on purpose. They'd shot a scene together, and for a guy who said he fucked guys for fun but loved girls, Scott's main talent in life had always seemed to have been giving blowjobs and rim jobs. He was *fantastic* at it, and that was no lie. Kane figured that maybe it had been the guy's sweet mouth that had kept Dex coming back. If Kane took out his mouth, maybe Dex could make the breakup stick. It was sort of like doing a public service, really.

"Go away," Kane said shortly, and he kicked one of the CD cases that hadn't shattered at him. "And take your shit with you."

And then he walked up the porch and shooed Dex inside so he could close the door on Scott before Talking Asshole could argue.

Dex was blinking at him, his eyes decidedly glassy and a little bit teary too. "Jesus," he muttered. "I can't take any of that back."

"Nope," Kane said, looking around. He'd been there before because Dex liked having people over for holidays and dinner and shit, and Dex's house was sweet. He'd always known it, but now it was even more important. Dark hardwood floors and brightly colored area rugs sat under the butter-soft mahogany leather couches. A big-screen plasma television dominated one side of the room, and the other side opened into a white-tiled kitchen with the big block thing in the middle, complete with dinette chairs so you could eat there, and a table in the corner so you could have a few guests over to eat too. The hallway went back into what was probably two bedrooms, if Kane didn't miss his guess, and that area was carpeted with sort of a teak-brown carpet, while the walls were painted a soft cream.

It was so warm and soft and… just frickin' classy, and Kane thought sadly that he should wait until morning so Dex could turn down his request when he was sober. Dex wasn't going to want Kane and his bullshit in this nice place. It was hardly fair to ask, but, well, maybe he'd let Kane crash in his guest room and borrow his pajamas for the night.

"God, Kane," Dex said after a little too much time had passed. He was sniffling and wiping under his eyes and nose. "What are you doing here?"

Kane sort of gasped and then grunted. "Going to fetch you Kleenex. Your nose is bleeding, Dex. Jesus, what did you do?"

"Cried like a pussy," Dex said, plopping on his couch like he'd sort of given up on something.

Kane came back from a bathroom with sky-blue walls (it was so damned cheerful it actually scared Kane a little) and gave Dex a wad of tissue and a damp washcloth. Dex looked at them both dumbly, and Kane put the tissue on his nose and his hand on the tissue and then wiped off his face around the Kleenex.

"I was asking what drug you did, but then your nose started bleeding, so I figure it was either coke or meth, right?"

"Coke," Dex mumbled. "And it sucks. It was great for a little bit. I was totally gonna tell him to go fuck himself. Wore off kind of quick, though."

"Yeah, that's 'cause you didn't do enough," Kane called from the kitchen. Damn—Dex's ice machine was working and everything. Dex did know how to live civilized.

"Wasn't even a line," Dex agreed. "Which is fine." He sighed. "I'm not doing that shit again. I don't see why anyone does it *ever.*"

"Why'd you do it in the first place?" Kane asked, coming back with the ice and cleaning Dex up some more. Dex's glassy eyes were half-closed, like he was crashing, and Kane thought he'd probably have to get his boy to bed in a minute.

"Because," Dex sighed. "I had to watch that fucking video with you and Chase. God. God, it was scary. He was…."

Kane swallowed. "Do I need to hear this?" he asked, and Dex looked at him and shook his head.

"It wasn't your fault," he said.

"Yeah, but it was what? Three days ago? I can't stop thinking about it." Kane shook his head. "I would have needed something to watch it too, you know?"

"There's nothing we can do about it," Dex said, and Kane could tell he hated that. "Chase was at the gym today. His eyes are like… like there's nothing there. He's… if I knew how to commit someone for their own good, I'd do it."

Kane grunted. "You'd think his girlfriend would pick up on it," he said, and Dex grunted back.

"Mine didn't," he said softly.

Kane looked at him and grimaced. "This thing we do? It complicates shit," he said.

Dex shrugged. "Allison knew what I was doing for money, but I didn't tell her I'd started doing it because I… I cared about someone." Dex's face darkened. "I'm not sure if it makes me better or worse than Chase."

Kane thought about it. "I think it makes this whole business complicated," he said after a moment. "That's why I don't sleep with women right now."

Dex squinted at him. "I didn't know you slept with guys off the set," he said, puzzled, and Kane shrugged back at him.

"Only *Johnnies* guys," he said, because that sort of made it different. The guys you worked with knew the score, right? Except when one of them said *I love you, be my booty call, but I'm not leaving my girlfriend.* There was no way to score that. Kane smiled a little to himself. Well, throwing CDs at him had been a nice start. "So," Kane continued, "you're gonna wanna go shower."

"Why?"

"Because you're sweating up a fucking storm and you bled all over yourself. And then I'll feed you—"

"I'm not hungry," Dex said, smacking his palate. "Mouth tastes like shit."

"Yeah, but you're gonna eat anyway 'cause I said so. Then you're gonna fuckin' crash."

Dex sighed. "I'll take that shower," he conceded, and he stood up. Sure enough, there were sweat stains at his pits and at the neck of his T-shirt. Dex turned around and looked at Kane, his pretty blue eyes all glassy from the drugs and red from crying as he stood. "He's a total asshole," he said, wiping his eyes with the palm of his hand. "It was worth getting high to get rid of him."

"Just don't make a habit of it," Kane said, worried. "That's bad."

Dex shook his head and started twitching a little. "I feel like ants are eating my skin."

"Ewww!" Honest horror. Kane had done some drugs in high school, some X and some pot and some K—but he'd never done coke because until he did porn, it was actually too expensive for him. "Is that normal?"

"I have no idea." Dex sounded totally forlorn, and his shoulders drooped, and it didn't look like he was going to make it to the bathroom after all.

Kane stood up because you just didn't leave a brother looking like that when he was down. "Here. I'm gonna put my arms over your shoulders, okay?"

Dex nodded and leaned into him. "That's nice," he said. "You don't have to do that."

Kane shrugged and kissed the side of his sweaty head. That bright-gold hair was wet on the sides, and Kane sort of wished if they were going to be this close that he could see it clean. It was soft, and it looked cool, and one of the perks of fucking guys for a living was that you got to touch them like that and check that stuff out. Kane liked to touch—stuff made more sense when you could feel it.

Right now, Dex's shoulder—he had one of those stringy athlete's builds, the kind that really made the muscles pop but that didn't get big or bulky, like Kane's—felt hard and bony but not so solid. Dex was usually the sort of guy who would manhandle you back when you were doing a scene, but right now he felt fragile, and Kane wanted to fix that.

"C'mon," he said. "Shower first. Food next. How's that?"

Dex leaned his head on Kane's shoulder, trusting as a kitten. "You feel so nice," he mumbled. "You could take care of someone, you know?"

Kane kept his arm firm while walking Dex toward the bathroom. “Only you,” he said truthfully. “And only ’cause you’re stoned. Otherwise you’d have too much good sense to let me.”

“You’re good people,” Dex said earnestly in the way of all stoned people everywhere, forever, since the history of fermented coconut milk and coca beans.

“I’m a psycho. You heard the man.” Kane pushed him into the bathroom, put two hands at the ribbing of the plain old gray hooded sweatshirt, and pulled it up and over Dex’s head. It was sopped with sweat and bloodstains, so Kane dropped it in the hamper. Wow—a hamper! What a fucking awesome idea! Kane made a note of that—he would need a hamper wherever he ended up living. When he was done, he moved closer to unbutton Dex’s jeans. Dex was usually a pretty slick dresser—leather jackets, tight jeans. He must have been needing comfort if he was wearing his baggy old 501s, so worn that everything was frayed.

But baggy or not baggy, Dex’s body underneath was just… damn.

Of course all the boys at *Johnnies* were just… damn, but Dex was special. He tanned well, which was a surprise since he was such a blue-eyed boy, but he didn’t tan often, so in the winter his skin was just a sweet shade of pale gold and rose. Kane found that he was running his hands down Dex’s hips and his thighs, framing that cut little diamond of a stomach with his thumbs, planing his palms down to Dex’s flanks as he pushed the jeans and underwear down to Dex’s feet. Kane sat down on the closed toilet (with a little cover, which was something else Kane had to think about), and there he ran into the time-honored snag of having forgotten to take Dex’s shoes off first.

Dex let out a tired little sigh, and Kane giggled. “Here, sweetheart, you can lean on me and I’ll get your shoes off.”

Dex grunted. “You know, I could probably muddle through.”

“Yeah, but I want you to remember that I was good to you tomorrow. I got a favor to ask you, and it’s sort of huge.”

Dex pulled his foot out of his battered tennis shoe while Kane held it, and then balanced while Kane peeled off his sock and shoved it back in the shoe, and then they repeated the process.

“Why don’t you ask me now?” Dex asked, and Kane shrugged.

"'Cause you're stoned and sorta weepy." Kane swallowed. "Man, I'm feeling bad enough after the scene with Chase. I don't want taking advantage of you on my conscience."

He looked up at Dex, that long, tanned body, and touched him some more. Dex's cock stayed at half-mast, probably because of the coke, but that was okay. He shivered at Kane's touch, and Kane looked up and smiled.

"Now see," he said proudly, patting Dex on the flank and standing up within inches of Dex's lean, naked body, "this is one of the bennies of doin' porn for two years. Three years ago, this would have weirded me the fuck out, and I would have bailed. But now? I'm just gonna turn the water on and let you get in there, okay?"

Dex nodded and then closed the gap between them and laid his head on Kane's shoulder. "Are you comfortable enough to give me a hug?" he asked.

Kane had been to enough parties to recognize that crash, the melancholy of having something that made you feel like Superman disappear like bubbles in the bloodstream, and he obliged.

Dex's sweat had cooled, so he was a little clammy, and he just relaxed in the circle of Kane's arms and sighed. "How much of this am I going to remember tomorrow?" he asked without a lot of interest.

"I have no idea," Kane said honestly. "I never did coke. That other shit just sort of left the world all blurry. I didn't like it. I'm not smart enough to deal with the world like it is, you know?"

Dex laughed softly. "You're smarter than you think," he said, and Kane shook his head.

"Yeah, whatever. Now I'm gonna turn the water on for you and get you in there and go make you a sandwich."

"I told you I'm not hungry." Dex took a step away anyway, and Kane held onto his elbow with one hand while he turned on the water with the other. He swore then, because he was wearing a hooded sweatshirt with his favorite sports team's logo, and he didn't want to get it wet. He let go of Dex long enough to strip it off and hang it up on the peg on the bathroom door and made another mental note. God, Dex's bathroom had more class than Kane's whole crappy house.

"I told you I don't give a shit if you're not," Kane said, down to his jeans, kicks, and one of those silky T-shirts that clung to his biceps and the heavy muscles of his chest. He turned to Dex and took his hand and elbow and put him under the spray, which was warm now, and Dex sighed.

"God, if I could just wash this night away," he said and hung his head beneath the spray.

Kane shrugged. "It could be worse," he said, meaning it. "You broke up with Scott. How bad could it be?"

Dex let out a laugh that sounded more like a sob, and Kane handed him the soap and the bath sponge for something to do, then closed the curtain and went to get him a towel. He found sleep shorts and a T-shirt while he was rooting around in Dex's bedroom, and left that on the top of the toilet seat too. Then he went to get Dex some tinned soup and a sandwich while Dex got out of the tub. He sat Dex up at the little island in the middle of the kitchen and made him eat the food, then swallow some Ibuprofen for the inevitable withdrawal headache. By then, the microwave clock (one of the few things that Dex had that Kane also had) said it was almost one in the morning.

"Okay," he said when Dex whined about not wanting one more bite of soup. "You go to bed and I'll crash on the couch, and then we can wake up and go work out tomorrow, okay? Is that good? You going to be okay?"

Dex shook his head. "I've been working out in the afternoon to check on Chase." He shuddered then. "Or whoever's running his body when he seems to have checked out of his head."

"He been showing for that?"

Dex shrugged. "Showed this afternoon—looked surprised to see me. Mumbled something about going out with Mercy tomorrow night and how he'd been sick." Dex sighed. "He's…."

Kane shook his head. "He scared me so bad," he confessed, and Dex nodded.

Kane's hand was resting on top of the tile island, and suddenly Dex's hand covered it. His skin was warm now, from the bath, from the soup, and when Kane met his eyes, he didn't look stoned anymore, just tired and terribly, terribly sad.

"He scared us all—is still scaring us," Dex told him. "And it's just all such a mess in my head. Chase, Scott, me, Dex…."

Kane startled. "You *are* Dex!" he protested, and Dex's smile was half bitterness, half bittersweet.

"I'm David," he said quietly. "Did you know that?"

Kane shook his head. "Yeah, you told me. You just always seemed like a Dex to me. But you always knew who I was. I sorta like Kane better."

Suddenly Dex's easy smile, the reason Kane stopped to get coffee just so he could see it, showed up. "There's no difference between Kane and Carlos," he said, and he sounded happy about that, so Kane grinned back.

"I'm not that complicated," he confessed, and Dex laughed.

"No. But that's not always bad." He closed his eyes then, and when he opened them, he was looking at Kane with such a humble need. "If I asked you nice and promised not to molest your body, would you sleep next to me?" he said after a moment. "It's, well, I know it's stupid, I just…."

Kane shrugged. "I ain't never woken up next to someone," he said, nodding his head. "That'll be fun!"

And then he hopped down and put the dishes in the sink and followed Dex into his bedroom. He stripped to his boxers in the dark while Dex turned off all the lights in the house and locked the door. When Dex got into bed, Kane scrambled into the other side.

He spooned up along Dex's back, no question, because Dex was the one who needed comfort, and Dex relaxed against him, that lithe body limp and helpless. Kane wrapped his arms around Dex's shoulders and nuzzled Dex's neck and purred a little.

"You know, Dexter, this ain't a bad way to sleep."

Dex chuckled. "Remind me to do it again sometime," he said through a yawn, and that was the last thing they said.

THE WORLD OF CRASHES

Dex

DEX woke up alone, but the other side of his bed was warm, and there was noise coming from the kitchen. Loud noises. Profane ones, with crashing and swearing—much of it in Spanish. Dex closed his eyes and covered his head and groaned.

"Ka-ane?" he moaned and was relieved when the noises stopped.

"Yeah?"

"I'll give you a blowjob if you could quiet that down."

There was a meditative silence.

"You'd give me a blowjob if I asked anyway. You're good like that. How about if I just bring you some painkillers and finish cooking while you're in the shower."

Dex didn't mention that he'd just taken a shower, because the thought of warm water sluicing down the back of his neck sounded like heaven. He grabbed a spare pair of boxers to put on when he was done, and hopped in the shower, wondering what the hell Kane was going to do with his kitchen but not really caring.

He was grateful. God, he was grateful. His breakup with Allison had been ugly. She was a sweet girl, thin and blonde, with a face more delicate than his. He was just vain enough to think that was a bonus—he knew he looked fragile and would rather not. She had looked on his involvement in the porn business like any other business—selling shoes, selling suits, whatever—and that had been nice. She'd been serious—so extremely serious. When he'd finally come clean about his involvement with one of the guys from *Johnnies*, she'd pursed her lips and thought for a moment.

"You know, Dexter"—in a year he hadn't told her his real name; that should have clued him in that it wasn't going to work—"I think you should rethink why you're in this business. It's gay-for-pay, not get-paid-for-your-secret-fantasies."

He remembered a slow, burning anger, which hadn't been fair since *he* was the one who cheated. "They're obviously not so secret, Allison, if I'm seeing a guy outside the office," he'd muttered. He'd seen firsthand how Chase had been ripped up inside about this, how betraying the girl who thought he'd hung the moon had fucked with his insides, even when it had been clear that the only place Chase felt comfortable in his own skin was in Tommy's reach.

Dex hadn't felt any of those pangs of conscience with Allison, and that bothered the hell out of him. In the end it had come down to the way he saw himself. He'd told Allison he was going out with the guys because he was going over to Scott's. Scott's girlfriend came over unexpectedly while they'd been sitting on the couch, watching a movie, and Dex had faked his way through a friendly good night when he'd wanted to cry like a child.

He wasn't sure why that had done it. He'd gone back to his apartment to a message from Allison, asking if he wanted her to come over that night, and he'd almost called her and said yes. And *that's* when it had hit him. He was doing to her what Scott was doing to him, and he refused to be that person anymore.

It was one of the reasons he didn't hate Chase when Chase broke up with Tommy. Chase didn't want to be that person either.

So breaking up with Allison had been rough, but the worst part of it was the moment he'd swallowed his anger down and conceded that she was right. He'd known. He might not have articulated it to himself, but he knew. The first seven years in front of the camera, he'd told himself a number of things. That nerve endings were nerve endings and it didn't matter who stimulated them had been the first and foremost, and that one had worked for a while. He'd practiced on his body with toys and had discovered that yes, having his prostate stimulated and his rectum stretched felt pretty good without a man attached to the thing doing it. He'd told himself that when you liked and respected a person, that made it easy to enjoy being touched by them, and yes, there was no difference between hugging a girl versus hugging a guy when you were just happy to see that person. A hug, any hug, offered comfort and warmth, and so for a while, he had been able to live with that. But the past two years he'd been doing mostly filming and editing. Once he was no longer fucking guys on camera, he finally recognized that it was the guys who had been turning him on.

He'd hated that admission. Hated it. He still did. The morning after Allison left, he looked himself in the mirror and said, "Dex, you're gay."

He'd seen Dex's eyes looking back at him. "If I'm gay, Davy, so are you!"

He'd wanted so badly to think that those moments with his first male lover had been special, had been perfect, not because of the word "gay" but because of David and Dex. Sometimes when he was with Allison, he closed his eyes and saw Dex, the real Dex, in his mind, the wicked bright brown eyes, the dimples, that one look.

Oh God, the look he'd given David as they'd lain there, side by side, naked under the sky. David had been *his.* He'd been claimed, made safe, taken in a way he hadn't been since. Sometimes when he was with Allison, he'd remember a scene with someone to make it hotter. He never wanted to admit why it was that being with a friend or a workmate and fucking him stupid, flesh sliding through flesh, nerve endings afire with pressure and pleasure, had been like a sensual supernova compared to the small hearth fires inspired by his girlfriends, from Allison to Kelly and even, when he tried to think about it, Sandra.

God—even when thinking about Sandra, he was forced to admit that part of the reason being with her had felt so good was that the whole time he'd been with her, he'd been thinking about telling the details to Dex.

So sometimes when he was with Allison, he thought about Scott or a guy from *Johnnies* to get hard. Sometimes when he was with Scott or one of the guys from *Johnnies*, he thought about Dex.

And last night, he'd kicked Scott out of his life for good, and it had been as ugly as Allison breaking all his dishes against the back wall of the kitchen before she'd stormed out. When he'd woken up from that breakup, he'd been alone without even a job to do in the morning. This time, when he'd woken up, there'd been—

Oh shit.

Kane's ruckus in the kitchen may have woken Dex up that morning, but it wasn't the first time that Kane had done something to wake him up.

Dex was in the shower when this thought hit. He ran his hands over his body, down the shower-sluicing water in the crease of his ass, where he fingered himself, looking for telltale signs of lube, of soreness, of—

Hard, bare flesh sliding between his ass-cheeks but not inside his ass. It was dreamy and slow and sleepy, and Dex's response was instant. Immediate. Necessary. Kane's hands wandered around his flat stomach, skating on his six-pack, over his sensitive ribs. Dex had wanted a harder touch, but he couldn't form a thought, foment a touch, even articulate that need.

The man behind him grunted, and wide, incredibly massy shoulders covered Dex's rangier body. A hand started to stroke the cut of Dex's planed stomach. Dex sighed, struggling to wake up, struggling to remember who he was with, why it felt so warm, so safe, and struggling to remember why it was wrong to feel this way. But it wasn't wrong, it was lovely, even through the struggle, and suddenly there was a hard hand on his neck and a laconic, faintly accented voice said, "Take it easy, sweetheart. I gotcha."

Dex held perfectly still, needing so badly to be touched with purpose that he whimpered for it.

"Don't worry, baby. Here." A hard hand wrapped around his cock and stroked expertly. It didn't take long before his body tingled, spasmed, and he came gently, spurting over the milking hand that continued to stroke as he came down. Behind him, still riding the cleft of his ass, there was thrusting, building, and a final grunt. There was wetness on his backside, but it was warm and not unpleasant, and as he came down from his own orgasm, it felt right. He knew what sex felt like, and that wetness was what it should be, if he'd done his job.

His breath was still shaky, and the hand at his cock moved, wiped itself off on the sheets above him, and then Dex was hauled up into the body behind him while that hand pressed against his middle.

"You better now?"

"Yeah," Dex mumbled. "Thanks."

"No worries, brother. Anything for a friend."

Bemused, he got out of the shower and dried off. As he was toweling off his hair, he wiped the steam from the mirror and looked into it, surprised like he often was to see his narrow, pretty face with his pouty lower lip and blue eyes looking back at him.

"Dex, you're a porn model, for God's sake," he told his image.

His image shrugged. "Yeah, but this wasn't like that."

He didn't have an answer for that, and after he wandered to his room and got a T-shirt to go with the boxers, then walked back into the kitchen, he still didn't have an answer.

Kane was in the kitchen. He'd cooked breakfast.

Dex blinked at the mess of scrambled eggs, cheese, peppers, and onions, and then at Kane, who was busy wiping the counter. He was wearing a pair of Dex's boxers, but his thighs were thicker with muscle, so the fabric stretched tight across Kane's ass as he moved around the kitchen.

Kane had a bubble butt.

It wasn't fat really as much as it was just… softness.

Most of the *Johnnies* models worked out until everything was diamond cut. From their toes to their necks, there wasn't a muscle that wasn't trimmed, defined, polished, and ripped—being naked on camera made you a stickler for such things. Kane was no exception, but his build was wider. Wide shoulders, heavy pecs, heavy thighs. And an ass that refused to chisel to diamonds.

Dex had been his first top, and Dex remembered that. It was one of two scenes they'd shot together, actually, and the sex had been secondary to the way Kane's soft ass had felt as Dex slammed into it. Sometimes a guy could get bruises when he was rabbit fucking diamond-cut muscle or bony leanness, but that wasn't going to happen with Kane. With Kane, it was… well, comfortable. Sweet. Fun.

And last night, those heavy shoulders had wrapped around Dex's and Kane had said, *Don't worry, sweetheart. I gotcha.*

Dex felt a little lump in his throat.

"Kane, gotta tell ya, breakfast looks awesome."

Kane turned around and smiled, his dimples popping at his cheeks and his head dipping a little to indicate that he was embarrassed at the praise. "You don't got no hot sauce," he said apologetically, "which is a real fucking crime. But here's some ketchup. This shit's always better with something red on it."

Dex had to smile. "Yeah," he said. "Ketchup would rock." Kane handed it to him and then shoveled the rest of the eggs in the pan—and there were a lot—onto his own plate. Dex offered him the ketchup, and he doused his eggs with about half the bottle.

"Holy God!" Dex said, his eyes wide open in admiration. "That's a lot of ketchup!" He took a bite of his eggs experimentally and then took a bigger bite. "'Kay, Kane?"

"Mmmph?" Kane looked up from his own bulging mouthful and swallowed through his scrambled eggs.

"The real fuckin' crime is covering this shit with ketchup. This is really good."

Kane ducked his head and smiled again. "Thanks. It was easy. You actually had shit in the refrigerator that cooks. I've got, like…." His face dropped for a second like he'd just remembered something sad. "I had, like, orange juice in my fridge, and frozen food. Like corn dogs."

Dex took another bite and realized how hungry he'd been. "Well you should cook here more often," he said when he'd swallowed. "Is there any milk in there?"

Kane swiveled and got him some from the fridge behind his chair, and turned back around to pour it. He was nibbling his lower lip with his teeth, an expression that made him look particularly vulnerable, especially because the distortion in his mouth made it easier to see the scarring from his cleft palate. Dex had noticed the place where his upper lip and palate had been carefully stitched together pretty much at their first meeting, but since he was still one of the most beautiful models Dex had ever seen, Dex hadn't wanted to pry about the scarring.

Dex realized he was staring. Kane's mouth was full and wide and mobile, and even though Dex had felt it on his flesh during the full range of sexual gymnastics that a scene required, that's not what he was thinking as he looked at it.

He was thinking of a simple kiss.

Dex startled out of his own reverie. "What?" he asked abruptly. "What are you thinking?"

Kane shrugged and put the milk away. "It's nothing. You got a real nice place here. I was going to ask you for something, but I don't want to…." Kane trailed off and took a halfhearted bite of his eggs. "It was a stupid idea," he said at last, his discomfort so acute Dex wanted to ease his mind.

"Well, tell me," he said and took another mouthful of eggs. "If it's stupid, I'll tell you."

Kane shrugged and leaned over the counter, supporting his weight with his elbows and sticking his luscious little bubble butt out behind him.

"See," he said, looking at his clasped hands and ignoring the eggs smothered in ketchup next to him, "the thing is, my sister just left her asshole husband because on top of everything else, he was beating on her."

Dex blinked. "Like, the sister with the baby with leukemia?" God. It was inconceivable. No one was *that* much of a fucker, were they?

"Yeah," Kane confirmed and then stood up and started a leisurely pace around Dex's newly furbished suburban dream kitchen. (Dex cooked a little himself, and he kept intending to take a class or something.) "I've only got one sister. Anyway, the thing is, I told her she could move into my place, but, well, you know how she feels about what I do."

Dex put his fork down. "So? I know she kicked you out of her place 'cause she said it's against Jesus or some such bullshit. But Jesus didn't pay for her kid's hospital bills!"

Kane shrugged like that was nothing, but Dex knew for a fact that Kane had worked two shoots a month for around eight months to make sure that kid got through her chemo so she could be healthy and grow up, and that Kane adored the little goober with all of his heart.

"My sister says she doesn't want no pervert sex fiend near her baby. But I don't want them being beat on either. And, you know, my place gots all that room. So I was gonna ask if maybe I could crash here. I'd help pay rent and everything! But you got a nicer place here, and I got the guys—"

"Guys?" Dex didn't know Kane had roommates.

"Yeah, my pets. No cats, which is too bad, I always wanted a cat, but my guys are sort of reptiles and things like that. I just don't want to leave them there. Lola's afraid of those things, and some of them just need some care, and I'm afraid she'd let them die because she's overwhelmed because the baby's still got some healing to do, right?"

Dex realized his hands were shaking. "Your sister is kicking you out of your own house?" he said, his voice tight. "Does she have any idea how many times you bent over so her kid could have the best care? How many guys you had to fuck so that baby could be all okay? I did the schedule, Kane. Hell, I helped put diaper rash lotion between your ass-cheeks because Cam rabbit fucked until the lube dried up—"

"I can't believe you remember that!"

"Shut up, I'm still pissed. *Kane*, how can you let her *do* this to you?"

Kane shook his head and swallowed, then started to run the water into the dish tub. "Can we just forget it?" he asked, his voice low and quiet. He didn't do great with crowds of people he didn't know, but one on one, Kane was usually a rabid, rampant extrovert, and Dex's stomach twisted again when he added, "It was a stupid idea."

Dex stood up and picked up his plate, then walked around the island and scraped the rest of the eggs—not too many; he'd needed the comfort food—into the garbage disposal. "It was a fine idea," he said after a moment of them standing side by side. Kane had picked up the scrubber sponge and started to take care of the pan with the scrambled eggs in it.

"You don't need this place full of cages and shit," Kane said softly, and Dex thought of that moment in the dark, where his life had fallen apart and he felt about as low and as lonely as he ever had in his life.

I gotcha, sweetheart.

"It's no worries," Dex told him. "Scott hates animals. They'll be better than watchdogs to keep that fucker away."

Kane shook his head and chuckled wickedly. "Since you don't got no more CDs."

Dex groaned. "Aw, shit. I'm gonna have to buy them all again, you know that, right?" He looked at the clock and then swore. "But first I've got to get my ass to the gym. Chase is working out in half an hour, and I don't want to miss him."

"Why?" Kane kept doing the dishes, and Dex felt the absurd urge to kiss him or hug him or something, because breakfast had been such a sweet idea, even if Kane had wanted something and had been almost too shy to ask for it.

"'Cause he's fucked-up," Dex said soberly. "I know you've been working out with Tommy because I asked you to, but Chase is… you want to come with me and see?"

Kane shrugged. "Yeah, why not? And then we can go get my lizards from Lola."

Dex burst into giggles. "You gonna write a song about that?"

Kane looked at him blankly. "Why?"

"Lizards from Lola—you know, Kane—it's an alliteration. The two *L*s?"

Kane looked at him and shook his head. "I'm lost. I have no idea what lizards and my sister have to do with music. Can I borrow some workout clothes and some clothes to put on after the workout and your shampoo and your—"

"Yeah, Kane. Whatever you need. You finish dishes, I'll go pack us a bag and get you some clothes."

Kane nodded, and on impulse, Dex turned back around, put his hand on the small of Kane's back, and leaned in to kiss his cheek. Kane looked at him in surprise, and their noses almost touched, they were so close.

"What's that for?" he asked.

For the first time, Dex noticed that his eyes were a true, rich brown, no green, no gold, very few black specks—just brown. They were solid and comfortable, and Dex swallowed, suddenly liking them very much. "For taking care of me," he said softly. Should he mention them, bodies in the dark? Should he ignore it? He swallowed, and his voice dropped. "You were a real friend last night, and breakfast this morning was awesome. Thanks."

Kane grinned and bounced on his toes a little, and Dex took a relieved step back. "Excellent! Does that mean I can pick out some more CDs? Because that shit you threw at Scott last night *sucked!*"

Dex grunted. "I liked that music."

Kane shook his head. "Naw, man. Let's get my guys moved in here and then I'll treat you to some *real* music."

THEY didn't get to the music that day. First they worked out with Chase, which sucked, because it felt like someone had Chase's brain in a little jar while Chase the robot followed them around and worked out.

"Chance, man, we're over here!" Kane said urgently. Dex thought of him as Chase, for some reason, which was weird, because besides Tommy, he had a real solid sense of most of the models as their porn name and not their real one.

Chase was standing by the barbells, where he'd just spotted Kane for an *obscene* amount of weight on a scary number of bench presses. His tall, rangy frame was limp unless he had a weight in his hand, and his blue eyes were vacant. “Sorry,” he said absently. “I forgot we hadn’t done those yet.”

Kane looked at Dex helplessly, and Dex shrugged. He’d been like that since the breakup with Tommy.

“So,” Dex said, looking again at Kane, who grimaced, “you talked to Donnie lately?”

Donnie was Chase’s best friend and a pretty decent guy. Where Chase was sort of quiet and introverted, Donnie was just like Kane, all Tigger, and a little like Dex, all about taking care of everybody else. Dex liked Donnie plenty. He might be healthy for Chase.

“Yeah,” Chase mumbled. “We lost our last game. No state championship for us.” He managed a little smile and picked up a set of free weights. He looked carefully at Dex, who was doing bicep curls, and then mimicked the motion.

“Yeah,” Dex said, a little concerned. “You told me that a couple of weeks ago.”

The free weight paused midway from Chase’s waist to his chest. “That long? Wow. Hadn’t realized.”

“So what’s Donnie up to now?” Kane asked from Chase’s other side.

Chase’s gaze drifted to him, like he’d forgotten that Kane was there. “Donnie? I don’t know.”

“What about Kevin? I need to take that brother to Thirty-One Flavors again. I’ve never met a guy who can eat as much ice cream as I can!”

Chase’s mouth lifted up at the corners. “I should call him,” he said. “Maybe tomorrow.”

“Why not tonight?” Dex made eye contact with Chase and switched his free weight to the other hand just to watch Chase mirror the move. He didn’t know why he did that—maybe because Chase was just so absent—but when it happened, he thought a little desperately that he needed a response, any response, to let him know this guy wasn’t gonna….

A thought tickled the back of his mind, a memory from a couple of weeks ago, when Tommy had made himself sick and Chase had broken it off, because Chase wasn't really a bad guy and it hadn't sat well to be with Tommy when he was with Mercy too. They'd stopped at a store after cleaning up Tommy's apartment, so Dex could buy some Febreze and some baking soda, and Chase had bought razor blades. Dex looked at Chase now, noted that the blond, almost invisible stubble at his chin was long enough to show, and wondered what Chase was gonna do with razor blades.

"Yeah, Chase," he said deliberately. "Why can't you call him tonight?"

Chase thought about it for a moment, then said, "Mercy wants to go out tonight. Some club off of K Street. Fuchsia—you heard of it?"

"Yeah," Dex nodded. "It's about three blocks from Gatsby's Nick. I know the place."

Chase smiled a little like he was remembering something pleasant. "Yeah. I remember. Anyway, we're going there."

"How's Mercy?" Dex asked, and if anything, Chase's expression became even more vacant.

"Fine," he said. "Why wouldn't she be fine?"

"No reason," Kane said, and he was jumping up and down on his toes. "Chance, Chase, whatever, are you on drugs?"

Chase squinted at him and put the free weight down after hardly any reps at all. "No. Why?"

"Maybe you should look into them. I hear they can make you happy too."

For the first time since they'd gotten to the gym, Chase's expression became animated. "Do you think that would work?" he asked, and Kane shrugged.

"Yeah, but you gotta see a doctor and tell him why you're sad."

To Dex, it looked like a door slammed shut, an iron vault sort of door, big and concrete and terrible. "I'm fine," Chase said, making direct eye contact for the first time that day. "I don't need to talk to anyone. It's all good."

He stalked off to their next routine then, and Kane looked at Dex with a furrow between his eyes. "Why don't I fuckin' believe him?" he muttered, and Dex shook his head and scowled.

“I have no idea.”

“Well, because he’s not really here, you know? He’s all funky and spacey and—”

Dex laughed and smacked him on the back of the head. “I know what you *mean*, you goober—I was being sarcastic.”

Kane’s mouth compressed uncharacteristically, and Dex realized with horror that he was a little hurt. “I don’t know when people do that,” Kane apologized. “They need some sort of sign or a light on their nose or something that says ‘this is when I’m being shitty and sneering at you.’”

Dex took all the puzzle pieces that he could see about Kane and did a flash reassemble. “I didn’t mean to be shitty, Kane. I’m worried. Aren’t you worried?”

“Well yeah! That’s why I didn’t want to use sarcasm.”

Dex nodded, because watching Chase move dispiritedly to the bench presses again, like he didn’t even remember they’d done those, made Dex think that sarcasm was pretty fucking overrated.

They left the gym and Chase went off to school, and Dex called Tommy before he even started his car—a big black pickup truck, fortunately for Kane—and told him about dancing.

“He’s gonna be at a dance club tonight,” he said without preamble as soon as Tommy picked up.

Tommy’s voice was bitter and sad, when usually he was so animated Dex had trouble keeping up. “So the fuck what?” God, he’d sounded like that for weeks.

“So I’m fucking worried about him, Tommy. There’s something not right in his head. He’s… you’re sad, and I get that. I get the being sad.” He didn’t tell Tommy that he was sad too. Funny—Chase knew about Scott, Kane knew about Scott, but Dex hadn’t wanted to bother Tommy about Scott, because Scott the douche bag seemed like such a minor consideration next to Chase, the lost guy who thought he was a douche bag.

“Worried?” Tommy’s voice hitched, and Dex let out a grunt. Kane was watching him avidly and taking in every word as they sat in the car, and Dex suddenly felt a little self-conscious, but he couldn't stop now.

"What, Tommy, this surprises you?"

"He walked out on me—twice!" Tommy's voice was a snarling, vicious mess, and Dex's voice dropped to gentle accordingly.

"Yeah! Because he loves you. Look, I had to throw a CD at Scott to make him go away, and I'm firmly convinced that's because he was having too much fun laughing at me to go on his own. But Chase—Kane, you psycho, give that back!"

"You're getting all sappy," Kane said, his nose wrinkled in distaste. "Tommy? Yeah. Look. Go to the fucking club and ambush him. You heard what I said. He's hurting. It's like being near him makes my skin crawl, he's screaming so hard inside." Dex watched as Kane gave an honest visceral shiver. "I don't give a fuck about your pride, asshole, you gotta make that sound stop, he's a friend!"

And then Kane hung up.

Dex stared at him, his mouth open. He closed it after a moment, and then opened it again, and Kane glared at him defensively.

"What?"

Dex shook his head. "Did you really hear him screaming?" he asked after a moment, and Kane shrugged.

"What would you call it?"

Dex felt like forming words was right out of his skill set. "I, uhm, I dunno," he said after a few moments. "I guess that was it."

Kane nodded like Dex had just totally affirmed his deepest beliefs. "See. Tommy's got to make it stop. Can we go now? I sort of want to talk to my sister when the baby's up."

DEX looked at Kane's spare room with some serious disbelief.

"Really?" he asked for what must have been the fiftieth time.

Kane had the grace to look a little embarrassed. "Sorry, Dex. But, you know. They're my babies."

"Not babeeth," said the toddler in Kane's arms. Frances was small, Dex thought sadly, and bald, and thin. But Kane said she was in remission, and all Fabiola had to do was keep feeding her veggies and doing healthy things—like not letting her douche-fucking ex-husband beat on her mother—and Frances would be all right.

And if that was going to happen, then they had to live here in Kane's house, because Hector did not know where that was. And given the way Fabiola had glared uncomfortably at them both as Kane and Dex had stood on the stoop of *Kane's own house* in the nice part of Natomas where the houses were huge and beautiful, the odds were good that if Frances was going to have a safe place to live, Kane was going to have to move out.

Dex couldn't help thinking it: the whole situation was *monstrously* unfair to Kane. Dex wasn't going to say anything, though. It was Kane's family, and—thank God—Kane didn't know jack diddly shit about Dex's own hang-ups, so Dex didn't have room to speak, did he?

So no, Dex didn't feel qualified to deal with Kane being abused by his own family. But this, seriously?

"Really?" he said again, and Frances looked back at him, her brown eyes huge in that thin hairless face.

"Weallwy?" she said back to him, and Kane shrugged miserably.

"They're my guys."

Dex looked back at the lovely large guest room with the white carpet and the white walls and *no* furniture. Instead of posters or books or music or any of the things that Dex might have put in there, there were four big terrariums, one smaller terrarium, and a big-ass cage. Kane's guest room was the habitation of lizards, turtles, frogs, and snakes, crickets to feed all of the above, and then (oh fuck, really?) a small cage for the feeding mice. There they all sat, with things slithering, skittering, spazzinating, and chirping inside. Dex tried and failed to count how many live creatures there had to be in that room, and then turned back around to Kane.

"You, uhm, want to move all of them?" he asked.

Kane nodded, and Dex's stomach dropped. Kane's normal smile—as happy as Frances's had been when she'd seen her Uncle Carlos—was compressed into a miserable, humiliated, sheepish expression, and Dex realized that he was embarrassed.

When Dex had gotten his first couple of checks, he'd gone out and bought the big black truck of manhood (as Kane had called it that morning), and then he'd bought a house. Tommy had done the same thing, except he wasn't really that into cars—but he *was* sort of a clothes whore. Some guys did stereo systems, some guys did big trips, some guys did blow and whores (but not that many of them, because everyone knew blow made your balls shrink).

But not Kane.

Kane did lizards and bugs. And Dex was the last person in the world to tell him he couldn't, because who in the fuck was Dex to say it was wrong?

"I don't see any heat lamps," Dex asked after a minute. "How do you keep them warm?"

Kane shook his head, his brow still furrowed and that awful look of mortification on his face. God, he so obviously hated to ask for this. "They got heaters under their cages. The cages cost, like, an arm and a leg, but see how they're all plugged in?"

Dex did.

"That's so we can keep them at the right temperature."

Dex gnawed on his lower lip and wrinkled his nose, thinking this through. "Okay, so Kane? It's like fifty degrees outside, and threatening to rain. We can't take these guys back to my place in the rain. What we gotta do is drive down to the Walmart and get a space heater—we can plug it into the jack in the back of the truck, okay? And we gotta get a tarp so we can make the truck all nice inside—"

"And we should get one for your carpeting and your bed," Kane said unexpectedly. "I don't want the cages messing up your shit."

Dex nodded. "Good idea—that's real considerate, thanks. So I'll go get the stuff and you can stay here and visit the baby. I'll be back in half an hour."

The furrows at Kane's forehead disappeared, and his eyes opened in a guileless look of naked gratitude. "Thanks, Dex. I'll do anything, man. I'll pay rent, I'll—"

Dex remembered the blur of being put in the shower, of being told that his one fuckup with drugs was not nearly as bad, not nearly as shameful, as it had felt in that moment, remembered Kane's voice, *I've gotcha.*

"No worries," Dex said, staring at the menagerie in the room. The snake was a big king snake that Kane called Tomas, and that thing had slithered to the end of his cage and was reaching up the glass, poking at the lid of the cage for defects. Just looking at it made Dex's stomach knot.

"Great. God, *excellent.* Here." Kane reached into his pocket and pulled out his wallet. There had to be three hundred dollars in there, and Kane peeled off most of it and shoved it in Dex's hand. "Go get what you need. I'll pay you back if it goes over."

Dex blinked at him. "What in the hell are you doing with all that green?"

But Kane didn't hear him. Frances had just said something about "beaw," and Kane wandered off to her room to go find "beaw," so Dex had to wonder how often Kane just walked out his front door with fucktons of cash in his pocket. Jesus, the man needed a keeper!

Kane's clothes were neat and simple—and most of them fit in the extended cab of Dex's truck. The terrariums barely fit in the bed with the oil heater, and the tarp turned out to be an excellent idea, because the skies opened up just as they were starting to leave. Kane relinquished his hold on Frances at the foyer of *his own home* (and Dex had to keep reminding himself of that, because Lola glared at them the whole time they were there) after giving the sleeping toddler a kiss on the temple.

"Tell me how she does at her checkup, okay?" Kane said anxiously. "She tired out so quick today, Lola. I don't want her getting sick again, okay?"

Fabiola's mouth relaxed, and between the dark hair and the oval face and the eyes, for the first time Dex suspected them of being related by blood. “The doctors said that’ll happen,” she said, rocking her baby in her arms. “She’ll be tired and sad, but she’ll feel better.”

“But you keep taking her, okay?”

Fabiola nodded. “Yeah, okay, fine. Don’t fuss. We’re going to be fine, just don’t stay with her too long. I don’t want her thinking it’s okay.”

“What’s okay?” Dex asked, because Kane just cringed and looked like he’d been socked in the chest.

“The gay thing. She don’t need to know it’s okay for Carlos to be with other men. Where’s he going to be?”

Dex gave her his address, and it wasn’t until he was done speaking that he realized his teeth were grinding. “You know,” he said when he’d made sure she would forward Kane’s mail, “you could try being a little fucking grateful. You’re kicking him out of his own home.”

Fabiola looked at him sorrowfully. “The money he used to buy this place, it wasn’t clean. We’ll move as soon as the baby’s better.” And then before Kane could kiss Frances on the soft bald skin of the back of her head again, Fabiola shut the door.

Dex and Kane stood there for a minute, surprised, looking at the thick blond-wood door of the white house in the middle of the block of all the other big two-story white homes, as the rain came down behind them. Dex threw a companionable arm around Kane’s shoulders and steered him toward the truck before Kane could yearn for one more hug from that baby (who hadn’t wanted Kane to put her down all day) or feel the full hurt of what his sister had just done.

They got into the truck and shut the doors, and Dex started it up so that the oil heater could start working and the guys wouldn’t get too cold. “After we get everybody moved in, what say we get some pizza?”

“Really?” Kane sounded incredibly hopeful. “You’re the one who’s always worried about gas!”

Dex had to laugh. “That’s before we shoot a scene, Kane. As far as I know, you don’t have a scene for another week, and I’m mostly behind the camera now. As long as we don't get fat, I think a day like this calls for pizza."

"*Excellent*! Think we can get some takeout on the way back to tide us over?"

Dex looked at him, at all that heavy muscle that might easily run to fat if he didn't work out religiously. "Maybe go home and have some fruit, what do you think?" he asked. "Then get the pizza."

Kane nodded comfortably, and Dex had a random thought. *I'll take care of you, Carlos. This'll be real good.* And then Kane started flipping through the stations on the HD radio and Dex was too concerned about not letting rap music contaminate the air in his truck to follow up on where that particular thought had come from.

UNLOADING the guys took some time, because fitting them in the guest room with the bed turned out to be like playing *Tetris*, except with terrariums and live snakes. Finally Dex had to concede to taking the bed apart and putting it into the garage, where the frame could sit in the corner by the tool bench and the mattress could rest in the rafters. It was the only way the snake, lizards, frogs, turtles, and moving dinner could all fit on the tarp on the floor under the Toulouse-Lautrec and Monet prints up on the wall.

Dex called for pizza, which was imperative because by now they were both starving. When he was done, he looked from the living room across the hallway, saw that Kane was lying on his stomach in front of the snake's cage with his chin propped in his fists and his bare feet swinging above his ass.

He was talking to the snake.

Dex hung up the phone after giving the order and leaned against the doorframe to listen.

"It's good here, you'll see. Dex is a nice guy, trust me on this, okay? He's being nice, and when the baby's better, Lola will take her and we can go back to the house, okay?" Kane's voice dropped like this next part was a secret. "I'll miss having her around, though. Don't tell anyone—Lola's afraid I'm some sort of pervert, but I like kids, and not in the sicko way. So you just stay healthy, okay, Tomas? You stay healthy, we'll be good, right?"

Dex followed a barely understood impulse and walked into the room and sank to his knees on the tarp. He put his hand under Kane's shirt to the silky skin at the small of his back and just rubbed pleasantly.

"You know something, Carlos?" he said gently.

"What?"

"It's not really a secret that you'll miss the baby."

"I know," Kane mumbled. "I just don't want to seem too needy."

Dex lowered himself to lie side by side with Kane and rested his weight on his elbows. "So noted," he said, and they lay there companionably, watching Tomas check out his surroundings with snakely interest. Kane deliberately didn't break contact until the pizza arrived—Dex could tell.

BY THE time the pizza got there and they showered, ate, and watched about an hour of television (*Castle*—Dex would do Nathan Fillion in a hot second), they were actually pretty tired. Dex opted to sleep in his boxers and Kane did the same. Kane's clothes were still in a pile on top of Dex's dresser, and Dex knew that the next day, they'd be dealing with that shit, so he had no problem lying down next to the guy when they were both almost naked.

They were porn models, right? What was one more naked man?

But then Kane rolled away from him, and Dex thought about his eyes that day as he'd turned away from Frances. Dex followed him, wrapping his arm around Kane's middle and drawing him close, being the big spoon this time, and Kane let him. They were tired and sleep came quickly, and Kane snuggled back into Dex's arms like that's how they belonged. Dex was just tired enough not to wonder at whether it was right or wise or even a good thing to do, and then they fell asleep.

At two o'clock Dex's cell phone rang on the bedside table charger. He answered it so tired he could barely remember how the damned thing worked.

It was Tommy. He was hella fucking freaked out. Chase had tried to slit his wrists, and Tommy needed moral support at the hospital.

Kane was diving for his jeans before Dex could even put the thought together that a guy he thought of as a good friend had almost died.

Kane

"WE CAN'T what?" Dex's voice grew shrill. For the first time since they'd scrambled out of bed and into their clothes so they could meet Tommy at the hospital, Kane heard that patina of "we can make this okay" crack.

Tommy had just gotten there when they arrived, and was pacing the halls of the ER waiting room, chewing gum fast enough to bite off his tongue if he missed his aim. Dex hadn't gone up to him and hugged him, which is what Kane would have done, but then Tommy had turned toward them, his narrow, long-jawed face screwed up into a fierce snarl, and Kane got it. Tommy had a bit of a shotgun temper. He was going to be pissed.

"Tango, brother," Kane said, trying very hard to radiate goodwill like the sun, "you gonna be okay?"

"I need a fucking cigarette," Tommy snarled, and Dex nodded easily.

"Okay," he said, "maybe after Kane and I get some news. Anyone know what happened?"

Tommy glared up at the pretty blond boy who was talking to the nurse at the front desk. "Ask him. Chase thought it would be dandy to call him when he did it. I got no fucking idea why."

"'Cause I made him promise," Donnie said, walking up to their little group. Dex and Kane shook hands with him because they knew him from a party at Chase's house about a month before. Kane went in for the chest bump and Donnie clapped him on the back warmly, so that was nice.

"So," Dex said, breaking up the sweet animal warmth of comfort, "what the fuck?"

Donnie gathered them to the side instead of the middle of the corridor and spoke quickly, looking at Dex the whole time. People did that, spoke to Dex—he always seemed to know what to do. It was comforting. It was the reason Kane had shown up at his house when he'd needed the help.

"So I made him promise to call me if he ever needed to talk," Donnie said. "I didn't really expect him to call me up in the middle of the night and tell me he needed to be taken to the hospital because he was bleeding out." Donnie swallowed tightly, and Kane realized for the first time that the side of his sweater, his shoulder, the top part of his chest, were all sopped with still drying blood.

"Why'd he do it?" Dex asked, and Tommy made a hurt noise and turned away.

Donnie looked at him sourly. "I don't know, but for some reason he thought it would be a fucking spiffy time to come out to Mercy while he was fucking bleeding in his own doorway. Told her all of it—gay, *Johnnies*, Tommy—said it was gonna set them both free."

Kane gaped. When he could close his mouth, he looked over at Dex and saw that Dex was gaping too. Tommy had turned away, but now he was looking back over his shoulder at Donnie, the resentment clearly easing.

"He told her?" Tommy asked, his voice thin and hopeful.

Donnie nodded. "Yeah. He told her. Had me throw his clothes over the rail so she wouldn't burn them. Kevin's getting them now."

Dex managed to close his mouth, which was good because Kane was back to gaping. Chase, Chance, whatthefuckever—he'd *said* all that? God… even when he was happy, the guy didn't say that much.

"Why?" Tommy muttered. He pressed a palm against first one eye and then the other, because apparently they were leaking. "Why would he tell her all that if he was gonna die?"

Donnie shook his head. "You don't get it, Tommy. Tommy, right?"

Tommy nodded. "Yeah. I'm him."

"Yeah, well, he stopped. He didn't slit both wrists. He slit one wrist and stopped. And had her get the phone so he could call me. We did all that shit—all that fucking breakup shit, like throw his clothes over the edge and tell his girlfriend he was gay and loved you and all that shit—before he even got in the car. He called *you* from the car, right? Because he got all that other shit out of the way…."

"He *planned* that?" Kane heard himself asking in horror. "He *planned* that? I can't even plan my next dump and he *planned* that?" Dex touched his shoulder, and Kane looked at him with eyes even he knew were big and startled. "Why's a guy who can do all that planning wanna go and hurt himself? Can't he fucking plan not to hurt himself? Wouldn't that be a better fucking plan?" Kane's voice was rising, growing shrill too, he knew it, but dammit, he'd *heard* that scream in Chase's heart, *heard* it. Why couldn't a guy who was so smart figure out a way to stop screaming that didn't involve blood? If Chase couldn't figure out how to be happy, how was Kane supposed to do it? Kane wasn't nearly as smart as Chase!

There was a hand then, clasping his, and he didn't care if it was girly, he clung to it. Dex moved in, blocking his field of vision, that perfect, pretty face, the hard little cheeks and the sky-blue eyes, and Kane felt his quickened breathing even out, just looking at him.

"Sometimes when you're hurting, your plans go to shit," Dex said, and he sounded like he knew.

"He stopped?" Tommy said, his voice was rising, and Kane realized he might have said this more than once. "He stopped?"

Donnie nodded. "Yeah, you heard me. He'd done one wrist, and then he called me."

"He stopped." Tommy nodded like he was trying to put that into a place in his head. "He stopped. And then he called you… because why?"

Donnie had wide blue eyes, but now they were all scrunched up as he tried to make sense of Tommy. "Because I've known him since the second grade, that's why. 'Cause if you've just fucked up your life, you want to get it in order before you call the guy you want to share it with—can you handle that?"

Tommy scrubbed his face with both hands. "I get this call," he muttered. "I'm lying in bed thinking that he made his first promise *ever*, that he'd try to leave her, and he calls me, and he says he's free, and then he says he's going to the hospital, and then he fucking passes out. What the hell am I supposed to do with that?" Tommy whirled around to the wall and threw a hard punch, fierce enough to split his knuckles as he howled, "*What the hell am I supposed to do with that?*"

Kane and Dex let go of each other's hand, and they each took one of Tommy's arms and hauled him away from the wall. Tommy fell completely apart on Dex's shoulder, sobbing hotly.

Kane got on his other side. "You're gonna help him get better," he said, and Tommy looked up, his pale skin blotchy and his brown eyes reddened and the skin around them puffy.

"How am I gonna do that?" he asked, and Kane flailed for words.

"He… he was all screaming inside. I'll bet when he wakes up he's not anymore. He's gotta learn to scream on the outside. You gotta teach him how to do that."

Tommy nodded and buried his face in Dex's shoulder again. "Okay," he said, and it was muffled and thick, but still, the word made Kane feel better.

Donnie came over to Kane's other side and shifted uncomfortably. Kane was shorter than he was—shorter than Dex, for that matter, but Donnie was tall enough to remind him that he missed being short by about two inches.

"His girl's not here," Kane said, and Donnie shook his head.

"Don't think she's gonna be, either. Man, there he was, bleeding out and babbling *all* his secrets. Being gay. Tommy. Porn. And we sat down in the car, and he's like, 'I got one more thing to do.' And then the sonovabitch held on just long enough to call Tommy and tell him he was going to be free. It was…."

Kane scrunched up half of his face. "*Twisted,*" he said with fervor. "Seriously. What is it with all these people who can frickin' do shit like that?"

"Like what?" Donnie asked.

Kane shook his head. It was hard to put into words, but the reason he carried cash only was so he didn't spend all the money in the bank. If he pulled out so much cash and stretched it out, he knew it would be okay. It was why he didn't decorate and his furniture was minimal—he was just being careful, was all. He had to make sure there was money in there when he sent the checks to the baby's doctors. At the moment, he was pretty sure he was safe, but that's why he'd been shooting all those scenes for so long. He needed to be sure, so he didn't let the baby down.

The actual balancing of a checkbook scared the hell out of him.

"Planning," he said at last, knowing it was lame. "How could he plan when he was bleeding out and I can't plan when I wake up in the morning and the house is quiet?"

Unexpectedly, Donnie grinned at him. "Because you're simple, Kane. But that doesn't mean it's bad. It just means that when something's important to you, we'll know, and"—Donnie's face fell—"right now simple is sounding really good, because… damn."

Kane remembered where they were again, and nodded.

They hunkered back on the waiting room couches for a while, almost cuddling. About a half an hour after Dex and Kane got there, Donnie's boyfriend, Alejandro, showed up with Kevin and pretty much Donnie's entire family. Donnie held Yandro to one side and kept up his huddle against Kane, and that was reassuring. Kane had actually fallen asleep against Dex's shoulder and was deep enough under to choke on a snore when the doctor came out.

Tommy and Donnie jumped to go see him, eyeing each other distrustfully as they stood.

"What's that?" Kane asked Dex softly, and Dex looked at him and shrugged.

"Whose dick is bigger."

"But Chase isn't like that," Kane protested.

"People get weird when they're sexually compatible," Dex said with a sigh, "and Tommy doesn't get how Chase can have a friend without benefits. God, I wish I knew what the doc was saying."

Whatever it was, it was bad, because Tommy's face was no longer blotchy and Donnie was no longer eyeing Tommy with distrust. They were, in fact, holding hands.

"They had to… what was it again?" Tommy asked distractedly, and Donnie filled in the blank.

"Resection his artery," Donnie said, his voice sounding a little flat. "They had to take a part of the blood vessel in his thigh out and put it in his wrist because he…." Donnie swallowed and a blood vessel popped out at his temple. "He did a number on himself. If he hadn't stopped…."

"You fuckin' finish that sentence and I'll fuckin' end you," Tommy said, his voice just as flat, and Donnie, who had never struck Dex as particularly cowardly, backed down.

"Yeah, anyway, he needs more blood."

Next to him, Dex perked up. "Blood," he said, looking at Kane like that was the answer to everything. "When I was in a wreck, half my town donated blood. Let's do that." He pulled out his phone and texted frantically for a minute, then hit Send. Kane's phone was in his own pocket, and when it buzzed, he took it out stupidly.

"We're all donating blood?" he said when he looked at the text, and Dex nodded.

"It's something we can do," he said, and Kane got it. Dex liked to fix things. Liked to make them better. Okay, then. If this would make things better, Kane would do it.

Except now, an hour later, the people in charge weren't letting them do it.

"What do you mean we can't donate blood?" Dex said again. About ten of the guys had turned out, which was sort of nice, and they were in the beige blood donor room at six in the frickin' morning, and Dex's voice was getting a little shrill. Kane had to admit, he didn't know what to make of this either.

The nurse—a large middle-aged woman with a face that was not unkind—looked Dex in the eyes. "Honey, I know what *Johnnies* is. My nephew's gay. If you are all models from *Johnnies*, and you're working, you won't be allowed to donate blood. You could all come in here and sit behind the partition and answer the questions, but I promise you, when we get to one section on the questionnaire, you'll be told in all confidentiality that you won't be allowed to donate. Gay men aren't—period. And neither are men who have had sex with other men, whether they're gay or straight. That's just the law."

Dex swallowed. "But… but we're *tested.* Every month, we're tested. Doesn't that count?"

The woman nodded and patted his hand. "It means you're going to live a long, happy life. But as soon as you started having sex with other men, the law says you're not going to be leaving any of that life here." She looked at Dex's expression, which was so devastated it made Kane uncomfortable, and said as consolation, "But you boys are welcome to some cookies and juice."

But that was that.

"But what are we supposed to do?" Dex asked, and Kane heard it, that need for something to do.

He walked up to where Dex was dealing with authority—that was sort of Dex's job with *Johnnies*. John was the big boss, but Dex was the little boss, and he organized the shoots and did the editing and took care of the guys, and that's what he was doing here. He was giving them something to do to make them feel better, and it wasn't working. And it hurt.

So Kane put his hand on the back of Dex's neck like he would if they were shooting a scene and Dex was getting too frisky, because

Kane liked his bottoms to sit still. "Dex, man, it's okay. We're gonna go back and wait for news, okay? You got us all here. That's good. We can say prayers, whatever, but we're here. You did good. You did your job."

Dex nodded, but his jaw was clenched and his face was locked, and his sort of pouty lips were thrust out. If anything, he looked more vulnerable here, when he was being in charge, than he had looked when he'd been coming down from the coke.

"Yeah," he said and then turned around to tell the guys. Most of them took it okay, but some were stunned, and some were angry. Ethan came up to Dex and burst into tears, and Dex spent ten minutes hugging him while he shuddered. Dex ran his hands up and down Ethan's massive biceps and shoulders and back, because Ethan needed to be petted sometimes just to be able to think.

Kane kept his hand on the back of Dex's neck through all that, and when Dex shuddered once, like he was thinking about breaking down with Ethan, Kane squeezed a little and shook and Dex got himself back under control.

And they were good right up until when the round little guy with the white fringe of hair like a hula skirt and the white beard and the yarn bag came out and introduced himself as the shrink. He talked to Donnie, Tommy, and Dex—and Kane, because Kane wasn't letting go of Dex yet. Dex just didn't seem that out of the woods.

"Does anyone know how long he's been planning this?" the guy asked when he was done with all sorts of questions that Kane forgot. He did that, especially when he hadn't slept in for-fucking-ever.

When Donnie and Tommy shrugged, Dex said, "Six weeks," without seeming to think about it, and they all looked at him.

"How would you know that?" Tommy asked, his voice thick, and Dex started shaking under Kane's hand.

"'Cause when you got sick," Dex said, "after we cleaned up your house. That's when he bought the razor blades. I was there, I just didn't know what they were for."

Kane almost dropped him, he was so surprised, but he didn't, which was good, because when Dex—*Dex*—came completely unglued, Kane just kept that hold on the back of his neck and turned him in to Kane's chest so Dex could sob on him while the rest of that hospital madness kept going.

CHASE came out of surgery eventually, and they said he'd be okay, so everybody but Tommy and Donnie went home. Kane drove Dex's truck while Dex sat, eyes glazed, and stared vacantly out the window.

"You couldn't know," Kane said at last. It was cold and gray again, and the sun barely made a glare against the high cloud cover. Kane wished it was bright and cold like it tended to get in November, but it was still early October. It was either going to be gray or too hot, and he liked the cold.

"Yeah, well, there's that," Dex said, and Kane grunted.

"I'm going through the drive-through. I haven't had anything since cookies and juice, and you need food."

"I need my fucking head examined," Dex said bitterly, and Kane waited until the truck was in the drive-through line at Jack-in-the-Box before reaching across the truck and smacking him on the back of said unexamined head.

"You need food and sleep, and you need to call John and fill him in if he didn't see the mass text," Kane said, all of his pragmatism coming out to play. "And you need to stop blaming yourself. Chase, man, he had that plan *down.* All we can do is be grateful he decided to change his idea midstream."

Dex nodded and wiped futilely at his face. "Yeah. Okay."

The car in front of them moved, and Kane got to the window and placed his order. He ordered for Dex too, figuring that there was only so much breakfast food Jack-in-the-Box had and Dex would probably eat whatever. The car moved forward, and Kane, tired and cranky, felt like he had to say it one more time.

"Honestly, Dex, how were we supposed to know what was going on in his head?"

"I should have known," Dex said, his voice falling away like dust from a shelf. "I used to feel that way too."

Kane's hands went cold on the steering wheel, and he looked at Dex—confident Dex, who welcomed everyone to the job and kept everybody's tempers all smooth and fixed the schedule so no one had to work with anyone they'd banged off-set by accident and couldn't stand anymore. His eyes were still open and still gazing sightlessly at the parking lot beside them, and Kane actually saw black spots in front of his eyes as he thought of Dex in the surgery like Chase was.

"When was that?" he asked, and something about his voice must have hit Dex, because he seemed to snap out of it.

"Long time ago," he said, sitting up and smiling reassuringly. "Right after I moved to Sacramento." He waggled his eyebrows then, and if Kane hadn't been there, right there at his side, for the past twelve hours, he would have been fooled. "Right before I met this freaky chick who suggested that gay-for-pay might help me get through college."

"Did you get through college?" Kane was surprised, and Dex shrugged.

"I've got about a semester to go. The schools got so impacted—I couldn't get the classes I needed even when I could afford them. I dropped out about two years ago. I should go see if maybe I can finish the damned degree."

At that point they were even with the window, and Kane reached for his wallet and then groaned. He had a five left, and breakfast was more.

"Dex, brother—"

Suddenly Dex had pulled himself back from wherever had been making him sad, and was there with Kane in the truck and looking a little concerned. He pulled out his own wallet and gave Kane his check card, and Kane gave it to the salesgirl, feeling flustered and uncomfortable.

"Kane, why don't you carry your bank card?"

Kane handed Dex his card and then took the food from the girl and put the bags between them. "I'm not good with money," he confessed. "I don't want to spend too much. Here. Have a sandwich. It'll make you feel better."

Dex started wolfing down the sandwich and didn't ask again.

THEY got home and Dex shed his jacket and shoes and jeans in the bedroom and was about to fall into the bed when Kane—whose own shit formed a little trail from the door to the bedroom—grabbed him by the back of the neck again. It was gratifying how quickly Dex's body went still.

"We need this," Kane said sincerely. He didn't have any good words. He wanted to talk about stress and human connection, but he just had those three words, and they were true.

Dex made a sound—it could have been protest or it could have been positive, but it didn't matter.

Kane shook him gently. "We need this."

Dex nodded and stood still, and Kane started to kiss his neck. Dex shuddered from his toes to the tops of his shoulders then, not just still but limp, and Kane continued to kiss under his jaw line and then nibbled his ears. Dex groaned and turned around, taking Kane's lips with his own, and Kane went with that even though he usually wasn't much of a mouth kisser on the set. With Dex, though, it was different. Dex's mouth was warm, and their breath wasn't so great because hey, woke up from sound sleep to freak out over bad coffee in the waiting room, but there was that constant, insistent tongue and the seeking heat. When Dex's hands came up to frame Kane's face, Kane suddenly felt accepted. It was like he was connecting with another person in a way he hadn't ever thought to during this one particular act.

He took over the kiss, putting his own hands on Dex's face. He growled from his stomach and devoured him, bearing him back against the mattress and stripping off his shirt to taste him some more. Dex tangled his fingers in Kane's hair and hung on as Kane kissed down his pecs and his ribs and then went up and visited Dex's nipples. Dex thrashed and moaned when he did that, so Kane put a firm hand on his lower abdomen and made him stop. He released a nipple with a pop and said, "Hold still," and Dex did. Kane grunted to himself in satisfaction. Good. He could make it better if Dex didn't wiggle so much.

And he wanted to make it good. He kissed down Dex's stomach and luxuriated in Dex's groan. He suckled some of that smooth pale-gold skin into his mouth and teased it with his tongue, and when Dex tried to wiggle some more, he put his other hand on Dex's chest. He released the marked skin and turned his head, saying, "I told you to hold still!" before continuing on down.

He'd always liked Dex's cock. It was a little longer than his own and thinner, but unlike Kane's cock, which had a wider head than base, Dex's was pillar straight. It looked like one of those sculptors had made a marble statue of what a cock *should* look like, and that's what he was pulling into his mouth. It even *tasted* better, which was weird, since they hadn't showered and Kane didn't usually do guys who hadn't showered. (He didn't do girls who hadn't showered either. It's one of the reasons he was such a fan of the "Keep the work area clean, hygienic, and eco-friendly" speech.)

But Dex tasted wonderful, and Kane pulled him back into his mouth and then back into his throat and then again and again. He relaxed his glottis, so Dex could get way back there, and tightened his mouth at the base, and he knew this drove guys crazy, but he was still surprised when Dex groaned again, grasped his hair, and said, "Kane, you've gotta stop! I'm gonna fuckin' come!"

Kane pulled back and licked a long line from the base to the head. "Can I still fuck you if you come in my throat? Some of the guys get all tender when you do that." It was why the shoots were structured the way they were—pull out of the bottom, let the bottom come, come on the bottom's face/stomach/thighs. They didn't always follow formula, especially after some of the guys got going and realized they could come under different circumstances, but it was a place to start. "Do you?"

He stuck a lizard tongue out and teased Dex's crown, just because it was so pretty, all fat and red and shiny like that, and Dex threw his head back against the pillows and moaned, holding his hand up to his mouth to silence it. Kane looked up—he was lying with his head on Dex's stomach—and pulled his hand away. "Stop that," he said absently. "I like the noises." Then he teased Dex's crown again because he couldn't help himself. Something about the taste of Dex's skin was making him crazy.

"You can fuck me if I come now," Dex managed, and then he groan/screamed into the open air, making Kane shiver. His own cock was all drooly, and he thought that was amazing, since he hadn't even given Dex a chance to touch it. Before he really went to town and swallowed Dex down and squeezed on his balls (because he liked feeling them clench when a guy came), Kane swung his hips over and straddled Dex's head. Dex whimpered and opened his mouth, then used his hand to grasp Kane's member and guide it in. Kane smiled a little and grunted, because Dex was good about swirling his tongue around the head and playing with the foreskin (not a lot of guys did that) and stroking Kane's taint when he gave blowjobs, and Kane enjoyed all of those little touches.

He especially enjoyed them when he was swallowing Dex's cock again. For a moment he was doing everything house style, with his chest pushed up off the bed and tilted a little to his right, and then he realized that there weren't any cameras, and that was *awesome.* He lowered himself to the bed and rested his weight on Dex's abdomen and sucked more of that wonderful cock into his mouth, swallowing and pressuring the base while Dex's movements on his own cock got more frenzied and less professional. Kane smiled a little around Dex's erection, then slurped back, sucking as he went, so he could talk.

"Take it, dammit! All the way to the back of your throat! I know you can!" He let out a gratified grunt when Dex obeyed him and sucked him from tip to base all the way back in and started a real blowjob again. It felt amazing, and his arousal built, but he really couldn't come and suck at the same time. He put all his concentration on Dex's dick so he could get around to fucking Dex blind. The prospect was so delicious that he shivered before he got serious. He sucked Dex back into his mouth and squeezed his balls and then used some of the spit sliding between Dex's butt crack to push against his entrance to make him all soft. Dex gave a cry then and started to shake, and Kane figured he'd better wedge two fingers in there to make sure Dex would stay loose after he came. When he was done, he wrapped his lips around his teeth and squeeze/sucked all the way to the top, teasing with his tongue as he went.

Dex's hands flailed at the tops of Kane's thighs as he made a loud, sexy, moaning howl and came. Kane swallowed happily while Dex was still convulsing underneath him, and then, before Dex had a chance to breathe, he sat up and dropped his balls into Dex's mouth. "Suck on those while I find the lube," he ordered, and when Dex did what he asked, he stroked Dex's stomach happily. God, Dex was good at this. It was a shame they'd never really shot more than two scenes together. Dex's tongue swirled and his mouth worked gently while Kane reached for the end-table drawer. Dex lifted himself up to follow Kane's balls, and Kane liked watching his stomach muscles ripple when he did that too. He rifled through the drawer, saw no more than the usual shit—no restraints, blindfolds, dildos, or cockrings; just lube, one plug, and condoms. He grabbed the lube and condoms and got himself gloved and lubed at warp speed.

He swung around and found that Dex was still lying in his back, gasping for breath, his mouth swollen and shiny from blowing Kane and his blue eyes as wide as an anime character's as Kane came back toward him. His usual grin was nowhere to be seen, and his fine-boned face seemed extremely delicate now that it was serious. Kane liked looking at him all stunned and blotchy from coming, so he decided not to make him turn around.

"Here, spread your legs," he said and smiled when Dex did what he asked. He parted Dex's cheeks and liked that little gasp that Dex made when he did that. Then he positioned himself at Dex's entrance and looked down seriously. "You good, Dex? This won't take long."

Dex nodded, his chest still heaving, and in a single thrust, Kane buried himself to his balls inside Dex. Dex gasped and clenched and threw his head back, and Kane, who usually only kissed because they told him to, had to capture his neck when it was all exposed and vulnerable like that. Dex moaned and Kane kissed him and kept moving, even though the angle wasn't optimum. Dex made an unsatisfied sound in his throat, and Kane pulled back.

"Kissing or fucking?" he asked, and Dex's laugh was a little desperate.

"Now I got a choice?"

Kane laughed a little and kissed him because Dex kissed so damned good, and then pushed up so the angle was better and thrust in again. Dex cried out and grasped the sheets in both hands.

"My chest," Kane told him. "Touch my chest, squeeze my nipples, I like that."

Dex nodded and responded, even while he groaned and raised his thighs up around Kane's ass.

Kane shuddered. "God, that's good. Keep doing that… God, next time, I'm gonna let you come when I'm in you. That'll be hot!"

"Kane?" Dex gasped.

"Yeah?"

"Please shut up and fuck me!"

Kane chuckled and went for it, strong, hard, and fast, loving his sounds and the way his hands shook and trembled on Kane's chest while Dex struggled to comply. Then Dex gave a particularly hard twist to one of his nipples and Kane was, without warning, *right there.* He didn't have a camera, so he could just keep fucking and come, shaking, falling on top of Dex, sweating and convulsing, comforted by Dex's hands in his hair and the soothing half noises Dex was making in his ear.

Kane didn't want to move, and Dex didn't complain, so they stayed there, tangled and merged, until Kane turned his head and saw Dex's eyes half-closed.

"Don't go to sleep yet," he said. "I'll clean us up."

Kane shivered as he rolled off and went to the bathroom for a cloth. When he came back, Dex was turned on his side, huddled under the blankets. He didn't resist when Kane wiped him down, but he didn't relax under the tending either. Something was wrong. Kane came back to bed and slid behind him.

"You're not going to feel bad about that, are you?" Kane asked, his voice thick with sleep, and Dex took Kane's hands and tucked them up next to his chest.

"You were wonderful," Dex said, still sounding distant. "It's not you."

"Then what?" Kane felt hurt blooming in his chest. He'd felt… warm and close during the sex. He didn't want it to make Dex feel bad. That wasn't how it was supposed to be. Dex shook his head, that bright, shiny hair sopped with sweat.

"It felt good," Dex whispered. "It felt great. And you were awesome. And for a minute I felt… like me. Like David. And then I remembered that you don't know who that is. David is a long way away."

Oh. Was that all? Kane hugged him so close he heard Dex grunt and his ribs creak. "David, Dex—you're the guy I just fucked blind. You're perfect, sweetheart. Don't stress about names. The guy right here, he's a good guy."

Dex laughed a little. "Aren't you supposed to be straight?" he asked, but his body relaxed into Kane's, and that made Kane happy.

"I am straight," Kane mumbled. "Except when I'm fucking guys, I'm plenty straight. Now shut up and sleep. And don't feel bad. That was amazing. You can't feel bad about it."

"God, you're bossy in bed."

"It's because it's the only place I know what to do. Now hush."

"Thanks, Carlos."

"My pleasure, David. Now do I need to gag you?"

Dex giggled tiredly. "Not today. We'll save that for later."

Kane thought about that, Dex with a blindfold and a gag, his thighs spread, his ass open and begging, and his cock got a little hard again, even as he fell asleep.

REFORMING THE WORLD

Dex

THREE weeks after Chase Summers survived his suicide attempt, Dex woke up to two things. One was Kane where he'd been for the last three weeks, jammed up against his back and holding him so tight that breathing was optional. That was familiar. That was the direct result of putting the critter cages in the guest room and packing up the bed, combined with the ease of having a live-in fuckbuddy who buggered Dex senseless pretty much every chance he got.

That was okay.

The other thing was a cool metal-slick muscular rope rippling smoothly up the inside of Dex's thigh.

That was *not* okay.

Dex's eyes flew open. "Kane?" he squeaked, and Kane grumbled in his ear. "Kane!" he squeaked again, and Kane grunted this time instead of grumbled. "*Kane!*" Dex's voice rose to a furious, hoarse whisper. "If you don't wake up right now I will never suck your balls again."

Oh, *that* got his attention. "What's wrong, sweetheart?"

Dex had been listening since that first time together. Kane didn't call anyone else "sweetheart." Not girls he talked to, not guys, not Tommy when Tommy was falling apart, not Chase when Kane was being that sublimely gentle person that so few people could see but who was so very apparent when talking to the wounded, mentally bleeding Chase. But Dex got called "sweetheart." Normally that would be very interesting, especially because Dex had never been big on endearments. He wasn't particularly big on using them, had never really gotten them—but Kane called him "sweetheart," and it was starting to make him feel like normal was warm.

But right now, being Kane's sweetheart was *not* something that concerned him.

"Kane?"

"Yeah?" Kane started to stretch—he did that, stretched his toes in bed first, then his calves; then he wiggled his hips and finally cracked his hands overhead and took care of his torso, shoulders, and arms—but Dex needed him *not* to stretch at this moment.

"Stop stretching and do me a fuckin' favor, okay?"

"Yeah?" Kane sat up like he was suddenly catching a clue from Dex's tone of voice, which was good, because the rippley, muscley coolness was slicking right up over his hip near the crease of his thigh, and Dex was very, very close to panicking.

"Kane, could you get your fucking snake out of my fucking shorts? If that thing touches my dick, I won't ever fuck again, and I've got a scene to shoot today, so that would be a real fucking shame!" He'd thought he was done with scenes, but everyone was doing an extra scene to fill in for Chase and Tommy.

Kane grunted again, but this time in acknowledgment. "Shit, Tomas, what you doin' out?" His hand was gentle on Dex's skin as he peeled Dex's boxers back and let the snake curl up his arm. "Oh geez, he feels cold! Dex—is the power on?"

Dex sat up, suddenly panicked for a whole other reason. Sure enough, the clock next to his bed was blinking and the heater had that dusty smell of having just kicked on again. Outside, the wind was blowing in what had been a killer thunderstorm the night before, and now that Tomas was no longer threatening Dex's livelihood, he could reach over to the phone and check the time. Okay. Good. Plenty of time to get ready for the shoot. But that was the least of their problems.

He looked at the time on the clock and then the time on his phone and did some subtraction in his head. "Probably about two hours," he muttered. "Okay, you go check the guys and I'll go get the space heater from the garage. We can warm them up quicker that way."

"But it's cold in here!" Kane sounded panicked, and Dex swallowed and said a quick prayer. Kane talked to them. He went in after his day and told them what he did. He picked up the snake and stroked its scaly black, scarlet, and gold body, and let the gecko ride the space of his shoulder. He had a small iguana that got to run around the room when the door was closed. He even talked to the mice before he put them in Tomas's cage for feeding. He told them they were good mice and would come back in their next life as good snakes.

Dex went into the guest room as little as possible—quite frankly it skeeved him out—but Kane? Kane could be found in there, sitting cross-legged, listening to rap music, on any given day. Dex was starting to think the gecko's eyeballs throbbed to Drake and Usher, but he didn't want to say anything in case Kane thought he was crazier than he already did.

"Okay," he said now. "You check them out and see what you need to do, and I'll go get the heater, right? Let's go!"

He didn't stop to put on slippers or anything, and the garage was fucking cold, but all he could think was that Kane's babies were going to need the heat before his creaky old heater kicked in. He got back into the guest room, pretty sure his balls weren't going to surface in time for his shoot, to find Kane cuddling the gecko in his hand with the snake still coiled around his arm.

He looked at Dex with abject pain. "He's moving really slowly," he said, and Dex nodded and plugged in the heater.

"Okay. I'm warming up the room, you stay in here. I'll go get the heating pad."

There you go—stroke of genius! Dex could fix this. He *could.* He couldn't go back in time and tell the shrink about the razor blades, and he couldn't warn the other Dex about the deer in the road. He couldn't warn himself that Scott was a douchefucker out for a piece of easy ass, and he couldn't tell his old self that he'd get so immersed in *Johnnies* that he'd rather edit porn than get his degree, but he by God *could* keep Kane's little green friend from dropping off planet Earth too soon.

He popped the heating pad in the microwave and got a wet towel to wrap around it. He knew reptiles and amphibians sometimes needed water—he figured it couldn't hurt. The heater always dried out the air, and Dex and Kane had taken to rubbing bee jelly cream on their hands and faces because it was odorless and they needed *something* so they didn't chap in the early November chill.

He brought the heating pad in and sat down next to Kane, holding it out to take the gecko, but Kane looked at him miserably and shook his head. Dex thought *Oh fuck* and reached out his hands anyway. Seriously, who knew with lizards, right?

Yeah, the lizard was dead. Its sticky little paws were flung out wide on the hilly surface of Kane's palm, and its pale-green skin was turning blue, and its little tongue was even flopping out between its gummy little lips.

Dex looked at it for a second and sighed. "Aw, man. I'm fucking sorry. Seriously fucking sorry. How's everybody else?"

Kane shook his head and clutched the lizard back to his chest, his lower lip thrust out like a little kid's. "I didn't want to check."

Dex nodded and looked around greenly. Oh holy fuckin' jebus. Ick.

"Here, let me give it a go," he said. He looked into the cage with the little breeding fancy mice first, because hell, at least they were mammals. Sure enough, two of the little bodies were still, and the rest of the mice were huddled into a corner, trying to keep each other warm. Dex swore and ran off to get a shoebox and tried to come back before Kane could even think to ask.

Quietly and without fuss, he gathered the little bodies of what were essentially snake kibble before moving on to the other cage. The iguana gave him a scare, but Ms. Darcy (Dex had no idea how Kane knew it was a girl) was huddled under her log and a bunch of wood shavings, her horned scales bristling along her skin, and apparently doing just fine. Now that the heating filaments under the cages had started warming again, she was starting to twitch, and Dex smiled in relief. For one thing, Ms. Darcy the iguana was about three feet long including her tail and might have been too big to fit in the shoebox.

The amphibian terrariums with the little frogs and the salamander and the turtle seemed to be doing okay. Apparently those creatures got used to temperature drops in the water, thank God. In the end, the worst casualty was the gecko.

Which Dex dreaded getting out of Kane's massive, delicately cupped hands.

Dex turned to Kane with a pained expression on his face. "Kane, buddy, I'm sorry…."

Kane nodded his head. "I hear you," he said roughly. "So just the two mice?"

"Yeah, everyone else is okay. They might need some reassurance, though—at least Ms. Darcy might." Tomas seemed to be relaxing a little around Kane's forearm. At least Dex hoped so. Kane's fingers were discolored from the lack of circulation.

Kane nodded, but those cupped hands stayed close to his bare stomach anyway. Dex sighed and came to sit next to him, their bare shoulders touching in the mercifully heating room. From the room next door, his cell phone buzzed, and Kane grunted.

"What's that?"

"That's John. I'm late for my shoot."

Kane bumped him at the shoulder. "You should go."

"John can wait," Dex said easily. He still had the shoebox of dead mice in his hands.

Suddenly Kane looked up from his hands, a brilliant smile on his face. "Hey, after this shoot, we can start fucking again, can't we?"

Dex had to laugh. Kane had done a scene three days before and Dex had one today—it meant they had almost gone a week without Kane holding him by the back of the neck and nailing him to the bed. Kane had bitched enough about the three-day moratorium on sex before a scene, but when Dex signed up to take Chase's place on the roster, Kane's whining got particularly acute.

"Don't you *like* having sex with me?" he asked when Dex came back from editing and told Kane he was filling in.

Dex smacked him on the back of the head. "Yeah, asshole, I like it fine. I'm doing a favor for a friend, okay? Two of 'em, if you count John, who already had plans to fly this kid out for this shoot."

Kane glared at him sourly. "You just want to know what it feels like to have a ten-inch dick up your ass."

Dex rolled his eyes. "Been there, been fucked by that. Besides, I'm topping. Chase was a real good top. John wanted someone to break this kid in gentle."

Kane's glare tweaked instantly to an evil grin. "So that's not me, right?"

They'd been sitting next to each other, watching *Dancing With the Stars*, because Kane never missed an episode and Dex had been sucked right into the madness. Impulsively, Dex leaned over and kissed Kane's temple with more gentleness than play. "No, baby. You need to be an expert to take you up the ass. That's why I'm lucky that way."

Kane's evil smile fueled his evil laugh, and they went back to watch the show with Dex hugged securely to Kane's chest. That night had been the last free night they had before Kane's abstinence started, and Kane had fucked Dex until Dex was tempted to wave the little white flag, but he hadn't. This was lucky because when he finally blew his third load—down Kane's throat—Kane had come just from swallowing. Kane had crawled up his body, apologetic and sheepish, but Dex had kissed him, the taste of his come still in Kane's mouth.

Kane had melted against him, soft and pliant like Kane was *never* soft and pliant, and Dex had that memory of him, sweet and gentle in the circle of his arms, to keep him satisfied during the next six days.

Which were supposed to end today (or tomorrow, after recovery) when Dex got his worn-out whoring ass to the set.

Kane reached out his hands and had Dex open the box. He set the gecko inside with a tenderness that made Dex absurdly bleary-eyed, and stroked the little body so lightly it hardly moved.

"Bye, Tree-Squirt. You were a real good little lizard—real sweet. You were the best first pet a guy could have. Sorry 'bout the fuckin' heater. Wasn't how I'd planned for you to go."

Dex thought wretchedly that if he walked into the set late with his eyes all puffy from bawling, John would fucking kill him. He closed the shoebox and pressed it into Kane's hands. "When the wind lets up, you can go out back and bury them in the flowerbeds or under the tree. I was going to put a pond in the center there this summer, so maybe not there, but you know. Somewhere he wouldn't mind hangin', okay?"

Kane nodded and then looked up at Dex, obviously embarrassed by his watery eyes but not able to hide them either. "That's real nice of you," he said softly. "I can do that before I visit Chase, how's that?"

"You say hi to him for me," Dex said, thinking with a little bit of shame that he was relieved not to be going there today. Usually he went and worked out with Chase at the mental institution gym, which was actually so crappy Dex had to come back to his regular gym to do the workout he needed to do if he didn't want to get fat since he was closer to thirty than twenty. Chase knew he wouldn't be coming today because of the scene, and Dex? Dex could see Chase fighting clear of depression and all sorts of horrible, nasty demons with every visit. But Dex usually visited Tommy after he visited Chase and found him rocking himself in a ball in his own bed, and Dex would sit and comfort him too. As much as this shoot was a favor to John and a favor to the company so they could keep up their schedule, it was a fucking relief for Dex to only have to go fuck with his body for a change, and not open his heart up for everyone else's pain to come fuck *it*.

But telling Kane that it was going to be all right and that he could survive the death of his little green lizard felt like something different.

He realized—and it surprised the holy fuck out of him too—that he didn't want anyone else in this room, sitting next to Kane, giving him a shoebox full of dead little bodies. That was Dex's job, and he didn't want to bail out of it.

Kane was still sitting there, his powerful shoulders drooped, and Dex wrapped his arm around them. "Kane?"

"Yeah?"

"Are you freezing your balls off yet?"

Sigh. "Yeah."

"Me too. If you promise not to do any kinky shit, we can shower together and get warm."

Kane shook his head and laid his head on Dex's shoulder with a touching faith. "I always want to do kinky shit to you. I don't know why. I mean, I done guys off set before, but that was always like, one and done, and they were guys from the set anyway, and they knew the score. You? This last week felt like school it sucked so bad. You need to go shower and do your enema shit and get out of here."

Dex grimaced. "You know, uhm, the night after I don't always feel like…."

Kane shrugged. "All I gotta do is jack off on your ass, man. I just need to touch you naked." He sighed and shifted like he was going to move, but Dex stroked his thick black hair and tightened the arm around his shoulder to keep him there. He didn't want to say it, but those were actually damned romantic words, coming from Kane.

THE shoot was… well, it was a porn shoot, right? Back when Dex had been telling himself that he was straight, he'd talked about nerve endings getting fondled, but he'd known better. There was an anticipation when you were getting touched by the person you wanted to touch you—even if it was just make and not specific model. There was an electricity, a singing in the blood, an incense in the smell…

It was *intoxicating*. Dex knew that. Even when he'd been with Scott, on those rare occasions when he'd found himself back filming a scene, he could still enjoy that cold electricity running under his skin from the idea of being with a guy for a shoot.

Dex looked at the sweet boy grinning at him, his ten-inch cock rampant and eager in his hand as they sat in the room and fluffed, and tried to summon some of that anticipation.

What was his name? Bambi? No—*Bobby*—that was it. Who had ever heard of a porn star named Bobby? Bob B. Long, maybe, but Bobby?

John was filming, because he and Dex had been working together a long time and he knew Dex's moves and Dex was comfortable with him. Dex didn't realize how much of his emotion showed on his face until John said, "Dex, get your hand out of your pants and get over here."

Dex was happy to get his hand out of his pants. It wasn't doing much in there anyway. He just kept remembering the way Kane had rested his head on Dex's shoulder, and how sad he'd been while he'd clutched that tiny little body.

"What's up?" Dex asked, and John shook his head.

"Was gonna ask you the same thing. You not getting it up? That's a first. You getting some on the side?"

Dex blinked. "Since when is having a relationship 'getting some on the side'?" he asked, and John sighted Bobby through the camera viewfinder.

"Kid?" John said kindly. "Maybe back off a little. You're gonna blow right here."

Bobby's hand stopped midstroke and he shuddered, and in that shudder, right there, Dex saw Kane, right the way he'd looked after Dex had come in his mouth: a little embarrassed, a lot turned on. Suddenly Dex wasn't having such a hard time getting his flag to the top of the mast.

"Don't worry," Dex said, and he smiled his most reassuring smile. "Give it a pat on the head and tuck it back into your pants. It won't be there for long."

The boy smiled back, his soft brown eyes going sort of moony, and Dex walked up to him while he buttoned up. Up close, Dex could still see the freckles on his cheeks. He had a long, almost horsey face, made pretty by the softness around the jaw and full lips, as well as the wild curly hair. He smelled like Old Spice, which was the smell of a kid who used his father's aftershave. Dex had skimmed his profile—he was nineteen, which was about a year younger than Kane, but Kane had never felt this fresh off the truck, and Dex felt a momentary pang of guilt.

Then Bobby looked into his eyes and smiled tentatively. "Is it bad that I really want this?" he whispered, and Dex suddenly felt honor-bound to tell the truth.

"Nothing we do here is bad," he whispered back. "It's gonna feel good, and you're going to enjoy the hell out of it. Don't let anyone tell you it's bad until it's not right for you anymore, you hear me?"

Bobby's smile was sweet and soft, and Dex gave John and the other cameraman the go-ahead signal for filming before he went in for the kiss. But it wasn't Bobby's smile that he thought of as the kid's lips surrendered to his own. It wasn't his smile or his youth or his ten-inch cock. All Dex could think about as he ran his palms up under Bobby's brand-new Aeropostale T-shirt was the trust in Kane's red-rimmed brown eyes when they'd been sitting side by side in a freezing room, honoring dead animals with brains smaller than sunflower seeds.

This kid, at least, Dex wouldn't let down.

WHEN they were done, Dex collapsed on top of him, looking down on his face while their bodies stuck together with sweat. Dex saw the softness in his eyes, his mouth, and sighed. This would be difficult. He didn't want the kid to be attached, but he didn't want to be a bastard either.

He kissed the kid on the forehead and said, "You were great, kid. It's going to be fun working with you in the future."

The kid blinked like he was waking up, and as Dex rolled off of him and put on his robe before they progressed to the shower scene, Dex saw him nod sharply.

"It's been a pleasure," he said. He sounded like a grown-up, and Dex was relieved. Maybe, if the shower scene went quick, he could finish editing in time to stop for something on the way home.

He called Tommy before he went, and Tommy came to help him select it because Tommy was working at PetSmart now and knew about these things. Tommy took him around PetSmart after his shift and told him what to pick out. He looked really tired.

They stood there looking at a terrarium full of turtles with a cart full of terrarium supplies, and Dex waited in the silence for him to say something.

"He's still crying a lot," he said after a moment.

Dex looked at him, not knowing what to say back. Two weeks before, Chase had broken down sobbing in the weight room for what had seemed to be no reason whatsoever. He hadn't taken visitors for a few days after that, but lately, Dex thought he'd seen an improvement.

"He's not doing that talk in his head thing as much," Dex offered, and Tommy looked up and smiled a little, his dark eyes glinting under the fluorescent light.

"Yeah—that's sort of cool. He told me to fuck off the other day and then looked just fucking baffled that those words came out of his mouth. He's *funny* now that he's not keeping all that shit in his head."

Dex felt suddenly better about Chase, the lost boy. "Well, that's something I don't have to worry about with Kane. That boy never did have a thought he didn't care to voice." For a minute, he wanted to clap his hand over his mouth. *Oh no! People don't even know we're rooming together!* But Tommy wasn't in a state to hear.

"Yeah, he's a total spaz," Tommy said, but he said it with a smile. "I took him clothes shopping two months ago, and you know where he ended up buying shit?"

"Walmart," Dex said, because he saw those clothes every day.

"And you know the thing that pisses me off about that?" Tommy asked in admiration.

"He makes it look better than all your high-end mall shit?" Dex said, even though it wasn't true—Tommy looked like a runway model, even if Chase was the only one to really notice that when he had his clothes on.

"Yeah." Tommy shook his head. "Fucking pisses me off. Here. See these guys? Good color, they're moving around good, they're eating. Sort of like my turtle Oliver, but these guys are sliders, so they get a little bigger. One of 'em'll fit into that outfit you got. You sure he's got enough room to fit a setup this big? You said he lost a gecko—their setups are smaller if it was only one."

Dex didn't know why he didn't tell Tommy then, not just about the roommate situation but about the fuckbuddy thing too. Maybe it was because he and Tommy had once had a one-and-done back before Tommy and Chase were set in blood and stone. Maybe it was because everybody had known about his thing with Scott, and Tommy had been undergoing a similar situation with Chase, and Dex just felt naked and exposed when Chase had done a nuclear detonation and Scott had proved to be *so* unworthy of all that pain.

Maybe it was because he was eight years older than Kane and he should maybe be treating this thing as not so serious, since God knew he'd managed to royally fuck up pretty much every other relationship he'd had since the real Dex.

But then, Scott had been his one relationship out of the closet too, and that had taken a cocaine-fueled implosion to kill dead, no grace necessary, thank you very much.

Maybe it was just because Tommy so obviously didn't need someone else's bullshit to contend with. Yeah, maybe it was mostly that. Tommy didn't need Dex's bullshit, so he'd keep that precious raw moment of Kane weeping on the floor over his dead lizard and some feeder mice tucked up against his own chest, and nobody else needed to have it.

So he didn't tell Tommy that he knew there was enough room because he knew how big the empty spot on the floor was, and that it could hold two grown men sitting down, plus enough room to walk around, plus a gecko terrarium that he no longer needed, and so it would probably fit some more turtles. He just bought the setup, thanked Tommy for his time, and told him he'd be in to see Chase tomorrow morning, and maybe Tommy and Kane could go out for pizza the next night, after Tommy's visit. Tommy brightened at that. When Chase got out of his mandatory psych time, he was going to live with Tommy, and Tommy could have him all to himself. But in the meantime, Tommy was lonely and scared, and he'd told Dex that he didn't know if his lover was going to be coherent or catatonic from one day to the next. Company for dinner? That sounded fantastic.

Dex gave him a hug as they got into their own cars, and Tommy clung to him fiercely.

"Tommy?" Dex asked when they separated. "How come it never happened with us?"

It should have, he realized. But it hadn't, in spite of the one-and-done when Tommy had been grieving for his mother and Chase had left him alone. It *seemed* to make sense—Tommy *looked* like the real Dex, even more than Scott, and that seemed to be his type.

Tommy squinted at the question, though, and pulled his lip up over those pointy canine teeth. When he spoke next, all of his South Boston was in his voice. "'Cause you like to plan and manage shit, Dexter, and I'm sort of plan-and-management resistant. All I need in my plan is one guy, and he's enough of a planner for the both of us. You got people goin' out for pizza, having barbecues and shit. I don't think that far ahead."

Dex laughed a little and thought that might be about right. "Well, I'll plan a barbecue for you any time," he said. He also thought that Tommy was a little too tough for him. Tough was probably a good thing for Chase but not so much for Dex. Dex liked a little softer, sort of like the softness of Kane's bubble butt, which might have been one of the reasons he'd never felt the need to kiss Tommy the way he was starting to yearn to kiss Kane.

Tommy nodded. "Good. You get all excited about planning. 'Cause Chase is coming home in three weeks, and I want the whole world to greet him." Tommy shook his head, his voice growing dark as the night sky. "I need that fucker to know that if he's gonna try and take himself out again, he's gonna leave a hole in the world. I gotta go now, he's waiting for me."

Dex swallowed, arrested by Tommy's intensity for a moment, and Tommy hopped in his car and took off. That was some serious love, Dex thought. Maybe that's why his lovers hadn't worked out so far. Maybe before you got someone who would fight to have you, you had to be ready to kill or die for them first.

He drove back home, very carefully not asking himself what the fuck he thought he was doing with Kane.

Kane

KANE had ordered pizza, because otherwise he knew Dex would come home and cook or at least try to tell Kane what to cook, and he didn't want to have to worry about food when all he wanted to do was touch Dex's naked skin. It was set in his brain now, this one priority. The day had sucked.

He'd spent the morning on the phone with Lola, trying to get her to take the baby to the hospital because she had a low fever, which babies couldn't *do* when they were recovering from leukemia, he *knew* that. Finally he'd shown up at the house, and Lola wouldn't put the baby in the Navigator with him because he was a sex pervert (it was all so casual how she said that, he had to believe it was true), but he followed her to the hospital and made sure she took the baby in. He'd waved to Frances over Lola's shoulder and the little girl had waved dispiritedly back, and he'd sat there in the parking lot of Kaiser, feeling helpless and miserable, until the asshole behind him honked his horn.

He went to work out then, and then went to visit Chase, and Chase had been… well, probably better than trying to off himself, but brother had been quiet. He was starting to lose muscle mass now that he wasn't eating well or working out so much. Kane still thought he was pretty, and he liked blond hair and rangy builds (and he was starting to like Dex's longer body even more), but Chase's cheekbones were getting pointier and his chin too. It was weird, though: every time Kane looked at him, he thought of Frances. He wanted Chase to get strong again because Kane liked hanging out with him. He was a little funny, and very quiet, but mostly just good people. He was smart, and Kane respected smart because he had so little of it himself, but Chase was also nice to people who didn't have that going for them. It felt good when someone smart was nice to Kane. Made him feel like he wasn't quite so deficient. It was something he liked about Dex too.

But Chase couldn't be nice to him when he was so sunk in his own head, like he was today. Chase had his own shit to sort.

By the time Dex got home, Kane was feeling… lost. Alone. Vulnerable. And Dex was late, which made him feel forgotten. So the last thing he was expecting, as he sat at the table and munched cold pizza and warm salad, was for the door to open and Dex to come staggering through with a big king-size terrarium balanced in his arms.

"Holy fuck!"

"Jesus, Kane, could you lend me a fucking hand?"

Kane dropped his pizza on the free paper plate and wiped his hands off on his jeans. Dex's blond hair was windblown because it was cold and still windy outside, and his cheeks were pale and blotchy with the cold. His jacket was dotted with water, but his angel-blue eyes were all for the terrarium, which Kane helped him balance.

"What in the hell?"

"Here… through the hall…."

They'd done this before with the rest of the cages, so it was easy for Kane to lead walking backward while Dex issued orders for which way to turn. They got to the door of the guest room and walked in, and Dex huffed, "Jesus, Kane, is it good for them to be this warm?"

"Shit!" Kane and Dex set the terrarium down in the empty spot—Kane had put Tree-Squirt's cage up in the garage, so there was plenty of room. Then he turned the oil heater down.

"God," Dex panted, unzipping his jacket, "I forgot what a pain in the ass that was."

"Yeah, it is. Why did we just do that again?" Kane was down on his knees, checking out the little guy in the terrarium. "A turtle? I already got turtles!"

"Yeah, but you got box turtles, and this guy's a slider. By the way, did you know those box turtles are gonna grow a lot bigger than that box you got? I grabbed a book on these guys. If we're not careful, they'll break my fuckin' house. We gotta be careful with 'em. In the summer, they need to go outside, and we'll have to make wooden enclosures and maybe a big brick box or somethin'. They're territorial too, so maybe two of 'em."

Kane looked up at Dex, whose narrow pretty face was all matter of fact as he made all these earnest plans for turtles, and he had to blink really hard to make sure this was what he thought it was. "If we gotta be careful with 'em, how come we got another one?"

Dex's full, pouty mouth compressed like he was biting back an answer. "Well, I didn't want to get you a gecko because for one thing, they were out. I thought about getting you something with fur because,

I dunno, a baby rabbit doesn't sound like a bad deal, but that didn't seem to be *your* deal, so I passed."

"Yeah, Dex," Kane said, still on his knees in front of what was apparently a gift. "But why get me anything at all?"

Dex's eyes darted restlessly toward the door. "Because you were sad, and I don't like you sad. Was there pizza? I could swear I smelled—"

Kane could move fast for a big guy, he knew it, so he knew he'd catch Dex by surprise when he launched himself up into his arms. Dex caught him, though, and in spite of the fact that he'd had a scene all day and that *nobody* felt like sex after they worked a scene, Dex turned his head into Kane's kiss and kissed him back. Kane relaxed after that, and the kiss wasn't aggressive or all lustful or anything. It was just… thank you. And it went on and on and on and on, and Dex returned every foray and met every stroke of Kane's tongue.

Although Kane could feel his arousal building, his body beginning that tingle he'd started to associate *only* with kissing another man and *especially* with kissing Dex, he suddenly remembered enough about Dex's day to pull away. Dex was tall and that was nice, because Kane could just rest his head on Dex's shoulder nuzzle his neck. Dex smelled good. He brought his own soap to the shower scenes like he was remarking himself after wearing someone else's skin smell.

"What's wrong?" Dex asked quietly, and Kane shook his head.

"Nothing," he said softly. "It's just a real nice turtle, that's all."

"You like?"

"Yeah. I gotta come up with a name. Besides Oliver."

Dex laughed, because he'd heard the story of Oliver the turtle from Tommy too. "I don't know, Kane. Given what I read about the damned things, we should probably call him Bruiser."

Kane nuzzled his neck again, licking experimentally, pleased with himself. "Bruiser—or how about Tractor. Tractor the Turtle."

There was more laughter, and Kane felt a kiss in his hair. He closed his eyes then and imagined… just imagined.

Dex's stomach grumbling broke the warm silence, and Kane pulled back far enough to look at him. "You ain't eaten yet?"

Dex shook his head. "Naw. Wanted to bring the turtle home too bad."

Oh. Oh geez. "I ordered pizza for you. Let me dish it up. I, uh, started eating it before you got here."

But Dex didn't hear that part. "Pizza?" he said dreamily. "I haven't eaten pizza in *forever*. I *miss* pizza."

"Yeah, we ain't ordered pizza in almost a month." Since Chase scared them so badly, but Kane didn't want to say it. "Why in so long?" Kane grabbed Dex's hand and pulled him to the kitchen.

"'Cause Tommy." Dex went to the sink to wash his hands, which was a real good idea after touching the turtles, so Kane joined him. "After he got sick or made himself sick or whatever, I started eating better to keep him company."

Kane grunted and took the towel from him so he could dry off too. "Too much of that'll make you nuts. Why work out if you're gonna eat carrots?"

Dex grinned and sat down at the island where they often ate as opposed to the dining room table. The table seemed to exist specifically to hold Dex's mail. "Because not all of us make it muscle! Some of us get spare tires around our middles instead of outrageously shaped man tits, Kane. But… mmlllmfff…." Dex grabbed a slice and dug in. "That doesn't mean I'm not still a fan."

"So how's the new kid?" Kane asked, picking up his half-eaten piece and going for it.

"Hung like a fucking elephant," Dex muttered, shivering. "God, I know I'm getting old, but seriously, I'm just as glad I don't have to ride that thing."

Kane looked at him assessingly. "Seriously? Some guys like 'em that big."

Dex shrugged. "Yeah, well, I guess if you cared about a guy it'd be different, right? You'd be all about the preparation and the foreplay—that'd be nice. But having to go through all of that to be stuffed like a sausage? It's got to be one fucking hell of an orgasm to make that worth it, and frankly? I haven't found one guy with a ten-inch schlong who was good enough to make it worth it."

Kane grinned at him. "What the hell kind of porn star are you?"

Dex grinned back between bites of pizza. "I'm the kind who's going into the business end instead of getting the business, that's what kind I am." Suddenly he sobered. "I may go back to school next semester, though. Tommy says Chase is. I've only got a semester—hell, less, actually."

Kane grimaced. "I'd go to school, but what're they gonna give me? A degree in snakes and bugs?"

Dex didn't laugh like Kane expected him to. "Entomology and herpetology," he said, and Kane gaped at him.

"Herpes *what?*"

"Bugs and snakes. That's what kind of degree you'd get. Entomology for bugs and herpetology for snakes. They're real studies, Kane. You gotta do all your homework and shit, and study English and history and everything, but you can get a degree in those things if you want."

It took a minute for Kane to remember to close his mouth. "Eat your pizza," he mumbled, not hardly able to put everything in his head in order. "You promised me we could shower together."

Dex grunted through the last bite of the slice. "I did what?"

"Well, I promised me we could shower together. And I just really want to touch your skin, so let's do that." He looked up and met Dex's eyes, which were wide and blue and amused—but kind too.

"That's fine by me."

"Good. Eat another slice."

"You are the bossiest little shit—"

"Please?" Kane said unexpectedly, and Dex startled and then nodded.

"Yeah. I want to touch your skin too."

Kane shooed Dex off to the shower while he cleaned up the rest of the pizza, and then joined him there, feeling curiously shy. Dex's eyes were closed under the spray when Kane stepped in, and he was soaping his chest and neck, and for a moment, touching him felt like such an amazing privilege. Stupid, right? They were porn models—they sold their personal space at the drop of a hat, and contrary to what Ms. Darcy the teacher had told him, putting a higher price on sex did not seem to make it worth more. He was starting to wonder if he'd misunderstood her—it was actually sort of nagging at him, because at this exact moment, the fact that Dex would *let* Kane touch him seemed really so far beyond money, and Kane had no idea why.

But not knowing didn't stop his hand from shaking as he reached out to curve it around Dex's shoulder. Dex shivered and sighed, and Kane pressed his entire body up against Dex's wet body, then reached around and pulled back on Dex's shoulders so Dex would lean fully on him. Dex did. He even tilted his head back a little so Kane could nuzzle his ear.

Kane reached to the shower rack in front of them and grabbed a sponge, squirted some soap on it, and started to bathe Dex from his neck down to his thighs, slowly, thoroughly, making sure the lather was thick before it rinsed away. Dex stood still in his embrace, and although Kane wanted *badly* and was even getting an erection, he was surprised at how much more he wanted to make Dex happy.

"Here," he said softly. "Turn around and I'll do your back."

Dex did, and they were suddenly front to front. Kane swallowed and soaped up the sponge, then dragged it down from Dex's neck to the tops of his thighs. In the meantime, Dex was… touching him, just like he wanted. Skin to skin. Those long arms draped over Kane's shoulders, their bodies rocked softly together, and Dex was leaning his temple against Kane's. Kane risked a look at him and saw that his eyes were closed and he was simply enjoying Kane's touch.

"Dex?"

"Hm?"

"This is nice. You ever done anything like this before?"

"Dance with a guy in a shower?"

"Or a girl."

"No."

Kane shivered, liking that a lot. "Good," he murmured, and his hard-on was suddenly really insistent. "Let me soap your privates and we can get out and go lay down."

"It's not that… ahhh… late," Dex hissed gently, because while Kane was being gentle, he was also being thorough. Even though this was Dex's second shower, the other shower had been with whatever the kid's name had been, and for some reason it was really important for Dex not to have any of that left on him when they were naked together.

"We'll watch television," Kane whispered. "There's a reason you have one in the bedroom."

"Ungh… Kane? I'm… oh dear God…."

It was just so logical. His entrance was all slippery, and Kane's blunt finger was just that shape, and suddenly Dex groaned and twitched in Kane's arms.

Kane had to bend his knees for a better angle, but he added another finger and Dex moaned, his breath dusting Kane's ear.

"I'm not… usually…."

Kane knew what he was going to say. Porn was sex for work. Who wanted to come home and work after they'd just finished working? It was one of the reasons Kane had never really sought out a girlfriend after he started working in porn. His experience with girls thus far had been that they wanted him for his cock, and he liked coming. Now that he got to come on a regular basis, he didn't have to cave to a girl who just wanted to use him. At least on set, whoever was with him was in it for the same thing he was. And the guys he'd banged off set had been in it for just that. The bang. It had been mutual. Kane hadn't wanted to go to all the trouble of being nice to a girl when the one thing he seemed to have going in that relationship was his cock, and he wasn't always going to want to use that thing on command.

But this was different. He and Dex hadn't fucked in *six days*, and Kane wanted it. He was sort of perpetually horny anyway, but six days? Only later would it occur to him that he hadn't gone looking for someone else in the past three days. But then, Kane was the first to acknowledge that he wasn't that bright.

So Kane didn't have an answer to why Dex seemed to want sex when usually most guys were pretty fucked out by the time they were done with a shoot.

"Did you shoot your stills today?" he asked gruffly, but he was sinking down to his knees as he said it.

"Yeah," Dex panted and then made a needing sound because Kane had to pull his fingers away as he got ready. "Doing the rushes and edits tomor… oh God. Kane… can we… lube?"

Dex's cock was fully extended, and since all the soap had washed off, Kane took it to the back of his throat. Dex's fingers clenched in his wet hair tight enough to hurt, and Kane just sat there, swallowing the crown, for as long as he possibly could before he needed to breathe. God, Dex tasted good. Clean, musty, didn't matter. *Dex.*

Kane gagged a little and pulled back. "Top of the toilet," he said, because he'd been jerking off in the shower the night before so he didn't come to bed and start poking Dex when Dex wasn't supposed to be fooling around before a scene.

Dex looked down at him for a minute. "Dare I ask?" he muttered, and Kane squinted back up against the water.

"Soap dries you out when you're whacking off. You know that. Get the lube." Kane was *going* to say *Get the lube and turn around!* but Dex was there by his mouth, and Kane needed to suck on him some more because he just fuckin' needed to! Dex rifled behind the shower curtain for a minute and made that sound again. It was a good sound—soft, almost whining, but mostly just needing. Kane didn't think he'd ever heard Dex make that sound on set. He held out his hand and took the lube from Dex and, keeping Dex's cock in his mouth, dumped some on his fingers. He reached around and teased Dex's crease, tickling the underside of his balls, tracing a line along his taint. Dex grunted and thrust deep into Kane's mouth, and Kane kept him there, trapped him in the heat and the suction, and slid his lube-sticky fingers up and penetrated Dex's ass with both at the same time.

Dex's weight came down on Kane's shoulders, and his pained groan echoed through the shower. "Oh God… God, Kane… oh God…."

Kane kept the hard, probably painful suction on Dex's cock until Dex jerked backward, embedding Kane's fingers in his ass to the second knuckle.

"Take it," Kane muttered, needing Dex to submit, needing to have him at his complete mercy. Kane had *needed* him, and Kane didn't like that. Kane needed to control him, here, in this way, so he could deal with that need.

"*Fuck!*" Dex cried, shoving his ass backward even further.

Kane chuckled and spread his fingers as wide as he could, and Dex's hands clenched on the skin of Kane's shoulders, probably leaving marks from Dex's blunt-cut nails. Kane didn't care—he welcomed the bite of it, and his own cock gave a throb and a jerk against his thighs.

Kane took Dex deeper into his mouth, sucking hard again, and Dex lowered his head, making a sobbing sound in his throat. He tried to arch his spine, probably to kiss Kane on his head or clutch Kane against his stomach, but Kane couldn't let him do that. He deliberately thrust his fingers against Dex's prostate, grateful for that one lesson before their first scene together, when Dex had told him where that was and what it did for a guy. When Dex let out a yelp and straightened his back and thrust his cock back into Kane's mouth, Kane had to chuckle around him.

No softness yet. Kane was quivering with *must* and aching with want—he needed to get that out of his system before he could allow softness and sweetness between them.

"Kane?" Dex whimpered, and Kane pulled his hand back, added another finger, and thrust.

"*Auughhhh….*" Dex spurted a little precome, and Kane needed him bad, so he figured the time had come. He pulled his hand back and stood, allowing Dex to collapse against him with his head on Kane's shoulder, and pant.

"I'm gonna fuck you, right?" Kane said into his ear, and he felt Dex nod.

Dex's blond hair was slicked against his face but not long enough to be in his eyes yet, and Kane made sure his fingers were good and clean so he could run them through it as they stood there. "Yeah," Dex whispered.

"I'm sorry it's so soon, but I gotta, okay?"

"Yeah, okay."

Kane kissed his temple and his cheek. "Thanks, Dex. Now turn around and bend over, okay?"

Dex let out what sounded like a relieved sigh. He braced one arm on bar on the side of the shower and the other on the side of the tub. His ass thrust out, all stretched and shiny with waterproof lube, and Kane thought regretfully that tomorrow, he wanted to lick that, soften it with his tongue, taste Dex all musty because that was good, but right now he needed to *fuck*, and that's what he did.

Cock, asshole, thrust… oh God yes! Dex's sounds… he didn't use words. On set he grunted and said things like "Good!" and "Oh fuck!", but in person he was even sexier. He grunted and howled, and right now? He was making random frenzied half word noises like "Oh God… pleeeee… geez… fuckin'… fuckin'… *augh! Augh! Geeeeaaaawwdd….*" And the more frenzied his noises got, the harder Kane had to fuck him, and Kane had plans, oh yes he did. He was going to fuck Dex until he was damned near facedown in the bathtub. But then Dex, without even touching his cock, shuddered around Kane, clenching tight and hard, and Kane watched over his shoulder as Dex came on his own feet.

It was the sight of it, hot and white, shooting on the blue tile of the bathtub, that sent Kane howling and coming in Dex's ass.

Dex's arms were shaking, and Kane reached around Dex's chest to pull him up. His ass was all loose and sloppy and hot, and Kane's come slid around his cock as Dex stood up, and that's when it hit them both.

"Oh no," Dex said, his voice, which had resonated and bounced, sounding suddenly flat.

"I forgot the condom," Kane said, really surprised.

"We forgot the condom," Dex echoed. He turned in Kane's arms, still wobbly, and Kane was feeling a little wobbly himself. The water took that minute to turn cold, and Kane reached behind him to turn the shower off. Dex was still pressed against his front, that white, muscular flesh still good to touch. They looked at each other, and Kane's nipples pebbled to rocks in the cool air. Dex reached outside over the toilet and pulled in two towels, and they both started toweling off and stepped out of the shower, still drying things like hair and shoulders and the backs of their thighs.

In the bedroom, Kane's clothes were in a neat stack on top of Dex's long, low dresser, so he grabbed his boxers and slid them on and then got into bed. He turned on the television and muted the sound while Dex slid on his own boxers.

They still hadn't spoken a word.

Dex slid into bed next to him, and Kane reached over casually and wrapped his arm around Dex's shoulders, *forcing* him to put his still damp head on Kane's shoulder.

"It's not like we don't get tested all the fuckin' time," Kane said, hoping that was true. It's what Dex had said the night Chase was in the hospital. He figured that was something.

"It's not like either one of us are fucking around outside of *Johnnies*," Dex offered.

"Yeah," Kane said, thinking on the bright side. "I mean, if I was gay, this would be, like, a monogamous relationship."

Dex made a sound like Kane had slugged him in the stomach.

Kane looked away from the television to see where that sound came from, and saw that Dex was staring at him with wide blue eyes and a pinched sort of tremble around his mobile mouth. "What?" Kane asked, feeling stupid.

"Nothing," Dex muttered. He tried to pull away, but Kane tightened his grip. He wanted Dex here. It was, if Kane could admit it, sort of where he'd been heading with that whole sex in the shower thing.

"Sounds like something." Kane put down the remote and bent to kiss Dex on the top of the head.

"It's nothing," Dex said, the tension sighing out of him like wind. "I just thought I'd learn, but I haven't, and there's nothing I can do about that. Not right now, anyway."

"'Kay," Kane agreed. "As long as we're good. We can forget a condom once. We'll remember next time, okay?"

"Yeah," Dex mumbled, turning over on his side and burying his face against Kane's skin. His face, still wet from the shower, maybe, itched at Kane's shoulder, and Kane wondered why Dex hadn't dried it off better. But then *American Idol* was on, and Kane was a sucker for reality shows. It was just so nice, Dex on his shoulder, a pleasant afterglow suffusing him, his favorite television show on. He dropped a kiss on the top of Dex's head and wished he could purr.

"You make me real happy," he said softly. "Thanks, Dex. You're like the best friend I ever had."

Dex nodded against Kane's shoulder and his body shook a minute, and Kane took that for a *You too*.

AN ADJUSTMENT IN THE TEMPERATURE OF THE TERRARIUM

Dex

A WEEK later Dex was *still* trying to figure out how to feel about Kane *still* being in his bed. He sort of wanted to have a knee-melty self-pitying crisis about it in a way he *hadn't* wanted to have about Scott, but a week after he brought the turtle home was not the day to have it. In fact, it seemed like the day to piss Dex off.

The first problem was that Kelsey the receptionist was late—in more than one way.

Dex answered the phones and directed people to where they were supposed to go. They were having three shoots that day, which was something of an anomaly, but John had decided to try his hand at het and bi instead of just gay porn, so, well, there were suddenly tits onstage. They'd had to split the locker room into two different sections so the girls could shower separately and get a break from dicks with dicks—Dex's idea.

Dex had been in charge of it too. It had taken a week, and the work had just been completed the day before—Dex had no idea how much John had paid to make it happen that quickly, and he didn't even want to think about it. He didn't even have *time* to think about it, because he'd also been editing and trying to find a *new* editor to help. As much as he liked drawing a paycheck from John, it wasn't big enough to cover the twelve-hour days. Between driving out to the hospital to work out with Chase and helping Kane with the critters Dex hadn't been left with a whole lot of time to visit the college and sign up. And being Kane's fuckbuddy hadn't made things easier.

Yeah, the fuckbuddy thing. He still wasn't sure how that thing had happened. Kept happening. It was just, the night with the turtles, he'd thought….

Well, it wasn't so much that he'd thought anything, but even after the "not gay" thing, Kane had been so….

It's just that being there, in the same bed together, touching after a long day had just seemed like….

Hell.

The problem was, Dex didn't want to finish *any* of those sentences, and until he could do it without feeling foolish, he couldn't have a coherent conversation with Kane about what exactly it was Kane thought they were doing together.

And every night, whether they had sex or not, Kane wrapped that hard, powerful arm around Dex, mumbled, "C'mere," and they slept the sleep of the just and righteous, whether Kane was gay or not. That's all it took: Kane's arm around Dex's stomach, and suddenly he was warm, safe, and cared for. Suddenly his sexuality had never been a question and never been a problem, and it didn't matter if he went by Dex or David or Milton—he was solid and real, and Kane's arm was his anchor to reality and his reason for staying. That muscular body at Dex's back (and, yeah, sometimes in his ass) meant that someone knew who he really was, and apparently still approved.

Dex found that after Scott, who had never stayed the night and who had laughed when Dex even suggested it would be nice, he could sacrifice a little self-respect for the solidness of Kane at his back.

Hell, it's not like he had a lot of self-respect left after Scott anyway.

But that's not what he was thinking as he manned the damned phone and waved people in and signed for packages at the front desk of the *Johnnies* office a week later.

He was thinking he didn't know where the fuck the receptionist was, and there was a reason they paid her every month when she, as of yet, hadn't gotten naked with anyone.

It turned out, the problem was that she *had.*

She came in about two hours late, looking pale and sad, her normally shiny dark hair stringy, her brown eyes puffy from crying, and the sort of cast to her skin that Dex was starting to associate with Chase right before he'd… yeah. That night had really sucked.

"Jesus, Kelsey—you could have called and told us you were sick!" he said, half concern and half irritation, and to his complete mortification, she burst into tears.

"Oh fuck." Tears? *Tears?* None of his girlfriends had done tears. He'd tended to go for strong women who thought only the weak cried. He'd found it sort of annoying, actually, and it hadn't prepared him for this *at all.* And she didn't even run away to the bathroom or anything, just stood there, helpless and vulnerable as a wounded hamster. He gaped at her for a second while the phone rang.

And then did what he did, apparently, which was get his shit together for other people.

"Okay, Kelse," he said, his voice dropping to the same gentle tone he used on Tomas the snake, "I'm gonna put the service message on and grab someone to come up and sit down here, and you and me are gonna have a talk, okay?"

Kelsey nodded at him, her lower lip thrust out and quivering, and her arms folded over her abnormally large boobs.

And the lightbulb went off in Dex's head, and he wanted to groan, but he didn't.

"Go ahead and go clean up in the bathroom," he said and then managed a smile. "There's a girl's side now—that's a good thing, right?"

She tried a smile too. It didn't really take, but he gave her points for trying while he lassoed Ethan (who had no earthly reason to be in today—Dex was going to have to ask him about that later) to man the phones and direct traffic.

"You can do this, right, Ethe?" Dex asked.

Ethan looked up at him, that broad Italian face open and guileless and his mouth, surprisingly pink and naked, with thick, downright pornographic lips, widely smiling. "Yeah, no problem," he said, nodding. "Sign for packages, direct people to John's office if they're on the list, don't fuck with the phone. I can do that. I'll just sit here and wait for Kane and Tommy."

"Okay, fine, thanks!" Dex said, and later he felt like a stupid dick because he had no idea why Kane and Tommy would show up at work, and didn't think to ask before he wandered through the adapted office complex to find Kelsey.

Dex had often thought about how deceptive the home office of *Johnnies* was. From the outside, it was a little complex—big enough for a couple of businesses, one floor, with a courtyard in the middle. It wasn't very old but had apparently stood vacant until John had leased it, about three months after Dex shot his first video. John liked to say that Dex made his down payment on the office, and Dex always laughed with quiet pride. Yeah, his videos had always sold really well—they'd always gotten five-star ratings on the website too. He'd liked it—*loved* it—the attention, liked being told he was beautiful. It didn't matter what girls said to him; the only places he'd ever gotten the same feeling of being perfect and lovely had been online after his videos had been posted and that one crystalline summer day, lying on a picnic blanket, looking at Dexter's brown eyes under the cloud-dappled shadows of the endless Montana sky.

So knowing that his performances had helped build John's place made him feel good. He was a good performer—he'd always been a good boy at home, and here, he was a good bad boy. And he liked this place. It *was* professional. They had a receptionist, they had a laundry service, and they only took trained cameramen. Dex had taken a couple of film classes and then passed that knowledge on to John, and their videos had improved.

Dex had taken all his accounting classes and helped John rework his payroll program so that it was more efficient, and John's finances had become pristine. And between Dex and John, they tried to make sure that none of the guys they had doing scenes felt exploited—or were exploitive. Sex wasn't going to be vilified or fetishized in John's business. It could be hot, it could be raw, it could be sweaty and a little rough, but it wasn't going to be dirty (unless it was in the good, happy way that made you want to fuck something), and it *wasn't* going to make the models feel like anything less than professionals at something a lot of people wanted to see.

So when John took his first year's profits and bought this office complex and then renovated it with Dex's suggestions, Dex was honored. He'd felt useful, like all of that college education his on-camera sex was paying for was actually something good. Silly, right? But true. True. He'd helped build a business, and he'd loved it. He'd gotten touched and caressed, licked and fucked, and he'd gotten to do the same things back. He'd traveled to France, Belize, Florida, and New York on the company dime. He'd had his dick sucked under a blazing blue sky in Cabo San Lucas, and he'd been fucked into a mattress in a penthouse in Las Vegas while the model who fucked him cried "Yee-fuckin'-haw!" at the top of his lungs. (That guy now had a family in Oregon—he still sent Dex Christmas cards.) He'd come frickin' gallons, and he'd enjoyed the hell out of it—and when he'd stopped loving it so much, the opportunities to help John had been fun too.

And this little office building, with its various bedrooms and its shower and its laundry service, its little gazebo and garden square with the easy-on-the-knees polyplastic ground cover, was a testament to how much he'd loved his job.

Gathering models in the hospital for Chase and knocking on the bathroom door to talk Kelsey out of the freaky tree were Dex's dues for that pride.

"Uhm, Kelse?" Dex muttered, knocking on the brand-new door at the opposite end of the hall from where the usual entrance was. He was unhealthily embarrassed. "Kelse? I can talk now."

"I'm—" Sniffle. "—I'm o—" Sniffle. "Okaaaaaayyyyy!" Sob.

Dex thunked his head against the door. It was painted pink—against his strenuous objections, but John insisted that he didn't want anyone confusing the girls' shower room with the boys' shower room. This might be porn, but goddammit, it was gonna be classy porn, right? At this moment, that classy locker room door made Dex think about Pepto-Bismol. He wanted some.

"No you're not," he said, wishing he was the kind of guy who could take that at face value, but he couldn't. It sucked. If he could turn around and walk away from this, he could have turned and walked away from Tommy and Chase, and he would have been spared that horrible moment in the hospital when he'd been faced with all the things he'd lost by being a gay man with a past in pornography. "You're not okay."

"Yes I am!"

"Do you want me to shout it all over the fuckin' complex, Kelsey? I have four brothers and a sister. I know what a—"

"Jesus, Dexter!" The door opened and Kelsey's hand reached out and hauled him bodily into the girls' room.

He wrinkled his nose as he looked around. "What the hell kind of soap do you guys use? It smells like vanilla and flowers."

Kelsey sniffed experimentally and then blanched. "Aw, fuck. Add something else to the list," she moaned and then ran for the toilet. Dex watched her go, then visited the shower, found the hand soap, scented candle, lotion, and air freshener, all of which emanated vanilla and flowers, and shoved them into an unused locker.

Suddenly the pink door burst forward and a willow wand in a fluffy robe, with dark hair and blue eyes, burst in, shouting, "Oh *God,* where do they find these guys with big dicks and no clue? Bobby? Seriously, Bo… uh. Bee?"

Dex's cheeks flamed. "I thought he was very sweet," he offered, and the girl's face flamed.

"I thought this was the girls' dressing room," she mumbled, and Dex shrugged.

"I thought so too. I didn't realize your scene was up so soon, and I was trying to talk to Kelsey."

"Who the hell is Kelsey?"

"I'm the receptionist, Rachel," Kelsey said, disgust written on her face as she emerged from the bathroom stall and washed her hands. "Jesus, I gave you a tour of the place."

Rachel looked at Kelsey and it looked like she caught herself midsneer. "I'm sorry. I'm sorry—I just… I sort of wanted some privacy to blow off steam. What are you doing in here? I thought this was girls only?"

"He's gay," Kelsey said, not mollified in the least. "Cool your jets, we'll be in the hallway in a minute."

Dex gaped at her. He'd been spending the last year, ever since Scott, his first nonporn affair, looking himself in the mirror and practicing that word. He wasn't just a straight guy boning straight guys—he was gay, and he needed to pony up. But he'd never heard anybody say it out loud.

Kelsey looked at him, a little color in her face, and suddenly clapped her hand over her mouth and grew a lot more color. "That wasn't common knowledge," she said, and he glared at her.

"Not even to me, Kelsey. Dammit, it's like our real names—you just don't fucking blow those out of the water, you know?"

Kelsey's head looked like a bobblehead's, and her eyes got suspiciously bright, and Dex wanted to swallow his tongue.

"I'm sorry," she whispered, and Rachel's eyes widened in horror.

"Oh fuck—is she gonna cry?" Rachel turned to Dex and actually stomped her bare little foot with the pink glittery nail polish on the toes. "Really? You gotta make her stop! Make her stop crying!"

Dex nodded and dredged up a panicked smile. "Look, Kelse—look. It's okay. It's okay, seriously. I'm not mad—I'm not. I thought I was, but I was wrong. I just want to help you out here, okay? You came in, you looked like hell, I thought maybe you could tell me what's doin' and I could help. But if you're not ready to do that, we don't have to. You know you can always—"

In that moment there was a crackle and a whine, and the PA opened up with a cacophony of voices.

"Don't touch that!" "Turn that off." "Not that button!" "Hey, I didn't do it on purpose!" "*Ethan you fucking moron, turn off the goddamned PA system, you're gonna get Dex in tr—*"

There was a sudden morbid silence, and it felt like even the air-conditioning stopped to listen.

Kelsey and Dex eyeballed each other in horror.

"Was that Kane?" she said curiously.

"And Tommy," Dex responded flatly, picking their voices out of that babble and trying not to think about the post-panic attack that was about to mow him down in his solar plexus. "Ethan, of course."

"Anyone else?" Kelsey asked, and Dex shook his head.

"I don't recognize the other voice. Did you know we have two scenes shooting?" Oh God. Two scenes. That sort of thing was hard to edit out. He was going to be here for *hours.*

Kelsey groaned and rubbed her forehead. "You're gonna be here for fucking *hours*," she muttered, and Dex closed his eyes and nodded.

"Are you feeling better?" he asked, and she grimaced.

"I think some soda crackers will help," she admitted.

"I'll send Kane, Tommy, and Ethan to get them. They seem to need something to do!"

As they turned around to walk out, Rachel let out a little whine. "Oh geez—what happened to my candles and stuff? This place is gonna start to smell like a locker room or something!"

Dex wrapped his arm around Kelsey's slender shoulders and resisted the urge to bang his head against the wall.

KANE looked miserable. "I'm so sorry," he muttered, and Dex clapped him on the shoulder and shook his head.

Ethan looked worse. "Seriously, man. I'm… I'm just… dude."

Tommy looked furious. "Jesus, Ethan, what the fuck were you doing?"

Ethan cringed, and Dex smacked Tommy in the arm.

"I… I wanted to see if the buttons had bumps on them!" Ethan protested. "Like Braille! I know that sometimes computer keys do, and

I just wanted to…." His voice dropped, because Dex wasn't the only one staring at him like he'd lost his mind. "Yeah, stupid idea," he finished.

Dex took a deep breath and looked around. He realized that the mystery voice was Donnie, Chase's friend with the white-blond hair, who was looking almost sick with apology. Controlling these situations: he sucked at it. Why did John leave him in charge? The real Dex had been a leader. He'd been the guy on the football field you could count on. He'd been the guy who'd told Davy what to do when they'd been alone together. David? David was just flailing around, trying hard not to make any bad situations worse.

"Okay," he said, planning like his life depended on it. "Here's what we're gonna do. Ethan, you're gonna go buy Kelsey here some soda crackers, a toothbrush and toothpaste, and some milk and fruit, okay? Don't ask why, she's got the flu and she's gonna man the phones since you monkeys can't even throw poo at a wall without missing, okay?"

Ethan nodded sheepishly and took off, and Kelsey sat down at the phones with a grateful, weary look at Dex.

"And you three," he sighed, turning to them. "What in the hell are you doing here?"

Tommy glared at Donnie and Kane. "I called psycho boy here to see where you were to help me plan Chase's coming home party, and he called blondie here, and I thought we couldn't possibly do this shit together without you!"

Dex closed his eyes and opened them and then looked at Kane, who shrugged.

"I tried to tell him you were busy today," he said, because Dex had spent the night before whining about what kind of day it was going to be. "I thought once you told him to fuck off, I could go with him and help."

Kane had dull red stains on his cheeks, and Dex wanted to hug him. "I think that's a fuckin' awesome idea," he said with feeling. "Tommy, Donnie, consider Kane my proxy. He'll tell me what you guys think, I'll give you a plan—but not now, not here, okay? The only way any of us get paid is if we pretend this is a real fuckin' job I'm doing, okay?"

Kane's full mouth quirked in and his dimples popped as he tried not to preen. Dex reached out and mussed his carefully gelled hair, and Kane's suppressed smile became an all-out grin.

"I got your back, bro!" he said, not self-conscious in the least.

Tommy cast an uneasy glance at Donnie and then reined in his general irritation. "Yeah, sorry to fuck with your day." Tommy glared in Donnie's direction again. "You need to keep your mouth shut unless it's something dire like a food allergy or something."

Donnie stuck an impertinent tongue out at Tommy and then gave Dex the brotherly clasp-hands-shoulder-bump, saying softly, "I'll be on my best behavior. Just keep him from strangling me, okay?"

Dex nodded, and Chase's friend and Chase's lover headed for the exit, turning back in time to see Kane hesitate in front of Dex.

Dex could feel it too. It was time for something: a peck on the cheek, a buss on the lips, clasped hands, something. But they weren't defined that way—Kane wasn't, by his own admission, gay.

But that didn't stop them from looking into each other's eyes in troubled silence for a moment.

"You're good at that," Kane said softly, and Dex smiled, feeling his face heat.

"You were trying. I wasn't so great when I was barely twenty." Feeling suddenly like they *had* to touch, Dex reached out and ruffled his hair again and then pulled Kane's head against his chest while giving a halfhearted noogie. Kane didn't burst out of Dex's hold around his shoulders, and Dex didn't let go of him immediately.

"Thanks," Dex said quietly. "You were trying to do me a solid. I 'preciate it."

Kane looked up from Dex's chest and beamed. "I'll let you know if they're still talking to each other, 'kay?"

Dex remembered Kane's mediator skills at the hospital. "I'd put money on it," he said, feeling proud, and Kane's beaming smile as he left lasted Dex for at least as long as it took John to come out of the shot he'd been filming to rip Dex a whole new asshole for the sound gaffe.

For once, Dex didn't take it personally. He had other things to sustain him besides John's approval.

AND finally, it was calm. The scenes were shot and in the can, John set up the second one for editing, and it was just Dex and Kelsey sitting at the reception desk with some takeout.

The quiet was unnerving. Dex ate his lean chicken and spinach with lemon juice and looked at Kelsey, who was eating something smothered with cheese and not looking the least bit repentant.

Kelsey caught his regard and sucked the last of the cheese off her fingers. "Say it," she said softly. "If you say it, then I have to believe it, and then I can deal with it."

Dex swallowed his last bite of chicken. "When are you due?"

Kelsey closed her eyes. "June," she said with a sigh. "I'm due in June."

"And Daddy…."

"Is a douche bag." Kelsey leaned forward and balanced her chin on her fists. "I mean, at first, I felt sorry for him, because he told me he'd just broken up with his girlfriend."

Dex raised his eyebrows. "How do you know he didn't?"

"Because he brought her into the office. Apparently she's into kinky shit like knowing he bones guys for a living. I still don't know where he got those marks on his face, though."

Dex's spinach and chicken abruptly turned into concrete and rubbing alcohol. "Marks? What marks?"

"I don't know—he had these… divots. Like someone threw something sharp at him and a fat lip that was split in the middle too. He didn't even want to shoot that day, but it was right after Chance… well, after Chance couldn't come in anymore, and John said nobody would notice."

Dex closed his eyes and swallowed, his mouth suddenly full of sand and grit. He hadn't picked up on it—he should have, when she said the guy had brought his girlfriend into the office.

"Kelsey?" he asked after sucking down the rest of his soda until it gurgled. "How did you know I was gay?"

Kelsey looked at him and flushed. "Uhm… how am I supposed to answer that? We work at a gay porn business."

"We work at a gay-for-pay business." Dex's eyes were narrow and his voice was flat, and he knew it. "Until August I had a girlfriend. I've barely said it to my closest friends. How would you know I was gay?"

Kelsey looked down at her cold french fries like she couldn't remember how they got there. "Scott," she whispered, and Dex stood up and took deep, grating, even breaths.

"Did he tell you how he knew?" Dex asked. He started gathering their trash and throwing it in the little can by her desk. It was full after a long busy day, and Dex bent over and started shoving the trash in, using his formidable strength to tamp it tight into the trash can, not caring if the bag around it popped or if the empty soda cup had burst and was leaking brown ice into the trash.

"No," Kelsey said, looking at her hands. "I… he was hitting on me, and I told him that if I was going to sleep with anyone from work, it'd be you, because you're a nice guy and I knew you best. He said you were gay, so give it up." She looked up at him, her eyes deep and shadowed and growing shiny again. "It sort of broke my heart, you know?"

Dex stood up and kicked the trashcan, sending it smacking against the filing cabinet behind Kelsey's desk and thundering a reverb through the office. It tipped over, but it was so tightly packed that nothing fell out. Kelsey jerked back and clasped her hand over her mouth in shock, and Dex looked at it numbly, not sure what to say.

"I'm the one." His voice was a hoarse surprise. "I threw CDs at him. Kane Split his lip. I… I didn't come in for the shoot because I was in the hospital with Tommy. I…." Dex shook his head and tried to pull himself together. He'd had a breakup. They happened. She was pregnant. That was worse.

He looked at her dead on. "Don't worry about me," he said sincerely. "I'm not going to go party with my uterus in eight months. Our health insurance is fucking awesome, but is there anything else you need?"

Kelsey turned her head so her cheek could rest on her fists. "Oh God. What a fuckin' douche bag," she whispered. "Why? Why would he even do that? It was like, I was invisible, and all of a sudden, he saw me. And…." She looked up and sat up and wiped under her eyes determinedly. "I mean, you're all so beautiful, and you're nice to me, and… and suddenly he was paying attention like he meant it. I thought…." She grabbed some Kleenex from the box by her computer. "Isn't that stupid?" she asked to the pained silence. "We work in porn. Isn't it stupid to think that he meant it?"

Dex walked around to the back of her chair and wrapped his arms around her shoulders. He rubbed his cheek against hers for a moment and then turned his head and kissed it. "When the cameras are off, it should be real," he said, thinking about Chase and Tommy. They'd never shot a scene. Not one. But Tommy had visited Chase in a freakin' mental institution every damned day. Chase had *stopped*, mid-suicide attempt, so Tommy wouldn't have to clean up his mess. Not one scene together—but Dex had shot scenes with both of them, and when they were in the same room, no one else mattered.

Kelsey nodded her head. "It should have been real," she echoed. "I thought it was real."

"Have you told him?"

Kelsey shuddered in his arms. "He told me to get an abortion."

Dex tightened his hug around her. Of all the things… nine years in gay porn, and *that* was the word that made his little Catholic heart quiver. He took a deep breath on his childhood repression and remembered this was not his body or his life or his mistake. He'd done blow and the effects had lasted a couple of hours. Kelsey's error in judgment was going to last forever.

"How do you feel about that?" he asked, and she whimpered.

"I always swore I wouldn't." She sniffled into her arms. "Dammit, Dex. I'm still in school. This was *not* my plan."

And Dex found he was smiling with all his teeth as a groundswell of bitterness erupted out of his pores like swamp water. "It never is," he whispered. "Trust me on that one, sweetheart. It never is."

There was a sound then as John opened the door from the hallway to the front office, and Dex straightened and squeezed Kelsey's shoulder.

"Did you guys hear something fall?" John asked. His eyes were glossy and his ginger hair was stringy from having his hand torn through it too many times.

Dex stood up with a scowl of irritation. Great. He'd knocked the trashcan over and John was on his *n*th bump of coke. Suddenly, in spite of his pride in his work, he was hit by the inescapable notion that Kelsey needed to find another job if she was going to be a single mother. It was okay for a bunch of single guys to fuck away their wonder years, but a baby probably deserved better.

"I kicked a trash can," Dex said, and his voice seemed to echo around the empty complex.

"Awesome. When you're done kicking trash cans, could you come in and help me frickin' edit this last frickin' video? You've fucked girls, right? You know what a pussy is supposed to look like?"

Dex winced. "Nice. Yeah. Sort of."

"Excellent. I need someone who can tell me if this shit looks hot or just weird." John whirled around and slammed the door, leaving Kelsey and Dex gaping at him.

"Oh God," Kelsey muttered. "I so do not want to be you for the next two to four hours."

Dex grunted. "I gotta call my roommate," he muttered without thinking.

"Roommate? Is that code?" Kelsey squinted at him. "I mean, you just scratched up Scott's face six weeks ago!"

"I threw CDs at him!" Dex snapped. "I did not claw him like some rabid… rabid…."

"Pussy?" Kelsey said grimly, and Dex grunted, uncharmed.

"I broke up with Scott a long time before the CDs," Dex said, so glad that was true. "I threw the CDs because he was showing up at my house asking for booty call. It was pissing me off."

Kelsey shuddered. "Yeah, he's been doing that." She sighed then, disconsolate. "I even gave in."

Dex had a sudden horrible thought. He looked at Kelsey, who was maybe five six and not teeny like a toothpick, but not two hundred pounds of muscle like Scott.

"Kelse?"

"Yeah?"

"Do me a favor. If Scott shows up at your place, lock the door and call me. I throw CDs and I make a dent. You throw shit at him and it just pisses him off."

Kelsey nodded, her eyes wide and apprehensive. "Okay."

"If I don't show up, someone will. This may be porn, but you're not alone here, okay? We'll take care of you."

Kelsey nodded again. "Okay, Dex. I hear you." She sighed. "You know, my mom retired and moved to New Mexico. She keeps telling me she's got a spare bedroom. I think she's lonely. Maybe I should take her up on it. I think she'd even forgive me for the kid, you know?"

Dex nodded. "We'd miss you. You finally learned the phone system."

Kelsey smiled. It looked watery and limp, but it was also a good try. "You can put that on my letter of reference."

Dex sighed. "Yeah. Make sure you have me write that up for you and John sign it. He'll probably put 'porn' on the letterhead."

"Yeah—what's with him, anyway? He looks way strung out."

Dex shrugged. "I got no idea" is what he said. "He don't usually let that shit get in the way of his work. Maybe it's the girl parts freaking him out."

Kelsey giggled and Dex walked away, aware that, like a total coward, he'd managed to dodge the "roommate" question—which was good, because with or without the talk with John, he didn't have an answer for that one.

LATER he would wonder why it hadn't occurred to him to talk to John. Maybe it was because Dex had learned to keep his personal business just that—personal. Nobody on the set had met Allison, or Ashley before her, or Corinne, or even Kelly, who had sent him to *Johnnies* because she'd thought the kink would be awesome. (He had to admit that for a while it had been, but he was really only a fan of threesomes on camera. Off camera, he found them way too exhausting for the emotional payoff.)

Maybe it was because although John knew about Scott and the cheating and the debacle of the whole thing, John had also spent a long time hitting on Dex when Dex had maintained stoutly that he was straight but just did the gay thing for kinks and kash. (He used to spell it that way in his head too—made it sound more like marketing and less like the complete moral degeneration his family would believe it to be.) John had understood about Scott—they'd both seen affairs start on location that ended badly off of it. But explaining about the breakup and how ugly it had really gotten, and maybe how Kane had comforted him afterward? That felt wrong. It was like those girls who dumped a guy and then called him to talk about their new dating life "because we're friends!" So Dex refused to do it for himself, and maybe that feeling bled into the thing with Kelsey.

And maybe it was because John was stoned—something he was doing more and more and that Dex was starting to worry about. In the beginning, it had been once every couple of months, maybe. The workload would spike, John would bump some coke and stay up and finish it, and that would be the end. But lately it was once a month, or every two weeks. Dex did the finances, so he knew John wasn't taking it out of the company yet, but still. He couldn't help a vague nagging worry that this entire enterprise that he'd put a lot of his uncredited (but well-paid) time into might eventually be snorted up his friend's nose. And the cocaine made John untrustworthy for Kelsey's secret too.

So Dex didn't confide in John. They sat in the editing room and polished three scenes together, and Dex said things like "Oh God—has that guy *ever* been in the same room with a naked girl before? *That* was your choice for our first het feature?" John would reply with things like "Nobody's gonna be lookin' at his tongue, Dex. I'm *still* obsessing about his wang!" and together they edited a porn film with unfamiliar parts. But not once did Dex tell John that maybe Scott needed to go, or that they were going to need to hire a new receptionist, and although he had the talk later, after Thanksgiving, it would bother him that he didn't do it *now*. It would bother him a hell of a lot.

What he *did* do was go home to his cozy little two-bedroom, which was now rife with scaly things, and look around in appreciation. There were remnants of pizza left on a plate with plastic wrap over it, and boxes neatly in the trash. Next to the plate (obviously meant for him) there was a list of things like *decorations*, *invitations*, *eats*, *victims/volunteers*, *clear it with the shrink*, and obviously some decent thinking toward the whole welcome home party for their troubled friend. The dishes were done, the recycling had been taken out to the outside can, and it looked like Kane had swept and vacuumed as well. Kane himself was on the couch watching an after-midnight episode of *Law & Order*, his cheek propped on his hand. His eyes were closed, and a very loud snoring rose and fell with his even breaths.

His hair was a mess, like he'd been running his hand through it, and when his mouth—usually moving in speech or expression—was slack, the faint scarring of his harelip was visible. He never talked about it, but Dex thought he might have been self-conscious about it. When he smiled widely, sometimes he held his hand up to his mouth. Even seeing Kane still enough to make out the small rectangular shape made Dex feel privileged. So much of Kane was on the surface, worn on his sleeve, completely unselfconscious and without reserve. Seeing this one private part made Dex possessive.

For a moment Dex just looked at him, feeling something warm and unfamiliar flooding his chest, stopping his breathing, making it hard to swallow. For someone who wasn't gay, Kane sure did seem to take awful good care of Dex when Dex needed it most.

Dex turned off the television and bent over the couch to kiss him on the cheek. "Kane?" he whispered. "Kane? C'mon. Let's go sleep in a bed, okay?"

Kane turned his head into Dex's mouth, and Dex lost himself in the heat and the wet of Kane's kiss, and then Kane pulled away and squinted at him.

"It's hella late," he muttered. "I want to jump you, but you'd probably rather go to bed."

Dex made a positive sound, affirming that, and then stood and offered Kane his hand. Kane took it and swung a friendly, supportive arm around Dex's shoulder as they walked down the hall, turning off lights as they went.

They climbed into bed in their boxers, and Kane wrapped his arm around Dex's stomach and just hauled him in, and Dex felt like he belonged there.

"Anything interesting happen?" Kane mumbled.

Dex, who thought they were just going to sleep, found the whole day pouring out, with Kelsey and Scott, with John and the coke, with crappy heterosexual porn and bitchy actresses and crying women and violent men. Kane woke up and asked questions and rubbed Dex's chest and listened. Just listened to all of it, and at the end, when Dex was all talked out and it was almost two in the morning, Dex rolled over on his side to face Kane because he had to.

Kane kissed him in the dark and swung a leg over Dex's hips and mumbled, "We'll fix it in the morning, sweetheart. You can't save the world after 1:00 a.m. Not even you."

Dex felt tears starting then and squeezed them back. God. *God.* The things he felt. The things he *wanted.* The things he thought he could imagine having, if only this kid eight years his junior was actually gay.

Kane

KANE looked at Tommy helplessly, not really sure what to do. Tommy's little house—which was painted gray and DayGlo orange on the outside, something that tickled Kane a lot, although Dex's brown and lavender blue was starting to grow on him—was full of people whose one connection was Chase Summers. It wasn't a bad connection as those things went. Chase knew guys from his baseball team and guys from *Johnnies.* Chase knew Donnie, and Tommy might want to strangle Donnie with his bare hands, but Kane liked him. Donnie was nice—always frickin' nice—and Kane could get behind that. And, of course, Kevin, Chase's other friend from high school, was just good people. Kane and Kevin could play video games for *hours*, and unlike Tommy, who made him feel stupid with his snarling sarcasm, or Chase, who was unnerving because he was always so *quiet,* Kevin was just…

Just like Kane. His entire soul was in his smile.

Now Kane looked at Tommy, who was picking at some carrots on his little paper plate (Kane had picked the plates out—they had turtles on them, and since Tommy had turtles too, it seemed like a good choice) and wished he could make his way to where Kevin stood next to Donnie and his impossibly beautiful sister. It would be an easier conversation.

"His girlfriend's pregnant?"

"Ex-girlfriend," Tommy snapped, and Kane winced because they'd worked too hard for the "ex" to happen, oh yes, and he needed to remember the ex.

"His ex-girlfriend is pregnant?" Kane rephrased, his voice small. He looked around the kitchen for Dex, but Dex was talking to Donnie, and Kane wished, suddenly, fiercely, that they were a couple, and that he really *was* gay, so that he could say, "Gotta go talk to my better half," and then walk over there and grab Dex's hand and kiss his cheek and let Dex, who always seemed to have shit like this together, comfort him and tell him that their friends were going to be all right.

"Yeah," Tommy muttered, and then he smiled. "It'll be awesome. We're gonna be daddies."

Kane gaped at him. "You're *happy* about this?" To make sure, right?

"Yeah. *Shit* yeah. She doesn't want the baby, 'cause she's fuckin' stupid, but I'm not holding that against her." Tommy smiled with some satisfaction, and the expression was a little bit evil. On the porn set, it was sexy as hell, and even now it made Kane's cock sit up and take notice. But Kane had learned a little since high school, and the unlimited sex on set had helped. He knew that his little fucker was hyper-fucking-active. If he let it sit up and bark, that was fine, and he could always pet it when it wagged, but he was getting too old to let it off its leash when it didn't need to be.

Kane shouldn't ask. He shouldn't. But he had to. "Why's she stupid?"

Tommy's scowl made Kane step back. "She should have seen it coming." Tommy's throat worked, and Kane's mouth went dry. "She should have seen it coming. He was falling apart, and it was her watch. And instead of saying 'Hey, baby, you seem fucking miserable!' she sabotages the fucking condom, 'cause she thinks she's going to lose her meal ticket."

Kane had met Mercy; she hadn't seemed that bad. It was all, he thought wretchedly, part of being complicated. If you kept things simple—this person's nice to me, this person's a bitch—you didn't have to get all mad about a girl who had maybe seen the same things in your man that you did.

"Maybe she was just scared," Kane said after a moment, and when Tommy looked at him this time, Kane remembered why Tommy was Dex's best friend.

"Yeah," Tommy said, his voice a little softer. "We can get down with that, right? Fuckin' asshole scared us all." Then Tommy brightened, and there was nothing evil or sexy about the smile at all. It was just all Tommy. "And you're right. She's giving us the baby if Chase agrees. I can fuckin' love that woman—bring her flowers, give her face, what the hell ever—if I can hold Chase's baby. It'll be good."

Tommy was watching Chase from across the room as they spoke. He'd gone to talk to a short, chubby blonde woman who looked a lot like Donnie and was probably Donnie's mom. They'd had a brief conversation, and now he was sort of wandering away down the hallway.

"He's tired," Tommy murmured. "He's still in recovery. His shrink"—and there he was, the shortish balding man with the bag of knitting and the homemade sweater-vest—"said that it'll take him a little while before he gets his stamina back." Suddenly Tommy's quicksilver smile landed on Kane, and Kane felt like Tommy knew he was there, really there, for the first time since Tommy and Chase had walked through the door. "So, mostly, he'll be a lot like you!"

Kane flushed. "Yeah, yeah," he grumbled, pleased that Tommy was in a good enough mood to give him shit. "You take one trip to frickin' Cabo San Lucas…." Kane had never traveled before, and for some reason jet lag had hit him *hard.* So the rest of the guys had been out sightseeing or getting busy between getting busy (it had been a fuckfest from the beginning to the frickin' end—Kane's dick had been rubbed raw by the time they left, and he hadn't needed to whack off for a *week*) or even finding different ways to work out, but Kane? Kane had been sleeping. He was lucky Dex had woken him up when he fell asleep in front of the pool the first day, or he would have been fried like a potato in oil.

Tommy laughed a little and clapped him on the arm, and Kane was comforted some more. Still Tommy. Tommy had always been a good lay but really intense in private. Kane loved him, but maybe it was good that someone like Dex, who was easygoing and got along with about everyone, was his best friend.

"Looks like Donnie's going to go see how he's doing," Tommy said. Kane heard the restraint in his deep breath.

"Donnie's good people," Kane contributed. Tommy looked at him—really looked at him—again.

"Donnie is," Tommy conceded. It sounded like it was hard. "I'm not really the jealous psycho I sound like. I…." Tommy grunted. "It's complicated, Kane. I know you like Donnie—you just keep liking him, okay? I think we're gonna be friends, the whole bunch of us. Me and Chase, we'll be the daddies. Donnie and Dex'll be the uncles. It'll be good."

Kane's heart made a painful misstep, and he grunted. Frances's little face—the eyebrows growing back, the blonde/brown stubble getting thicker on her bald head—swam in front of his vision. He didn't get to be the uncle to that baby no more. Lola would barely let him in the house to fix shit when she needed it, and he was still making the payments.

"Can I be the uncle too?" he asked, and if it wasn't for Frances's big brown eyes, thickly lined with dark lashes now that they'd grown back, he would have been really embarrassed by how much need was in his voice.

Tommy's smile was absurdly gentle for how fierce Tommy could be, and he looped a companionable arm around Kane's shoulders. "Yeah, Kane. No worries. You can be the uncle too."

Dex came up that moment on Tommy's other side. "Who's gonna be an uncle?" he asked, and then Tommy told him, and Kane spent a few smattering heartbeats watching the play of emotions on Dex's face.

"Is he sure about this?" Dex asked after a moment, and Tommy shook his head.

"Not yet. Not yet. But he's gonna be." Tommy had a deceptively square jaw, and it jutted out now as he watched Donnie come back from the hallway, glare at his mother, and say something sharp to her. A girl who looked like Donnie's sister was smiling at Donnie in that quirky way that said she thought he could probably do no wrong, and Kane wondered if Lola had ever looked at *him* that way. If she had, she didn't now, he thought and turned his attention back to Tommy, who was telling Dex in a few simple, specific words how very sure he was that Chase would raise his own child.

Dex looked at Kane, expecting eye contact, and Kane gave it with a nod, wondering if Dex was thinking about Kelsey but not sure. He was suddenly tired. He knew why maybe Chase might want to go to sleep sometimes and not wake up. The world was confusing and hard when everybody could think faster than you, feel faster than you, so when he turned around and saw Ethan sitting alone on the corner of the couch, Kane ambled over to sit next to him.

Just that quickly, Ethan had his arm over Kane's shoulders and was resting his chin on Kane's chest.

"Put your arm around me, man, I need a hug."

Kane did what he asked, aware that Ethan was one of those people who needed to be petted constantly, like a cat. When they were shooting a scene, it was great. Any little bit of attention made Ethan's cock swing north, and he made some of the greatest noises. Ethan made work so fucking easy, it was almost not fucking—it was almost like eating pudding instead, except that sounded really gross when you were talking about coming and sex. But doing a scene with Ethan was effortless—it didn't even require any teeth or chewing, just slid down nice and smooth and you got a whole lot of bang for your buck.

Off the clock, Ethan needed stroking too, just not the sexy kind. Kane loved the guy, but he was glad he hadn't ended up rooming with him, even though Ethan had been his second choice. If he and Ethan had ended up sleeping together, Kane would have had to touch him constantly, and if Kane liked being body humped that much, he would have gotten cats instead of snakes.

But now it was perfect. It was like borrowing a friend's cat (Kane had seen Chase and Tommy's kitten, Paulie, haul ass for the back room when he walked in, or he would have been playing with it now), and that was always fun. Ethan laid on him and Kane petted him, and Ethan snuggled.

"Heya, big guy," Kane said, relieved. Ethan was like him—uncomplicated—and Kane was looking forward to some of that. "How're they hangin'?"

"So low they're getting squashed flat," Ethan said glumly and then snuggled in a little deeper.

"Oh Jesus, Ethan—what the fuck?" Kane's balls shriveled up and hugged his groin in sympathy.

Ethan burrowed against his chest some more. "Sorry. Horrible thing to say about the guys. It's just that…." Ethan let out a whimper just like a puppy's sound.

Kane wanted to cry. God. He wanted his people to be *happy.*

"What's wrong?" Kane rubbed a solid palm along Ethan's huge bicep, and Ethan sighed.

"Does your family know about the porn?" he asked, and Kane got a nasty clenching in his gut. *God, not this.*

"Bad?" he asked, not wanting to talk about Lola and Frances and the house that wasn't his house anymore and how happy he was at Dex's. He *really* didn't want to talk about how happy he was in Dex's house. It felt like he would jinx it if he brought that up. It was funny—he'd brought the guys over to Dex's house, and nobody had even questioned how he'd gotten in. But as everyone was leaving, Tommy had turned to him and said, "Thank Dex for letting us use his place, okay? You gonna stay here and give him back his key?"

Kane's stomach had dropped a little, and he realized that somehow, he and Dex had become a secret. "Yeah, that was the plan." He hadn't even tried to keep a secret from his sister—he sucked at it. But just that suddenly, that moment, every night of hauling Dex's body next to his, of relaxing his big bulky muscle against Dex's leanness, became sacred, something he didn't want to talk about to anyone, especially Dex's acerbic best friend.

But now, confronted with Ethan's open-skinned misery, he could understand how Ethan might want to say something.

Ethan shuddered and Kane hugged him harder. "How bad?" Kane asked again.

"I… it's going to be a lonely holiday," Ethan said quietly, and Kane dropped a kiss on his hair, because that's what Dex had done for him.

"We'll find someone," Kane said. "Don't worry. I mean, yeah, I know we all fuck for money, but that doesn't make us bad people. We'll find someone. I promise."

Ethan sat up a little and just rested his head on Kane's shoulder. "Thanks," he said softly, and Kane sat there in the corner, hugging his friend, until the party started to break up and Dex quietly came and got him to take him home.

"You guys ride together?" Ethan asked, and Kane won the fight not to take Dex's hand and say, *We are together!* He didn't think Dex would like that, at least not without a conversation, but hadn't Kane just proved he sucked at those?

"Yeah," Dex said. "See you tomorrow!"

"You'll see all of me tomorrow." Ethan leered, Dex winked, and Kane wondered how come he got to see Ethan fall apart when Dex would have handled it so much better.

They got outside and the air was damp and cold and foggy, like it could get in late November.

"Nice place," Kane said, pulling on the coat Dex had been holding for him. It was a leather jacket, business-suit cut, with a soft fleece lining. He didn't spend a lot on clothes, but he and Dex had been at the mall because they'd needed to go to Sears for sheets (Dex's were wearing out from being washed so much), and Dex had seen it in a store and shoved Kane in there after it.

"But what am I going to do for a hat?" Kane had complained. That's why he liked his old school lettermen jacket—it had a really nice lined hood on it, and he hated it when his ears got cold.

"I'll get you a fuckin' hat—hell, I'll get my mother to knit you one."

That had stopped Kane. He'd written his parents several times in the last year, but Lola must have told them about the porn, because they hadn't answered back. She told him that they were fine, so he figured it must only be him.

"Would she really?" he asked plaintively, and Dex had paused in the act of smoothing the coat over his shoulders.

"Yeah," Dex said. Then he added honestly, "As long as she doesn't know about you and me or *Johnnies*, yeah. I mean, I've never asked her before, but do you want me to?"

Kane looked at the jacket and decided he liked it. "We'll buy a hat on the way out," he said quietly. "I don't want your moms making me anything that would be a lie."

Dex nodded and avoided his eyes, and Kane felt bad. But that night, when they got home, Dex caught him in the hallway and framed his face with both hands, then kissed him slowly, sweetly, with such terrible softness and tenderness that Kane almost embarrassed himself by crying before he came. All of that fucking—and he'd be the first to admit he'd done his share and the neighbor's share and their kids' share and even people they hadn't met's share—and he didn't think he'd ever felt that good when he was coming.

"Yeah," Dex said now, pulling him away from his spiffy new warm coat and the purple Kings stocking cap he'd put over his ears. "It is a nice place. They're going to have Thanksgiving there, if you want to go."

Kane brightened. "Not so many people?" he asked. Dex smiled at him, a quiet, real smile that told Kane he hadn't been able to hide his discomfort at all the people—Chase's baseball team, Donnie's family—that he hadn't known.

"No. Mostly *Johnnies*, I think, maybe Chase's friend."

"Good," Kane said, putting his hands in his pockets. The temperature was in the low forties, and they'd parked around the block because there'd been so many cars. Dex had leather gloves on, and Kane thought wistfully that he planned to get some every year, and every year he forgot. "That way we can bring Ethan. His folks told him not to come this year."

Dex grunted. "Fuck. How'd they find out about the porn?"

Kane shrugged. "I didn't think to ask. He just needed… you know. He needed pets. You're the one who gets into why and shit. I'm just muscle."

Dex's hand felt comfortable around his bicep as he squeezed. "Yeah you are. Hey—Chase is back home, and Tommy's actually working at the pet store. You want to go work out with Chase and me tomorrow?"

Kane grinned. He liked routine, and having Chase in the hospital had seriously screwed his up. "Yeah! I like working out with you, man. I can't remember the last time I had fun at the gym!"

Dex hadn't let go of his arm, and when he squeezed again, Kane patted his hand so he'd know he could leave it there, that Kane didn't mind. "Yeah—it is fun with people, isn't it?"

"Yeah. It's fun with you."

"How bad do you want sex when we get back?"

Kane smiled, completely content. "So frickin' bad. I hope you stocked up on lube and rubbers, man. I'm gonna nail you into the fuckin' mattress."

Dex made a sound suspiciously like a purr. "Fan*tast*ic. Can't wait."

And it was awesome. But at the end, when Dex was a puddle of goo (not literally—Kane had gone and gotten the cloth and cleaned him up this time) and Kane had dragged him against his sweating body in the cooling dark, Kane stopped fighting the urge to smother Dex and just draped his body over Dex's shoulders, practically smashing him into the mattress.

"Kane, you psycho, I can't breathe!"

"Yeah," Kane admitted. "I know. I'm sorry. I just need to."

Dex's chest fought up and down, and then again. "Yeah, okay. Just resuscitate me when you decide to climb off, 'kay?"

Kane laughed a little, but he stayed there for a few more of Dex's hard-fought breaths. When he finally rolled off, he clenched Dex to his body harder than usual, and Dex grunted.

"Something I should know about?"

"I got no words," Kane apologized. "When I get words, I'll let you know."

It was just that there was something missing, in a way. When he held onto Dex, it was all perfect—best part of his day perfect, best part of his life perfect. Just… just sunny spring day perfect, with soft grass where you could see worms and spiders under your feet perfect, and even lizards sunning themselves on granite boulders. *Perfect.* But when they weren't touching, there was something… empty. Kane couldn't figure out what it was. Was it because Dex was a guy?

Kane pulled him tighter, felt his cock come alive again just at the brush of Dex's ass through his boxers, and thought that couldn't be it. It wasn't the guy/girl thing, was it? They were happy, right? What was the problem? Why the need? The craving? The fear that he'd wake up one day and Dex wouldn't be there?

Kane had no words. He just didn't. But Thanksgiving—yeah. Thanksgiving blew it all out of the fucking water. At Thanksgiving he found his words, and he was lucky he found them in time, because it was almost Fucked-ups-giving, because Kane didn't have no words.

THEY made pies that morning, and Kane enjoyed the hell out of that. Dex looked up two recipes, and Kane went out and shopped the day before. On Thanksgiving Day, while Dex was in the shower, Kane started reading the directions. In the past he hadn't been great at that, the directions part, but he thought he could handle it now. By the time Dex got out, Kane was pouring the pumpkin/cream cheese mix into the graham cracker crust, and Dex was damned impressed.

"God, Kane, it looks awesome! Here, you shower and I'll make the next one!"

Kane preened under his praise and then remembered to take off the apron, which he'd worn over his boxer shorts as he'd worked, and put it over Dex's dressy shirt and slacks.

"You don't want to get that shit dirty," he said seriously. "You look real good."

And now *Dex* was preening under *his* praise, and Kane was so warm in his chest he had to grab Dex behind the head and pull him in for a kiss. He pulled back and saw that Dex's cheeks—which were really, really pale pink, even in the summer, when he was pale gold almost everywhere else—were blotchy, like he wasn't just turned on, he was pleased. Kane's warmth spilled over to his face and he pulled away, thinking if he didn't, they'd end up in bed again, and they had shit to do.

He felt bumbling and awkward as he stepped back, and then he noticed that Dex was biting his lower lip like an adolescent girl and looking purposefully at the recipe like that was the only thing on Earth. For a minute Kane was tempted to make a dirty joke or something, but something—the angle of Dex's head, something—made him think that suddenly they were beyond dirty jokes, and he just kept going to the shower like nothing had happened.

When he got out, though, Dex was done with the pie, but he was still standing in the kitchen with a little bowl of chocolate pie filling and some graham crackers.

"There was some extra," he said, smiling so wide his dimples popped. "You want to help me eat it?"

"Oh man, that's *awesome!*"

Together, they leaned over the counter and dipped the graham crackers in the filling, eating very carefully to not get the pie remains on their nice shirts. Dex had taken Kane shopping again, and instead of a Henley and jeans, which is what he was pretty sure he *would* be wearing at this moment, he was wearing something sort of silky, in black, with little geometric patterns on it. He was wearing jeans too, but they were black, and they were a little more fitted than he was used to, with white stitching on the inseams. He had to admit that with as much time as he spent making his hair look good, the new clothes made sense, but right now, being very careful not to get them dirty, he was a little embarrassed. Usually getting his clothes dirty wasn't a problem.

"So—mmm… God, this is good, Dex. I hope my pie tastes this good."

Dex giggled and wiped his finger on the corner of Kane's mouth, then licked off the chocolate that had been there. "I've tasted your pie, Kane. Trust me, it's great."

Kane was about to protest that his pie was in the refrigerator, perfectly unmolested, when he had a sudden vision from the night before, in the shower, when Dex had surprised him by going down behind him and licking him from balls to the small of his back, paying special attention to Kane's asshole. Kane could still feel Dex's tongue penetrating him, licking all over, being dominant and hungry, and just like that, he was blushing over pie and getting a hard-on *and* a double entendre.

"Yeah," he muttered, "well, I didn't mean like that. But that's fine too. You should taste my pie more often, I liked it."

Dex turned his head sideways a little, looking at Kane from the corner of his eye. "You don't usually let me… I don't know. Taste anything. It's usually the Kane the Dominator show."

Oh God. Would he ever stop blushing? "It's what… I don't know. I'm good at it. On set. It's my boy-sex mode."

Something… weird happened then. Something cold, and alien, and sad. Dex's face closed down, and the space between them, which had been intimate and close the moment before, was now chilly and vast. Kane straightened, feeling that horrible inarticulate fear again, that thing that had made him practically crush Dex to the bed a week ago. He wasn't sure where it came from, but suddenly he had Dex's shirt in his fist and Dex back against the refrigerator and Dex's mouth open under his. Dex was responding, but his back and arms were tense, and Kane wasn't satisfied with that.

He kissed more, hissed harder, until Dex's arms grew fluid and soft around his shoulders and his spine melted a little, leaving him pliant and boneless, with his eyes closed and a sort of pained resignation on his face as Kane pulled back.

"We've got to go," Dex whispered, his eyes still closed, and Kane rubbed Dex's temple, next to that bright-blond hair, with his tingling lips.

"Yeah. Okay. Just don't."

"Don't what?"

Kane closed his eyes and kissed that spot again. "Whatever you did to make the day go dark. Don't do that again."

Dex swallowed and nodded. "Kane, we're going to have to talk about us soon, you know that, right?"

Kane closed his eyes. God, no. Not relationships. He'd never had one. He didn't know how they worked. "No," he said, because he didn't want to go there. He didn't want to hear Dex tell him it was over. "No. No talking. We're good."

He pulled away abruptly so he didn't have time to say anything else that would make him feel stupid or completely lacking or unable to deal. Him and Dex. They slept together at night. They functioned in the day. He didn't want to disturb that. It was all he dared to ask for. Hell, he was a *porn star*. It was more than he figured he had coming anyway.

He trotted to the hallway and got his coat and Dex's, made sure Dex's gloves were in Dex's pockets along with the hat he'd bought Dex the same night he'd bought his. Dex's hat was sky blue, because Kane liked the color on his bright hair, but that's not what he'd said. He hadn't said anything, in fact. He'd just bought it and stuffed it in the pocket of Dex's fleece-lined leather coat when he hung their stuff up. He'd seen Dex wearing it, and he'd been content.

He brought the coats into the living room. Dex was wrapping the pies in foil, carefully not looking at him, when he walked in. Kane waited patiently and then walked up to him when the pies were wrapped, and held the coat out for him.

Dex let out a bitter laugh and put his arms in the sleeves. "I'm old enough to put on my own coat," he said, and Kane cringed.

"Yeah, but I'm not old enough to know how to talk about this."

Dex looked at him closely and held up a hand to his face to touch Kane's cheekbones with tender fingertips. "You need to grow up soon, Kane. I'm tired of having my heart stomped on."

Kane's own heart gave a bloody pump in his chest. "I've never stomped on—"

Dex shook his head. "Not on purpose. Look. Let's go."

"We're early, you know."

Dex still couldn't look at him. "Yeah, but I'd rather be uncomfortable in their kitchen instead of uncomfortable in ours right now. C'mon."

So all things considered, running to Tommy and Chase's just to get away from each other, from the painful, uncomfortable things ripping the air between them—that was like, *salvation* right there. Kane ditched Dex in the kitchen with the pies while he went to chase the kitten, who went beyond his expectations and chased him right back.

He played that game for an hour as the house filled with people. Not as many as for Chase's welcome home party, but still, Kane wasn't really ready to go talk to all those people with that conversation with

Dex still aching in his chest. The kitten was simpler. Kane was stalking the little fuzz ball on all fours, coming out of Tommy and Chase's bedroom, when he almost ran into a very fine pair of legs emerging from the bathroom. The legs had red pumps at the bottom and a short hem toward the top, with round calves that were so perfectly muscled that the owner of the legs was either a dancer or a workout fanatic.

As Kane's vision traveled up to a diamond-cut butt, tiny waist, and flat little chest, all wrapped up in a white wool shirtwaist, his cock gave a nostalgic little throb. He sort of missed women sometimes. Yeah, sure, they all assumed that because he wasn't that bright, he wasn't worth much, but they had soft skin and really amazing smiles. This one had fluffy short-cut blonde hair and pretty blue eyes and a full, wide, smiling mouth. If he'd thought about it, he'd have realized she looked a lot like Dex, but thinking about Dex made his chest hurt, so he didn't think about it.

Instead, he just looked up and waggled his eyebrows. "Hel-lo, pretty lady! Did you see my fuzzy little friend come by here? Unca Kane is gonna play with him!"

The girl's mouth turned up at the corner almost lazily, and Kane was reminded of the look on that damned kitten's face right before the little fucker took a piece of Kane's hand with a tiny claw. "Yeah, Unca Kane—I think he went into the living room. But I warn you, the people in there are pretty much on his side."

Kane stayed on the floor—the view was better from down there—and looked up at her coyly. "Well, maybe I should just stay in here and wait. Little fuzz ball's gonna get too hyped out with all those people anyway. Eventually he'll come back down here, and then I got him! Wanna wait with me?"

It was cheezy with a capital Z, but it worked. She looked into the hallway and then back at him, and he recognized the same feeling he had: better a quiet little corner than the big raucous room with all the noise.

"Yeah, fine, why not?" She slid down across from him, sticking those long legs out in front of her. For a tiny little woman, she really did have pretty spectacular legs, and she crossed them demurely at the ankles. "So, how do you know Chase and Tommy?"

Kane didn't even think about blushing. If she knew Chase and Tommy together, she knew what they did. "We work together," he said.

Her eyes widened and her mouth made one of those adorable little O shapes that girls had always been able to level him with. "Really?" She looked behind her shoulder for a second like she didn't want anyone to hear what she said next. "So," she asked, her eyes sparkling impishly, "how is he in the sack?"

Kane grinned at her, liking her style. "Which one?" he asked.

She looked, if anything, more avid. "Chase. I've thought he was beautiful since he was like, sixteen, but I'm way too old for him, right?"

Kane nodded. He got it. "He's hella good. Him and me, we were, like, gladiator gods when we shot scenes, 'cause he's like a total dominator and so am I. It was awesome."

The girl's grin widened, and her nose wrinkled, and she looked like an adorable little chipmunk woman as she lowered her voice conspiratorially. "How's Tommy?" she asked.

Kane's grin amped up. "I'm surprised the house hasn't exploded," he told her truthfully, and she burst into peals of tinkling laughter that made him smile some more. "So how do you know them?"

He caught it then—that first moment of "You really don't know?"—and knew that when she spoke, he'd feel stupid. "I'm Donnie's sister, Chelle," she said. "Donnie and Chase have been best friends since they were little."

Kane nodded then and felt stupid. Of course. He'd seen them at the welcome back party—they looked like twins. "Yeah, I should have known. You look just like him." Kane thought about it for a second. "What was Chase like as a kid?" He had to wonder. What kind of little kid grew up into the kind of guy who would cheat on his girlfriend while doing gay porn and then try to kill himself? Because Chase as a grown-up was nice. Quiet, but nice. What made a guy like that?

Chelle looked thoughtful for a moment. "He was lonely," she said softly. "Even as a little kid, even when Donnie and Kevin were all around, he was lonely. My mom used to try to mother him, give him things, and he always looked really… pleased, but he never got excited. It was like even with a Christmas present, he was always waiting for the other shoe to drop, you know?"

Kane thought about the young man he'd visited in the mental institution, who had looked at him the same way. "I know," he said, and then he remembered how that same young man had smiled when he and Dex had walked through the door. "But maybe that's what growing up gets you. You get better. You stop waiting for the bad stuff to happen and maybe enjoy the good, you know?"

Her smile at him was warm and fuzzy, and suddenly the pit in Kane's stomach was warm and fuzzy too. And at that moment, the kitten came stalking back in, looking at him like he'd dropped the ball.

The conversation was getting too serious anyway, so Kane went chasing the little goombah all over the house again, except now Chelle stood in the hallway and cheered him on.

Eventually he got poor Paulie too wound up, though, and got his face scratched into the bargain. Before dinner was served, Chelle sat him down at the kitchen table. Dex raised a sardonic eyebrow at him while she dressed the scratch across his nose.

"That's what you get," Dex said, his voice sharp, and Kane looked at him sheepishly.

"Yeah, I know better," he replied. Perversely, he wanted a kiss on the nose and a pat on the head, and he wasn't sure where that need came from. His mother would have done it, yeah, but his father? No, his father would have told him to be a man about it, it was only a little blood.

"Well, I think that kitten just overreacted," Chelle said, and she placed a playful kiss on his nose then pulled a bemused Kane to his feet. "Here, go put this back in the bathroom and I'll get you a plate. It looks like they're almost ready to serve."

He ambled away and as he did, he heard Dex's voice at its most acidic.

"Needs. A. Keeper."

Well, maybe not *needed*, but he'd been sort of hoping Dex had wanted the job. Now he wasn't so sure.

Dinner was good. They served themselves in the happy yellow kitchen, buffet style from a laden table, and ate in the living room, which was as dramatically colored as the bedroom. There was turkey and gravy and stuffing (with too much of something weird in it—Kane didn't like the stuffing) and all sorts of stuff that most of the *Johnnies* models usually avoided like the plague but were eating in limited quantities today. Even so, while the food was good, the video games were better. Kane and Donnie's friend Kevin dominated the deep-blue video couch in the living room until Dex came by and whispered, "I think Ethan needs a turn," in his ear. Kane looked up and saw Ethan looking forlorn in the corner of the living room, and realized that he'd been sort of sad and alone for most of the evening. He looked at Dex and nodded and hollered, "Hey, Ethan! You go next!" and then tanked his player before throwing the controller at Ethan's head.

Ethan caught it, of course, because he was an athlete and so was Kane and it was a good throw, but still, he shouted, "Kane, you psycho! You could have killed someone with this!" before he stood up and took Kane's spot in the game without even losing any points.

Kane got up from his spot and stretched and looked at Dex to see if he'd done good.

Dex winked, and Kane thought wistfully that something as small as an expression of approval was the difference between a happy Thanksgiving and one that really blew chunks.

Kane followed Dex into the kitchen, and so did Chelle and Donnie. With Tommy's help, Chelle and Donnie pulled Chase into the front room to soundly thrash Ethan in *Halo*, and Dex and Kane stayed behind to do dishes. It was a familiar thing, something they did when they were alone in their own… or in *Dex's* home, and for a moment, all was right with the world.

"Chase looks good," Dex said, and Kane had to agree.

"I've never seen him smile so much."

"Yeah, well, Tommy neither. It's a little scary."

Kane laughed. "People can be happy," he said, thinking that might be what Dex wanted to hear.

It wasn't. Dex just looked at him levelly like he'd said something much more important than what that was really supposed to be, and nodded. "I'll finish up," he said quietly. "Your girlfriend's waiting."

"She's not my girlfriend," Kane answered, but even as he said it, he heard the same sound in his voice that he'd heard when he was in the sixth grade. Suddenly he had to ask it. "Is it because I'm younger than you?"

Dex looked honestly surprised, and then his narrow, pretty angel's face hardened. "Yeah," he said spitefully. "It's because you're younger than me." And with that, he turned his back and started wiping off the golden marble counter. At that moment Tommy came in and said something about serving pie. God, it wasn't like anybody knew about them. It wasn't like it was a *real* relationship, right?

Except it felt real. It felt real, and Dex's turned back felt like a shiv in the gut, and Chelle's pretty face and happy, flirty smile as he walked into the living room didn't make up for the uncertainty of maybe not having Dex where he should be when they got home.

Chelle got his number before she left, and made a big production about pushing her digits into his phone and taking a picture of herself to go with the number. Kane played along and flirted back, because he'd had fun with her while Dex had been all grown-up having the what're-ya-gonna-do-with-yer-future talk in the kitchen, or so he assumed. Then Kane walked out with Dex after hugging Chase and Tommy and wishing them a good holiday.

Kane was glad to leave. He loved them—hell, he loved pretty much everyone in the house, after they'd had dinner and played video games, even Donnie's snotty little standoffish boyfriend, Alejandro, who kept trying to speak Spanish to him when all Kane knew was Mexican. (Sure, his teachers in high school had kept trying to tell him it was the same fuckin' language, but Kane wasn't buying that any more now than he had when he'd been in high school!) So, yeah, he loved them—but for once, he didn't want to take care of other people.

For once, he wanted to take care of his own house, and that meant Dex, and Dex wasn't good.

Dex drove home through the fog so vicious it was like volcano smoke, looking for a break in the weather to erupt. Kane tried to make small talk—didn't so-and-so look nice, wasn't the stuffing gross, what did Dex think really happened with Ethan? But Dex gave one-word answers, and Kane was at a loss.

Dex parked the Navigator (which is what they'd driven, and it was weird how Dex always ended up driving even if it was Kane's car) in the driveway and slid out, then headed straight for the door, leaving Kane to scramble behind him, grabbing his little packet of turkey and wondering what went wrong.

He got into the house and shut the door and put the turkey on the counter. Then he followed Dex down the hall, where Dex made a surprise right into the guest room and turned on the light. He bent down and grabbed the new turtle terrarium—probably the smallest of the cages—yanked the plug out of the wall, and brushed past Kane into the hallway.

Kane was at a loss. "What in the fuck are you doing?"

"I'm moving half of them into my room," Dex said shortly, his back toward Kane, and Kane managed to pass him in the hallway and put his hands on the tank.

"Well, don't. You're upsetting them," he said. He looked carefully into the terrarium at the box turtles, who were still fast asleep. "Why are you moving them at nine o'clock at night?"

Dex gave the tank, which was pretty heavy, a solid yank, but Kane held on. "'Cause if I move half of them into my room, we can put up the bed, and you can sleep in the guest room," he said. His eyes were narrow—and red, like he was on the verge of crying—and his mouth was pushed together and pouty, and his jaw was squared and surprisingly stubborn.

Kane wasn't any of those things. "Why in the fuck are you going to do that?" he asked, hearing the thread of panic in his voice and not caring. "Why? We're good in the bed together. Why would you want to move the guys and fuck that up?" He kept his arms locked on the terrarium, thinking that his one saving grace was that he could bench press about 150 pounds more than Dex, so he *would* be able to keep this from happening, even if it was by main strength.

Dex looked up at him and spoke, and for the first time since that moment in the kitchen, Kane saw the real Dex—and the real Dex was in pain.

"I can't do this," Dex said.

"But we're good—"

"Yeah! We're good! We're great in bed! Don't you see? That's all we are! You… you don't even know you're in a relationship, Kane! You spent all night flirting with that girl because you don't think you're gay! Well, that's fine! You flirt with girls. You sleep with them. That's great! But leave my heart out of it, okay? I know I'm a guy, so I'm just a piece of ass to you, but that's not what's happening to *me,* all right? I'm getting *feelings.* I'm getting *attached.* But all that shit you're doing that's making me fall for you, that's just boy-sex stuff to you, and it's *killing me.* I just got out of a relationship where I was in love with the guy who used me for a booty call. I'm not *doing* it again! *It fucking hurts!*"

Oh Jesus. Oh fucking Jesus. Kane looked at him in horror. Oh Christ. *He'd* done this. *Kane* had done this. *Kane* had let Dex think that he was booty call.

"You're not booty call," Kane muttered, halfway to himself.

"I know that's not what you're trying to do—" Dex started patiently, and Kane's panic snapped.

"Put the fuckin' terrarium down!" he yelled, pulling at it. "Put it down, Dex, and *let me fuckin' talk*!"

Dex let go of the terrarium and Kane stumbled backward, running into the wall (fortunately) and grunting as he took the full weight of the tank. He put it down right at his feet, ignoring the fact that it was still cold in the house because neither one of them had turned on the heater, and pulled out the phone.

"Turn on the heater, wouldja?" he asked absently, because Dex was the one next to the thermostat, and Dex did, still staring at him while he scrolled through his phone for Chelle's number and then punched it in over Chelle's smiling face.

She answered on the first ring.

"Hullo, Unca Kane," she said, her voice all silky and liquid, and Kane wanted to groan. Oh fuck. He'd been having fun, dammit, and *she'd* been picking up a guy. Fuck. Fuck, fuck, fuck. No wonder he was better off with men. God, he just wasn't smart enough to deal with women.

"Hey," he said and looked at Dex from under his brows. Dex's eyes were still red, but now they were spilling over a little, and Kane felt like shit. He reached out then and used his finger to brush some of the wetness off Dex's cheek. Dex looked back at him, and suddenly Kane saw how tired he was. This had been eating at him, hadn't it? Just like that fear had been eating at Kane. Oh God. Dex had worried too! The knowledge gave Kane some confidence when he started talking to Chelle.

"Chelle?"

"Yeah?" She sounded amused.

"Look, I know we had a real good time tonight, and I'd love to go to the movies with you sometime like we talked about but"—Kane made sure Dex was looking him in the eyes when he said it—"but really, only as friends, okay? I'm sort of in a relationship right now."

"Oh," she said, and he heard the disappointment in her voice and wanted to kick himself.

"I'm sorry. Yeah. I didn't really think about how all that could be… how it could… fuck, what's the fuckin' word?"

"Misconstrued," she said gently. "Or mistaken."

Kane swallowed, thanking God she wasn't a bad person either. "Yeah. The way I was acting, it could be misconstakened. I had a lot of fun tonight, but I got somebody, and I didn't want to waste your time, okay?"

"Thank you," she said softly. "Most guys would be okay just leading me on."

Kane reached out and brushed another tear off Dex's cheek with his thumb. "Yeah, well, most guys would be smart enough to know they were doing it when they were really just looking for a quiet place to sit in a noisy house. Thanks for not bein' mad. I gotta go."

"Bye, Kane. Don't forget to call me about the movies. I promise I won't misconstrue anything. We'll just go as friends."

"Bye. I'll call later."

He hit End Call and put the phone in his jacket pocket, and he and Dex regarded each other levelly over the turtle terrarium.

"You didn't have to do that," Dex said after a moment that was so quiet, Kane could swear he heard the November fog settle and the turtles breathe.

Kane snorted. "The fuck I didn't!"

Dex arched his eyebrows, and another tear plopped down on the carpet. Kane reached out to brush the next one away, and Dex caught his hand. "Why did you?"

"'Cause." Kane swallowed and turned his hand so they could clasp fingers. "Anything that ends up with us in separate beds, that's the wrong thing. You hear me? Whatever I have to give up or stop doing to keep us in the same bed, that's the right thing. I'm not smart. I'm not. But right now, that's the only thing I know."

"Kane, you know that means you're gay—or at least bi."

Kane shrugged. "I don't care," he said helplessly, unable to convey how little that really mattered right now. "I just…." He tried to drop his hand, but Dex kept their fingers tightly laced. He looked down past their clasped hands to the turtle terrarium and tried, for once, to put things into words.

"I just kept being afraid that I'd wake up and you'd be gone," he said softly. "I don't know how to make it so I know that'll never happen, but if telling people I'm gay and you're mine is the way to do that, then fine. I don't care. Whatever you want. I just need us to keep waking up in the same bed, David. I need to know you'll be there when I go to sleep. Good day, shitty day, the only thing I want at the end of it is for you to be there when I go to sleep. You tell me how to make that happen."

Dex brought their clasped hands up to his mouth and kissed Kane's knuckles. "Okay, asshole. Repeat after me: 'I'm sorry. I'm in a relationship.' Can you say that?"

Kane looked up at him and smiled, so relieved that Dex was smiling back that he felt his eyes get warm and salty-bright too. "I'm sorry. I'm in a relationship," he said softly, and Dex took a step forward like they were going to kiss, and then stubbed his toe on the terrarium.

"Fuck," he muttered and then bent down. "Go get undressed, okay? I'll be there in a sec."

Dex bent to pick up the terrarium and put it back. Kane did what he said to do, making sure to hang his coat up in the hall with his hat in the pocket. He threw his shirt and undershirt in the hamper they'd been sharing, and folded his jeans neatly and put them on top of the dresser pile with the rest of his clean clothes. Then he jumped in the shower quick to rinse off, and when he got out and put on his boxers and ambled into the bedroom, Dex was rearranging the clothes on top of the dresser.

"What in the hell are you doing now?" he asked, his voice pitching. God, he just wanted sex! Not plain sex but *Dex* sex, which was apparently worth giving up all other sex except for *set* sex, because *Dex sex* was that special. But he'd said the good thing, he'd made Dex feel better, and he'd meant it—didn't they get sex now?

"I'm moving your clothes into my dressers," Dex said patiently, and he did. He put the big pile of plain white underwear in the top drawer of the big dresser, and the big pile of T-shirts and Henleys in the next drawer, and then looked at the pants and jeans, then into his closet, which wasn't that big and was sort of full. "I'll take care of those tomorrow," he said softly, and then, while Kane still waited at the bedside, he came forward.

"Why'd you do that?" Kane asked, looking at the blank spot on top of the dresser. Maybe they could put a terrarium on that after all.

"When I lived in the other house, I kept most of my shit on the dressers anyway."

Dex smiled a little, but his eyes were downcast as he flattened his palm against Kane's muscled stomach. "I know you did," he said, and Kane sucked in his gut and let his skin ripple across it in response to Dex's touch. "I visited, remember? Before you got the guys?"

Kane's shoulders twitched. "I was embarrassed," he apologized. "I knew you'd have a better place than that. I bought that expensive house and everything, but I didn't know how to make it a good place."

"You like my place?" Dex said, moving closer.

Kane always forgot how tall Dex was, and when they were standing toe to toe like this, he had to look up. "I do." Kane framed Dex's hips with his hands and pulled him close not in a crude way—although when Dex's thumbs brushed his nipples, his cock woke up big-time—just closer, that was all.

Dex lowered his head and brushed Kane's shoulder ever-so-gently with his lips. "Good," Dex said. "I'm glad you like my place. Your slimy things are taking up my spare bedroom, and you've bought groceries for a month. Now that I've moved your shit into my drawers, it's officially your place too, until you want to bail."

Kane swallowed. "I don't even pay rent." God, he was dumb. He'd meant to, but he'd totally spaced the day he should have. It had just occurred to him too. But obviously it hadn't just occurred to Dex.

"Yeah, Kane. You're a freeloader. I don't give a shit. Just don't… don't deny me in public. Don't fuck around with girls and say it's not cheating. Don't… don't treat this like it's not special."

Kane rubbed his cheek against Dex's, thinking about all the guys he'd fucked on the set, all the girls he'd fucked in bathrooms, behind buildings, whatever. "I'm not smart," he said, his voice rough. "But I know special. It's special. Anything I gotta do to sleep next to you. That's what I'm gonna do."

"Anything?"

Kane's lips came to that spot just under Dex's jaw, and he turned his head and kissed it. "Yeah."

Dex stepped back and took Kane's face in both hands, then pressed forward, stopping when their lips could barely touch. "Then let me lead tonight."

"Okay—"

Dex captured his mouth and kissed him, but not their usual kiss. Not the dying of starvation kisses they were good at. This kiss was slow, and slower, and exquisite and tender, and it played with the sweep of Dex's tongue and the pulling of his lips and the playful bumping of noses until Kane was happy and aroused and tried to push forward for more.

Dex didn't let him. "My turn," he warned and then kissed Kane back until his legs bumped the bed. Dex kept pushing, and Kane put his arm behind him and took their weight, lowering them both onto the bed until Dex was lying on top of him, still kissing.

Oh God. *Still* kissing. And it was wonderful. Kane spread his knees so Dex was lying between them, then lifted his ass and ground up against Dex's lower abdomen. Dex ground back aggressively, then pulled away enough to whisper, "Don't get pushy, Carlos," as he kissed down Kane's jaw to his ear.

Kane groaned, and Dex nibbled on his earlobe again. "Say it again," he muttered.

"Don't get pushy?"

"My name."

"Carlos," Dex murmured, his breath hot in Kane's ear. "Carlos Ramirez."

"José Carlos Ricardo Ramirez," Kane whispered, because it was his baptism name and he didn't think he'd ever hear anyone else say it when his parents stopped writing.

"José Carlos Ricardo Ramirez," Dex said soberly, rearing back to look him in the eyes. He did something odd then: he leaned forward and kissed Kane's upper lip, licked it softly, and Kane realized that Dex could see his palate scar—and apparently didn't give a fuck. "José Carlos Ricardo Ramirez, I'm David Calvin Worral."

Kane's grin felt like it stretched his ears. "Calvin?"

"It's my grandfather's name. My brother got the other grandfather, and everybody else got aunts and uncles. Not a lot of imagination in our family." Dex punctuated the speech with little kisses all over Kane's face, and Kane loved that, but he was fully aroused and starting to squirm.

"Okay, David Calvin, are we gonna start fucking soon?"

"Yeah, José Carlos Ricardo, but first I'm gonna stick my tongue in your asshole and suck your balls. You ready for that?"

Yippee!

Kane grabbed Dex's hips and forced their groins together so the counterpressure could keep him from coming. "Dirty talk," he gasped. Guys didn't talk that dirty at *Johnnies*—a lot of 'em were too self-conscious. But to hear those words coming from Dex's plump, smiling mouth with those angel's eyes twinkling when he said it? "God! You'd better fucking follow through!"

Dex kissed down his jaw and across his pecs. Kane closed his eyes as Dex took a nipple in his mouth and laved, and laved, and laved until—

"Oh crap! Dexter! David! Whatever!"

Dex pulled away from the one nipple and pinched the other. Kane groaned, and Dex pointed his tongue and traced a path over each rippled muscle in Kane's stomach, then down, circling his belly button, and to his happy trail, which Kane left unwaxed.

"I like this hair," Dex said between licks and then slid Kane's boxers off and shoved his feet up on the bed, leaving him exposed, erect and splayed for Dex and Dex alone, with the light still on.

Kane's cock was lying hard and long across his abdomen, his cockhead exposed because the foreskin had retracted, and Dex's breath on the head made Kane shiver. Suddenly he *needed* a touch there, *needed* Dex's mouth there, but after one brief tantalizing touch of Dex's tongue right on the slit to lap at the drop of shining precome, Dex traced a line down the ridge of Kane's cock down over his balls (which he tried to shave regularly) and down, down….

The flat of Dex's tongue on Kane's freshly washed taint was *so* good, Kane let out a bark of surprise.

And then started wiggling his ass because he wanted more.

Dex kept licking, and with every lick, he moved down, down, until he grabbed one of Kane's thighs in each hand and shoved up.

"Part your cheeks for me, 'kay?" Dex ordered roughly, and Kane did, realizing that even though there were no cameras here, he'd never felt more vulnerable.

That was okay, though. Dex used that moment to lick *down,* into Kane's asshole, and start licking, poking his tongue into the entrance, and Kane's whole body started to quiver. He moved his hand to his cock because he *fucking needed it,* and Dex knocked the hand away.

"No," he said between licks. "No. 'Cause I'm gonna top tonight, Carlos, and you're going to want to hold on to that thing when I'm pounding your ass." Dex punctuated that with another lick, and Kane grunted.

"You'd better hurry, then, 'cause I'm gonna shoot!"

Dex peered up over Kane's crotch. "Yeah?" he said, sounding pleased. "Really?" He stuck out his tongue and licked again. "From a rim job?"

"*Dexter!*" Kane begged, and Dex rewarded him with a finger in his ass. Kane groaned low and happy, because it felt good, and Dex added a second one, and then, oh thank God, took Kane's cock down his throat in one slow mouth caress that left Kane's hands scrabbling in the sheets for purchase while he tried to focus on something, anything, enough not to come. He reached backward instead and scooted out of the range of Dex's mouth, and Dex followed him with those twitching, invading fingers never leaving his ass. Finally *(finally!)* he was in range of the end table, and he pulled out the lube and the condoms and threw them at Dex, careful not to clock him in the head.

Dex dumped the lube over his fingers and penetrated him again, and Kane wriggled, hoping Dex would get the hint. He'd always liked bottoming, he had, but he'd been so forceful as a top that John had scheduled him to do that instead.

"No condoms," Dex said suddenly, and Kane tried to open his eyes, but he couldn't. If he opened his eyes, he was afraid he'd come.

"What?" he asked instead. God... Dex's one finger had found his prostate and was rubbing, and Dex's hand was on his cock, and... oh fuck.

"We use condoms on set," Dex said, and his voice was serious, so Kane forced his eyes open and forced his hips down on the bed. "You and me, you and me only? We're no condoms."

Kane tried to do the math and failed. "Is that safe?" he asked, and Dex kissed the inside of his thigh. It tickled and turned him on unbearably at the same time.

"Only if neither of us cheats."

Kane nodded and wiggled and whined and tried one more time—his last for the night—to think like a grown up. "Won't cheat. No condoms. God... Dexter... whatever. Fuck me."

Dex's fingers disappeared, and Kane keened at their absence. And then Dex was suddenly there, his cock wedged in Kane's entrance. Kane often forgot that Dex's cock was longer than his and almost as wide, and suddenly he remembered that thrill of having someone about to invade him in a way that was intimate and private and potentially painful but... ahhhh. Dex's cockhead breached him, and it burned, but it felt unbearably good, and his entrance clamped down on Dex's cock as his whole body started to shake.

"Oh God!" Kane gasped, and Dex just kept pushing his way in. "Oh God... oh God... Dex... slow is killin' me... oh God...."

But Dex kept pushing slow until finally he was there, all inside, and Kane's whole body was shaking with sweat, just having it there. Oh, *fuck*, it felt so good. Dex pulled back a little and moved forward, and Kane groaned and his hand flailed for his cock, because he *needed, needed, absofuckinglutely had to fucking come right the fuck now!*

As soon as Kane gripped his cock, Dex pulled back and slammed into him, nailing his prostate and burning the holy hell out of his ass, and Kane squeezed himself hard and stroked and howled.

Dex laughed breathily and did it again. "Jesus, Kane, the neighbors are gonna think I'm killing you!"

Kane couldn't answer. "Fuck me faster," he begged and stroked again, right as Dex pulled back and pumped in some more. Oh God. Oh

God. He'd forgotten how good this was. How amazing it was when someone else took care of him, did this for him. And Dex was good. So good. Dex pulled back and thrust again, and again, and again, his hips picking up speed as Kane jerked on his cock, yanking the foreskin up and over the cockhead and using that delicious precome-slicked friction to pitch himself up, up, up high… oh God, so high….

Dex plowed into him with a brutal thrust and Kane was over, spurting all over his abs, his hand, his arm, and he howled out his orgasm as Dex kept fucking him. This wasn't the porn set, and Kane realized that specifically when Dex didn't pull out to come. He just kept hammering away until… oh God. Kane felt it. Dex's face scrunched up and he gasped and fell forward, his hips jerking, and Kane *felt* it. He'd never realized you could feel someone else's come up your ass, and it was hot and sticky as it started to leak out around Dex's cock, and it was so sexy… God… so sexy….

Kane's cock hardened again even as Dex fell forward, breathing heavily into Kane's ear. Kane moaned, so sensitive it would take the slightest touch to send him off, and Dex chuckled. "Again?"

"Your mouth," Kane begged. And Dex did. He pulled back, and the flood of come over Kane's backside made him whimper, because it really was fuckin' *hot*, and… and then Dex's skilled and gentle mouth engulfed his cockhead while his strong hand stroked, and that's all it took for Kane to go off one more time.

Dex hauled himself up and collapsed on Kane's shoulder, sweating and breathing hard—Dex, who ran about ten miles on the treadmill every day. "Done?" he asked, that thread of gentle humor in his voice, and Kane nodded, palming Dex's bright, sweat-soaked head with his own wide, sweaty hand.

"For now," he said and turned his head so he could kiss Dex, come-breath and all.

"Happy Thanksgiving, Kane," Dex said when Kane let him up for air.

Kane just laughed softly because it really was.

SCOUTING NEW TERRITORY

Dex

DEX was watching him sleep. Sometime in the night, Kane's tight hold on Dex's waist had loosened, and his arm was flung out under his head, and his dark hair was tousled over his bicep. His head was tilted back and he was snoring. Not gently and not like a gentleman either—it was mouth-open, no-holds-barred, rattle-the-windows-and-scare-the-snake-in-his-terrarium snoring.

It didn't really wake Dex up anymore. It was official. If Dex could sleep through Kane's snoring, he could sleep through fires, tornadoes, thunderstorms, tax collectors, and yet another escape from Tomas, the snake who liked to sleep nestled in Dex's balls. (Twice. Twice more, that snake had crawled up Dex's boxer shorts. If Dex hadn't learned to sleep like the fucking dead, he would never sleep at all. He would, in fact, be crouched up on his empty dresser with a flashlight and a metal pan, waiting to warn that fucker away from his fucking boxer shorts!)

So Kane's snoring hadn't woken Dex up this cold, foggy Friday after Thanksgiving. What had actually woken Dex up was the knowledge that he'd been planning to buy his plane tickets home today—but he didn't wanna.

It was a completely childish emotion, and he knew it.

He usually loved going back home. It was like two weeks to be a kid again. He and his brothers would help Dad with the livestock and talk about the planting. Dex's older and younger brothers had both stayed to work the farm, and they'd built houses for their families on the property. (Well, Sean didn't have a family yet, but he would eventually.) Dex got to play with children and ride horses in the snow. He got to milk the family's few cows and herd the small flock of sheep they kept to sell wool to local vendors, and be glad he wasn't there come harvest time. He got to help his mother cook and his sister-in-law tend her two kids, and everybody in the house would call him David.

He never mentioned *Johnnies* by name, he just referred to it as a business, and the porn tapes as product, and the models as guys at the office. No one judged him, and no one expected him to look at sex any differently, and no one knew he was gay.

On the one hand, it was enormously comforting to be there for Christmas. It felt amazingly normal.

On the other hand, sometimes he felt like standing in the snow that blanketed his parents' front yard, stripping off his clothes, and shouting "*See me*!" at the top of his lungs until they knew him for who he really was, and proved that they could still love him after all that.

Every Christmas he watched Catholic Mass on television with his mother, who could recite to him all of the edicts the Pope had issued that year, and who had loudly and proudly voted no on everything from gay rights to abortion rights to equal salary rights to… hell. Name something Dex now believed in, and his mother (and, less obtrusively, his father) believed the exact opposite.

So those two weeks were like being someone else, someone he used to know, someone with a different name.

He'd lived so long as Dex that he now felt like he was both of them—the best of Dex and the worst of David, fused solidly into one person.

But not lying here, watching Kane snore.

Kane… Kane didn't have any of those hang-ups about the different names or the labels or the beliefs or being two different people. God, Kane was simple. Dex had been sure—absolutely sure—that Kane would just do it, just move out of his room and go back to fucking anything that moved. But Kane's simplicity had turned out to have a whole different direction. *Anything that ends up with us in separate beds, that's the wrong thing.*

Dex reached out and traced a finger down the curve of his thickly muscled shoulder. So monogamy—outside the office, of course—was really that easy to achieve. Anything that made them sleep in the same bed was a good thing. Anything that separated them was bad. Was it really that easy?

Either way, the thought of leaving Kane alone in this house while Dex went off to be somebody else for Christmas just wrecked him.

Kane's snores stopped. He smacked his palate, made an "mm-mm," sound, and rolled over onto his stomach, hunching his shoulders protectively over his hands. His eyes opened a little, and he squinted at Dex. "Did I wake you up?" he asked. "Was I snoring?"

Dex laughed softly and rolled from his stomach to his side so he could rest his head on the pillow.

"Not at all, Princess. You were as delicate as a feather made of snow."

Kane's lips curved up in a smile. "You're so fulla shit."

Dex nodded. "As are you. It's why adding another bathroom is on my to-do list." He had a sudden thought that it wasn't a bathroom he needed to add, and a whole actual to-do list for Christmas appeared behind his eyes, and he thought he might make this one actually work.

Kane snickered again and then reached out casually and hauled Dex into a kiss, morning breath and all. Dex went, closing his eyes and sighing. God. Kane had it right, didn't he? Anything that made this impossible was a bad thing.

"What's wrong?" Kane asked when the kiss ended, and Dex had to hand it to him. For a guy who claimed he wasn't bright, Kane was damned perceptive.

"I want to ask you something, and it's going to sound really nice, but if we do it, it could be a whole lot of trouble, and I don't want to do that to you."

Kane squinched his eyes shut and opened them and squinched them shut again. Then he squinted at Dex like he was trying to put things into focus. "I'm sure you could have made that more complicated, but I'm not sure how."

Dex pressed his face into the pillow and giggled. He turned his head back and reached out to touch Kane's coarse dark hair, which was standing up in six different directions from the top of his head. "Trust me, oh simple one, I'll find a way." Kane pushed his face against Dex's hand, and Dex touched his temple delicately with skating fingertips. "I don't want to leave you alone for Christmas," he said. Maybe just touching Kane gave him magic powers to cut to the chase. "The thought of you alone here with the turtles makes me want to cry. But I already promised my mom that I'd go home, and I want to take you with me, but…."

Kane grinned and bounced up, sitting on his knees with avid eyes. "You want to bring me? Really? To *Montana*? You want to take me with you? That would be *awesome.* Would we see mountains? I'd love that—would there be *snow*? I'd have to get new boots, right? Really, I can *go?*"

Dex couldn't decide whether to laugh or cry, so he started with propping himself up on his elbow and smiling. "Yeah—but only if you hear me out, okay?"

Kane snapped his mouth shut and nodded, and Dex patted his spot—still warm—so he'd calm back down again. Kane settled right back into his warm spot, but he was still grinning, and Dex had never hated himself more than right now, when he had to make this simple thing complicated and squash some of that innocent enthusiasm.

"It's not as easy as that," Dex said softly. "See, here's the thing. My family doesn't know I'm gay, or in porn, or any of it."

"I knew that," Kane said, surprising Dex. He couldn't remember mentioning it.

"You did?"

"Yeah. I heard you talking to your mom. She was trying to get you to vote some way on some proposition, you know, back in October? I remember I was surprised because she lives in Montana, and anyway, just the way you were talking about it with her—you were voting for gay rights and she was voting against, and you had that sound in your voice. You knew something she didn't. Anyway, so what? They don't know. So?"

Now Dex was the one squinching his eyes shut. "Okay, so I take you with me, like I want to because I don't want you spending

Christmas here alone. Anyway, so who are you? Right here and now, what are you to me?"

Kane blinked and then smiled. "I'm your friend," he said smugly, and Dex didn't blame him. It was true.

"Great. Now who am I?"

Kane pulled up one side of his mouth. "You're Dex!"

Dex shook his head. "No, I'm David."

Kane shrugged. "Why can't you just tell them it's a nickname?"

Dex looked down and spoke to the hollow of his shoulder and the pillow. "Because it's not just a nickname," he mumbled. "It's the name of someone they'd know."

"Will I get to meet him?" Kane asked, his voice so guileless, so sweetly curious, that Dex wanted to cry.

"No. I'm sorry, he's uhm… he died, more than… almost…." Oh God, really? That long ago? And Dex—*David*—was *still* this hung up about it? "Nine and a half years ago," he finished, not able to look at Kane. Geez, Kane thought Dex sort of had his shit together. Dex flashed back to that first night, when he'd been stoned and needy, the night that had pulled Kane into his bed, where he didn't want to leave. Well, maybe not *that* together.

"He was important to you?" Kane asked, and Dex closed his eyes.

"If I say yes, can we leave it like that?" he mumbled. "My parents… they thought I was sad because I lost my friend."

Kane was suddenly there, his face near Dex's, the space of his enthusiasm diminished to breath. "Nobody knew? Ever?"

Dex's throat was thick and his eyes burned. "You do," he rasped. "See, and that's the hard thing." He pulled himself together, started to push himself up, but Kane put a hand on his shoulder and kept him down, with his head turned sideways on the bed, and then slid down and joined him there, their shoulders overlapping, their breath mingling. Kane reached down and pulled the comforter up, and for a moment, Dex remembered David and the real Dex, six years old and playing blanket forts. But Kane's skin was silky against his, and Kane's eyes were wide and accepting, and Dex was suddenly aware that for all that he was only twenty, this man had supported his sister, had paid for his niece's doctor's bills, had bought a house and taken care of a menagerie and, right now, was listening to Dex's heart with more attentiveness than *anyone* else in Dex's life.

They weren't six, and Kane wasn't his first lover, and this was real.

"What's the hard thing?" Kane asked, blinking owlishly in their little space. His eyes were such a wonderful chocolate brown.

Dex swallowed and wished they were fucking instead of talking. "The hard thing is that if you come with me, one of two things will happen. One is you'll have to call me David and you're not used to it, and you'll have to not kiss me or touch me the whole time, and that will feel like a lie. The other thing is you'll slip up or I'll slip up or, hell, I'll just lose my nut and fucking tell them, and it will be ugly—Kane, it'll get ugly. And I will have hauled you across the country to fuck up your Christmas all on the basis of you don't want us to sleep in separate beds."

Kane grunted. "Will we have to sleep in separate beds?" he asked, and Dex shook his head.

"Probably not. I had a queen-sized when I was in school. Shared it with my younger brother. It's where I stay now when I go back for Christmas—Mom made our room into the guest room."

"Mm." Kane nodded then. "Okay, so what's the problem?"

Dex squinted at him. "Hello? Two options? Hiding and lying or a big ugly scene? Did you not *hear* that part?"

Kane nodded. "Yeah. But we won't be in separate beds. I haven't changed my opinion on that, Dex. As long as we're sleeping in the same bed, it's a good thing."

Dex smiled a little. "Okay, then. After we're up and we eat, I'll call my mom and get you a ticket."

Kane's smile was broad and wide, but he did not whoop and jump up and down like Dex expected.

"What?" Dex asked after a moment of just them smiling at each other.

"I know something about you that no one else does," Kane said softly, and Dex's cheeks burned.

"Which thing? At this point, you know a lot of things about me that no one else does. Which thing is it?"

Kane's grin cranked up. "I know you watch me while I sleep!"

Dex howled with indignation and snatched the pillow under his head so he could try to beat Kane to death with it. "Auuuughhh! You psycho, yeah, I watch you! I wanna see if you suck any flies in that big mouth of your—mmmffff…."

Kane caught Dex's flailing pillow easily and clasped both of his hands together at the wrist, then pinned them up over his head against the bed and ravished his mouth before Dex could even finish the sentence. Dex kissed him back, suddenly so hungry, so needy for those big arms around his shoulders that he couldn't kiss him enough. His body went pliant, bones liquid, and his knees came up around Kane's hips, his feet pushing against that surprising bubble butt so Kane would mash his groin against Dex's.

Kane groaned into his mouth and pulled his head back, although his hips kept undulating. "God, Davy, what you do to me! How 'bout I make this quick and then we can go eat, okay?"

Dex groaned and frotted desperately against him, but he was just a little too far away for really good traction. "Food?" he complained. "I've got a hard-on like steel and you want *food*?"

Kane chuckled and bit his chin. "Don't worry," he said, punctuating it with a lick on the neck. "It'll take five minutes, ten minutes tops. Here." He reached down and grabbed Dex through his boxers and squeezed, and Dex groaned. Kane kept his hand down there and started to scoot his hips up while moving his head down. "See, if we do this, it'll save time."

And there he was, his mouth hot and wet, clamped over Dex's cock like the vice of heaven, and there was Kane's cock, beautiful and thick and mostly erect, the foreskin covering it like a half-torn wrapper on a big white-chocolate truffle. Kane slurped him down hard and Dex suddenly *needed* Kane in his mouth. As his brain went bye-bye, his body started screaming *yes, yes, yes, yes, oh God, Kane, fucking* yes*!*

Dex had maybe a moment to think that Kane might change everything for better or worse, before he was just an electron in the power surge Kane sent streaming through his body.

THEY went out to breakfast at Denny's, which was low-rent, but Kane liked their hash browns, so he ordered, like, four plates of them. Dex ordered fruit and toast and looked so longingly at Kane's sausage and hash browns that Kane gave him his own plate.

"I'm gonna get fat," Dex said through a full mouth. His eyes were blissfully closed.

"Good," Kane said after he swallowed his own mouthful. "Good. 'Cause then you can't be in porn anymore, and I can have you all to myself."

"You're not gonna want me when I'm fat." Sausage. God. Ever since Tommy had gone on his nonbulimic binge-and-purge thing, Dex had been eating health food as a show of support. He'd lost five pounds, but… oh God. He missed sausage. He'd been raised on it.

Kane actually paused in the middle of his second plate of hash browns and sausage, the fork halfway to his mouth. "That's stupid," he said, his nose wrinkled. "Why wouldn't I want you? I *like* you. I mean, I could fuck any pretty thing that moved, but I couldn't *live* with any of them."

Dex cocked his head. "You know, I've mostly quit porn as it is. I get a decent paycheck from helping John out with the rest of the shit. You want I should tell him I'm done for good and forever? Not even to help out when the schedule's thin?"

Kane looked stunned for a minute, and then he blushed, looking really pleased. "You'd do that?"

Dex thought about it, thought about Bobby with the giant schlong and anyone else he might end up banging. Yeah, sure—there was always a hot guy out there. But then, there was always a Chase, who could break your heart, or a Tommy, who Dex was glad wasn't in the business anymore, because he would have felt weird banging his friend when his friend had a boyfriend.

And a Kane, waiting for him at home.

"Not really a sacrifice," he said, meaning it.

Kane looked down at his plate and, wonder of frickin' wonders, put his fork down.

"What's wrong?"

"I… I can't really do the same thing," he said apologetically.

"How much money do you have?"

Kane shrugged. "I got no idea. I deposit my shit and the money disappears. I have to go get my mail from Lola." Yeah—Lola had said she'd forward Kane's mail, but they hadn't seen any of it yet.

Dex blinked. "How much did you have two months ago when you moved in?"

Kane toyed with his hash browns for so long Dex actually saw them congealing.

"Eat your food, Kane. We'll go get your mail from Lola after breakfast."

"She won't be home."

"We can get it from her on Monday, then."

"Okay, fine." Kane took a bite, but he still didn't look happy.

"Now what?"

Grunt.

"Look, Kane, you've got an unhealthy amount of potatoes here that are gonna get gross if you don't quit fucking around and get your momentum back. I don't expect you to quit tomorrow, so just say what you gotta say and turn the steam shovel back on."

"What do I do if I've got enough money to quit?"

Dex blinked. "Whatever you want, right? That's the purpose of having enough money to quit!"

"But the only thing I know is bugs and snakes!"

Dex grinned. "'Kay, Kane. Two words. Two lousy fuckin' words. I want you to memorize them, all right?"

Kane had slicked his hair to the side, which was hard because it was so thick. But he'd also put on his other good shirt, and his new jeans. Dex knew—just *knew*—it was to look good when they went out, so it made him proud when Kane looked at him with trust and hope in his eyes.

"Two words?"

"Yeah. Two words."

"I'm listening."

"Entomology and herpetology."

"Every time you say them, they sound like more than two words."

"Trust me, Kane. You're gonna love them."

Kane shoveled half the hash browns, smothered in ketchup, from his plate into his mouth. He was halfway through swallowing the giant mouthful when he spoke again. "How would I go about loving those two words?"

"Trust me. Just trust me, okay? But we have to wait until Monday."

Kane wiped his mouth and moved on to his next plate, sausage first. "Monday? So everything's happening on Monday. What're we doin' for the rest of today?"

Dex looked around them. The place was a madhouse, because it was Black Friday and shoppers were losing their fucking minds. "I'd say Christmas shopping, but *Jesus.* I guess we should work out in an hour—"

"Fuck it," Kane said, taking another one of those huge ketchup-coated bites. "We're goin' back home and humping like some sort of farm animal."

Dex had been in the middle of taking a sip of milk, and now he got caught between spitting it out and choking on it. He ended up grabbing a pile of napkins and using it to wipe off his face, so he didn't even have a reply. That was okay. Kane didn't need one.

"See? You need to go wash your shirt off anyway. We'll go do that, and if we can still sit tonight, we can go out and catch a movie, you think?"

Dex paused in the act of wiping off his shirt. "I think you're a born fucking romantic. I also think you're going to need another nap after you finish that last plate of potatoes."

Kane looked at it judiciously. "Maybe we can go running after we fuck."

Dex had to laugh. God. Well, maybe this was what having a regular boyfriend really was. "Yeah, I'm not complaining," he said, and Kane grinned at him wickedly over his potatoes.

Complain? Seriously, who would?

Kane

"YOU want I should come in with you?" Dex asked, his voice gentle, and Kane felt weak and sad as he looked at him in the passenger's seat of Kane's Navigator.

"I'm just asking for the mail," he said apologetically. "It's not like we need a whole gay security force to ask for my own mail." He'd insisted on driving today. For some reason it felt like he owned the problem more if he drove them to it.

"If I'd called Tommy and Chase, then we could have had a security force," Dex said pragmatically. "Or, you know, Ethan alone."

Kane nodded. "Yeah, Ethan's ripped. Okay, like I said, I can handle it."

Dex's hand, warm and surprising, covered his own as it rested on his thighs. "Carlos, you think I'm going to kick you out if I see your ugly?"

Deep breath. Another. Kane turned his hand palm up and accepted Dex's hand in his. Dex kept his nails nice and neat, and his hands were long and sort of arty.

"No," he said, looking to the front of the house again. Fabiola knew he was coming. She usually took the baby outside so he could see her and he didn't have to go inside and be in the same space with the baby. He never really got the point of that. He fucked grown men in front of a camera—that didn't mean he was going to start doing ugly things to little girls, and he couldn't make his brain figure that out.

But then, it wasn't his baby, either.

"Maybe she's not feeling well," he murmured, almost to himself. "Maybe she's having a relapse. I called the doctor to make sure the baby was good, but… oh fuck. Goddammit. *Dammit*, Lola!"

The garage door opened, and parked in the two-car garage was a small red coupe and a big silver Navigator, about five years older than Kane's. A stocky Hispanic man in his thirties was getting into the Navigator and Kane wanted to throw up. Jesus, Lola—Hector? Fucking really? The Navigator pulled out, and Kane looked frantically at Dex, pulled the handle on the seat so it slid way the hell back, and ducked.

Dex looked down at him crouched between the seat and the steering wheel and then looked back up. The Navigator had pulled up alongside Kane's car, Kane was gesturing for Dex to roll down his window.

Dex did.

"What you doin' out here?" Hector asked, and Dex pointed to the house across the street.

"Waiting for my friend to come out over there," he lied cheerfully.

Kane wanted to kiss him.

"Yeah, okay. Don't wait too long."

"He'll only be a minute," Dex said.

Kane wrapped his clammy hand around Dex's ankle in thanks. He felt Dex shiver from the contact, and in a minute, the engine noise faded and Dex creaked in the leather seats of the Navigator as he twisted around to watch Hector drive away. "He's gone."

"Thanks, brother," Kane said, sitting up and throwing himself back against the seat. "I didn't want to cause a fuckin' scene, but if Hector saw me here, it would have been yelling and shit." Kane closed his eyes and banged his head against the steering wheel. "Christ," he muttered. "I just wanted to get my own fucking mail."

Dex turned his head back around and watched Lola's buzz-cut supposed ex-husband drive away. "How bad a guy is he?"

Kane glanced at him, all blond and pretty and shit. When Dex got into a fight with *his* ex, he threw CDs at him. "When I moved in with you, it was so Lola could get away from him. She'd just gotten out of the hospital when I brought her here."

Dex grunted. "Kane, if he's that much of an asshole, why didn't you name the snake after him?"

"'Cause I like the snake."

"Who'd you name the snake after?"

"A guy whose girlfriend I slept with in high school."

Dex grunted again. "None of this is making me feel any better about how much that snake likes my balls."

Kane grinned in spite of himself. Sure enough, Tomas had gotten out again this morning and had made himself at home in the warmth of Dex's boxer shorts. Kane patted Dex's lean thigh. "It's 'cause you let off so much natural heat, baby. And you tend to sleep real still. If you thrashed around more, he'd just stick to the foot of the bed."

Dex laughed and took his hand again. "So, should we start from scratch? Let's go get your mail!"

Lola couldn't even look Kane in the eye as she opened the door. She was still wearing a bathrobe even if it was in the middle of the day, and there was a faint bruise forming on her cheekbone.

"Don't start on me," she muttered, letting them both come in. "Mama and Papa, they talk about you like you're dead. Don't you tell me how to live my life."

Kane grunted. "Can I see the baby, Lola?"

Fabiola made a pained sound. "I just put her down, Carlos. She's barely—"

Kane walked quietly, Dex on his heels, into the baby's room, which used to be the reptile room. To Lola's credit, she'd put up pink contact paper as a border on the walls, hung up a mobile, and installed shelves in the room—it looked like a real nice place. Frances was lying in the middle of her crib; at almost three, she was long enough now to take up a good size of it. She was wearing a real nice little outfit, something with leggings and a skirt, in orange and brown, which girls had been wearing a lot this year. Her hair was a little longer—about a half an inch of fine, downy brown covered her scalp—and even sideways, Kane could see she was getting a little plumper. She was inhaling and exhaling like she'd been crying a lot. On every exhale, her quivery lower lip went "f-t-f-t-f-t-f-t-f-t," and Kane just wanted to pick her up and protect her, keep her away from all of this bad stuff, make sure she was okay. He approached her carefully, laid his big hand in the center of her small back, and stood there for a minute, just breathing with her, waiting for her breath to even out and calm down. He looked up and Dex was in the doorway, nodding at him.

Kane nodded back and took a couple more breaths, then ran a finger down the baby's cheek and followed Dex out and into the living room.

"My mail, Lola?" he asked, not even wanting to look at her. He was so angry.

"Don't sound that way," she said, her voice weak. She handed a sheaf of envelopes to Kane, and Dex took them out of his hands and started sorting through them. Kane looked at her, relieved at Dex's help, because he couldn't focus on two things at once, and right now, she was the thing he needed to pay attention to.

"How do you want me to sound? All excited that he's in here beating you up where she can hear? In *my house?* The whole reason I let you live here was so he couldn't find you. How'd he find you, Lola? How long did it take before you called him back up?"

His sister couldn't meet his eyes. "It was his mother," she said quietly. "She called me up to ask me to Thanksgiving, and I went, and he was there. He followed me home. And he's the baby's daddy, Carlos. It's not like I can just cut him out of my life!"

"Why not? You cut *me* out of your life!"

"That was different! You're doing bad things!"

Kane reached out to her, touched her bruised cheek with his finger, and remembered when they were kids and she used to throw him a Frisbee in the backyard for hours, or play tic-tac-toe with sidewalk chalk in front of their apartment. She'd been the smart one, the one who did good in school and never got in trouble, but she'd always had time for him, because they were family.

"This isn't a bad thing?" he asked, feeling something hot and horrible in his throat. He didn't know how Dex could be afraid that Kane would see the ugly in Dex's life. Kane knew about the ugly. The ugly was everywhere around him. With Dex, it was like they could be a little spot of pretty in the middle of all that ugly.

Fabiola turned her head. "He's my husband—"

"You're my sister. I don't like seeing this, and I don't like the baby being near it. I'll sell the house, get you an apartment—"

"The hell you will!" Dex said sharply, squinting at one of the envelopes in his hand.

Kane looked at him, surprised. "Dex—"

"No! She needs to let you see that baby, dammit!" Dex's voice was weird, wobbly, and thin.

"He's making those movies—" Lola tried to protest, but Dex cut her off.

"Yeah, I know. The movies. He's making the bad movies—well, that's great. If you don't like the bad movies, why are you so excited to spend that money he's making off of them? Kane, did you really give her access to your money?"

Kane blinked. "Well yeah, Dex. She had to pay the doctors and the electricity and the garbage bill and all that other shit."

Dex's eyes were narrowed and his hands were shaking. "Wonderful. I get it. She's living in the house—on your dime—so she's paying the bills, again, on your dime. She's also grocery shopping on your dime? And going to buy clothes on your dime?" Dex glared at Lola for a minute. "And not at Target, either, huh? No, I've got bills from Pottery Barn and Baby Gap and Wet Seal—this is prime shit, Lola. You won't let your brother in the house 'cause of what he does for a living, but you're not too proud to live off of it, are you?"

Kane grimaced. "Dex, Christmas is coming up and—"

"Yeah. She's buying the baby gifts and she's buying herself gifts. Isn't the house a gift, Kane? And what about you? Don't you want to buy that baby some clothes and some toys and shit?"

Kane's heart fell. It was really one of the things he'd been planning to do in the next week. That and find Dex something, anything, that would be special without being stupid.

"He's got lots of money!" Lola objected. "I see those bills too!"

Dex looked at her bitterly. "Yeah. He's got lots of money. He does. But he doesn't have lots of family. He's got you and he's got the baby. And he's got the guys where we work. And now he's got me. Did you even ask yourself what he was doing Thanksgiving, Lola? Did you even care who he was staying with?"

Fabiola looked away, and Dex said, "Kane, get her bank card."

Kane looked at him in shock. "What?"

"Get her bank card."

"I'm not kicking her out!"

Dex shook his head. "No, no, you're not. And you're not cutting her off and you're not gonna be the bad guy, 'cause that's not in you. But this isn't our last stop today, remember? We had plans. We had plans for *you.* Not me, not Lola, *you.* We're gonna make that happen, if you still want to. You still want to, right?"

Kane looked at him, suddenly remembering that they were going to Montana. What was he going to tell Dex's parents if it didn't get ugly? *Yeah, I'm in porn. No, I got no plans for the future. Yeah, high school graduate, barely.* What was he going to tell Frances when she got old enough? *Yeah, sorry, baby. I'd like to hang out and be your uncle, but I fuck guys for money. No, I got nothin' else. Here, have a couple hundred and go hang with your woman-beating pops.*

And then, pure as light, he had a vision of Dex the night before. Kane had taken him, slow, face-to-face, and Dex? Dex had buried his face in Kane's neck and groaned and climaxed, the come splashing between their sweating bodies. It was not porn sex. In porn sex, you came for the camera, your body splayed and open and on display. But last night, it was Dex, his body covered by Kane's, his eyes closed, his shoulders hunched forward, and in that moment, he was Kane's, just Kane's. No one else was going to see that moment, no one else was going to know what that felt like, because from now on, Dex was only gonna do that for *him.*

Afterward Dex smiled tiredly, his eyes half-closed, and Kane planted little kisses over those eyes, over his cheeks, down his jaw, on his neck, even his ears. Dex fell asleep then, curled in his arms like Tomas, or Tree-Squirt when he was alive. Dex's hair was sweaty against his scalp, but still bright and soft against Kane's shoulder. His breath heated Kane's skin right at his neck and chest in moist little pants. Kane looked at him—gold eyelashes fanned out on his cheeks; pink, full mouth slightly parted—and fought the urge to hold him so tightly he couldn't breathe.

That was *his.* Freely offered, happily given, Dex was his.

"Yeah," he said now, looking at those angel-blue eyes. Maybe they were even the color of the Montana sky, and Dex was gonna help him get there and see. "I remember those plans for the future."

Kane turned to his sister. "Lola, I helped with Frances's doctor bills—I'll keep doin' that. I'll buy your groceries and shit—I will. I can give you an allowance, and you can get a job and daycare or even go to the state until you get on your feet. I'm here for you. But I'm not Mom and Pop. I got plans for me. I need some of that money for *me.* I worked for it—"

"On your *back*!" Fabiola snapped, and Kane nodded.

"Some of it. But some of it was earned for showin' up when I was supposed to and working out and watching my diet"—he ignored the soft snort from Dex because he knew it was just to make him laugh—"and being a nice enough guy to give other guys a hard-on, even if they didn't like guys to begin with. And it's okay work—more honest than you think. But if I ever want to do something different, I gotta take what I'm makin' and put it into something else I want to do. And I deserve that, right?" Kane fought not to cry like the little kid he'd been, the chubby little kid who'd run to his sister when he'd been knocked on his face by the other kids because he couldn't keep up. The little kid who spoke with a lisp in a new language because he wasn't used to the way his mouth worked yet and had to work really hard not to get laughed at. Lola had known *that* kid and loved him. Why couldn't she know him now?

Fabiola looked away. "Yeah, Carlos," she said after a minute. "Yeah. You deserve to do something else. You give me what you think is right. I got my papers in at Welfare."

"And he gets to visit the baby," Dex said, and Kane looked at him, almost begging him to stop. His sister said he deserved to be happy. It was almost like a blessing from the frickin' church! Why would Kane want to push it now?

Fabiola looked at Dex for the very first time. "Who are you?" she asked, and Dex smiled, the kind of smile Kane used to watch him use on rookies when he was gentling them in, or on girls if he was trying to date them.

"I'm his new family," Dex said, and for the first time, maybe, Fabiola looked at the two of them, Dex at his elbow in his shearling jacket, taller than Kane, but also rangier and unassuming in spite of his absolute beauty.

"You look smart," she said, because *she* was smart, and she'd seen the way Dex was sorting through the mail even as he stood there, using crisp, efficient movements and quick scans of the content.

"I must be, if I'm with your brother," Dex said levelly, and Fabiola raised one corner of her mouth.

"My brother's a nice boy, but he's not too smart. You probably just like him 'cause of his—"

"Please don't finish that sentence," Dex said with deceptive mildness. "And don't try to change the subject. Look—let him take her out for ice cream once a week. Let him take her to the park. Tell him what clothes she needs, let him pick them out for her. I swear to you, Fabiola, your brother wouldn't hurt a fly unless it was to feed it to his turtles, and the only part of him your baby would see more of than right the hell here is his big frickin' heart. He just wants to hold the baby, see that she's okay. She's his family too."

Fabiola nodded her head. "Just don't come here when Hector is here," she said, looking away. "I don't know what he'll do."

"Why's he even here in the first place?" Kane asked, trying to breathe through the rush of gratitude. He was gonna take that baby to see Santa. He was gonna buy her the fuckin' world. He wanted to just hug Dex and pound his back until the whole world could hear the echoes, but he didn't do that. Not here. Not for Lola to see and judge. He had Dex all to himself until his next shoot. He wasn't ready to explode that all on the world now.

Fabiola looked away. "You should know," she said bitterly. "Just because it's wrong don't mean it's not easy."

Kane wanted to protest about the wrong part, but surprisingly enough it was Dex who spoke up.

"Most of us know that," he said. "We've all had that, you know? The hard part is to say no and mean it. You let us know if you ever want to say no and need help, okay?"

To Kane's surprise, Fabiola nodded and wiped her hand under her eyes.

"If he ever hits the baby," Kane said, keeping his voice gentle, "I'll either kill him or take her, okay?"

Fabiola kept nodding and kept crying, and Dex bumped Kane with his elbow. "Give her the grocery money, Carlos, and give her a hug, all right? I think we all need some freakin' space."

Kane nodded and pulled out his wallet and looked at Lola. "Can you get your bank card for me?" Dex bumped his arm. "Actually, get your wallet. I think Dex wants to make sure your credit cards ain't on my dime too."

Fabiola gave a glum nod, and Kane wondered wretchedly if Dex could just tell him how much money he had and how much to give her, and leave out the details of how bad things had gotten when he hadn't been paying attention.

THEY went to Sac City College next, and then to Sac State for Dex. Dex did all the talking.

"'Kay, he's been out of high school for what?" Dex turned from the registrar to Kane, who was looking around the registration office in the forty-year-old building and thinking that he needed to buy more lottery tickets if this was the best they could do.

"Kane," Dex said patiently, getting his attention, "how long have you been out of high school? Three years? Four?"

"Two and a half," Kane said, and Dex grimaced, then turned back to the girl.

"Two and a half years," he said. "Christ, I'm old. Anyway, does he need his high school stuff or can we just pretend that never happened?"

The girl grimaced. She was maybe Dex's age, but she dressed older and had one of those plain expressions on her face that said she wanted to be taken seriously. "Why would he want to do that?" she asked, eyeballing Kane like he was a weird species of bug.

Kane lifted a corner of his lip in response. He wasn't sure what that looked like, but her eyes got big and she went back to her paperwork in an all-fired hurry.

Dex looked at Kane apologetically. "Because I'm betting he spent his high school years getting laid and not getting educated."

Kane cocked his head to the side and nodded. "That's fair," he agreed, and the girl's eyes got *really* big.

"So, uhm, why are you interested in education *now*?" she asked, and Kane looked at Dex in exasperation. God, who the fuck cared, right?

"Because I'm tired of banging the whole goddamned world and I'd like to do something else for a while," he snapped, and he could tell it was probably the wrong thing to say by the way Dex's eyes got big and his mouth pursed tight like he was trying not to laugh.

The girl turned crimson and open and closed her mouth a few times, and she looked at Dex for help.

"So you're helping him sign up for college?" she asked when she could breathe again, and Dex nodded, still with that suspiciously bright-eyed look on his face. "So, who are you to him?"

Dex's eyes narrowed, and Kane could tell Dex was fucking done with the personal questions too, but he still wasn't prepared for his answer.

"I'm his pimp, sweetheart. Now do you need his high school transcripts, or can he just pay his tuition here and sign up for classes online?"

The next day Chase came over so they could all go Christmas shopping together, and Kane told the story with great gusto.

Chase—the new, quietly smiling Chase, who answered questions with real words instead of wisecracks like he used to—laughed appreciatively and then actually asked about Kane's life. "So, you're signing up for classes? That's great! What are you signing up for?"

Kane flushed. "Well, Dex made me sign up for biology, because he said that's what I'm gonna love and that'll keep me interested. Then he made me sign up for English A, because he said I'm not gonna get through anything else without it. And I had to sign up for basic math for the same reason. And then"—Kane brightened a little—"then we both signed up for cooking!"

Chase was up on one of the stools at the little tile island in the middle of the kitchen, and he practically spit out the soda he was sipping. He turned to Dex and said, "What in the furry hell?"

Dex rolled his eyes, and when he spoke, he spoke directly to Chase like two grown-ups spoke when there was a kid in the room. "He didn't want to do all that learning by himself. I said we could take a class together."

For a moment, Kane felt something red and ugly in his chest, and then he caught the thoughtful look Dex aimed at him. Chase didn't know. *Nobody* knew. It was a good story—Kane wanted to tell it. But

Chase didn't know, and if they were going to tell the story, they would have to tell Chase, and suddenly, they'd be a real thing.

Chase turned around and looked at Kane, then back at Dex. "I've gotta pee," he said, startling them both. "I mean, I don't gotta pee, but I'm gonna go pretend to pee, and then when I get back, maybe you two can tell me about cooking class."

Chase got up and walked out of the kitchen toward the hall, and Dex opened his mouth to say something. And that's when Chase let out a startled squawk.

"Dex! Dex! Holy fuck, Dex, there's a *snake* in your house!"

"Oh Jesus!" Kane went trotting into the hall and brushed by a freaked-out Chase to go pick up Tomas. Fucking snake was slithering across the hallway like a sinuous four-foot-long ruby, black, and gold rope on his way across the carpet to the bathroom. They didn't know why he went into the bathroom—snakes weren't supposed to like tile or even carpet for that matter, but when he got out, they could either find him curled up in Dex's balls (Dex's least favorite way to wake up) or asleep behind the toilet. Dex once said sourly that he just liked to smell the place when Dex missed, and Kane had to admit, he didn't mind smelling like Dex either. (Not his pee, but, well, just Dex.)

"Tomas, buddy," Kane mourned, taking the snake low down on his neck so Tomas had some movement while Kane lifted the middle of his long body up. Tomas coiled his tail behind Kane's wrist, and Kane helped him drape the rest of himself on Kane's arm, so he could hold the guy by his chest and warm him up a little. "Tomas, it's not good to bust out in the winter. Man, you got everything in there, you got heat, you got water, you got food. I come and visit every day. Why you gotta be like that?"

"Maybe he's still pissed you slept with his girlfriend," Dex said dryly from the hallway. He came up and got into Kane's space, stroking Tomas's neck with a sort of reluctant tenderness.

"Naw," Kane mumbled, checking his body temp to see if the big guy got too cold during his little sojourn. "If he was that upset about the girl, he wouldn't keep trying to climb up your ass all the time. Here, I'm gonna take him in the room and warm him up."

Kane opened the door, aware that Chase was peering over his shoulder curiously as he walked into the room. They had the little heaters in the terrariums on, but they left the oil heater on too, so the room was tropically warm, and Tomas seemed to relax on Kane's arm as Kane walked in.

Chase looked at the little sea of big glass enclosures and said happily, "Turtles! Tommy's got turtles!" and Kane relaxed a little. He'd lost his curiosity about the new pink scar on Chase's wrist—he'd seen it at the welcome back party and at Thanksgiving—but sometimes he still wondered what to say to someone who had been as much in pain as Chase had without ever really telling anyone.

He'd mostly talked about bugs, really, and now that he knew Chase knew something about turtles, he had another topic.

"Yeah," Dex said. "Tommy helped pick out one of these too."

Chase took in the room then, and Kane could almost hear his eyeballs shift. "Uhm, Kane—don't you have a house in Natomas?"

Kane looked at Dex, who shrugged. "Yeah," Kane said. "But my sister and her baby are living there right now."

Kane saw Chase looking at Dex, who shrugged again. "So, uhm, if this is the guest room, where are you sleeping?"

Dex looked at Kane, and this time Kane shrugged. "I'm sleeping with my boyfriend. Is that a problem?"

Chase looked at the two of them, and suddenly Kane saw a wonder of wonders on his thin face: a smile. "No," he said quietly. "Not to me. It explains why Donnie's sister was so disappointed on Friday, but I'm pretty happy for you both." He winked at Dex. "Glad to see your taste improved. Now, are you gonna tell me about cooking class or not?"

"Yeah," Kane said, and he held Tomas over the cage to see if the snake was ready to slide down or if he still wanted to cuddle. The vote was to slide down. "We'll tell you about cooking class if you'll agree to help Ethan watch the guys over Christmas while Dex and I go meet his folks!"

Chase's look at Dex was thoughtful, and Kane wasn't surprised when Dex said, "Spit it out, Chase. You're not allowed to do that anymore."

"I am when it's something that's none of my business," Chase replied mildly. "I know. I asked."

Dex laughed a little. "All right, I'll help you out. No, my parents don't know. No, I don't know if I'm gonna tell them. And no, I don't know how that's going to work out over Christmas. Did I answer all your questions?"

Chase nodded. "All except the cooking class. And whether or not I can hold one of the turtles."

"You can hold the iguana if you want!" Kane said excitedly, because not even Dex had warmed up to Ms. Darcy the iguana yet. "She doesn't get a lot of attention. But you gotta be careful she doesn't bite. Her spit's poisonous."

"Charming," Chase said dryly. He found an empty spot among the terrariums and slid down to sit on the carpet. "Hand me the lizard and tell me the story quick. Ethan and Donnie are gonna meet us at the sporting goods store in an hour."

Kane lifted Tomas out of the terrarium again and handed him to Dex, where Tomas was more than willing to go. Then he reached into the terrarium to pull out Ms. Darcy.

Ms. Darcy weighed around six pounds now and had a good eight to ten to go. When he'd first gotten her, she'd hissed and tried to bite him more than once. But Kane had wooed her. Sweet fruit, sweet grasses, fresh veggies—oh yeah, he bought her the nutritionally balanced pellets and cleaned and disinfected her food dishes twice a week, but that's not what really made Ms. Darcy melt like butter. The trick was, while she was eating, he'd reach in and stroke her between the eyes, or even on the neck and along her spine and sides. When she'd allowed him to pick her up, he'd continued to feed her delicacies, until now, as long as she'd been fed, she was as docile as Tomas. Kane pulled her out gently and hefted her up, giving her tail room to swish. He looked up at Dex and said, "Could you get her some of the mango in the fridge?" and Dex turned around to do just that while Kane set the bright-green lizard delicately in Chase's hands and told Chase about cooking class.

The problem had been, Kane told him, that they were getting ready to take all these classes, but none of them were *together.* All the classes Dex needed were at Sac State, and Sac State wouldn't even let Kane through the doors if he didn't pass some classes at the community college.

"Yeah, that sucks," Chase said, stroking Ms. Darcy along the back. He seemed to have a knack for it. Ms. Darcy was relaxing right into his hands as Dex came in with the mango.

"So I didn't wanna do it," Kane said frankly, looking at Dex with the remnants of his little snit-fit from the night before. "I mean, I like hanging out with him. Why would I want to make our whole week so we couldn't even frickin' see each other, right?"

"Works for me," Chase said mildly.

"Damned straight," Kane said, and he didn't mind how much I-told-you-so was in his voice when he did, either. "Anyway, so I was gonna dig in my heels—"

"And not in the fun, sexy way either," Dex said dryly, and Chase grinned at him.

Kane ignored them and went on. "—and Dex said that maybe we could take a class together at the community college. I was like, sure, what? He could get a degree in running a pet store? I mean, business and enterpetolomy—seriously. Where's that come together?"

Chase was crossing his eyes a little and moving his lips—Kane was pretty sure he'd gotten one of the damned words wrong, but he didn't care, he was on a roll.

"So Dex said how about something we both liked, and I said what? Cooking? 'Cause Dex cooks, you know."

"No, I didn't," Chase said, raising his eyebrows meaningfully. "How about next time we get together, we come here? Tommy's gonna frickin' kill me with tarragon over Christmas, I know it!"

"Have him make fried chicken," Dex said seriously. "No tarragon in that recipe at all."

"Can I finish?" Kane complained, and Dex gestured for him to go on. "Anyway, so Dex cooks, I cook, but I'm not sold on the idea. I'm like, 'Cooking? Like food?'"

"And I'm like, 'No, cooking like poison, genius!'" Dex chimed in. "'Of course cooking like food!' And this guy looks at me and says—"

"Two gay guys take a cooking class!" Kane quoted. "And Dex says, 'What's the punch line?' and I say"—and they finished this together—"That *is* the punch line, I saw it on a sitcom last week!"

Chase laughed throatily, looking from one of them to the other, and Kane smiled, feeling like he and Dex had accomplished something, making Chase laugh like that.

"Okay," he said when he caught his breath. "I get it. Cooking class. Like in the television shows. It sounds like fun."

Dex rolled his eyes. "I hope they've got a 'Cooking with Ketchup' chapter, just to make Kane comfortable."

Kane nodded, because he'd even do extra homework for that one, and then they both looked at Chase, cuddling Ms. Darcy to his chest and looking at the lizard fondly.

"Look at her, I think she's thinking about falling asleep." Ms. Darcy's eyes were partway closed, and she was swaying hypnotically in tune with Chase's breathing.

"She likes you." Suddenly Kane found a reason to pout. "She likes you, Tomas likes Dex—when's one of these stinkin' guys gonna like me best?"

"They *all* like you best," Dex soothed. "You're just the mommy. Most mommies get taken for granted while their kids go out and find a playmate. You're gonna have to get used to it."

Kane perked up. "I'm the mommy? That's awesome. I've always wanted to be the mommy!"

"Good," Chase said. He was suddenly sober. "So you'll be able to help me if I decide me and Tommy can be the daddies, right?"

Dex was the one who spoke into the charged silence. "You ready for that, Chase?"

Chase looked up, and suddenly Kane saw that this guy, the guy they'd all thought had it together and then lost it, this guy who had some sort of mythic mystique in Kane's mind, because he'd just been who he was, was really just as lost as Kane had always felt. "No," he confessed with a smile, "but Tommy wants it more than anything. For Tommy, maybe I can fake it."

Kane bent down and took Ms. Darcy gently from Chase's arms so the lizard could stay asleep and happy when they left.

"I got a niece," he said into the sudden quiet. "I love her a lot. I don't never get to see her, although, you know, thanks to Dex, that might change. I'd love to see a baby, raise a baby, who knew who I was. I'd really love that. You know. I'm Mexican. We like babies."

Chase stood up and dusted himself off, and when Kane was done putting Ms. Darcy back in her terrarium (she was getting too big for it—Kane needed to build her an actual enclosure with some higher trees and stuff), Kane looked at his thin face with those haunted blue eyes and saw another one of those wonderful smiles.

"Good," Chase said. "If you guys can help us, I think maybe we can do this, you know?"

Dex hugged him first, because Dex and Chase had been closer, but Kane stood by, waiting for his turn, until Dex grabbed him by the front of the shirt and hauled him in. It was a real good hug, and Kane felt that warm thing, that warm thing that more and more opened up in his chest, grow bigger and softer and friendlier, just from standing there with Dex and their friend.

CONCEDING THE MENTAL CONVERSATION

Dex

DEX gave Kane the window seat on the plane, because he'd flown with Kane before and knew what would happen.

For the first twenty, twenty-five minutes on the plane, as it powered up and took off, Kane was like a little kid. He pressed his nose to the window and watched as the farmland of Sacramento and Woodland disappeared beneath them. Most of the fields were green after the December rain that had besieged them since Thanksgiving, and etched with lines of service roads and the matte black ribbons of freeways.

As soon as that disappeared and they were over the cloud cover, Kane turned around to Dex happily, laid his head on the seat rest, blinked twice, and fell fast asleep.

Dex was tired—exhausted, in fact, because those last few days hadn't been easy, getting ready to go, finishing up at work, not to mention those fully realized covert plans for home renovation to surprise Kane—but still. He waited for Kane to fall asleep, because it was perfect and without self-consciousness. Kane's descent into sleep was as sweetly trusting as Frances, who had cried on Santa's lap but calmed down when Uncle Kane took her to their place and let her look at the turtles.

Dex just wanted to see him sleep. It was soothing, and it put a soft blanket on the wicked edges of worry in Dex's chest that had been catching and fraying on his well-being since he'd called his mother.

"HEY, Mom. I was just wondering if I could bring a friend with me this time."

Dex called his parents while Kane was out with Chase, buying Christmas presents and shopping for Chase and Tommy's nursery. Dex felt something alien and warm at the thought of the two men teaching each other how to spoil children. He'd spent the last nine years watching from the outside as his brothers and sister grew up, married, began families. As off-kilter and broken as his life was, he'd yearned for that. As many times as Tomas made himself at home in Dex's balls (four now!), Dex thought he could deal with it, because that snake was Kane's baby.

So was Kane's niece.

So Dex had gone shopping with Kane most of the week, getting ready to spoil Frances rotten, but on this day, he gave Kane a break. Kane had been hinting, begging for a hint, anything, about what to get Dex for Christmas. Dex already knew what he was getting Kane—he'd set it up with Tommy, Chase, and Ethan while they were watching the critters. He'd been a little uneasy about how to give it to Kane with a bow, but Tommy told him they had his back. As far as Dex knew, none of the three of them had ever befriended Scott or even talked to the guy when Dex hadn't been there, and he thought that should have told him something. God, the older he got, the more he was convinced he was the dumbest motherfucker on Earth.

But just like Dex was worried about getting a present for Kane, he knew Kane was worried about getting him a present, so on this day, he gave Kane his space. And thus, he had a chance to lie to his parents without Kane hearing, because the lie shamed him more than usual this year.

"Oh, honey!" His mother sounded happy, and he thought a little bitterly that he'd worked hard for that happiness. "Is it Allison? Or do I know her?"

He almost flinched. Had it really been only seven months since he'd broken up with Allison and then broken up with Scott, who was the reason he'd broken up with Allison in the first place? Had he really only been sleeping with Kane since October? It seemed like longer.

Surely it took more than two and a half months to form a froth-at-the-mouth, shaking-hands-without-a-fix addiction, right?

"No, Mom. It's not a girlfriend. He's a good guy. We're rooming together. I can't leave him here alone for the holidays." He didn't say why he couldn't. He didn't say that he wasn't sure he could let the plane take off with Kane here on the ground without him. He didn't say that nothing he could think of would be worth not sleeping next to Kane for two weeks, when everyone was supposed to be happy and joyful and celebrating. There was no celebration without Kane. There just wasn't. Sometimes Kane was right—things were that simple.

"Okay, honey. He's welcome. I think the only place we'd have to put him is in bed with you. Will that be okay?"

Perfect, he thought. "That's fine, Mom. We don't mind."

"Good. So, when are you landing?"

THEY were landing in Butte in six hours, and then Dex was going to remember how to drive in the snow all over again and rent a car for the three-hour trip home.

It was okay, he told himself stoically. He'd seen Kane's ugly, and Kane had been like a shiny, rough diamond in the midst of it. Whether Dex's ugly came down to the lying or the ugly that happened if he told his family the truth, now at least Kane would know who Dex was in the middle. That was only fair.

DEX was still looking at Kane when his eyes opened slowly.

"What's wrong?" he murmured, and Dex shook his head. They would land in the morning, so it was dark outside, and he peered out the window like magic answers might appear on a little cube against the glass.

"Driving in the snow's gonna be a bitch," he said, and Kane squinted at him.

"I've never seen you do that before," he said softly.

"Do what?"

"That thing Chase did before he tried to off himself. That thing where what you're thinking isn't really what's going to come out of your mouth."

Dex laughed softly, thought about putting his hand on Kane's cheek, and decided what the hell—it wasn't like he was going to get a chance to do it that much at his parents' house. Kane's was soft at the cheek and a little stubbly at the jaw, and the soul patch under his chin was surprisingly silky. His blunt, wide-palmed hand came up and trapped Dex's hand, right there.

"I'm thinking that I wish this was normal. That I could tell my mom I was bringing home a boyfriend, and she'd be happy for me. I'm thinking I'd rather this get ugly than do this as a lie."

Kane looked troubled for a minute. "Why? I mean, it's just me. You and me know we're good, right?"

Dex leaned forward in the darkened cabin, pretty sure that no one could see the two of them and even if they could, no one would care. "You may not believe this, Carlos, but you're sort of a big deal for me. You don't have to feel the same way, but it's the truth."

Kane closed the difference and kissed him, his lips and breath warm. Dex shut his eyes and tried not to wish too hard for their bed and their smells and their room and their books and their snakes and turtles and iguanas.

"I ain't never been anyone's big deal before," Kane said, his voice barely audible under the engine noise. "How come I get to be yours?"

Dex wiggled for a minute, and Kane clicked the little wooden armrest up and undid both their seat belts so he could wrap his arm around Dex and haul him close. In spite of the fact that the little plane only sat four across, in the tight half circle of Kane's muscled arm, Dex suddenly felt like there was air to breathe.

"You're my big deal because you were nice to me when I was at my lowest," Dex said softly. "And because nobody asked you to, but not once have you let me down. You're my big deal because you're kind to animals—even ones nobody would think about—and because you would rather blow off a pretty girl than have us sleep in separate beds. You take care of the people at *Johnnies* like they were yours—"

"So do you," Kane said, sounding surprised, and Dex relaxed, warm with his cheek against Kane's shoulder.

"You make me feel like I'm not alone," Dex told him. "Not when I do that, not when I make dinner or watch television or go to bed, even if we're not having sex. You just make being with someone a good thing. A *great* thing. You're a big deal because…." His breath caught. How long had it been? Nine years? Nine and a half years? "Because just talking to you makes me happy. Can you deal with that?"

Something hot hit his temple, and Kane's breath got harsh and shaky, like an airplane engine before it took off. "I'm only stupid sometimes, David. I'm not gonna blow that shit off when it comes from someone who makes me happy too."

"You're not stupid," Dex said softly, and Kane leaned over and kissed his temple, and Dex knew the taste of the salt sliding down from the deepening creases of his eyes.

"Then I must be crazy, because I think you and me, we're not ever going to sleep in separate beds again."

"So I'm not alone?" Dex felt it necessary to clarify.

"Not if you'll let me stay."

Dex fell asleep then, safe against Kane's massive chest. A part of him felt like maybe he should apologize for seeking shelter there, for unloading on Kane right before they were supposed to go meet his family, but most of him was just grateful. All those girls who had shared his bed but hadn't really known him, all those boys he'd fucked who had been all about the nerve endings, and the whole time, he was just looking for that one thing he'd had once, on a long-ago summer's afternoon.

He'd been looking to not be alone.

Even in his sleep, he could hear the beating of Kane's great heart.

DEX was all set to drive the SUV—complete with chains—in the snow to his parents' house, but Kane wouldn't let him.

Over the hood of the car, Dex looked at Kane, all warm with his hat over his ears and a cashmere scarf and gloves (yes, Dex had bought them for him! The big doofus was going to freeze to death if he didn't wear some warm clothes!), and wondered when his life had gotten so damned askew.

"I'm driving because I've *driven* in snow before," Dex said patiently.

"You were up for forty-eight hours before we left," Kane said evenly. "You need to sleep."

Oh yeah! Dex had the cowardly thought that maybe *that* explained his near-meltdown over the irritating man in front of him. Sleep deprivation. He hadn't thought of that!

But Kane set his mutinous jaw and stared Dex down with those sweet brown eyes, and Dex found that he was more than a little aroused. Men who made eternal declarations of love on sleep deprivation alone did *not* get aroused when they were pissed off and confused. Dex loved Kane even when the guy was pissing him off—it *had* to be real.

"I slept on the plane," Dex said weakly, and Kane did that thing—that *thing*—where he lifted the left corner of his mouth and his right eyebrow. Kane wasn't big on irony, but that *thing* expressed an amazing amount of skepticism.

"I know you slept on the plane, David," Kane said patiently, like he was talking to Tomas or Frances. "You slept in my arms. It was nice. But it was about three hours. Our boss kept you up for two days before you left, and you did that without coke, which is good, but you're not going to drive."

"*You're* not going to drive!" Dex said, suddenly panicked. "You don't *know* snow! You don't *know* these fuckin' roads—"

"I can read a map! It's pretty much straight for two hundred miles, and then you hang a fuckin' right!"

Dex closed his eyes, opened them, tried to put his thoughts in order. Kane was right. He *was* tired. John couldn't get his fuckin' shit together. Dex had set the schedule so that everybody shot their scenes early (including Kane, who had been a bastard for the three days before without fucking apology, which had made Dex's life a joy), and then nobody had to work over the two weeks for Christmas. It was a great idea—everyone had been real fuckin' grateful—but John had forgotten to hire the goddamned cameramen, and Dex had been scrambling to do that and edit the scenes, because John was moving hella slow for a guy snorting so much coke. It had been a nightmare.

If Kane hadn't been home, shopping for their friends, showing Ethan, Tommy, and Chase how to care for the critters (and telling Ethan he could stay in the house, but if he was going to have sex, he had to wash the fucking sheets!), and generally doing the home front thing, they never would have made it out the door.

But that didn't mean Dex was going to let another man drive down fucking Highway 135 again if he didn't have to.

"Carlos—"

"José Carlos Ricardo, if we're gonna go baptismal names here, David Calvin. I'm a better driver'n you, you know it. You keep *asking* the car to do shit, and sometimes you gotta *tell* it to do shit, just like your skinny ass in bed. Now how 'bout you hop in the car and get some sleep and I'll get us there, all right?"

Dex swallowed his temper and would have scrubbed his gloved hands over his face, but they were caked with snow. "Kane, please. Deer jump out in front of cars here, moose—"

"Deers? Really? Mooses? That'll be cool!" Kane's eyes lit up, and Dex had a vague out-of-body experience.

"*Not cool!*" he shouted, surprised at himself. "It's *not* cool, Carlos! Those fucking things jump out, and one minute you're smiling at a guy you've known since kindergarten, and the next you're waking up in a fucking hospital and he's *gone*! It's *not* cool, it can change the course of your entire fucking life, do you understand me?"

Kane's entire body went still, and his mouth opened a little, and then he shivered. "Get in the car, David," he said after a moment. "It's fucking cold out here, and we've got to let it warm up."

Dex's hand was shaking too hard for him to open the door, so Kane got in and turned the car on, then opened the door for him. Dex slid in and took off his gloves, blew on his fingers, and tried to figure out exactly how his life had slid so sideways.

It couldn't possibly be when Kane slept with him. Had it been when he'd left home, trying so hard to leave the memory of Dexter Williams in his rearview that he'd forgotten who David Worral was in the process?

Maybe. Maybe it was that moment—he could remember it, specifically—in the hospital, when he told himself that he would grieve for his friend and not for his lover.

And then set about trying to replace his lover with a hundred different porn models, giving them two or three auditions at twenty-five minutes a pop.

But not Kane. Kane wasn't twenty-five minutes. Kane wasn't months of being a dirty little secret. Kane had climbed into his bed and then decided that was where he belonged. Friends first. Lovers second. And then lovers first. Lovers *all.* How in the hell had that happened?

"Stop worrying about it, David," Kane said quietly next to him, and Dex couldn't turn and look.

"What am I worrying about?"

"How there's an us. You're just going to make yourself crazy. You said all that deep shit on the plane and then woke up and wondered if you meant it. Of course you meant it. You don't lie about shit like that, or you would have been sleeping with John all these years and he wouldn't be doing so much blow."

Dex's brain officially shorted out. He couldn't think about that right now. "I don't give a shit about John," he said, consigning nine years of friendship and mentoring to hell. "I just don't want you to hit something on the fucking road!"

Kane rolled his eyes. "Since I'm not going to be driving with my brains in my fucking johnson, Dexter, I think maybe I can handle it!"

Dex squinted at him, his eyes sore and gritty. He'd been practically walking in his sleep as they'd disembarked and then taken the shuttle to the rental car agency, and it felt like his brains had frozen in the white wasteland of his home state.

"How did you know his brains were in his johnson?"

Kane grunted. "I didn't," he said gruffly, checking the brakes and the steering wheel and generally making himself familiar with the interior of the car in that way he had of touching everything at once. "But you were… what? You just turned twenty-eight this summer, and I went back and watched all your videos—"

"You did what?" Dex's eye started throbbing, and Kane paused before he put the car in reverse.

"I looked at all your old videos. I wanted to see if you were touching me different than you did the guys in the vids. I mean I *thought* so, 'cause we'd shot a few, but I wanted to see if I could spot it."

Dex almost whimpered, because he'd thought his brain was going to explode. "Yeah? What'd you see?"

Kane smiled softly like he was remembering something. "You and I would shoot lousy porn right now, Dexter. It's a good thing that's not what we do in bed."

Why? How? Explain? "So what does that have to do with—"

"With the real Dexter?" Kane asked, still pausing with his arm over the seat, getting ready to look behind him. "It's easy. I've seen your scars, you know. The ones in your arm where your bones popped through? They were there nine years ago. You keep saying things like 'God, I'm old!' and your family lives in Montana, so I figure you came right out here after high school, and your guy? He was probably there when you got those scars and not there when you were done getting them. And the way you freaked out just now? Tells me he was driving."

Dex moaned. "My head hurts," he whined. "My head hurts, and you know too much about me. Nobody knows that much about me.

And you keep taking care of me, and you're barely twenty. You think I don't know that you're barely twenty? If *was* out to my parents, they'd *still* kick me out of the house for taking advantage of you."

Kane let out a growl. "God, I need some fuckin' coffee, and you need two Advil and a sledgehammer. I know all this shit about you because you been my fuckin' homework since October. Now give it a rest. You'll go to sleep, you'll wake up at your family's commune or farmhouse or what the hell ever, and you can introduce me as your buddy Kane and it'll all be fuckin' okay. Now I wanna see some horses, some cows, and some fuckin' sheep, and I seem to recall you promised me bunnies and kittens and shit too. I always wanted a fuckin' rabbit, but I don't trust Tomas, the fucker, so no rabbit for me. But that doesn't happen if you get to your parents' all wired on lack of sleep and fuckin' insecurities, so get the Advil out of my backpack"—he shoved it at Dex from between the seats on the floor—"and hold your horses until we get some decent fuckin' drive-through coffee. Now the only thing I want to hear you give me are directions to a goddamned McDonald's, are we clear on this, Dexter?"

Dex fished out the Advil and a bottle of water gratefully. "Follow the airport road to the freeway," he said. He palmed the Advil and washed them down. "Go north. The highway will take you through the main drag. You'll see signs past Helena to Forsythe. Wake me up when we get past Helena, we need to turn right about forty miles before we get to the next big city."

Kane smiled and cuffed the side of Dex's head like a bear cuffing her cub. "Good boy. Now kick the seat back and let me fuckin' drive. God. Dexter, it's a good thing we don't have a fuckin' cat, or you'd be telling it how to untangle the goddamned yarn."

KANE woke him up shortly after they cleared Helena, and sure enough, Dex felt much more himself and much less… what? David? Whatever. He felt like the guy who took care of things, who gave orders, who organized shit. He liked that. He could deal with that.

"Turn right in about a mile," he said, sipping at the hot chocolate Kane had gotten him in Helena. "You'll see a yellow T sign telling you the road's coming."

Kane grunted. "You weren't talking out your ass about the fucking roadway, were you? How much snow we driving on?"

Dex grunted back and watched Kane order the car into a straight line, when for Dex, it would surely have been a spinout. "They cleared the roads, Kane—you can see pavement. But yeah. In February, they use the upper-level stop signs and just drive on top of it."

"Yeah, well, I'm glad you got your little nap, 'cause I'm gonna need one when I get there. I hope your parents don't hate me for that!"

Dex smiled. "My mom'll think you're adorable. She used to just sort of dote over us when we were teenagers—that's how she'll see you. A teenager."

Kane *hmm*ed to himself. "My folks left when I was like, a junior in high school. Had too much of the promised land, I guess, wanted to go back where nothing was promised but it was all easier. I don't know. Moms woulda liked the baby, maybe. I don't know if she still woulda spoiled me."

Dex smiled at him. "Someone oughta spoil you, Carlos. You do a real good job of keeping me from falling apart."

Kane sucked his teeth. "You don't fall apart—you get a little frazzled sometimes, but you keep it together. I just don't like to see you making yourself crazy." Suddenly he flashed a wholly grown-up grin—but he flashed it forward and didn't turn his head to the side, which was reassuring, 'cause it meant he was taking Dex seriously about watching the road. "That's my job."

Dex chuckled and then groaned. "Crap. No sex for two weeks. God, you just reminded me how much that's gonna suck."

"That's the problem," Kane grunted. "No sucking at all. Okay, here we are, slowing down and turning right. How much further do we have to go?"

"About five miles." Dex's cock gave an enormous throb, and he wondered that he could even get a hard-on so close to home.

Kane apparently had no problem with that, though. He made a sound of discomfort and took one hand off the wheel just long enough to adjust himself. "Two weeks," he muttered. "We're gonna have to find a quiet place in the barn, Dexter, because I ain't gonna make it. So when do we get to your parents' property?"

Dex looked around, noticed the outbuilding his dad had built to hold supplies. "We're here. As soon as we turned, we were on it—it's to our left."

Kane grunted. "Wow. That's a lot of… whatever the hell it is!"

Dex shrugged. "Everything. It was sheep first, but they tear the hell out of the ground, so Dad just has a small flock of the kind with the real good fleece. He makes a lot of money for the fleece, and the little herd leaves more of the land for cattle, and we have a small herd of dairy cows and a bigger herd of beeves, and there's some land we can farm, but Montana is a lot of rocks in the middle of all that flat, so not as much as you'd think."

Kane grunted. "Yeah, uhm, Dex? Whatever that word was that there's a herd of, you're not gonna make me say it, are you? I don't know how I could work that one into conversation."

Dex laughed and pointed out three guys on horses, riding by the road. The horses were picking their way carefully through the snow, and the guys were in shearling coats, with Stetsons on over stocking caps, leather gloves, and probably long underwear on under their jeans. "Looks like Dad and the guys are out already. Maybe after we unpack, we can join them."

Kane made a disbelieving sound. "Me, on a horse."

"Yeah!"

"In the snow."

"Yeah?"

"Dex, do you not remember Cabo? It was warm, sunny, and frickin' beautiful there, and it was all you could do to get me to wake up enough to fuck! I'm napping by the fire, if that's okay with you. If your mom needs help in the kitchen, I'll go help there."

"Oh." Dex felt an absurd disappointment.

"Oh what?"

The car hit an ice patch and tried to buck. Kane apparently was not into letting that happen and told it to behave with an easy flex of the bicep. Dex, who worked out just as much as Kane, felt a sudden flush of pride. Oh yeah, Kane could drive a car in the snow. Dex tried to swallow it down. It wasn't like Mom and Dad *knew* what Kane was to him, but Dex did. Kane was someone to be proud of.

"I wanted you to ride a horse," Dex said, not sure how to make this sound less lame. "You just… you get excited about shit like that. I thought, you know… it would be sort of a reward, for coming out here and dealing with this shit."

Kane looked at him quickly and then immediately back to the road. "Don't get me wrong, Dexter"—the more Kane called him David, the more Dexter sounded like an endearment, like "sweetheart" or "baby" or "darlin'"—"I do want to see the horses. I just want to pet them in their stables. Is that so wrong?"

Dex laughed a little. "No," he said quietly.

"I gotta ask, though. I know you made me pack the thermal underwear and the wool-flannel shirts and shit, but seriously. Is it *always* so fuckin' cold here?"

"Sometimes it snows in July," Dex said with a smile, although his parents lived in the eastern part of Montana, so that was a little less likely.

"Get the fuck out!" Kane said, clearly delighted. "Any other shit I should know?"

Dex gathered himself up and waved at the three riders, who were urging their horses along the trail that led to the house. His oldest brother—at least Dex thought it was Travis—waved at him, and Dex waved back, smiling a little.

"Yeah," he said, something in his body melting a little. "Montana is on the continental divide. If you take a leak in Helena, it winds up in the Pacific Ocean, but when we piss out our coffee at my folks' place, it ends up in the Atlantic one."

Kane laughed over that until they turned off the road into the driveway, and Dex's greatest regret before he got out of the car was that he couldn't haul that laughing, happy face near his for a kiss.

KANE tried to keep him from unloading the car. Instead, he shooed Dex up to the porch while he opened up the back for their luggage. Predictably, Dex's mom opened the door to greet him and then to chide him for not helping his friend.

"Told ya," Dex said as he grabbed his own suitcases out of the back.

"White people," Kane muttered, popping his wide mouth up until it dimpled on the side. "My mother would have had you eating by now."

"Give her a minute. You know us white people—first there's suffering, *then* there's food."

Kane's low chuckle warmed Dex up as they threw their backpacks over their shoulders and grabbed a suitcase in each hand and made their way up the porch. Dex's sister, Debbie, was there, holding out her hand for the smaller one.

Dex eyed her with a grin. She had their mother's blue eyes, blonde hair, and slender build—like he did, actually—but not the hours and hours at the gym to bulk up the muscles.

"Don't think so, little sister," he said, bending forward to give her a buss on the cheek. She rolled her eyes but hugged him back. "I've got it. Here—we'll just drop our stuff in the hallway and take it up after we strip off our boots."

Kane made a wounded sound. "We gotta take off our boots?"

"We do if we don't want them to rip up the floor inside. Don't worry. I packed your slippers."

"I've got slippers?" Kane wondered as they set down their bags.

"You do now," Dex said grimly.

"Nice, Davy—you buy your roommate slippers? Do you serve him breakfast in bed too?"

Kane grunted and bent down in the hallway—which was really just a bare-boards entry platform with a double row of shoe racks and coat racks on either side—and started to unlace the pricey waffle-stompers Dex had made him buy before they left.

"Yeah, you want me to get on back of a horse, David, you'd damned well better not make me take these things on and off more than once."

Dex saw in his head the thing he *would* do—pop the grumpy fucker on the ass, throw an arm over his shoulder and lean down and talk in his ear, make a crack about how quick Kane would get those things off if a blowjob was involved—all of those things he would do if they were by themselves, or with their friends even, or even with people who didn't know them.

"It'll be worth it," he said mildly, and Kane looked at him sharply. Yeah, so now they both knew what it had been like to be Chase, saying things in your own head when they were screaming to be said out loud.

In the meantime, Debbie walked over to his suitcase and tried to heft it up. "Damn, Davy—what in the hell? You guys just picked those things up like…."

Kane took off his jacket then, the simple flex of his arm straining against the knit of his long-sleeved shirt and the thermals underneath it. Dex looked over at his little sister and started to crack up as she almost swallowed her tongue.

"What, Deb?" he said sweetly, and then he reached over and hefted the suitcase with little effort himself, and Debbie blinked really hard.

"David," she said, some of the fun leached out of her, "those are really heavy!"

"Only if you're teeny and pregnant," Dex said, wiggling fingers at the little five months of baby bulge that barely showed under her sweatshirt.

"No, they're heavy for anyone. Mal's in the *army*, you idiot—and I can pick up most of what he does. How come the two of you look like that?"

"I told you, sweetheart, I work for a modeling firm—you think I don't work out with the models?"

Kane's shoulder made a suspicious twitch as Dex rehashed the cover story he'd been using for the last nine years. Underwear modeling. He had enough stills of him with his shirt off for his parents to think it was true. He'd told them he was unsuccessful but that the firm had taken him on in the business part of the works. Close—damned close—to what had happened.

But that little teeny splinter of truth he left in the wound? Oh yeah. That was a doozy.

Deb looked at Kane again, her eyes getting bigger and more appreciative as he turned around in his stocking feet and picked up his luggage again. "I take it he's a little more successful than you?"

Kane slid his eyes to Dex, his expression a little bit inscrutable. "Don't kid yourself, sweetheart. Your brother could have been a top model, he just had better things to do with his time."

"Deb, Kane. Kane, Deb," Dex said belatedly, and Kane gave her a quiet smile.

"C'mon, Davy," Kane said, "let's dump this crap and meet the fam."

"David!" called his mother's familiar voice from the kitchen. "David, make sure you bring your friend in here after you're settled."

"Told ya," Kane said. He popped his dimples again. "Nice to meet you, Deb. Back in a sec."

Dex chuckled softly as he led Kane down the hall to the attic stairs. He and Henry had shared the small room as they'd been growing up. Until Dex started high school, Henry had slept in the bed with him, and then there had been some general chaos about "Mom, David won't stop whacking off!" Since David had been whacking off in the shower by then, this was really cover for the fact that Henry *wanted* to whack off, but it worked. The ruckus had generally made their mother uncomfortable enough to get Henry moved into Joey and Sean's room, which was big enough for bunk beds and a twin.

Dex brought them up the narrow stairs, their luggage bumping at their thighs, and walked into the room, ducking because the ceiling was made for a junior high kid and not a full-grown man. The raw beams were padded with insulation between them and then backed up by drywall. The drywall had been seamed and plastered but never painted, and Dex had covered it with posters—football teams, the occasional cheerleader. Henry had come along and plastered things with boobs all over the place, and those were still up there. Kane looked around and grimaced.

"Whatsamatter?" Dex smirked. "You don't like the décor?"

Kane wrinkled his nose. "I mean," he said, thinking hard, "I remember the appeal, but seriously—this is a little overkill."

Dex laughed, stacked his suitcases in the corner, and shivered. "God, I forgot how cold it is up here."

"Yeah, well, your parents want it to be a little colder. Dexter, what in the fuck is that?"

Dex looked in the corner and grimaced. "That, Carlos, appears to be a foldout cot."

"For a kid in junior high," Kane said, his eyes narrowed. "Do me a favor, Dexter, and pull that thing out?"

Dex complied, but he couldn't resist the reminder: "Hey, if you fuck up and call me Dexter in front of my parents, shit's gonna get weird."

"The hell it will. Set it up. Good. Yeah, I don't know why you're waiting for me, I don't know how it works."

Dex unhinged the thing in the middle and stretched its creaking frame out, looking in disgust at the thin mattress and the sleeping bag—admittedly warm enough but that smelled like mothballs. "Jesus," he said. "If I didn't know better, I'd think they knew we *were* having sex and this is punishment."

"Yeah, not gonna happen." Kane walked over to the suitcases and hefted his smaller one up, then his larger one, and then eyeballed the cot. "Hm… okay. I think the smaller one's actually heavier. That'll do it. Hold that end."

Dex did and watched him bemusedly as Kane hopped up on the queen-size bed holding the suitcase up to his chest and assessed the cot again, which was about two feet from the bed. Sometimes the shit that Kane did was just completely out of his—

"Holy shit!"

Dex's gasp was masked by Kane throwing the suitcase at the corner of the cot, while Dex barely remembered to hold on to the other end of the cot with all his might. The clatter of the suitcase hitting the rusting iron frame came first—and the squeaky wail of the frame breaking at the hinges came next.

"David!" His mother's voice approached from the bottom of the stairs. "David! What was that noise? Are you okay?"

"Fine, Mom!" Dex called down. "Fine. Kane just dropped his suitcase, that's all. We're fine, but the cot's busted. It was a nice idea, but he'll have to sleep in my bed anyway."

"Okay, honey!"

Dex looked down the stairs, and there was his mother's face, young looking in spite of her being nearly sixty, narrow, with a wide, plump mouth. Her graying blonde hair was pulled back into a ponytail, and she was wearing jeans and a sweatshirt—and an apron. Dex's heart gave a happy little thump in his chest, and the lie that he was telling seemed like nothing for the moment, because he got to see his mommy, and he was home.

"We'll be down in a sec, Mom! And I hope you're ready, because we're starving!"

That face widened into a smile, and Kane looked over Dex's shoulder. His hand on Dex's/David's back—warm and large and solid—was completely welcome as Dex's boyfriend smiled at David's mother. "We'll be down in a minute, Mrs. Worral," Kane said seriously, and Dex's mom nodded.

"Okay then—we've got stew and potatoes, I hope you're ready!" And with that she turned around and left.

Dex closed his eyes and leaned back just to feel Kane's body behind him, and Kane kept his hand where it was.

"Nice with the Mrs. Worral thing," Dex said softly. Kane hadn't even asked what to call her—he'd just seen Dex's driver's license and the name on the house and had figured it out. "And the cot…." Dex shook his head and turned back into the room to fix things up. He started by folding the cot, hanging iron bar and all. “Man, I was not ready for that.”

Kane shrugged and helped him shove it in the corner, where it just sort of leaned there, the blue lining of the mattress peeking out between the bent springs. “Yeah, well, Dexter, like I said, anything that makes us not sleep in the same bed, that’s a *bad* thing.”

Dex laughed and set up his smaller suitcase on top of the dresser, then grabbed Kane’s smaller one and did the same thing on the semisolid old maplewood kid’s desk that Dex had done his homework on through high school. “So why is it okay to call me Dexter?”

Kane shrugged and dragged his bigger suitcase next to the desk, then stood it up on its end. “Because,” he huffed, straightening up, “that’s what you call the smart kids, Mr. I Got One More Semester to Graduate. You’re the brainiac in this scenario. I’m the bully who calls you Dexter.”

Dex looked at the cot again and laughed. God, he wanted to sleep next to Kane tonight. He was so glad he could. “I’m the brainiac? Really?”

Kane shrugged. “I’ll be the evil criminal mastermine if you want.”

“Mastermind?” Dex clarified.

“Yeah,” Kane said, nodding because they were done. “Yeah. I’ll be that.”

“You’re on, buddy. Let’s eat!”

Kane

IT TOOK most of the rest of the day for Kane to learn everyone’s name. Part of it was that the brothers all looked a lot like Dex, and there were four of them, and Debbie’s husband, Mal, didn’t look far off from the lot of them, and that made five.

Part of it was that the whole family tended to talk over each other—they all lived nearby, except for the husband and the brother who were serving together and on leave, but even then, Debbie stayed with her parents and filled them in on the gossip.

Kane was welcomed with a smile and an invitation to sit down and eat when they first walked down the stairs, and he did just that, staking out the corner of the table farthest back in the kitchen, grateful when Dex sat close enough to him so they could bump knees.

Which they did.

It got to be their communication, their sort of Morse code, as the chatter from the kitchen washed over them.

"No, Dad," the oldest brother—Travis? Yeah, maybe—was saying while his oldest, a string bean of an eight-year-old boy, crawled on his lap. "I don't think we should move the sheep yet. Yeah, I know they got wool on them, but the barn's plenty good for another day until it warms up a little."

Dex's dad was a squat man, built like a fireplug. Two of his sons had his build, but none of them had his brown hair or green eyes. "Warm up? Warm up in December? Did you grow up somewhere I don't know about? We've only got so much hay, Travis—it's got to last until March or April or whenever the hell it's going to not snow so damned much!"

Kane watched Dex's older brother send his eyes heavenward and count under his breath before he spoke next. "All right, Dad. You let 'em out now, and when we get sheepsicles like we did last year, you be sure to write 'I told you so' on the insurance claim, with my name at the bottom."

Kane would have laughed then, which would have been bad, because Dex's father had done nothing but glare at him since the men came in from the cold. Instead, he bumped knees with Dex frantically and was soothed by Dex's dancing eyes. Yes, it was funny; no, Kane wasn't delusional; and yes, they could wait until later to talk about it.

"Mom, you got any more stew?" Dex's slightly younger brother asked, and Kane looked at him, sitting next to Dex. He was squarely built like their father and had the family blue eyes and blond hair just a couple of shades darker than Dex's. He was sitting in the spot at the kitchen table closest to the stove, but Dex's mom got up to get it for him anyway.

Yeah, the only person at the table to say anything was Dex.

"Geez, Henry, your legs broken?" Dex asked, and the young man turned slightly and shrugged.

"Sorry!" he said. "What, you still haven't shaken off that whole PC thing of California? What's next—you'll be trying to teach us to surf?"

"Nothing wrong with treating women right," Dex said evenly, and Kane bumped knees with him again and scowled. Yeah, Dex had cheated on a girl. Yeah, he felt like crap. He needed to let that shit go. Couldn't they both see that figuring that shit out with the gay or the straight or the porn or the not porn or the touching or the hearting—that was all complicated and shit? Dex had forgiven Kane for flirting with Donnie's sister; now he had to forgive himself for cheating on the dumb bitch who couldn't figure out that he wasn't straight in the first place. (Kane dimly realized his perspective may have become skewed, but he was annoyed at Dex for feeling like a family tradition of sexism was his to get rid of. So his mom waited on people. So what? So did every woman in Kane's family. As long as no one was smacking her around, Marlene Worral was one up on Kane's sister.)

Dex scowled back. Yeah, well, communicating in code didn't mean you couldn't bitch at each other with your eyes then either.

"Nothing's wrong with a woman taking care of her men," Dex's mother said mildly in one of those voices that Kane could tell was meant to soothe people.

"Besides," Dex's sister said with a little bit of innocent malice, "all of that liberal crap doesn't seem to be doing you any good anyway. If women are all excited about that crap, why can't you keep any of 'em?"

Kane double bumped his knee in commiseration, but Dex seemed to have this one covered.

"Didn't want to keep the last one. Pretty much drove her off. If she's not doing your dishes or your laundry, Debbie, you've got to think of a *real* reason to keep her around."

Kane clapped his hand over his mouth and tried hard not to cackle like an evil chicken. Dex bumped his knee back and raised his eyebrows, and Kane looked hard at his stew (his empty bowl of stew—Dex's mom could cook) so he wouldn't paw the guy's head over to him and plant a big one on him.

Then Dex did something stupid and weird, but Kane was the only one who noticed. He stood up with his bowl, grabbed Kane's from in front of him, took them both to the stove, and filled them up again. Henry and Debbie were still giving him shit about not having a girlfriend, Travis was still arguing with their father about what to do with the sheep, and there was Dex, in front of his family.

Being the little woman.

He set down Kane's bowl in front of him, sat down himself, and plowed back into the chow. Their knees bumped, and then Kane felt Dex's hand, ever so gently, patting him there.

Kane swallowed hard. He hadn't held a damned thing against Dex for coming here in the closet—not a single thought. But if he had, that there would have put paid to anything, anything at all.

"David!" The voice of the family patriarch cut through the crap like a sharp shovel, and Dex jerked up like he hadn't been expecting it.

"Hi, Dad—wasn't sure if you saw me here."

"Who's that you brought with you? You were supposed to bring a wife!"

"He's my roommate, Dad. I didn't want to leave him there by himself."

There was a low titter then, a breath of gossip.

"Honey, I thought you said he was your friend!" his mom said, more than a little surprised.

"Well, I'm not gonna room with someone I don't like!" Dex said, twinkling his eyes at her. "Certainly not someone with all of *Kane's* baggage!"

"What sorta baggage you bring with you?" Travis asked, and for the first time, Kane was being spoken to directly.

"Reptiles, sir," he said between bites of stew. "They sort of took over the fu—" He looked at Travis's other child, five years old and clinging to her mother's hand behind Travis's shoulder. She was a slightly built woman with big brown eyes who hadn't said a thing, just stood there behind her husband, being quiet. Creepy.

"Freakin' house," he finished lamely.

"What kind of reptiles?" said the little girl shamelessly.

Kane smiled at her and just her, and ignored all of Dex's freakishly cloned family staring at him. "Well, we had a gecko, but he got too cold and died, so we're left with a snake and an iguana and two box turtles and two slider turtles—"

"Why four turtles?" Sean wanted to know.

Kane remembered Sean too—he was the youngest, the one who looked most like Dex in those videos when he was brand-new at *Johnnies*, but there was a softness around his chin and his eyes that said that maybe Sean couldn't have done what Dex had, and couldn't have made himself a new person because the old one was a little lost.

"'Cause PetSmart was having a sale that day," Dex said with a wink, and Kane socked him in the arm and grinned.

"Naw, 'cause doofus here didn't know what sort of lizard to get me to make me feel better after the first one died."

"Aw," spoke up one of the big guys—Kane couldn't keep them straight, but since this guy *didn't* look like a blond guy, he figured it must be Debbie's husband, Mal. "That's cute. How long have you two been a couple?"

And before Kane could think, *Oh fuck, we're done for!* all of the grown-up David clones started throwing crackers at him.

"Jeez, Mal!"

"Get your mind out of the gutter!"

"Ohmigod, make me sick whydoncha!"

"Maa-aal! That's my brother, you moron!"

"Malachi, did we really have you at our table to suggest such a thing?"

And so on. For a minute—an entire minute—Kane thought that he and Dex were safe. This could just be a family visit, and it would be fun.

Then Kane saw Dex looking at something, his expression troubled. Kane followed his gaze and saw Malachi and Henry bitching at each other with their eyes.

TOWARD the end of lunch, Dex's dad suggested they go out on the horses. Dex took him up on it but told Paul that Kane got to bail.

"He sleeps on vacation, Pops. Don't fight it."

And sure enough, Kane felt sleep pushing behind his eyes and a yawn building up in his chest. He smiled sheepishly and allowed Dex to shoo him up the stairs.

Kane turned around to him before he got halfway and said, "You going to be okay?"

"With my own family? Yeah." Dex gave him a weak smile, and Kane knew he was thinking about things he wanted to talk about and do but couldn't.

"Remember what's important, Poindexter. That's why you're smart."

"You make me look brain damaged," Dex said rawly. He bit his lip then, cast a frantic look over his shoulder, and patted Kane's cheek like he was being friendly. Kane felt it, though. His skin was softer than just a friend's.

KANE woke up in the afternoon and came down to help Marlene with dinner. She had him peeling potatoes and chopping up bacon in no time, and Kane didn't mind. Brainless activity—he could deal.

But then Dex's mom started to talk to him—*really* talk to him, and Kane had never been so glad to be trying to be an honest man in his life.

"So, Kane, you're a model where David works?"

Kane nodded and grunted, because parents weren't his strong suit.

"Are you working your way through school too?"

Kane shrugged and tried to take a peel off without breaking it. "I am *now,*" he said honestly. "Dexter had me sign up for classes."

Marlene was mixing stuff into a big hunk of ground beef, and she almost dropped a handful of onions. "Dexter?" she asked carefully.

"Poindexter, cause he's smart?" he told her, feeling really smart himself to have thought of this. "Not like his friend who died."

Oh no, not at all.

Marlene's laugh was a little forced. "Oh good," she said. "Otherwise, you know, if he was telling people that's his name… well, a mother worries."

You should have worried nine years ago. Letting him wander off to another state—you couldn't hear him being sad? I could hear him being sad, and it's an old sound by now!

"I think he was lost after it happened," Kane said carefully. "But I didn't know him then."

"No, of course not—you're pretty young, aren't you? You would have been what? Ten?"

"Twelve," Kane lied. He'd done the math when he thought Dex was going to leave him because he was too young—back when he was watching all of Dex's old films. He would have been eleven when Dex shot his first video. Dex had still been nineteen.

"So you're a model, and you're going to school," she said, sounding happy, like that made her view of the world fit. "What are you studying?"

And even though Kane had been practicing, his brain suddenly froze and he couldn't say the words. "Bugs and snakes," he said, feeling dumb, and she laughed like he'd made a joke on purpose.

"Well, isn't that high up and fancy. David said he's finally gone back for the rest of that degree. That's a relief. I know he got frustrated when he couldn't get the classes he wanted, but it's good to see him back in the ring."

"He wants life after the modeling agency," Kane said, and he felt some pride here. Kane was going to school; Dex was going to school. Suddenly he realized that in a year, they could both say they were porn stars to work through college—and it would be the truth, and people would laugh at it because it made a good story.

And they would be together still, because what they were doing wasn't a *Johnnies* thing, it was a real thing.

"Yeah—he never could explain what he does for them. He just says random business, but I don't know. I mean, I know he gets a paycheck, but I don't know what he *does.*"

Kane blinked. "He does *everything!*" he said, a little upset. "He arranges shoots, chooses the shots, hires the staff, comes up with shot idea, sets up the website—"

"I didn't know they had a website!"

"They're under construction—you can't find it on the web yet."

Oh *fuck.* "Oh *fuck!*"—because right when he'd been spazzing about telling a lie about the website not being up and almost getting caught, he'd slipped with the potato peeler and taken off a slice of his finger.

He looked at it blankly, saw the blood well up, and had a sudden flash to Chase. Yeah, he thought with wonder. Of course Chase had tried to kill himself. If Kane had to keep his lies straight in his mind for his entire life, he'd want to end it all too.

By the time Dex got back, all cold with red cheeks and what looked like perma-frozen dimples, Kane's mother had recovered from hearing the F-word in her home and Kane's finger had started to numb out with all of the antibiotic ointment and bandaging on it. He'd been exiled from kitchen duty and told to just put his feet up in the living room and had spent the time prowling from kid photo to kid photo until he found the ones with Dex.

And Dex.

'Cause damn if every picture on the mantel didn't have that other kid in there.

Kane heard *his* Dex clattering in after hauling off coat and boots and gloves in the entryway, and when he walked in and looked over Kane's shoulder, Kane yearned to turn and touch his cheeks and see if they were cold, take his red hands and rub them, let Dex bury his cold nose in Kane's neck.

He looked sideways and saw where Dex was looking—the original Dex and the original David, about twelve years old, looking thrilled and triumphant in front of a bizarre apparatus that had a sail, a surfboard, and what looked to be bicycle wheels. The original Dex had dark-brown hair and wild black eyes—he looked a little like Tommy. The original David looked…

Sweet. Tow-headed, blue-eyed, with that big, wide, dimpled smile and the little grooves around his mouth, even as a kid. His teeth were a little bucked, mostly because he hadn't grown into them yet, and his ears still stuck out.

Kane wanted to go back in time for him, go back in time to the day those two perfect boys were separated, and tell them to watch out for the thing in the road. He didn't know if he'd ever seen Dex, *his* Dex, smile that wide. He didn't know if he'd ever seen that much joy, that much unguarded happiness, shining out of *his* Dex's face, and for a moment, he felt cheated. He thought he'd give up his spot in Dex's bed just to be able to see Dex, *his* Dex, smile that way as a grown-up.

"We still have that thing," Dex said over his shoulder, and Kane turned to him, surprised.

"Yeah?"

"Yeah. It's in the barn. Dad kept it."

"What's it do?"

"When there's no snow, it's like a sailboard. Dex and I took it out for about three miles one day. We had to walk against the wind all the way back, but it was worth it."

Kane looked at it again. "Could you make it work without the wheels? Maybe turn it into a sled and do the same thing?"

Dex was just close enough for Kane to smell him, and he smelled like unfamiliar things. But Kane knew that slow-expanding smile, the mischievous bright-eyed look of him—it was the look he had when he brought home the turtles or when they stood together, shoulder by shoulder, and ate pie filling and graham crackers.

"Wanna try?" he asked, breathless and happy.

"Damned straight!" Kane said, so thrilled to see his Dex was real.

At that moment there was a clatter behind them and Henry said, "Jesus, Davy, give the boy time to breathe! Didn't you see he wounded himself?" on his way down the hallway.

Kane held up his bandaged finger sheepishly. "I'm sort of a klutz today," he said, and Dex looked at it sadly, then checked to make sure Henry was gone.

"I'll kiss it better later," he said, and Kane nodded, wordless. He was going to need that kiss when they were alone in a bed together with nothing else to prove.

THE dinner table was just as raucous as the lunch table, and Kane picked at the meatloaf and the potatoes, needing some reassurance like he hadn't needed since he was a little kid. Suddenly Paul Worral's over-hearty voice broke into his thoughts.

"You keep eating that way, son, I'm gonna think Mal here is right. Don't need those people at my table, so you'd better eat!"

Kane blinked, feeling stupid. "What people?" he said, remembering too late the not-funny joke cracked earlier.

"Chase and Tommy's kind of people," Dex said, his voice hard. "Dad, you gotta not make those cracks here, okay? Not in front of us. Just for two weeks, do you think you could keep that opinion to yourself?"

"You know gay guys in California, Davy? I thought that was a stereotype." Marlene's voice was sweet and trying to make the peace, and Kane heard Dex's deep breath before he spoke.

"Kane and I know a couple of guys," he said. "We know one guy who was so afraid of people like you, so afraid of being told he wasn't good enough to eat at the table, that he got engaged. He lived for two years with the sweetest girl—and he was miserable. He had himself a guy on the side that he really loved, but he broke it off because he knew it was wrong. But remember the miserable? Remember the miserable, Mom and Dad, because it's important. He tried to kill himself, Dad. He'd rather die than live like that. But you and Mom, that's not what you see when you make cracks like that. You see an old man a million miles away on television, telling you not to do shit. I see the look on Tommy's face when we came into the hospital, and he didn't know if Chase was going to live or die. I see Chase breaking up with Tommy and then buying razor blades. I didn't know what they were for, right? I was just there as a friend. Well, I should have known what they were for, because my friend almost died. So I don't want to hear it, Dad. I don't want to hear it this year. My friend almost died because he didn't want to disappoint people who kept telling him that he was a bad person when he was actually a really good person—right up until he felt like he had to be straight."

The table had screeched to a halt. Everyone was looking at Dex with horror and embarrassment, but Kane got it.

He'd been thinking about Chase all day too.

"We're, uhm, sorry about your friend, Davy," Marlene said.

Paul didn't say anything. He looked down and kept shoveling his meatloaf in. One of Dex's brothers, Joey, the one who obsessed about sports and that shit, started talking about the Super Bowl of all things, and the table built up to its usual level of noise.

Dex and Kane ate silently through the middle of it, not making eye contact at all. Their knees never stopped touching.

BED.

They were almost cockblocked at the last minute. Yeah, sure, Dex called it "thwarted," but Kane knew a cockblock when he heard one. Kane, true to form, started to get a little tired around nine o'clock, but that didn't seem like a bad thing, since pretty much the women were sitting around doing thread things with needles and colored floss and charts and shit, and the men were playing poker. Kane had seen a lot of yawns, and since everyone claimed to have a fuckton of work to do in the morning, he figured he'd go to bed early and spend a little time in his own skin, remembering that having Dex get in bed with him was the whole purpose of this trip.

He stood up from the poker table after his loss to Henry, the one who couldn't stop talking about girls and looking at his sister's husband, and said, "Night, everybody" without a lot of fancy talk around it, and turned down from the living room to venture up those incredibly narrow stairs at the end of the hall.

"Hey," Malachi said amicably, "you know, Deb was gonna sleep over at Travis's place tonight so she and Cathy could talk." Cathy! That was the name of Travis's wife. No one ever actually said it. "I could bunk up there and you guys could have the twin beds in our room."

Sure, Kane thought irritably. *And your boy Henry isn't going to be sneaking out of his room and up those stairs anytime soon.* God—at least Chase had stopped before actual marriage. Hell, he'd tried to kill himself just to not do what these two guys were doing to Dex's sister.

"I've got a dent there already" is what he really did say. "I'm good." He saw Dex's jaw tighten and the way he glared at his younger brother. Henry didn't meet his eyes, and Kane suddenly wanted bed in the worst way.

He woke up when Dex showed up, though. It was dark—much darker than in their house—but Kane knew the different patches of darkness at this point. He was not surprised to hear Dex rooting through his suitcase for pajama bottoms, and he spoke up.

"Boxer shorts."

"But—"

"Boxer shorts, Dexter. I'm not fucking around. I need to touch you."

Dex grunted and slid into bed next to him. The bed was pushed into the corner of the room—they had a wall on two sides and a dresser on the third. Kane actually liked that. He felt protected. He needed to feel protected. Even more, he needed to protect Dex.

"I'm sleeping on the outside," he said before Dex could get too comfortable under the heavy comforter and three wool blankets and the sheets. Kane was grateful for all of them—it was around fifty-five degrees up there. "Here. Lay down, I'll roll on top of you."

"Just like at home," Dex snapped, and Kane kissed that smart mouth while his body was crushing Dex's into the mattress. He started out hard and irritated, but the way Dex melted into him, soft and sweet and very, very needy, made his own touch softer.

He finished his roll and crushed Dex so close to his chest he was pretty sure the boy couldn't breathe, and he didn't care. Kane would be his breath.

Dex didn't object. He accepted the hug and returned it until Kane could no longer clench his muscles that tight.

"I'm sorry I brought you here," Dex said after a few minutes of silence. "You would have been happier at home."

"Naw. The only thing that makes it home is you."

Dex made a sound in the dark that was difficult to hear. "It's like you read this whole book on the right shit to say when we were on the plane. I need to read that fucking book."

Kane didn't know what to say. He was going to have to read a fuckton of books after winter break—that scared the shit out of him. He certainly wasn't going to do it now just to talk to his… whatever. Just to talk to his Dex.

"I really want to make that sail sled," he said after a moment, because it was true. "I mean, the wind here *sucks.* It would be awesome to see if it did something good." The wind did suck—he'd felt it battering at the car the whole drive and knifing through his coat like a scalpel. He thought houses here probably didn't collapse, they blew away like a doctored photo that took out the house pixel by pixel.

"I'm looking forward to it," Dex said softly, bringing Kane's attention back to good things. "There's someplace I want to take you."

"Yeah. That'd be good. I wonder if we'll feel free."

Dex's sigh shook his bones. "Free. I think… I think when I left, nine years ago, feeling free was all I really wanted. Now that I've been free, I just want something to keep me here on Earth. But not this part of it. I want our little house and your creepy slimy guys and our friends who are unbelievably fucked-up. All the normal on the planet can't make up for not being able to say the things in my head or love the person I love…."

Dex trailed off, and Kane felt his face heat next to Kane's chest. For a minute he wondered why he'd get all embarrassed, and then it hit him.

Oh shit. Really. How could he not know that? Know that's what they were supposed to say now?

"I love you," Kane said into that painful awkward silence. "Too, I mean. I love you too."

Dex's soft laugh was broken. "God, Kane. I love you so fucking much. I thought I knew what this was supposed to feel like, but it doesn't feel like any of the other ways I thought love was."

Kane swallowed hard. "You know if we were home, I'd fuck you into the mattress so we didn't have to talk about this, right? 'Cause nothing I've got to say is going to sound as huge as this is."

"I know, right? And it's stupid too, because all day I've felt like if I could only say the shit in my head, I'd be able to breathe. It was like, I *finally* understood how fucked-up Chase must have been because—"

"I know, right? Because if he was doing that same shit I've been doing in my head all day, but doing it for his whole fucking life—"

"Oh my God! No wonder! No wonder! I wouldn't have made it. I would have crumbled. I would have run my car off the goddamned road or—"

"Stop it!" And now Kane's voice clogged. "You wouldn't have. You wouldn't have." He thought of Dex running the hell away from this happy, loving home when he was eighteen and hurt, and his breath made a breaking sound in his chest. "You know how I know? 'Cause you didn't do any of that. You went to the world's shittiest town and made porn. And you were good at it. You were fucking beautiful. And you went to school. And you tried to have a life and you tried to fall in love and you tried again and again and again…."

Dex's hands came up on either side of Kane's face, and he realized his cheeks were wet. "Shh…."

"No, don't shh me," Kane told him, but he lowered his voice. "Don't make me keep this locked in my chest. You were brave, sweetheart. You were so fucking brave. And I'm so proud of you, coming from here and learning how to be Dex."

Dex's body shivered in his arms. "That's the dumb thing," he said, but it didn't sound dumb to Kane when he said it. "It's just so stupid, because the thing is that Dex was always the brave one. I was always the one following in his shoes."

His cheeks were wet too, and he wiped them on Kane's chest.

"I didn't know that guy," Kane said. "I didn't know him. But you're the guy who tries to take care of all the guys at *Johnnies* and the guy who's going back to school. You're the guy who buys me gloves and makes sure I don't do stupid things with my money and my life. You're the guy who got Lola to let me see the baby. That's the guy I love. That's you."

"It is, isn't it?" Dex said, his voice muffled with wonder, and Kane closed his eyes and held Dex tight and didn't let him go, hardly let him breathe, until sleep claimed them both.

THEY slept like they always slept—Kane had his arm anchored around Dex's middle, drawing him close. Kane hadn't counted on being awakened by a small person with too much curiosity while they were sleeping that way, but hell, if Dex could wake up with Tomas in his balls, Kane could keep his head, couldn't he?

"Heya, uhm, short person," he mumbled, looking over his shoulder.

"Heya. I'm supposed to wake you guys up and tell you that if you want to go out with the men, you need to be at breakfast in fifteen minutes."

Kane squinted. It was the *really* short person, the little girl. "Are you going out with the men?" he asked, and she shook her head, her blonde hair—not brushed yet—flying everywhere.

"I'm not a man," she told him, and he wrinkled his nose.

"I don't know if I like horses enough to be a man in Montana," he told her frankly. "Maybe I'll just be a girl here and stay inside where it's warm."

The girl clapped her hand over her mouth and smothered the peal of laughter that threatened to break free. "You're funny! How come you and Uncle David are sleeping so close together?"

Kane wrinkled his nose again. "It's not a very big bed," he said, and it was true. Usually, in their own bed, Dex would try to escape a few times and Kane would have to capture him and pin him back against Kane's body, but not here. Nope. Here, he stayed mashed up against Kane's front all night. Kane thought that if they got a queen-size bed at home, maybe he could fit some terrariums in the room *and* sleep with Dex like this. It was a good thought. He liked it very much.

Dex heard the conversation, though, and propped himself up on his elbow, and then rolled over in bed so he could come partially out and talk to her. "Morning, Tanya," he mumbled, propping his chin on Kane's shoulder. "We're not going out with the guys. We'll get our own breakfast, okay?"

"Are you going to hang around the house all day? 'Cause grandma says your friend is as useless as tits on a bull!"

Dex grunted and Kane said, "I'm *what*?" and Dex poked him to make him quiet.

"He's usually a better cook than that, sweetheart. But no. We've got a project outside we were going to work on. You can come too, if you want. It's in the tool barn."

Tanya shook her little blonde head again and wrinkled her nose. "I don't like it in there. There's spiders. But if you're going in there, you *must* be real men! Daddy kept saying you're not, and I'm confused."

Dex buried his face in Kane's bicep for a minute and made a growling sound, then looked up. "Tanya, sweetheart, I want you to go downstairs and remind your father that I saw him wet himself when a jackrabbit surprised the hell out of him when we were branding, and he was fifteen years old. Tell him I'll put that story out on the Internet with his name and picture if he doesn't shut his trap about real men, okay?"

Tanya's eyes got really big. Her mother must have had brown eyes, because they were dark brown in her broad-cheeked little face, and she nodded gravely. "Okay, Uncle David. He's not going to be happy!"

"Well then, tell him to keep his opinions on real men to himself, okay?"

"Okay, Uncle David." She looked around. "Uncle David, I see presents in the suitcase. Are those for *us*?"

Dex buried his face in Kane's arm again, and Kane patted the back of his head. Kids. You had to love 'em, 'cause you couldn't give them to other people to put in a cage.

"Yes, sweetheart. Would you like me to put them under the tree?"

Again that grave-eyed nod. "Can *I* put them under the tree?"

"You gonna get help?" Dex asked. Kane noticed that his voice got more… more *Western* when he was here with his family. It was cute.

"Yeah. Hold on a sec." And then, after barely turning her head over her shoulders, she yelled at the top of her lungs, "*Garth, you get your skinny butt up here and help me with the presents!*"

Kane and Dex looked at each other, surprised and a little horrified, and Kane did what he'd been longing to do since he'd woken up with the little girl staring at him.

He pulled the covers over his head.

"Coward," Dex muttered, but when Kane gave him a hand under the covers, Dex grabbed it and squeezed, so Kane knew he wasn't really mad.

Kane heard more feet up the stairs, and then Dex talking to probably the string-bean little boy, and then there was rustling and talking and more pattering and Dex hollering "And could you close the door, Garth? Thanks a lot" before he tugged the covers back and then pulled them over his head so it was him and Kane in the blanket fort.

"They're gone," he whispered, and Kane grunted.

"That's what *you* think. Those kids were never gonna leave."

Dex laughed softly, his warm puffs of breath filling the space between them. "Let's wait another fifteen minutes and then get up and shower. After breakfast, we can go out and look in the tool barn. With any luck, we can have that thing all adapted before lunch. It'll be like a workout, right?"

Kane brightened. A workout? Awesome. His muscles were starting to tense up as it was. And then—"Dex, so you think it'll be private in there?"

Dex nodded. Kane smiled, knowing it was the same wide, childish, greedy smile that the little girl had given. "Good. I'd really like to kiss you!"

Dex laughed low and quiet, but they didn't kiss. Kane didn't expect them to. Not in the daylight, and not in this house.

THEY cooked together for breakfast—a sausage egg scramble, and because Dex knew what to do for seasoning, Kane didn't need quite so much ketchup. Dex's mom was there with Dex's sister and sister-in-law, and they were making something at the kitchen table—something that involved hot glue, fabric bits, weirdo little craft store jib-jobs, something called "raffee," and buttons.

Kane had no idea what it was, and he didn't want one in Dex's house, but when Mrs. Worral asked Dex if he'd like to have a centerpiece for the table when he got home, Dex smiled thinly and said, "Sure, Mom. That would be really sweet of you."

Dex turned around then to brown the onions in the bacon grease, and he crossed his eyes and stuck out his tongue at Kane, who nearly swallowed his tongue not to bust up. Kane was chopping up leftover baked potatoes from the night before, and he dumped them into the grease too. While Dex stirred them in, Kane went and got the eggs from the refrigerator.

"Mom, you don't want to give him one of these! They're girly! Any girl he brings home is going to see this and think he's got a girl already!"

Kane set the eggs down at Dex's elbow and tried not to cringe. God, Debbie's voice was really starting to grate on his nerves. One of the best parts about coming clean to Lola about where the money was coming from was that Kane hadn't had to hear her try to shove him into a relationship anymore.

Dex looked at his sister and grimaced, then started cracking the eggs into the pan. "If I wanted a girl that badly, I would have made Kane get rid of his snake. That thing would pretty much scare off anyone not serious about the job."

Kane heard the double meaning—he wasn't good at that, but he heard it this time, and he grinned. "Yeah, Tomas isn't really subtle about staking his claim," he said. He was throwing away the eggshells in what Dex had called the compost bucket as Dex finished with them.

Dex finished cracking and started stirring, and Kane looked over at Mrs. Worral when she shuddered. "I really thought you were joking about the animals, Kane. Why would you bring critters like that in the house? Why do you like them, anyway?"

Kane cocked his head, thinking about the answer, while Dex continued to stir the eggs so they didn't stick to the bottom of the old-fashioned cast-iron frying pan. "I dunno," he said after a minute. "They're just all muscle, you know? And their skin, it's pretty and functional and silky. And they're really affectionate if you give them a chance."

"Yeah right!" Debbie scoffed, and Kane kept his face impassive while he imagined squishing her head between his finger and thumb.

"No, it's true," Dex said. He kept stirring and scraping, which was good because that meant the eggs were getting brown, and Kane liked them that way. He had a thought and went rooting into the refrigerator for cheese while Dex spoke. "Tomas? He likes me. He keeps escaping and crawling into bed with me. The first time it happened, I about crapped my pants—"

"David!"

"Mom, it was a snake crawling up my shorts while I slept—"

"Oh heavens!" Mrs. Worral shuddered.

"See? You would have too. But he really was just cold. After that, he just kept coming to snuggle when he got cold or lonely. I mean, I stop by his cage when Kane's not there to say hi—"

"I didn't know that!" Kane said, startled, as he opened a bag of pre-grated cheese. Dex took a handful of the stuff out and threw it on and Kane closed the bag.

"Well yeah. I mean, I was like my mom here. I wanted to know what made them so special." Dex winked at him, and he smiled back and turned around to put the cheese away.

"Yeah?" Kane said, straightening and going to fish the plates from the drying rack.

"Yeah. They were… they were nice. They moved in their own time. They were… they were thoughtful. Even when the snake or iguana moves quick—and they can—it's a real powerful move. It's sort of soothing after a while, you know?"

Kane smiled, happy. "Yeah, I know."

"That doesn't mean I wouldn't want a rabbit eventually."

"Why not a cat?" Cathy, Travis's wife, asked unexpectedly, and Dex grinned at her.

"Because isn't a cat a little average, after having snakes? I don't know—I think Kane set the bar pretty high."

Debbie laughed shrilly, but Dex's mom and Cathy were exchanging weird looks.

Kane ignored them. "Those eggs about cooked, Dexter?" he asked, a little bit starving, and Dex looked at him.

"You always ask that, but you never like them runny. You want them dry, you're going to have to wait a minute, okay?"

Kane grunted. "Right. Of course. But I'm gonna make you suffer when I'm making tamale pie, you know that?"

Dex grunted right back. "That's different. You always try to cook it until there's a crust on top. I like it when it's all juicy. That sauce you use is amazing."

"Yeah, there's supposed to be a crust on top," Kane told him, but he was pleased anyway. Dex liked his cooking. That's why they were taking a class. Together. Where they could get better at it.

Kane looked up then, and it wasn't his imagination. The women were all having silent, maddening, eye-humping conversation while he and Dex cooked. It was just rude, that's what it was.

"What?" he asked, irritably and Cathy spoke up hesitantly.

"You guys cook together like you're married."

And then Debbie pitched in and both saved their asses and confirmed Kane's deepest suspicions.

"I still think you two are crazy," she muttered. "Henry and Mal are just like that when they're putting together a car."

Kane looked at Dex and saw his jaw locked so tight it was twitching, and decided not to say anything. "It means we know each other," Dex said, and Kane nodded, not wanting to look at anybody. Instead, he held up the two plates again and Dex dished up the eggs, then turned off the gas and grabbed the ketchup. He knew just how much ketchup Kane liked, which was good. When he was done squirting ketchup, they both moved their plates to the spare, clean corner of the table to sit down to eat.

"Well, I think it's neat," Cathy said encouragingly. "I mean, I don't know what it'll take to get Travis to cook, but I'm betting it would be dire."

Kane grinned at her. "We just like to eat," he said gratefully.

Cathy winked at him, and he and Dex dug into the chow.

THEY washed up after themselves and then put on their five hundred protective layers of clothes to walk out between the house and the tool barn, which was about three hundred yards off the house. There was a path, but it was still icy and under about a foot of snow, and Kane felt like he was getting a workout just walking in it.

"Yeah," he muttered when they finally got to the barn, "your dad was right. This shit ain't for pussies."

Dex looked at him with that grin—God, Kane was starting to treasure that openmouthed ear-to-ear smile more and more. "When'd he say that?"

Kane shrugged. "I dunno. Every time he breathed in and out when I was in the room?"

Dex turned around and gave Kane's scarf—something dark and brown and soft that Dex had just sort of put in his luggage—a tug. "Don't be intimidated. This shit is all he knows. He obsesses about where to put the sheep because it's the hardest thing he's ever had to think about, okay? Doesn't make him not a good man, but it doesn't make you a worse one."

It took Kane a couple of steps before it sank in. "Did you just say I have to think hard? 'Cause I've got nearly thirty videos to prove thinking ain't what I do hard."

Dex stopped suddenly and looked him in the eyes. "If you ever tell me you're dumb, Kane, I swear to Christ I'll deck ya. And then I'll *top* ya for a month." Dex shook his head and started trudging to the barn, muttering, and Kane had to make himself blink because his eyes dried out.

SCREAM FOR ME GENTLY

Dex

THE tool barn was just like Dex remembered it when he was a kid. It was bigger than the house, and dark, but also neat and orderly. He made his way through the stacks of spare engine parts and the upright organizer drawer that held everything from the head gasket to a tractor that was parked near the entrance to a set of wheel bolts to a car his father had sold after Sean had been born. All of it was organized, right down to the placement of spare parts alphabetically from the front left of the shed to the back right—axles, brake lines, carburetors, door handles, electronic ignitions, and so on. Dex kept his gloves on as he turned on a light. Montana wasn't known as spider country, but he'd always been a little afraid of them in here. (He was glad, in fact, that Kane's critters hadn't included tarantulas. He knew some people kept them as pets, and he was pretty sure that's where he'd have to draw the line.)

The single bulb flared to life so Dex could find the bank of lights on the wall near the workbench and turn them on. They flickered fluorescently overhead, and Dex started to hunt.

"Okay, sailboard… sailboard… *S*… or *B*?"

"*D*," Kane said practically. "For David."

Dex looked at him and then looked over the piles of parts, set up as close to order (the smaller parts in those stackable drawer things, with labels) as one man could make them, and sure enough, there it was. Right next to two doors from a Ford pickup and one from a Dodge Charger.

"Or *D* for Dex," he said thoughtfully, and Kane snorted.

"What?"

"Isn't David his son?"

Dex thought about it. "Dex was a better son," he admitted. "Dex was going to stay here for his father, I was going away. Dex was the quarterback, I was the receiver—"

Kane snorted, and Dex smacked just enough of his head to catch hair.

"We didn't get that far," he said sternly, and Kane made a sound.

"You didn't what?"

Dex looked away. "It was a day, Carlos. A day. We had a… a spare two hours on our way home from town. About all we knew before we hit that fucking deer is that we wanted to do it again."

Kane let out a pained sound. "But… but why *Johnnies*, if that's all you knew?"

Dex took a breath and then another. God. It was a good question. It was a *fair* question, after the terrible discomfort of the last two days. That didn't make it any easier to answer.

"'Cause," he said after a minute of restlessly searching the cannibalized banks of real-life leftovers for an answer. "'Cause, I told myself that… that it had happened because it was *Dexter*, my best friend. That it wasn't something in me, it was something in him. I didn't know how to find a new best friend." He swallowed. "I didn't. No girl I was with was doing it for me. One of them suggested *Johnnies* for kink, and I thought, 'Well, I already have that kink. And there's never going to be another Dexter.' So that's why I took that name. 'Cause there was never going to be another Dexter, and David was always gonna be empty, but *Johnnies*, that would come close."

He still couldn't look at Kane. He couldn't. It sounded so… so young. So lost.

Kane had taken off his gloves in spite of the chill that wasn't hardly scratched by the oil space heaters that came on with the lights. His fingers were cold as they fit under Dex's chin and jerked Dex's face around to make him look Kane square in those chocolate-brown eyes. Yeah, there were the muscles, the dimples, the little flat bottom on the square chin and jaw, but truly, everything a man needed to know about José Carlos Ricardo Ramirez was in those eyes.

"How'd that work out for ya, David?" Kane asked evenly, and Dex managed a limping smile.

"Better than I thought in October," he said softly, and Kane put both hands on his shoulders to bring him in for an almost chaste kiss.

"Yeah, well, you were always David. I didn't know that brown-haired kid in those pictures. I knew you. I'd recognize that grin in a blizzard. Your eyes? I mean, on the website it says blue—but your eyes are a better color than that. The guy who was nice to me on my first day—hell, on my first *scene?* That was always David. It was David I knew would let me sleep in his spare room when I needed help. David's name is on all that school stuff that's got us going to cooking class. David's the name on your diploma. I mean… you're *my* Dex, but that doesn't mean you've ever been anything else."

Dex smiled and blinked hard. His eyes were watering—he told himself it was the cold and used his palm to clear away the moisture. Kane wasn't having any of it. He framed Dex's face with those big blunt hands. Dex's father would have said they were pansy's hands, because they were smooth and moisturized, but Dex knew better. Dex knew they could hold him down and master him and ground him. He knew they were powerful, confident hands, and that they'd never, ever do anything to hurt Dex in any way.

"You can't do this now," Kane said, and Dex nodded, because just hearing the words made him want to get control of himself. "You do this now, I fuck you in the corner. I fuck you in the corner, we're gonna get caught, 'cause you're loud, Dexter—no two ways about it. You get caught, we're not gonna be able to make the sailboard, and that'll suck, because right now, I'm thinkin' that alone will be worth the plane ride, you hear me?"

Dex found himself grinning in spite of all the nice attention his body was paying to hearing Kane say things like "fuck you in the corner" and "you're loud."

"It's gonna be awesome," he said, and then he stepped into Kane's arms for a hug, because he needed one.

Kane held him for a moment, tight, like he'd held on the night before, until they both shivered in it. "Let's do this shit, 'kay? I need to fly with you in the worst way!"

"Yeah."

IT TURNED out to be not that hard.

Dex took the wheels off first and then had Kane look around for stuff that could be a fin and a rudder. They found one better—an old sled left over from when Dex's parents were kids, with the rudders still intact. Dex wrenched a little and pulled the skids off the sled, then used the drill and the press and some hot glue and clamped the runners onto the bottom of the sailboard and set it up with a couple of vice grips to dry.

"We can get some rope out of the tack room in the barn," he said as they were wrapping it up for lunch. "I'm thinking if we use that steering apparatus but sit back further on the sailboard, it'll be easier to steer."

Kane nodded his head and took Dex's word for it, mostly, and Dex took a quick look toward the door of the barn and pulled Kane in for a kiss. They separated just as they heard voices, and both of them were busy moving the whole apparatus from the workbench to a set of sawhorses when the door burst open. Dex looked over and saw Henry and Malachi pushing and pulling at each other and laughing excitedly as they touched.

Dex and Kane made eye contact. You didn't work in porn for any length of time without knowing your touches. They weren't just touching like friends horsing around. These were very specific touches Dex was seeing between his brother and his brother-in-law.

He spoke loudly. "Hey, guys! We were just going in for lunch. You guys coming in, or you want Mom to make you some sandwiches?"

Both the men on the far end of the garage looked up, startled, and Dex met their eyes evenly.

"We'll... we'll have some sandwiches later," Henry said, smiling gamely.

Dex knew that smile. When Henry was ten, he cut off the hair of Debbie's favorite Barbie. That was the same smile he'd used when he said he didn't do it.

"Yeah," Dex said. "Okay. We'll tell Mom that."

Malachi's face was flushed and his breath was coming in little pants. As Kane and Dex passed them, Dex saw that his eyes were dilated and he was standing oddly—probably sporting wood.

"Maybe lock the door," Dex said, keeping his voice expressionless. "It's kind of freaky when people just bust in here."

They walked out the smaller door next to the big one used to drive the tractors in, and Dex heard the bolt shoot home behind them. He looked at Kane, expecting to see judgment in his eyes for pimping out his brother to his brother-in-law, but how could he explain? He hated them—hated them both, because Debbie didn't fucking deserve this.

"They got everything to lose, don't they," Kane said, and Dex grunted. Yeah. Kane was smarter than everyone thought.

"Everything," Dex muttered. "That doesn't mean they deserve to have it, but they got so much more to lose."

"But the army doesn't kick you out anymore," Kane said hopefully, and Dex sucked frigid air in through his teeth.

"They don't give you a parade either. But it's more than that. Right now they serve together. They go back and they're a couple, and that's not gonna happen."

Kane grunted. "God. And it's not like your parents are gonna accept either of 'em with open arms... *especially*...." Kane couldn't say it.

Dex swallowed. "Chase... God. I cannot even imagine how much worse that whole thing would have been if he'd known about the baby beforehand."

Kane grunted. "Yeah. Probably no trip to the hospital, but...."

"But no Tommy either."

They were quiet for a minute, and then Dex said what they were both thinking. “And there might not have been a trip to the hospital, but you can bet your ass there would have been a trip to the morgue.”

Kane let out an explosive burst of air. “Jesus, Dexter, and I’m the one everyone says needs to watch his mouth.”

Dex patted him on the back. “Sorry, baby. Sometimes you just gotta look the fucked-up in the face.”

“Yeah,” Kane replied glumly. “Except it’s gotta be hard seeing it in the face of your baby brother.”

Dex swallowed hard, and all of the triumph of the sailboard completely dissipated. “You know something, Carlos? You *are* the one who needs to watch what he says.”

Kane’s pats on his back were just as sincere as Dex’s had been. “Sorry, baby. Looking the fucked-up in the face just makes it look more fucked-up.”

“Fuck.”

“Yeah, and not in the good way either.”

NOBODY asked where Henry and Malachi were over lunch—apparently they were going to the tool shed to fix a nail gun to use with the fencing by the road, and Travis already knew to give them sandwiches to bring when they went out to the barn. Kane and Dex met eyes when they heard this and then simply let the matter drop.

Kane had nailed the issue—Henry and Mal had too much to lose. Dex and Kane weren’t going to help them lose it.

They pounded down lunch and then got their gear on to go back outside again.

“You found the sailboard all right?” Dex’s dad asked, and Dex smiled at him.

“Yeah, Dad. Under *D* for Dex.”

Dad nodded. “I figured you’d find it there.”

"Why wasn't it under *D* for David?" Kane asked, and Dex's father looked surprised, like he didn't expect Kane to talk ever.

"'Cause it was Dex's idea."

"It was my idea," Dex said with a wink to Kane. "I just didn't expect Dex to follow through."

"Yeah, well, the follow-through was never your strong suit," Paul Worral grunted.

"He's getting his degree this semester," Kane defended, and Dex wished he could grab the guy's hand, because he sounded like Tomas the snake did when you reached into his cage too fast.

"Yeah, I'll believe it when I see it." And with that Paul Worral stomped out of the house, leaving Kane making growling noises at the closed door.

Dex grabbed his arm and ignored the look Cathy sent him from the entryway as she stood there with a bag of sandwiches and the censure his mom was sending him from the kitchen as she started clearing the table. "It's complicated with family," he said quietly. "You know that. C'mon. It gets dark in, like, two hours. If we can't get the wind to take us *back*, it's gonna be a long and cold walk home."

BUT *oh*, that thing was just as fun as Dex remembered it.

Kane sat in the middle, arms around the mast, keeping his head down as the sail played above it, and holding the front steering apparatus by the rope they'd gotten out of the stable. Kane had spent half an hour rolling the sail up and repositioning it on the open bolt that circled the mast while Dex bored out the skids and bolted them to the board. Otherwise the damned boom would have taken his head off.

Dex stood on the back of the board and propped the tiller with his ankle while holding onto the sail. They didn't try for sailor's jargon—Dex just barked out simple orders.

"Left! Left! Over up that hill *but not toward the tree*! There you go! *Whooee!*" Because the hill was steep both ways! On they raced, over a landscape made unfamiliar by time and snow but along a path Dex could have walked (or sailed) in his dreams.

He knew the exact moment the sailboard passed off his parents' property and onto Dex's parents', but he wasn't sure *how* he knew.

Maybe he just recognized the little stand of evergreens by the burial plot, but that didn't explain the lifting of his shoulders, like he had sails for wings there too.

With a little bit of effort, the two of them leaned to their left and steered to the right, kicking up snow and letting the sail collapse in a suddenly hushed heap. Dex tied the boom upright so the thing wouldn't take off without them, and laid the board on its side, and then grabbed Kane's hand through their gloves.

The top was barely visible through the snow, but Dex got down on his knees, glad the snow was dry so it didn't seep through his jeans and long johns, and dug away the snow in front of the headstone until you could see his name.

"Dexter Allan Williams," Kane read, his voice rasping. "God, he was so young."

"Not too much younger than you," Dex said, and Kane rolled his eyes.

"Young enough," Kane said seriously. "Think about it—he never had a kid or owned a snake or lived out on his own. He never got to say he loved you—that was pretty young."

Dex smiled and stroked the shiny granite of the headstone, then turned to Kane. "You've gotten to do those things," he said soberly, and Kane nodded without any irony at all.

"The 'I love you' part needs practice," he admitted. "That's why it's not good to go out young. You got to say that shit a lot before it sticks."

Dex nodded and felt his face, his shoulders, his neck, everything relax as he gave up the burden of being anyone but himself, put it to rest on Dex's headstone, and let Kane see the real him, just like Kane had seen all along.

"I love you," Dex said, feeling it so hard it threatened to burn out of his chest. "I love you so much. You saved me, Carlos. I was so lost, and you just… just tied me to the ground until I remembered how to walk my own path… you saved me."

"Yeah. You're the one who let me sleep in your bed until it stuck. I love you too. You got to promise me I get to say it a lot when we get back home, okay?"

Dex nodded, and he didn't care that they were two men standing on a lonely ridge and that anybody driving or riding by could see him. He just cared that they'd exchanged vows of a sort, and they needed to seal it with a kiss.

Kane captured his mouth first and then cupped the back of his head and pushed forward. Dex liked it when he did that, liked being moved, positioned, liked knowing what he was doing was right.

He opened his mouth, felt the warmth of Kane emanating out, and the lonely stone in the middle of his chest began to warm for the first time since the airplane had left the ground. The kiss deepened, intensified, became passionate, until Kane forgot what they were doing and slid a cold glove still caked with snow under Dex's jacket until it touched bare skin.

Dex gasped, then laughed, and Kane did too, looking heartily embarrassed.

"I'm sorry," Kane muttered, and Dex smiled and kissed him on the chilled cheek. They'd both worn their scarves over their faces as they'd ridden, but once they stood up, they'd unwound them, and the cold didn't take a coffee break while you kissed your boyfriend senseless under the iron-gray sky.

"Here," he said softly and then turned toward Dexter Williams's grave. He moved forward and crouched, talking softly, and Kane let him have his privacy.

"Hey, Dex," he said softly, and the name sounded funny when he was talking to someone else. "I hope you like him. He's not much older than we were when this happened, but I think that's okay. I think a part of me got stuck here, right here on this hill, trying to say good-bye to you. He's sort of a shock when you're not paying attention. He busted me loose and set me free. I hope you don't mind if I keep the name. Maybe the best of you can live on, and me too, if people know there's a Dex out there who's fearless. Just as long as Kane knows I'm David, I'm fine with that if you are."

There was no answer, just the lonely wind under the big sky. There were mountains on three sides of the ranch, and David could name them all, but at this moment, this ridge over the slight valley of his father's farm felt like the palm of God.

Dex shuddered and stroked the headstone again. "Bye, Dexter," he said softly. He wasn't sure what was going to happen when he got home—and he certainly wouldn't have predicted what *did* happen—but he was pretty sure this was the last time he'd be visiting this place for a while. Maybe even forever. It was important, that was all, that Dexter Williams got to know his memory was treasured, even while David said good-bye.

THE wind had pushed them up the hill, so that meant they could ride down the hill like the sailboard was just a big hard-to-steer sled. This was good, because tacking wasn't easy in a sailboard, and they had to do that for the last mile or so.

By the time they got back, Dex's back, neck, arms, core, thighs, and calves were all complaining from the strain, and he practically fell off the damned board as they pulled into the little windless area left by the house and the two barns.

Kane laughed and unfolded himself and then stood and stretched with Dex. They'd both done enough extensive workouts to know that a few yoga stretches would put paid to a lot of pain later. Twilight was darkening to night, and the temperature was about to become unlivable. Dex was glad it wasn't snowing, because he could tilt his head back and see stars.

"Look," he said, and he watched as Kane did the same thing. They stood there, hands laced behind them as they stretched out their chests and arms, and watched the simplicity of the stars, with a full moon cresting over the animal barn.

"Think the guys are in already?" Kane asked after a moment. They couldn't stretch too long or the cold would start to set into their bones.

"Yeah—probably long before this. Not too much to do in the winter. Milk the few cows, muck the stalls, feed everybody. If they were riding out to fix fences, they would have finished that up after lunch."

Kane kept his head tilted up. It was such a simple sky—deep, thick, syrupy velvet black and clean, sparkling, crystalline white. Then Kane had to make one of those simple observations that messed up everything Dex had been thinking because it was profound too.

"So clear here, you can see the reds and the blues in the stars," Kane said. "You can see the moon like a little planet, with sand and stuff on the surface and not like just a glowing light in the sky. It's funny how you get rid of all the weird city stuff and you can see things for what they are."

Dex turned his head, saw Kane's face lit up by the moon. "Yeah," he said softly. It was like he'd hung the moon there just so Kane could look at it and be enchanted. He'd do anything to give that sort of wonder to Kane.

But it was getting cold, so they finished their stretch and clomped in, passing through the threshold into a surprisingly silent house. Dex looked around as he and Kane took off their coats and unlaced their boots.

"Where is everybody?" Kane asked, and Dex shrugged. Come to think of it, the driveway, which had a cover big enough to accommodate four vehicles, had been missing some cars too.

"I wonder if they went out to eat. It's a little late notice—"

"They're at my house," Travis said, coming out of the kitchen quickly enough to startle Dex. "And don't get comfortable."

"We're going to your house?" Kane asked in confusion, but Dex took one look at his older brother, that square jaw grim and those lowered eyebrows even grimmer, and shook his head.

"No, baby. We're going home."

Except it was never that simple, was it? Dex was all for making it simple. He walked into the kitchen and there was Dad, his eyebrows and forehead as grim as Travis's and his mouth pinched in and sour, and there was Mom, her eyes all red and puffy and her mouth open and vulnerable.

Dex walked in there, sock-footed because he'd taken his boots off, and looked at them both. "How'd you know?" he asked, and his father scowled.

"Greg Williams called me up. Said a couple of faggots was necking on his son's grave. I didn't know what the hell it had to do with me until he told me one of them was you!"

Dex wrinkled his nose. "Weird. I didn't see him out there at all!" He looked at Kane. "You?"

Kane shook his head no, and then they both looked expectantly at Dex's father. In that moment, that shared movement, it was like they were in their own little bubble, their own little Dex-and-Kane planet, like the moon. Yeah, they could see changes on the Earth's surface, but they were cold changes, far away, and had nothing to do with planet Dex-and-Kane, which would weather all those changes with equanimity. Dex wasn't startled or even surprised when Kane grasped his hand and moved closer, shoulder to shoulder, as his family ties were savaged and mutilated in one painful moment.

"So you don't deny it? You went up to… to what? To deface your best friend's grave with this bullshit?"

Dex swallowed. "Leave Dexter out of it," he said quietly. "I was there to say good-bye."

"To Dexter?" his mom asked, confused. "You were going to say good-bye to Dexter by… by being perverted with this… this…?"

Oh shit. Suddenly his moon was way too close to planet earth, because he'd thought he wouldn't have to talk about this, but now it seems he would.

"He's my boyfriend," seemed like the first matter of business, mostly so his mother wouldn't swallow her tongue. "He's the first person I've really loved since Dexter—"

His father stood up so fast Dex didn't even have a chance to step back, and the crack across his face shocked his breath away. "That boy's not even here to defend himself!"

"From what?" Dex asked, hearing a child's tears in his voice and wanting to be back on the moon. His face stung, was bruising, his cheekbone throbbing because it had been the sort of open-palmed smack that would have bruised a slab of frozen beef. "From falling in love? We were in—"

His father's hand went up again, and suddenly Kane was there in front of Dex, catching Paul Worral's stringy arm in his own strong hand. "You hit him again and I will end you," Kane said, his voice as steady and even as a snake's.

"Carlos—"

"We're done here, David," Kane said. His other arm was bent behind his back, because he'd never released Dex's hand, and now he gave it a squeeze. "We're done. Whether we stay here and do this scene ugly or leave now and let them wallow in it alone, they're going to ask you to leave. We're going to leave now, before he gets a chance to hit you again and I have to lay him out."

Dex took a breath, and he wasn't proud of the next thing he said. "Mom?" Oh God. Growing up, his father had always been the hand of God, but Mom? She'd been the mercy of the goddess, the gentle supporter, the voice of kindness.

"David, is it true? Are you and this boy…? Did he make you…?"

"Gay?" Dex said, and hearing it out loud should not have been such a shock. He'd been in *gay porn* for nine years. He'd been *fucking guys for money* for seven of them. Why, then, would the word *gay* sound obscene when uttered once, while holding his lover's hand, in his mother's kitchen and under his father's roof? "He didn't make me gay. *God* made me gay. Dex made me realize it wasn't a bad thing."

"And this boy?" his mother asked, like Kane wasn't still holding on to Dex's old man's wrist with a grip of steel while Paul Worral's arm trembled with exertion as he tried to follow through on that blow. "Who is this boy to you?"

Dex squeezed Kane's hand back. "He's the first good relationship I've had since Dex Williams died. He's the first person to accept me for me since we hit that damned deer in the road." His voice rose, and he felt that whole useless year yearning for Scott fading away, all those failed relationships with girls while he fucked men for money disappearing like one of those pixelated pictures of stuff disappearing one small photoelectron at a time. "Are you really going to kick us out because he's not who you thought I'd want?"

"Oh, honey." Dex's mother was crying, and she wasn't looking at him. "You know how strongly we believe this is wrong!"

"Yeah," Dex said. He remembered lying in the hospital, needing someone to understand so badly, being so afraid that they wouldn't that he'd made plans to bail from his entire home state before he could find out. For the first time since he'd done it, that felt like a good plan. "I just thought… I still hoped that maybe you could love me more than you loved your damned beliefs. C'mon, Kane—you're gonna break his arm."

Dex's father was sweating by now, his whole body shaking, and Kane simply let go and stepped back. Dex's dad lost his balance, had to windmill his arms to keep upright, and he glared at Kane and spat, "No goddamned idiot faggot's gonna touch me in my own house!"

And suddenly the moon was far away, and Dex was there in the ugly, and the ugly had made him, and he was wearing it like skin. "Faggot?" he said, his voice thin and a little shrill. "Faggot? You want to know how I made it through school, Dad?"

Kane turned toward him, horror on his face. "No… no, Dexter, no—not like this!"

Dex shook his head. "No one calls you shit. No one. You think he's an idiot faggot, Dad? You want to know what an idiot faggot *I* am? Guess. I dare you. *Guess* what I am."

Kane squeezed his hand hard. "David… David, baby, trust me—you can't take this back."

"I don't want to take it back. I don't want to. They're gonna kick us out? They're gonna call *you* names?" He pitched his voice over Kane's shoulder. "He's the gentlest man in the world, do you know that? In the *world.* He gave his sister his own house so she could get away from her husband. He spent more money than you've made in ten years making sure her baby gets better from cancer. And you're gonna call him *that*? You *deserve* to know everything. If you're gonna give up on me, you need to know what you're giving up on."

Dex's mother was looking at him with absolute confusion in her eyes, and Travis, who had watched the whole thing dispassionately from the doorway, was suddenly curious. "All right, Davy. I give. What the hell did you do?"

"Porn," Dex said, feeling evil. He didn't deserve to be clean like the moon. "Gay porn. Over a hundred movies. *That's* what *Johnnies* is. *That's* the modeling agency I'm working for. *That's* the place that's giving me a dick up in business. That whole time, those girls I was dating? They were the kind of girls who would know. You want to know why Kane calls me Dex? Because I missed Dex… I missed him so bad I *became* him. I became someone fearless, and when I was Dex, I could sleep with any guy I wanted, and I could look for someone to fill that place in me that was missing. Seven years. It took me *seven years* to figure out that Dex wasn't the only man I could ever love. It took me seven years to figure out that he wasn't a fluke, and that it wasn't a woman who would make that ache in me feel better, and that sleeping with all the guys in the world was *not* going to make up for not having one to love." He wasn't crying. He was surprised. His voice was a little shaky, but he was going to do this. He *had* done this.

His parents had no words, and he was still shaking, his chest heaving with the need to shriek at them, to rage, to scream, to be that little part of himself who had mourned to the heavens when he was eighteen years old and whom no one had heard. Suddenly Kane was there, and Dex was engulfed in a massive embrace.

"Keep it together," Kane murmured in his ear. "Keep it together. Shoes on. Jacket on. I'll go get our shit. You take it out to the car. I'm driving. Little things, David Calvin. You can scream when we're done." Dex nodded into the hollow of his shoulders, and Kane rubbed their cheeks together. "You heard me?"

"Shoes on," Dex rasped, taking that lifeline and holding on with two hands. "Jacket on. You get our shit."

"I'll be right down."

They separated, and his mother burst into sobs, and Dex turned away from the kitchen, from his parents, from that little pocket of the boy he used to be, the family he used to have, and into the truth he'd tried so hard not to face.

Kane

KANE could hear it, even though Dex was quiet.

The roads had been cleared and it hadn't snowed in a few days, but still, it was cold enough that there were nasty little patches of ice, and Kane couldn't take his eyes off the road for any stretch to check on Dex. What he *could* see wasn't reassuring.

Dex was leaning against the window, the glow from the occasional streetlight blooming across his face with icy regularity. He didn't even blink when that happened. His chest was still heaving in and out, and Kane remembered when Frances was a baby, back before she'd gotten sick and before Kane had told Lola about the porn in the misguided thought that knowing there was a steady source of income would comfort her when the leukemia was diagnosed. Frances had been playing with blocks and had smashed her finger against the coffee table—poor little sausage-shaped thing was black and blue for a week—and she hadn't cried right away. No, no, she'd done that baby thing, that thing where they suck air for a couple of breaths and then just belt it out and deafen you.

Kane had known it was coming. He'd held her and tried to calm her down, and still he'd felt her sucking the power out of life, getting ready to just rip it loose in a shriek that would melt skin and flay bone. Those moments, those breathless moments between knowing when it was coming and hearing it come, had been suffocating, horrible, agonizing things that had crawled by like turtles were supposed to. Turtles moved faster.

Right now, this sound that Dex was making—it was the same thing.

There was a little thermometer on the dash of the rental SUV: it said -10F. Kane wasn't sure what people in Montana thought was cold—he'd been freezing his ass off for the last two nights in that bedroom—but he was pretty sure he couldn't just roll down the window and let Dex scream his way into Butte in this weather.

He thought if it had been just a little bit warmer—maybe without that minus in the number—he would have tried.

But he knew that back about thirty miles was a small town—big enough to have a Costco and a Holiday Inn but not much bigger than that. He figured if he could hold on, keep Dex breathing in until they got there, he could deal with that scream on his own.

An hour. It took an interminable hour to get to the Holiday Inn, and Kane told Dex to wait while he checked in. He took a room with a king-size bed and didn't give a fuck that the kid looked at him funny. If he had to knock the entire staff of the Holiday Inn on its ass, he was going to get that boy alone and make him better.

Kane didn't have to knock anyone on their ass, but the thought made him feel better. He just kept remembering that crack across Dex's face, the easy, careless way that muscle-knotted father had just taken his kid out. If Kane had to guess, he'd guess that those kids in that house had a few days from their childhoods where they couldn't walk. If he had to guess, he'd guess there was a belt involved. It wasn't like the guy threw violence around like popcorn, but he wasn't afraid of it either.

Kane tried very hard not to think of Dex alone in a hospital bed, mourning his first lover with a silent scream. It was easier to think of him getting knocked around a little as a kid—not a lot. Not enough to scar them all for life. Just enough to know that opening your mouth and screaming out of grief was not going to get you any sympathy. Just enough to make running to the ends of the fucking Earth the best option in the world.

He got out to the SUV and opened Dex's door, then started unloading the luggage.

"Get the suitcases. Here's the extra key."

Dex nodded, clearly on automatic, nobody home, everybody working on the great scream suppressor in Dex's head.

Yeah. Kane was going to take care of that.

They got inside, shut the door, and Kane dropped the suitcases then bent down to unlace his boots. He shucked his jacket, coat, gloves, hat, scarf, all that shit, and reached into his suitcase for something necessary while Dex shucked his winter crap off too. Dex sat down dispiritedly on the bed in his sweatshirt and jeans—the same wet jeans he'd worn when they'd been sailboarding—and Kane said "Stand up and take them off" in a crisp enough voice to make Dex comply.

Kane was a little bit faster.

By the time Dex had wiggled out of the jeans and the long underwear, Kane was in front of him, angry at his quiet, terrified of his complacence.

"You all undressed now?" he asked gruffly, and Dex looked at him, those angel-blue eyes flat and dead, and nodded.

Kane planted his wide-palmed hand on the back of Dex's head and hauled him close. "C'mon, baby, scream," he whispered and then hauled Dex in for a blazing, punishing kiss. He made it hard, hard enough to bruise, to draw blood maybe, and as Dex started to struggle against the pain, Kane came back and whispered, "C'mon, baby, scream."

"What in the fu—"

And then he mashed them together again. He used his thumbs to force Dex's mouth open, and wider, and Dex did, groaning as Kane invaded, welcoming Kane in. Kane plundered, kissed hard, long, deep, and took everything he wanted from the kiss because Dex needed it that way. Kane pulled back a little and peppered Dex's closed eyes with hard, purposeful kisses.

"You think you can keep that shit bottled up?" he said between kisses. "You think so? I don't fuckin' think so." He kissed Dex hard again and this time shoved Dex's underwear down while their lips were still locked, and Dex was sucking Kane in like Kane was water and Dex was a fucking camel. Kane stepped back long enough to haul Dex's shirt and sweatshirt over his head, then dropped to his knees and took Dex's erection into his mouth quick and hard, needing him aching and sensitized. He used his teeth lightly around the crown, listening for Dex's groan. When he got it, he dropped lower, sucked Dex's shaved balls into his mouth, and tugged on them a little roughly, waiting for the little pain sound before he let them go. He pulled back then and turned Dex around, grunting "Bend over" so Dex would bend over the bed and stick his taut little porn star ass in the air.

Dex was sweaty from their afternoon, but Kane didn't care. He sat up on his knees and buried his face between Dex's cheeks, probing with his tongue and fondling Dex's cock and balls roughly from the front.

Dex buried his face in the cheap sateen comforter and groaned, but not loud enough for Kane. Kane stood up and ripped back the covers, then started shoving off his underwear and shirt.

"Lay down there," he said gruffly. "On your side."

"On my—"

"Stretch yourself out. Make yourself ready." Kane fished out the little lube tube from the pocket of the jeans at his feet and threw it at Dex.

Dex caught it automatically and then… just complied.

Kane had known he would. Knew now what that little part of Dex was, the part that had been alone for too long, that liked to be told what to do because it made him safe. Kane liked telling him what to do, because that way Kane could *make* him safe, *make* Dex want him, *make* him be there the next morning with kindness in his eyes. The fact that Dex would have been there anyway just made it even better to tell him what to do.

Dex cracked the little tube open and drizzled some lube on his fingers, then reached back and thrust them between his cheeks.

"Show me," Kane muttered roughly, because he really wanted to see. Oh God, yeah. There were Dex's two fingers buried in his own flesh, spreading, stretching, separating….

Kane threw himself on the bed behind Dex and gave his wrist a jerk so his fingers would come out. They did, and Dex made a half-pleasured, half-pained sound, and then Kane was bare against his entrance and pushing in.

It was rough—but then it was supposed to be. Dex let out that first anguished gasp of pleasure/pain as Kane breached him, and Kane took that for a sign. He shoved his bicep under Dex's head and wrapped his arm around so he could clap his hand over Dex's mouth. He didn't want the neighbors to call the police, and this was going to get loud.

"C'mon, baby, scream," he growled as he drove his cock in to the hilt.

Dex's scream rattled, smothered against Kane's palm, and Kane pulled his hips back and thrust again. Dex screamed again, and again, and as Kane pummeled him from behind and restrained him in front, Dex's screams became less about the sex and more about the pain, and that's what Kane wanted.

They hadn't had sex in too long, and they had been in touching distance all that time. God, Kane was close. He wrapped his free arm around Dex's hips, and Dex was enough of a pro to throw his leg backward so Kane could grab his cock. Kane squeezed, and Dex screamed again against his other hand.

"Good," Kane panted, still pistoning his hips. "Don't keep that shit inside. Scream, Dex. C'mon… scream, dammit!"

Dex's next scream was long and low, as much a groan as a scream, but it exorcised all of it—the pain, the hiding, the longing, the bitterness, all of it purged against the sweating insides of Kane's palm.

Kane groaned then, because he was close, and he *needed* Dex to come first so Kane would know he'd be all right. "C'mon… c'mon, David, you're close… let go… let go… I've gotcha…."

Kane was pounding hard, and between Dex's ass clenching down on his shaft and Dex's increasingly frantic screams, he had a good barometer of when Dex was going to come completely apart. It was gonna be… gonna be… oh *God* that was tight, and hard, and suddenly Dex bit down on the flesh of Kane's palm and spasmed almost hard enough to squeeze Kane out of his body (like Kane… *thrust*… was gonna… *shove*… let… *pound*… that happen!) and spilled hot and urgent all over Kane's hand.

The scream that tore out of Dex then felt like it ripped through both their guts, and Kane arched his neck and bit down on Dex's shoulder *hard* as he thrust in one last time and came.

Kane's grip on his body relaxed, and the soft sounds of Dex sobbing filled the room.

"Shh…," Kane whispered in his ear. "Shh… it's okay, Dexter. It's okay. We're gonna be okay."

Dex took one of those deep child's breaths and let it out on more tears. Kane brought up his hand—still covered in come but he didn't really give a crap—and smoothed back Dex's hair, ran his hands over Dex's shoulders, clasped his arms around Dex's chest, and pulled tight, crushingly tight, while Dex fell apart only because Kane was there to hold the pieces together.

Kane stayed awake until the sobbing stopped and Dex had fallen asleep, and then he got up and washed off a little, but he wasn't thorough. He found the thermostat and cranked that motherfucker up to seventy degrees because he was *tired* of being cold. He found his sleep pants and then a takeout menu, because he realized it wasn't even nine-o'clock and they hadn't eaten yet. Chinese food arrived and Kane ate half of it (okay, well, maybe a little more than half, but then Kane tended to eat for bulk anyway) and still Dex stayed on his side, his face turned into his arm, without moving. Kane packed up the food and figured they'd have it for breakfast, and climbed back into bed with the remote. After an hour of television, he was finally ready for sleep, and he turned off the light, then slid one arm under Dex's head and the other around Dex's middle, like it should be, and pulled Dex back until his bare ass was even with Kane's groin.

"Can we take the sleep pants off?" Dex said, his voice muffled by his arm.

Kane used one hand to drag off the side of his sleep pants and then kicked them the rest of the way off. "I thought you were asleep," he said, more than a little surprised, and Dex turned and met him bare chest to bare chest in the soda lamp darkness of the hotel room.

"I was for a while," he said against Kane's lips. "I was asleep for almost ten years. And then this big goober with all these fucking weird animals moved into my house, and I was suddenly awake." Dex wrapped a leg around Kane's hips and pulled him close, and moved his hand up to cup Kane's face. He stroked Kane's cheek, tangled his fingers in Kane's thick hair, which was long enough to curl after the day they'd had, and even stroked Kane's lips with his thumb.

"How's awake treating ya?" Kane asked, and he realized a part of him was apprehensive.

"Better than I deserve," Dex said, and he pushed forward into a kiss.

Kane opened his mouth and allowed Dex in, and let Dex have control this time. Every touch in that darkened room was soft, every brush of lips against skin was tender. When Dex captured Kane's nipple in his mouth and suckled, there was no bite of pain, just the easy stroke of his tongue. The same when Dex moved down to Kane's cock, and his balls, and his… oh geez, Dex knew how to lick down there. He was a little more assertive around Kane's taint, but his tongue, right at Kane's entrance… gentle… gentle… gentle… his fingers sliding around in the moisture before they penetrated… gentle… gentle… gentle… until Kane's back was arching and he was grabbing his thighs and spreading himself out and begging, because sometimes too much gentleness hurt.

"Please," he whispered. "Please. Please."

Dex's thrust inside him was gentle too. Every bit of pressure, every thrust, added another layer of want to Kane's skin, and even Dex's breath against his shoulder, or his neck, or his lips, hurt him with desire.

His air was sobbing in and out of his chest when he said it again. "Please. Please. Please."

Dex sat back, grabbed one of Kane's thighs in one hand and his cock in the other, and started to pound him so quickly, the slap of their flesh filled the room.

This time Kane screamed as he came, and Dex groaned and filled Kane's body, jerking and thrusting uncontrollably, until when he fell forward into Kane's waiting arms, Kane felt his come sliding between his ass cheeks and his thighs, warm and sticky and real.

They panted together in the darkness, Dex on top of him without fear, and Kane was proud because that meant he knew Kane could take it. Kane squeezed him so tight his breath hitched, and then rolled over a little so they could be side by side, skin to skin in the darkness. The unfamiliar bed squeaked beneath them, and Kane reached down and pulled the stiff sheets, blankets, and comforter over their shoulders.

"I love you, David," he whispered then, aware that he could see the outside light reflected in Dex's shiny eyes.

"I love you too, Carlos," Dex whispered back.

"Can we go home?" Kane asked plaintively, shivering in the sheets and the bed that weren't theirs. "I want to be home with you."

Dex closed his eyes, and Kane saw the last few tears trickle through, silver in the shadows. "You are my home," Dex whispered, and Kane kissed the tears away.

"Yeah," he said, "but I can't make the bed suck any less."

Dex laughed then, and kissed him, salty and sloppy, and they didn't care. "Carlos?"

"Yeah?"

"If you wake up in the middle of the night with a hard-on, promise you'll share."

"Don't I always?"

"Yeah. But tonight it's really fuckin' important."

Kane kissed his cheeks and wondered if anyone else looked hard enough to see the freckles that had been there when he was a boy, and hadn't quite been erased by time. "I hear ya, David. I promise."

Dex tucked his face into Kane's chest then and fell asleep for real, and *now* Kane could sleep himself, because it just might be all right.

THEY woke up in the morning to a pounding on the door and Dex's brother's voice shouting, "David! David, are you in there? I've got Mom out here and we're freezing our asses off! Wake up!"

Kane sat up immediately and looked at Dex's face as he struggled with panic. Kane had woken up in the middle of the night—twice—and Dex actually had flakes of white still on his face and his chest from the last time. His hair was standing on end and stiff with it (from the first time), his lips were swollen, and Kane had left hickeys on his neck and jaw from probably every frickin' time. None of it masked the bruising on Dex's cheek from his father's backhand, but still. Normally just looking at him like this would have Kane fucking him again, slowly, on their sides, until climax roared over them like a long languorous wave, but right now?

"Dexter, get your ass in the shower and I'll let 'em in!"

Dex nodded and went to root through his suitcase, but Travis pounded harder on the door and Kane hissed, "I'll throw them in for you—but *now*!"

Dex's bare (stretched, sticky) ass disappeared around the corner, and Kane threw the comforter around the disheveled bed before pulling on his sleep pants commando and grabbing a T-shirt from his open suitcase as he passed.

He threw open the door, stepped back, and pulled his T-shirt on as they walked in, all bundled up and shit because apparently Montana *had* invented that slogan "when hell freezes over."

They came in and Travis shut the door, and Kane lunged for his suitcase for his sweatshirt and those moccasin things Dex had bought him while they were looking for a place to sit.

"You got the two shitty chairs or the bed," Kane said as he pulled the sweatshirt out. The place *reeked* of sex—it overpowered the Chinese food, and that was saying something. "You guys make your decision, I'm gonna get him some clothes."

Kane already knew Dex was the crowned king of *Tetris* packing. Kane could tell his dirty clothes from his clean ones, because the dumb bunny actually folded his underwear, which was all kinds of wrong, but it made his job easy. Jeans, underwear, T-shirt, clean sweatshirt, socks, and moccasins. Took him two minutes while he ignored the two people behind him uncomfortably choosing the chairs.

Kane shoved the clothes on top of the toilet, and Dex poked his face out of the curtain and wiped the water from his eyes. "What are they saying?"

"They're talking about *American Idol*. It's all good."

"Sarcasm isn't your thing!" Dex snapped, and Kane grinned at him just to piss him off. It didn't work. Dex's face softened, and he nodded, and Kane nodded back.

"Take your shower, Dexter. I've got it from here."

"I'll be out in two seconds."

Kane's look heated, and he didn't care. "Take longer than that. You're messy."

He loved watching that color spread across Dex's pale chest to his stomach. Made his morning. Dex dragged the shower curtain shut, and Kane chuckled softly to himself as he walked into the room and threw himself facedown on top of the bed before rolling to his side and propping his head up on his hand.

"So, what can I do ya for? I'd offer you some Chinese food, but he didn't eat last night, and he's got dibs." Yeah, it was cruel. He knew it. Reminding a woman who loved with stew that she'd kicked her kid out without feeding him? Salt in the goddamned wound. He was perfectly capable of being a real asshole sometimes. Not often—he certainly didn't try to flaunt that side to Dex—but sometimes. When it really fucking mattered.

And it worked. She made a hurt sound and looked guiltily to the leftovers on the table. Then she swallowed, reached into her purse, and pulled out a familiar small box and an unfamiliar card wrapped in a gold foil envelope. "You boys left so quickly you forgot these," she said shakily, and Kane dropped the casual pose and grabbed.

"Fuck," he swore, snatching the box back like she might have contaminated it. "I would have been fucking pissed if we'd left that there." Jesus. Dex's present. It must have been taken downstairs when the kids had invaded their room. And Dex's present to him. He looked at the gold foil envelope and pushed his finger along the edge, feeling a moment of wonder. As he'd gotten older, he'd realized that sometimes the best presents really *were* the ones without boxes. He glared up at Mrs. Worral for a second, really hating that he was going to have to do this. "Thank you," he said stiffly. "It would have sucked to drive back to get these."

"We would have sent them," she said hesitantly, and Kane squinted at her.

"And that would have sucked less?" He got up and tucked both boxes in Dex's luggage, because it was neater, and then turned around to them. "Is that all? Because if there's a way we could manage to not rip his heart out again, I'm all for you guys getting the fuck out of here." God, he really wished he was home. If he was home, he could order them out of the house. His and Dex's house. Dex said it was his too.

"That's no way to talk to my mother," Travis barked, and Kane looked at him dispassionately.

"She lost any respect I had for her last night. So did you, dickweed. So, can I ask again, what's your agenda here?"

Travis looked at his mother for a moment, and to Kane's surprise, he looked a little bit shamed. "Last night was not my idea," he said quietly. "Dad told me I needed to be there in case things went wrong. I didn't know… I had no idea how bad that was going to get."

"But we couldn't let them… just…."

"And Henry and Mal are okay?" Travis snapped, shocking the hell out of Kane.

"You can't blame that on us!" Kane said, just to make sure that wasn't going to happen. "Whatever is happening there was going on *way* before we showed up!"

"*Nothing* is happening there!" Mrs. Worral was so upset she actually stood up, wringing her hands around the strap of her brown leather purse. "*Nothing.* That's you people making them dirty!"

"Yeah," Kane muttered, wanting Dex's little house so badly his stomach cramped with it. "And David wasn't grieving when he ran all the way to Sacramento to get the hell away from you people. God. You know, he warned me. He said that we were either going to be hiding the whole time, or it was going to get ugly. I lived through the hiding and it sucked. Now I'm living through the ugly and it sucks. But you know what? It's gonna be fucking worth it just to get back to our house and know we're not going to have to come to your balls-freezing state ever fucking again, and you idiots aren't ever going to be able to hurt him like you been doing. Do you have *anything* good to say to him, or do I get to kick you out before he gets out of the shower?"

"You'd like that, wouldn't you?" Mrs. Worral snapped. "Dragging my son back to your nasty little porn factory—"

"Mom, he's like, what? Five years younger than David?"

"Eight," Kane said, "but who's counting. And we don't get *dragged* into porn—we all got a reason."

"What's yours?" Travis asked him frankly, and Kane shrugged.

"I got tired of being used for my body by girls, figured I'd be able use my body on my own terms."

"And David?" Travis demanded, and Kane's whole posture softened.

"Your brother…." He swallowed. "Your brother… you know, my niece got diagnosed with cancer, right? And that's a lot of doctor's bills. So I tell my sister not to worry, I got the porn gig and I can pay for all of it. My sister says that's great—but I gotta move out. The only person I tell—and I mean the *only* person I tell—is your brother. And in an hour, he's got me scheduled in the highest-paying gigs, and I've got a real estate broker. That first time? I crashed on your brother's couch for a month while I got my shit together. And this time my sister moves outta her husband's house, but it's the same deal, right? I gotta go. Only this time…." Kane shook his head and looked past Travis's shoulder to three months earlier. Had he known this the first night, when Dex had needed the comfort? Had he known it the second night, when they'd both needed someone to cling to? Had he known it before he'd even asked? "This time, I wasn't gonna sleep on the couch. And once I didn't sleep on the couch for the first time, I wasn't ever goin' away."

"Oh God," Dex's mom moaned like this was horrible, but Travis didn't.

He looked at his mom and then back to the bathroom. The shower turned off in the silence, and it was apparent that Travis had only a minute to make up his mind.

"Mom, remember when he saved Sean's life?"

His mother didn't answer—she'd dropped clunkily into the cheap chair again, so Travis explained.

"So I was like, thirteen, right? Which meant David was eleven and Sean was like, what? Three? Anyway, we were going on a hike with Mom, and Debbie was being a demanding little shit, because that's just what she was like as a kid, and suddenly we look up and we don't see either of 'em. No Davy, no Sean, and then we see them catching up, and Davy's got Sean on his back and Sean is wet and muddy and bawling. 'Cause the thing was, about a hundred yards back, Sean had fallen into the creek, and Davy, he was always checking up on us. We used to joke, you know? If we went on a walk, he walked twice as far, 'cause he'd always go back and check on the youngest and come back up and check on the oldest, and this time—this time it saved Sean's life. And he was like that his whole life! Dex Williams was one wild motherfucker, but not with David there. David made sure he was sober and made sure he was throwing the right plays and checking up on his homework—"

Dex walked out right then, fully dressed and still drying his hair, and stopped, just stopped while his older brother spoke. He looked up and Travis nodded to him and just kept on talking.

"So that thing he did for you, when you needed help, that's just my little brother. So you see, Mom may not see David in your guy, but I still see my little brother—there's not a damned thing that's changed."

"Travis—" Marlene Worral looked scandalized, but Kane figured him and Dex's mom had most likely had their last conversation, so he ignored her.

"Sorry, Mom. You may be done with him, but I've got a house too." Travis nodded at Dex again. "You're welcome to come to our house for Christmas, Davy."

Kane's chest started to work, because he couldn't say no to that, but God, oh-my-fucking-God did Kane want to go *home*. Dex came up alongside him and squeezed his hand right there in front of his brother.

"That's… that's really nice of you, Trav," he said, and Kane's whole body went liquid in the pause, because he heard the next word before Dex even said it. "But I think we've put Kane through enough this year. Maybe we'll come back in the summer sometime, okay?"

Travis nodded and grimaced, and Kane suddenly didn't hate him as the older-brother-master-of-the-universe that he'd seen this whole time.

"Yeah, Davy. Cathy said you'd say that. She's real smart, Cathy, but she doesn't say much. She had you two figured the minute you walked through the door. Dad found out, and I wasn't surprised. I didn't think they'd kick you out." Travis shook his head. "If I'd known they'd kick you out, I would have screened that fucking call."

"Travis—"

"Go ahead and tell Dad," Travis snarled to his mother. "You tell him that. You have him kick me out and see how much longer he's got a farm."

"Trav—" Dex said softly, and Travis shook his head.

"Yeah, I know." To his mother he said softly, "Mom, here's the keys. Go warm the car up. We'll start home. You can pretend you didn't see this next part, okay?"

But Marlene didn't leave, and she did see Travis haul Dex into a hug that Dex returned. "Call me anytime," Travis whispered, and Dex hugged him tighter.

"Backatcha," he said. "Maybe talk to Kane if I'm not there."

Travis backed away and reached out his hand. Kane took it. "Looking forward to it. C'mon, Mom."

And Travis turned back around and Marlene followed. Neither of them had even taken off their coat. Travis opened the door, and Mrs. Worral paused for a moment.

"I thought...," she said softly. "I thought we could talk you into coming back alone. I'm so foolish. I should have seen you were already your own family. Bye, David."

"Bye, Mom."

The door closed then, softly, and Kane sank to the bed in relief. "Thank God. I'm sayin', if one more person goes outside in this fuckin' country without giving me fur undershorts, my source of income is gonna shrivel up and fuckin' *die!*"

Dex sank down on the bed, sniffly but seemingly okay. He wrapped his arms around Kane's waist and buried his face in his shoulder. "That would be a real shame," he said against Kane's shoulder. "I'm sort of attached to the big guys. They're awesome at motivation."

Kane laughed. "Well, maybe you eat some food—"

"Oh hell no!" Dex looked at the aging Chinese food, offended. "There has *got* to be an omelet place somewhere nearby."

Kane nodded. "That's a deal, Dexter."

"Yeah, well, we'll look for tickets outta this dump while we're at it. We need to charge my cell phone, though, because tomorrow's Christmas Eve, and I need to make sure your present's on schedule."

Dex had sort of tipped his head back, so even though he was usually a few inches taller than Kane, Kane got to look at him protectively. His hair was still damp, so Kane amused himself, running his fingers through the part that hung over his forehead, waiting for it to dry. "I thought my present was in that envelope your mom brought."

Dex shook his head and smiled a little, looking so content there on his shoulder that Kane eased them back so it was like they were in bed again.

"No," Dex said, curling up on his side. For the first time since they'd gone to bed in the deep a.m., Kane looked at the clock and realized it was only four hours since they'd closed their eyes.

"If that's not my present, what is it?"

"It's just an explanation of why your present is your present," Dex said sleepily. "It's why I didn't freak out when we left it at my folks'."

Kane grunted. "Well, I shoulda freaked out—your present *was* your present, and I just left it there."

"Yeah, well, you were looking after me. I forgive you."

His voice was getting muffled with sleep, and Kane rolled over quickly and gave him a quick kiss on the forehead before sitting up. "And I forgive you for dragging me out to this icehole and exposing me to family drama. How 'bout you take a nap and *I'll* take a shower."

Dex chuckled sleepily. "You smell like lots and lots of sex, Carlos. You can wash it off, but it can't change the fact we had it."

Kane pulled him close and spoke softly to the whorls of Dex's ear. "Yeah, well, who wants to change that?" he whispered and then slid out from under Dex's body, which was already soggy with sleep. He dragged the comforter over Dex as he lay there, because it was fucking Montana and he could have set the temperature at ninety, the hotel room would still be chilly, and then went to take his shower.

THE WARS AT HOME

Dex

IN THE end it took them two days, four planes, a bus ride from Reno, and everything but a canoe to get the hell home. They walked into their own house on Christmas Eve, dropped their luggage, kicked a groggy (and naked) Ethan to the couch, hit the shower, and passed out for the next twelve hours.

They were surprisingly happy.

Of course they were happy to be sleeping in their own bed—that was a given. And they were happy to wake up together on Christmas Day—that was actually the best part. But the best part *before* that had been that the nightmare of a trip, the multiple layovers, the time off the ground and in the plane, and even in that lonely, miserable, cold bus from Reno to Sacramento and the shuttle ride home, was accomplished together.

They said very little, played a lot of games on their phones, and spent a lot of time sleeping with their heads on each other's shoulders or, at least until security in Dallas made them stop, working out with their luggage. (Admittedly they'd been a little punch-drunk then—throwing the big suitcase back and forth at each other at the luggage check had probably not been the wisest choice in the world.)

Waking up on Christmas morning *in their own house* was the best gift *ever.* Judging from Kane's erection prodding Dex in the back, Kane thought so too.

"Merry Christmas," Dex said softly, and Kane nuzzled his ear.

"You gonna tell me?" Kane said wickedly, and Dex laughed to himself. It had been a tough secret to keep, it really had, especially when they'd been bored shitless in the middle of the Helena airport and both their cell phones had been charging. But the next five minutes were going to make it all worth it.

"Go check on the scaly things. I'll make coffee," he said and snickered to himself as Kane muttered "Killjoy!" and slid out of bed and into his moccasins. He wasn't too upset, though, Dex could tell. He wanted to see the scaly guys too.

"Oh my God! Dex, get in here, somebody fucked up your guest room!"

Dex was already halfway out of bed, which was good, because he was crippled with giggles as he put on his moccasins and padded in his boxers and a T-shirt to watch Kane unwrap his present.

"Ohmigod, *David!*" Kane was bouncing from enclosure to enclosure, checking on the newly rebuilt floor-to-ceiling heated iguana and snake cages that Dex had installed on the brand-new porch attached to the guest room. "Ohmigod. You can get to them from the outside too!" he said, getting between the two cages and seeing the door. "You built a *porch*! In *six days!*"

"I didn't build shit!" Dex laughed.

Ethan came wandering in (thank God wearing sweats), and he laughed at that too. "You can say that again. No, Dex hired the whole frickin' world to come in as soon as you left. Me, Tommy, Chase, Donnie, Kevin—we had to move all the guys into the house proper and keep 'em warm, and then move them back when we were sure it was all set. We were real fuckin' lucky, Dex. We got rain comin' in *tomorrow*, and they finished up yesterday morning!"

Dex shuddered. God, he'd been worried about that. He even had a contingency plan with Tommy that involved moving everybody to Tommy's place for a month while they finished, but he was so glad they hadn't had to use it.

"Yeah, well, I owe you," he said softly, and Ethan rolled his eyes.

"Bullshit. We found the presents in the garage, you know, when Chase came and got the stuff he bought for Tommy? There they were, everybody's name on them, like you were fuckin' Santa and we were the elves."

Dex grinned. “You guys like your shit?” Yeah, he’d bought presents for everybody—something small for the guys he didn’t know really well, a couple of good things for the guys he loved like brothers. He sent everybody else their stuff in the mail, but Ethan, Tommy, Chase, Donnie, Kevin, and Kelsey all had presents waiting in the garage this year. Usually when he went to his parents’, he left gifts under the tree in his house and left someone (usually John) his key, but since there was going to be all the construction, he’d thought the tree would get in the way.

The night before, as he and Kane had dragged themselves in like zombies, he’d noticed that Ethan, faced with the prospect of having Christmas alone this year, had set up a small tree on his coffee table.

“Don’t know,” Ethan said guilelessly. “Haven’t opened my shit yet.” He smiled, and it was a little self-conscious. “I figured I needed something to do on Christmas Day since dinner at Tommy’s isn’t until later.”

Dex was going to say something, try to make that aching hole less big and painful, but at that moment, Kane turned around from the newly remodeled porch with eyes so big and bright that they really were like a little kid’s.

“For *me*? Dex, you did this for *me*? This is… this is *permanent.* You did this thing to your house—”

“Our house,” Dex said, swallowing. “See, this way it’s our house. ’Cause I don’t want to live here if you’re not here. I mean, I know it hasn’t been that long, but, see, that’s what it says in the card. That maybe when Lola moves out, you could maybe sell your place and—”

Kane’s hurtling body pinned him to the wall, and he was lost in a hug so vast and powerful it stopped his breath. “Our house. It *is* our house!”

Dex nodded and palmed the back of Kane’s head, losing himself in that clean, curly black hair. “And in the summer we can dig a turtle pond and put a brick wall around it, and they can live out there,” he said softly, wanting Kane to approve—to *love* this plan. They were Kane’s guys, so now they were Dex’s. It was good, right?

"Our house," Kane said, his voice wobbly. "David Dexter Calvin… this is like… like the *best* thing. *Best* Christmas present ever. Best." He smiled, and it was the watery kind. "Please tell me this isn't just because I almost froze my balls off in Montana."

Dex shook his head. "It's because you got on the plane."

Kane nodded. "This makes it worth it. I'll even go visit your big bossy-assed brother for this. I can't even believe you did this for me."

Honesty. Complete honesty. "If you think it was for you, you're mental." Dex lowered his head then and kissed him, wondering how this had happened, that he'd remade his home just to make this man a part of it. He didn't know—hadn't known when he'd made the plan and gotten Tommy and Chase and Ethan to be a part of it—and he still didn't know, but Kane tasted wonderful, and his happiness fed Dex in ways Dex had forgotten he could be filled.

There was a sound next to them, and Dex looked up at his audience and saw Ethan trying to edge his way out of the room. Dex bumped noses with Kane, and they both looked up at Ethan, who was getting all shy, and that wasn't a good look for him. They made eye contact and both of them reached out and grabbed his shirt and dragged him into the hug.

He snuggled like a kitten. Just snuggled, his head on Kane's shoulder, his arm around Dex's waist, and they stayed there and petted him for a while. They had pets to spare—why the hell not? When the group hug was over, Kane said, "Oh, God! Dex! Lemme get your present, 'kay?"

Kane went running off, and Dex and Ethan went into the kitchen for coffee. Dex pulled out the pancake mix and fixings and was pleased to see there was milk and juice and some fruit in the fridge—Ethan had shopped, which was nice.

"Hey, Ethan?" he said as he cracked an egg into a bowl.

"Yeah?" Ethan was cradling a cup of coffee while leaning up against the island where Dex and Kane usually ate.

"You still living in that crappy apartment?" Dex had found it for him after he'd been kicked out of the house for the porn thing. He'd been living there for around six weeks, and Dex couldn't help thinking about that little Christmas tree.

"Yeah." The syllable was flat and almost unfriendly.

"If we move the turtles into our room, the lizards and baby frogs and shit into the living room, all that would be left for that room is the crickets and mice. That porch is heated, so the room might get a little warm, but it's winter. You… you wouldn't want to sleep in our spare room instead of the crappy apartment, would you?"

Ethan's hug over his back was completely platonic and full of so much gratitude that Dex felt bad for not asking him sooner. Well, the room had been full, after all.

"You wouldn't mind?" Ethan said wistfully, his head resting between Dex's shoulder blades, and Dex shrugged. Very carefully he set down the egg he'd been about to crack before Ethan had assaulted him with sheer stinking joy.

"We'll have to ask Kane. Maybe when Lola moves, you can move into Kane's house for cheap. It's something to think about."

"Oh God. That would rock." Ethan wiped his face against the back of Dex's T-shirt. It was wet. "I'm telling ya, Dex, I'm just not made to be alone. I feel bad, 'cause you and Kane have this thing going…. I mean… it's special, and it's you two, but… God. I just miss my family so bad."

Dex turned around and wrapped arms around Ethan's shoulders. He never would have been able to put that into words, he thought. Tommy? Maybe. Chase? He *literally* would have died before saying something like that. Kane? Yes. Kane wouldn't know how to hide that.

But Ethan? "You're going to be fine," Dex said softly.

Kane came into the room, the little present box in his hand, and he walked up and started rubbing Ethan's back while Ethan stopped trembling.

"You're going to be just fine. We can be your family 'til you find your own, 'kay?"

"Yeah," Kane said, "but only if you let him go. Dammit, Ethan—he's fixing the chow!"

"Evan," Ethan said, backing up and standing shoulder to shoulder with Kane. "Just, you know, so someone knows."

Kane rested his head on Ethan's shoulder. "I'm Carlos, Evan. This here's David. Dexter, why in the fuck aren't you making my pancakes?"

Dex stuck his tongue out. "Fine." He turned around and started working. "Ethan's moving into our spare bedroom. You need to go get the bed out and set it up with him, okay?"

"What happened to *our* house?" Kane asked, but he didn't sound mad.

"Kane, can Ethan move into our house?"

"Yeah, Dex, I got no problem with that. As long as he doesn't mind us having sex in the next room."

Dex had not been sure he could still blush. Now he knew he could. "Oh God. Thanks a lot, you psycho. Now go move the bed so I can finish breakfast."

They got the terrariums shifted before the pancakes were done, and after breakfast (and before the rest of the work) they opened presents.

Ethan got clothes and a gold chain (because he wore that sort of thing) and tickets to a play in San Francisco, which made his eyes widen. "How'd you know?" he asked, breathless, looking inside the little box.

"That you like musicals?" Kane asked, disgusted. "You're the only guy I know who sings *Stop the World—I Want to Get Off* under his breath."

"Yeah," Dex said, smirking, "but with him we could have taken that as a come-on!" Ethan's on-camera orgasms were legendary—he was the Energizer Bunny of come.

"The world does stop when I come!" Ethan said with a wink, but he was looking pretty damned pleased.

And then it was Dex's turn, and the small box was jewelry, which he expected, but… but not.

"I thought it would be tags," he confessed, floundering for words. There were two of them, one for him, one for Kane, and they weren't tags or anything playful like that. "These are serious."

Rings. Two titanium rings with rounded brushed-black surfaces and a rainbow titanium beveled strip right down the center. Dex pulled out one of the rings and looked at the inside for engraving. Some of his awe disappeared. The inside of the ring said "Property of: Dex." The other one said "Property of: Kane," of course, and he looked at Kane again, wanting so very badly to put his on.

"These are serious," he said again. "These are real."

"And wrecking your house wasn't?"

Dex's throat got tight. "Yeah. Yeah. But that's just my house. This is my…." He trailed off, because Ethan was looking at him seriously, and Dex grabbed Kane's hand and shoved the ring on. "This is my heart, asshole. I'm not gonna say you're too young, and I'm not gonna tell you we've only been doing this for a couple of months, and I'm not gonna ask you if you're sure. I'm gonna shove this thing on your finger and make you wear it, because you don't give a guy a thing like this and take it back."

Kane took the other one from the box, and almost reverently took the class ring off Dex's ring finger. Dex blinked. The inside of the ring said "Dexter Williams, Class of '02." Kane had seen it before. It was the only piece of jewelry Dex wore.

"This is my place now," Kane said and put the ring on, looking really serious indeed. "No one else is here."

Dex examined it soberly, and Kane grinned at him suddenly. "Don't be so serious, Dexter. I'll think you don't like my gift!"

"I love your gift, Carlos." His voice was shaky and tense—and fervent. "But I think it's going to make shit complicated, and you don't do complicated."

Kane's grin was positively evil. "Bring it the fuck on."

FISCALLY Kane hadn't been able to quit porn. Dex had spent a week sorting his tangled finances and thinking that his strategy of taking out just enough money in cash and only spending that much had stood him in pretty good stead. If his sister hadn't been siphoning money out of his account like a delinquent siphoned gasoline, he would have been able to sell his house and walk away.

Hell—even if he couldn't sell his house, Dex could support him through school and he could still walk away. But he couldn't walk away and support Fabiola, and even if Dex thought Fabiola might want to learn how to support herself, he knew that jerking the rug out from under *her* meant jerking the rug out from under the baby, and that was never going to happen. Dex couldn't even blame Kane for not letting it happen. But the fact was, Kane had started that ball rolling by making porn star cash. He couldn't keep supporting them making night clerk cash, and Dex couldn't support them either—not and keep his house, which was their home.

So what porn started, let no commitment taketh away—and Dex was pretty sure he could live with that. He knew the business. He knew the difference between sex and love—hell, he'd *lived* the difference between sex and love for most of his life.

But he knew for damned sure it wasn't going to be easy.

It was especially not easy when he went the day after New Year's Day to set the schedule and call everyone to remind them that the next day, a Tuesday, was business as usual.

He'd made the schedule, but he'd been working on fumes, and somehow (denial?) his brain had not made the connection about putting Kane on the schedule and shooting him while he worked. He sat at the little desk next to Kelsey's, where he kept his computer and did all of his office things, and groaned.

Kelsey, slightly rounder than she had been in early November but not quite pregnant looking, turned around and said, "What?"

He grimaced, feeling embarrassed, his eyes on the schedule. He knew this was going to happen. He had a handle on this, right? *Right?*

"Nothing," he muttered, twisting the ring on his hand. It was familiar to have one there, but every time he looked at the rainbow winking from the middle, he felt a little warmer than he used to.

But Kelsey noticed what he was doing, and her eyes got wide.

"Nice ring!" she said and looked at him sideways.

He grinned for a moment and then looked back at his computer, like looking at the schedule was going to *not* show Kane scheduled to do a tag team with two guys Dex didn't know that well while Dex helped man the camera.

"Thanks," he said, and still, the awkwardness of the schedule couldn't kill his pride. It was the first time someone had noticed. Ethan hadn't said a word to *anybody*, and Chase and Tommy had gotten all of the attention over the holidays (and rightly so) because they'd told Chase's girlfriend that they were going to take the baby if she still wanted to give it up. Dex had gotten them in touch with a lawyer—a *really good* lawyer who would get them as iron-clad a custody agreement as possible—and he and Kane had been content to sit in the background at Christmas dinner at Tommy's. The same for New Year's Eve, which had been at their place this year. Everyone had played Monopoly and Scrabble and drunk beer until the ball dropped, and then crashed on the couch, the loveseat, or with Ethan in the guest bedroom or even on the floor until the next day. (Dex told Kane as they were going to bed that night that it would be just a peachy night for the damned snake to get out, but the new enclosure did its job, and Tomas stayed happily ensconced in his big snake palace without terrorizing all the porn stars in the morning.)

And no one had noticed the ring.

Until now, when he recognized that he *wanted* someone to notice. Hell, he was *dying* for someone to notice, because that ring differentiated him from the two other guys who were going to have sex with Kane in a week, who didn't have a ring and would never get one.

"Does the ring *mean* anything, Dex?" Kelsey wheedled, and Dex's grin erupted full force. He pulled the ring off and let her see it.

When he heard her gasp, he actually closed his eyes, bit his bottom lip, and did a little happy dance in his seat.

"Kane? *Kane?* Oh my God. Ohmygod! Omigodomigodomigod! *Dex!* Really?"

Dex looked at her sideways, still smiling like any besotted blushing bride—or groom. "We haven't had papers drawn up or anything," he apologized, but he took the ring back from her as she stared at him in bemusement.

"But you have rings?"

"Yeah. And I remodeled the house for his animals."

Kelsey clapped her hand over her mouth. "Dex, that's huge! Have you told anyone?"

Dex shook his head, looked at the schedule, and sighed. "No," he said, and she backed her ergonomically perfect wheeled office chair up and looked over his shoulder.

"Oh, hells. Dex, have you told *John*?" she asked gently, and Dex shook his head again.

"He knows we've been, uhm, yeah, that, but Kelsey, it was like… it wasn't anything, right? And then it was *everything.* And we didn't know how you make an announcement about that. Because when you go from it's not anything to it's *everything,* you know that it's the *real thing.*"

Kelsey put a hand on his shoulder and squeezed. "Well, you need to tell John that it's the real thing, hon. Otherwise you're going to have to shoot his porn and edit his porn and market his porn, and no one's going to offer to step in and do it for you."

Dex sighed and dropped his elbows to his knees, all the better to prop his chin in his hands. "Was it that obvious?"

"That you were obsessing about how to deal with him in a scene you had to film? Only a little."

"Yeah, well, I need to pull my shit together about it. He's got obligations, you know? I'll be out of business school in a semester—he's just starting. Until I'm making enough money to pay all his bills…."

Kelsey looked at him as he trailed off at the obvious conclusion.

"What?" he asked seriously, and she shrugged.

"You're both the nicest guys in the world," she said with a little laugh. "I mean… *really* good guys. You'll make it work. God." She dropped her hand self-consciously to her stomach. "If you can put up with that goofball, I can put up with this one, can't I?"

Dex suddenly found her problems much more interesting than his own. "What are you going to do, sweetheart?"

She smiled. "Well, I'm going to keep her, and that should make you happy!"

"It's a her?"

"Yeah. It's a her. But I'm going to stay here. Here in my home. I talked to my mom about it when I went out for Christmas, but… well… I like *Johnnies.* So far I can't see a reason to go."

Dex looked at her sideways. "Have we fired Scott yet?" he asked, thinking he needed to talk to John *again* about that. He'd said something right before he left, about maybe asking Scott if he could find another house—another *business* house—and John said he'd look into it. But then, John's brain hadn't been working too clear in the past few months, and Dex wasn't sure how likely that was to happen.

Kelsey looked down. "No," she said lowly. "But he hasn't harassed me either."

Dex shook his head. "Kelsey, until that guy has been fired from here, I'd still make plans to move."

Kelsey shook her head. "Dex, this place has the best health insurance in the *county.* Hell, maybe even the *state.* And it's not like nobody here is on my side."

He still wasn't happy about it, and she gave his shoulder a shove. "Buck up, little camper!" she said happily. "You've got a *ring*!"

Dex looked at it just sitting on his finger, announcing that he didn't have to be asleep or lost anymore, and that someone was out there who was going to keep him safe.

"It's a pretty cool ring," he said, and she laughed, because yes. Yes it was.

THE three days without sex were rough but sort of good too. Dex thought he'd spend them helping Kane do his prereading for his classes. Kane was appalled that there was such a thing. When Dex told him that college was like that, Kane had a semiserious argument about not going, and then Dex pointed out that the science department probably had lots of the critter things to take care of, and Kane was sold.

"If they lose me in the first day, though," Kane warned, "I'm gone."

Dex shook his head. "If they lose you in the first day, you start bringing a tape recorder to class, and then we listen to it together. Now, we're reading this chapter"—they'd prebought the textbooks—"and we'll see how it goes."

It went slowly. Dex found hidden reservoirs of patience that first night as he listened to Kane sound out each word on its lonesome. By the time they'd finished a page of reading, Kane had forgotten what they were reading about, and Dex realized that he really was in over his head.

The next day he dragged Kane down to the student services department and made him take a reading assessment test. He was not surprised when Kane scored somewhere between a fourth- and a sixth-grade reading level on it. Dex was there when the counselor sat down with Kane and explained the results of the test, and Kane looked like he was going to cry.

"See!" he said, shoving the test results in front of him in a loud scatter.

Mrs. Hendrickson, a plump, comfortable woman with a loose bun of gray-blonde hair and a naturally smiling face, jumped a little, but she didn't look surprised.

"See! I told you this was a bad idea! I *told* you I was too stupid for this! You got me all excited about… about… *fuck!* I can't even say those words!" Kane stood up and would have stormed out, but Dex beat him to the door.

"Get the fuck outta my way!" Kane looked like he really might have decked him too, and then Dex would have been in trouble, because Kane's body mass was way bigger. Dex couldn't back down, though. He put his hands on Kane's neck and pulled him close, touching foreheads with him, and waited until Kane's breathing slowed down enough that Dex knew he'd listen.

"You've got a scene in two weeks," he said and watched Kane's eyes widen at the change of subject.

"Yeah. So?"

"So I don't wanna watch you fuck other guys. I will. And you will. Because you've got responsibilities and that's just who you are. But how often do you want to do that, Kane? Tell me. Give me a number. 'Cause… 'cause…." Dex shook his head. "I don't want to count," he whispered. "Not with you."

Kane closed his eyes. "But… Dexter, the only thing that got me here was the animals. How'm I going to study the animals when I can barely read?"

Dex nodded his head like he had an answer to that. "We're gonna go ask the nice lady with the test results, okay?" he said, and he prayed too. *God, let Kane find a way out of porn.* They'd only just found each other—it would be nice if that could last.

Turned out, they had special reading classes that could help Kane catch up in a year. Turned out, they had biology classes that didn't have a lot of reading. They wouldn't transfer to the bigger colleges as science, per se, but they'd give Kane some elective credits, and they'd keep him interested.

It turned out, there was a way.

The day was exhausting, though, and after they got home and made dinner and showered, all Kane wanted to do was climb into bed and watch television. He curled over on his side, not even interested in holding Dex or anything. They both turned out the lights, and when the darkness was over them, they were separated on the bed, when this whole thing had started because Kane didn't want any space between them at all.

Dex gathered up his courage and rolled over to press his chest against Kane's back. "What's wrong?" he asked to the unhealthy silence.

"I'm sorry I'm so stupid," Kane muttered. "I… I gave you that ring, but you can give it back if you want."

Dex's stomach went cold. "Why in the holy fuck would I want to do that?" He sat up in bed and turned on the light and grabbed his pillow and *whumped* it with as much force as he possibly could across Kane's stupid fat head.

"Hey!" Kane sat up. "Dexter, what in the fuck?"

"That's my ring!" Dex snapped, his voice treading the same thin thread that Kane's had earlier in the day. Logically he knew what was going on. He knew why Kane would feel this way, why he would say something like this. Logically it all made sense. But Dex couldn't think with his head right now. Not about this. Not about *Kane.*

"But look at you, Dex! You're almost done—you can do anything you want and—"

Whump! "And you… you come deal with my shit and you take care of me and hold me together through my stupid bullshit family shit and now you want to *leave me*?" *Whump!*

Kane rolled up into a little ball, and Dex smacked him a couple of more times on the head.

"Fuck you! Fuck you, and fuck *that!*" Dex was standing up in bed shouting at him, not even sure how that had happened. He floundered for a moment, looking for words, and bounced on his mattress trying to find them.

Kane looked up at him from under his arms, his brow puckered in an uncharacteristic show of concern. Suddenly Kane's expression lightened, and he smiled faintly. "Having fun up there, Dexter?"

Dex squashed his smile mostly flat. "Not so's you'd notice. My stupid boyfriend just said something so totally boneheaded it makes me want to kick him!" Dex threw out his foot, trying to get Kane in the chest, and Kane grabbed his ankle and gave it a yank. It was a good thing the damned bed was so big, because Dex fell on his ass on top of it and not on his back on the floor, and Kane rolled over on top of him, his lower lip thrust out, his thought-pucker still there.

"You realize you've called me stupid about six times," he said.

Dex scowled up at him, realizing the expression was as uncharacteristic on his face as thoughtfulness was on Kane's. "Well, until just this fucking minute, I'd never heard you say anything quite that dumb." Christ, his eyes were watering. "Fucking idiot. You gave me a fucking ring and you want to take it back, like, what? Two weeks later? I hate you! You fucking gave me hope!" He pounded weakly on Kane's chest, and Kane captured his fist in a wide-palmed, blunt-fingered hand.

"I'm sorry, Dexter," Kane said softly. "I didn't mean to hurt your feelings."

Dex's anger and panic leaked out of him. "Well, you did. If I want to give the ring back, I'll give it back. You want it back, you ask for it back. You ever say anything that chickenshit to me again, I'll beat you for fucking real."

Kane chuckled then, still looking weary and as old as Dex had ever seen him. "You'd like to think so, but you haven't been to the gym in weeks!"

"Went this morning with you, asshole!"

Kane grinned then and looked younger. "Yeah, well, when you're as old and wise as I am, sometimes you get senile—mmmm…."

Dex raised his head and made him stop talking. Kane wasn't stupid, but sometimes talking wasn't the smartest use of his mouth either.

Kane

KANE looked at the two guys in the room, their hands down their pants, their eyes closed. They were probably dreaming of the girls in the titty mags, and Kane wondered when he'd stopped being one of those guys.

When had he stopped thinking about girls when he did this? Had it been when he'd moved in with Dex? No, probably before that. After his first few months, when he'd first started hooking up with *Johnnies* guys after hours—maybe *that* was when he'd started to think about a man's mouth on his cock instead of a woman's.

But whenever he'd started to think about the world different like that, right now, everything in his brain was centered on Dex.

This was Kane's third shoot since they hooked up. For the first one, he'd been *thrilled* to get on the set and start fucking. He'd gotten used to sex every night with Dex, and being deprived for three days had made him ready to fuck fire hydrants, couch arms, and small animals. (Well, maybe not small animals, but he had been rubbing up against the countertop in a suspicious way the night before.) For that shoot, all he had to do was to get in the room, think about Dex, and he'd been good to go.

For the second shoot, he'd had to do something wonky in his head. When all of the guys had been talking and fluffing and bandying about sexy talk, Kane had been in the corner, eyes closed, remembering the way Dex had looked that morning, fast asleep.

He'd wanted *so* badly to wake him up by kissing down his spine. Dex had that long body: when he arched his back, it looked like poetry. That thought had sustained Kane through the shoot. He'd been doing his thing on the set, following the basic directions the cameraman gave before the shoot so that they knew where he was going and could follow him without getting in his way or caught by the mirrors. In his head, he pretended he'd awakened Dex in the early morning and they were doing poetry.

But now Dex was in the room, and while the rest of the world might just see Dex, that's not what Kane was seeing. What Kane was seeing was David Calvin Worral, whose jaw was held too tight and whose eyes were for once looking closer to thirty than twenty, and who kept twisting the ring on his finger nervously, like he was afraid someone was going to take it.

Oh fuck. His ring.

He'd been about to reach his hands down his pants and start massaging himself through his underwear, but he jerked his hand out like his cock was on fire and he didn't want to get burned.

Quietly, when Dex was all alone checking out his handheld camera, Kane walked up to him and thrust the ring into his hand. "Hey, Dexter," he said, trying to be all cool and shit, "do me a favor and hold this for me, will you?"

Dex looked at the ring in his hand dumbly and swallowed. "When do you want it back?"

"After I shower," Kane said matter-of-factly. "The real shower. The one by myself."

Dex nodded and then leaned in close enough for Kane to smell his sweat and realize that he had stains under his arms from the effort of keeping himself together. "Carlos?" he said, his voice uncertain. He tried a smile and couldn't quite make it go.

"Yeah?" *God. Say anything, Dex. Just let me know we'll be okay when this is over.*

"It's okay if you think of me."

Kane's grin was all relief. "Oh thank God," he said, totally serious. "I feel *so* much less skeezy now!"

Dex laughed then, and Kane wanted to kiss him, but not here. Not on the set. He found suddenly that he didn't *ever* want to kiss him on set again.

"You going to be okay?" Dex asked, and Kane nodded, suddenly feeling like he could do this.

"Just give me the ring back at the end," he said cockily. Yeah. He could do this.

HIS eyes were closed a lot. He'd open his eyes and he'd see this guy he'd had lunch with a couple of times, just to get to know him, and then another guy he and Dex had taken out dancing on the same principle, and if there hadn't been something going on in his pleasure spots, his woody would have died a sad and shriveled death. So when the camera wasn't on him, he closed his eyes and thought of Dex, imagined it was Dex's lips touching his skin, Dex's hand gripping his cock tight. At the end, after the bottom (Nick) had come and the other top (Bobby) had come all over Nick's face, Kane kept his eyes closed and just kept fucking away, imagining the noises Dex made beneath him, but he knew. He knew it was someone else. Nick's ass was a little tighter, his chest and thighs were bigger, his hair was brown and silky, and instead of waxing, he'd mowed.

Kane felt a moment's fear then that he wouldn't be able to do it, wouldn't be able to come. Oh Jesus, how was he going to pay his bills if he couldn't come on command? His whole life, the one thing he'd been able to do with any sort of competency was fuck, and he wasn't going to be able to do it!

He opened his eyes in sudden fear and saw Dex, the camera whirring in his hand, his eyes fixed on the viewscreen. There was no time to register expression or intent—for the moment, it was just *Dex*, and that's all that mattered.

Kane hardly had time to pull out and rip off the condom before he came all over Nick's hard, rippled stomach. He closed his eyes tight when he came and just let the explosion wash over his nerve endings like purifying fire. He barely registered that he was being pushed into the kiss for the end of the shot, even when Nick's tongue, tasting of Bobby's come, licked inside his mouth.

"Shower scene optional." Dex's voice was tightly packed—Kane heard it. "We've got plenty of footage."

Kane pulled away from the guys and forced a shaky smile. Guys were often a little lost after a shoot—even guys who'd worked together before and knew each other. Some guys, like Ethan, could kiss and cuddle, and it felt just right. Tommy had always been practically ready to go again, and Kane almost wanted to just rebound and go run a race with him. Chase had always seemed to need a friendly arm over his shoulder. Dex had had this smile, this sweet "Well done!" smile that let everyone know the touching time was over. But if you weren't with guys like that, guys who had their manner, their personal space, completely geared for the gentle disengage, things could get awkward.

Kane pulled away first and grabbed the offered robe from the gaffer (another porn model working extra shifts) and smiled, wondering if it was his usual smile or some other smile that stretched his face funny, because that's what it felt like. "You guys go if you want," he said graciously. He didn't do irony or sarcasm. He was completely sincere. "I'll sit this one out." Yeah, the extra money would have helped, but he couldn't do it. Not today.

Dex looked at his other cameraman and gave a little nod, and Kenny and the gaffer trotted off to follow the guys into the shower.

Kane sat down on the soiled bedspread before his shaky knees went out from under him. "Think they'll go for it again?" he asked disinterestedly, and Dex shrugged.

"Only if Bobby bottoms," he said, sinking down next to Kane. The bed jiggled a little under his weight. "You fucked Nick raw." He lifted his arm to put it around Kane's shoulders, but Kane blocked it clumsily.

"Don't touch me," he said gruffly. "Don't touch me when I'm like this."

Dex's voice was just what it always was, and Kane gave thanks for it. "Like what? Sad?"

Kane couldn't look at him. "Please, Dexter," he said softly, staring at his hands, which were clasped loosely in his lap. "Give me this, okay? Go away for now, but… but could you do me a favor?"

"Yeah."

"Be there when I'm out of the shower, okay?"

Dex nodded and stood up, carefully not touching him, and walked out, probably to upload the shoot into the computer.

Kane sat in the room gazing into space until the gaffer stuck his head in and said they were done. "You shoulda seen it, Kane! It was epic! Bobby totally bottomed—ate his own come!"

Kane nodded. "Impressive," he said sincerely. "Everybody done now?" He'd managed for that fifteen minutes to be nowhere in his head, and it had been wonderful. No thoughts, no Dex, no pain. Maybe he could keep that, right? Maybe he could just be… empty, right? Empty of sex and desire and come? Empty?

He stood up and walked into the bathroom, relieved that everyone was gone. He stepped under the shower, and that sudden blissful emptiness was filled, hot and tight in his throat and his chest, and he let the warm water loosen it as it sluiced the contact from his body. He thought wretchedly that he shouldn't have any hickeys or razor burn or bruises—he'd given. Given. *He'd* sucked, *he'd* fucked, *he'd* nibbled, kissed, handled, pushed, pulled, prodded, and stimulated.

He'd done that so he didn't have to feel anyone else's hands on him when they weren't Dex. His chest heaved, and he kept forgetting to move his face out of the water and sucking water in through his nose on the inhale because he was so busy sobbing on the exhale, and every time he tried to make it stop, it just felt worse and worse.

Suddenly the water stopped and there were two arms around his shoulders and he was left gasping on a shoulder covered in the gray sweater Dex had worn out the door that morning as they'd walked to work.

"I'm getting you wet," Kane mumbled, but he didn't try to pull back.

"I know, dickhead," Dex said, kissing his sopping wet hair. "You'd better bring me something dry when you're all done. I'll be here until five o'clock, you know."

"Thanks," Kane mumbled. "That's a fair trade."

Dex grabbed the towel from the side of the shower and started to towel off Kane's back and hair, and Kane let him. He just submitted and let Dex tend him, let Dex touch him, because he didn't want to make Dex dirty with his own touch.

When Kane was dry, Dex led him to the bench by the lockers and sat him down while Dex pulled the clothes out of his locker and set them on Kane's lap. Kane waited until he was done, then captured his hand. "Dexter?"

"Yeah?" Dex turned to him anxiously, and Kane smiled a little.

"There's really only one thing I want to put on right now. You got it?"

Dex's smile was warm and real, and he fished it out of his pocket. "Gimme your hand."

Kane put his hand out, and Dex held it steady because it was shaking, and slid the ring on gently, so Kane's skin didn't pinch.

Kane swallowed and nodded and grabbed Dex by the hips and pulled him closer so he could rest his head against Dex's middle while Dex finger-combed his wet hair.

"That got harder," he confessed and was relieved and blessed when Dex bent and kissed his head.

"I know it did," Dex whispered. "It should get harder."

"It never got harder for me!"

Both of them turned to the voice in horror, but it was Dex who moved first. "Jesus, Scott! You douche bag! Get the fuck out of here, you don't even work today!"

Scott smirked. "I came in to talk to John. I didn't expect to see something this sweet going down! Jesus, Dex, it's a good thing he's pretty!"

Dex lunged at him, and Kane stood up and caught him around the waist.

"Say it again!" Dex snarled. "Say it again, motherfucker!"

Scott looked legitimately surprised as he backed up, and Kane struggled to hold Dex back.

"I'd get the fuck out of here," Kane snarled. "Because if you say something to piss him off again, *I'll* go in for the hit, and I don't think your nose would survive that!"

Scott put his hand up in front of his face protectively, and Kane knew his expression was twisted beyond reason.

"Jesus, you two!" Scott snapped, backing out of the bathroom not fucking quick enough. "Lighten the fuck up! It's only sex!"

And then he was gone, and Kane was left feeling crumpled and lost like a condom wrapper. "It's not," he said, half to himself. "It's not. He's wrong."

Dex came to himself and he stopped fighting in Kane's arms and turned around to hold him. "Wrong about what?" he asked, and Kane started shaking again, holding his hand against Dex's chest and looking at the ring.

"It's not just sex," he said weakly, and Dex, bless him, Dex just held him in the echoing space of the locker room, and Kane gave it up and spent the rest of his tears cleanly on his lover's chest.

SCOTT was gone when Kane and Dex got out front. They didn't hold hands or do anything obvious, just bumped shoulders, but that was enough.

"I'm gonna go get you some clothes," Kane said quietly when they got to the big glass doors in front of Kelsey's desk.

"What're you going to do with the rest of the day?"

Kane had a moment of acute discomfort. He didn't want to be home alone, but he didn't want to talk to anyone either. Ethan had been a stellar roommate over the past two weeks—he did the dishes, hit the center of the toilet, and pretended not to hear when Kane and Dex had noisy New World primate sex in their bedroom. Once he realized that Kane was, as Dex stated in no uncertain terms, the grand royal prickweenie king of the fucking remote control and that Animal Planet and *Dancing With the Stars* were *not* optional, he'd been absolutely perfect. But Ethan wasn't there—he was out with Chase and Tommy, so it would just be Kane alone. And even if Ethan *was* there, Kane just didn't have enough asshole in him to sit in a corner and brood while a guy who'd been so grateful for company wanted to talk. So going home was out, and going to a movie alone just sucked. He could work out, but he'd already done a light workout that morning, and for once, he was just tired. He didn't *want* to do anything. He wanted to sit in front of the television under a blanket with Tomas around his arm, just being, except that would mean he would be home alone again!

Dex seemed to know exactly what his problem was, though.

"Go get your homework," he said quietly. "You start class next week—bring those new books in. If you have a problem, ask Kelsey or me. It'll be good."

Kane cast a furtive glance at Kelsey. "Kelsey?" he asked, feeling a stab of shame. She was a nice girl, but she was pretty and funny and quick with the words, and maybe she'd be like all those other girls who made fun of him in junior high and high school.

And Dex read his mind again. "Kelsey'll be fine with it," he promised. "No one's going to hurt you on my watch, 'kay, Carlos?"

And Kane nodded, knowing his lip was pushed out with a little bit of vulnerability. "I'll be right back."

After Kane had scared the shit out of the reading services lady, he'd made up for it by being particularly charming. She'd bent over backward for him, and he'd ended up with a bunch of what she called college-age hi-lo books. Dex had been the one who'd asked what that meant, and she said it was short for high interest, low readability—so books that would appeal to someone who wasn't a kid (mostly) and that wouldn't make Kane feel like a fucking moron. He could get behind that. After some discussion, she'd gone to the resource center and come back with what she said was every book about animals—snakes, insects, dogs, cats, chimpanzees, leopards, and wombats—that she could find. Kane hadn't been able to take them all home, but she'd set them aside for him and told him that as he progressed through the reading class, he could go through them when he needed to.

He'd been so happy he'd hugged her, and then Dex had hugged her, and she'd told them both that they were adorable. He had no idea what that meant, but it had made Dex wink at her, and that had been fun to watch too.

So Kane brought back a couple of those books (and some lunch, which Dex was grateful for) and hung out in Dex's roller chair, leaning the back against the wall and propping his feet up on a trash can as he read.

It was soothing.

There was background noise—Kelsey was constantly on the phone or talking to someone at the front desk, but Kane was mostly hidden behind the filing cabinet next to Dex's desk, and nobody talked to *him.* Dex would come by and put a hand on his shoulder or knee, and then he'd go out of the room again, leaving Kane feeling cared for, and for about two hours, he could almost forget that this job that he'd sort of loved for coming up on three years suddenly constricted his chest like a big fucking anaconda and he couldn't do a damned thing about it.

He was so deep into a book about primates and trying to sound out the word "macaque" (Mackakwee? Maquay? Makag?) that he almost didn't recognize Scott's voice until he heard something wrong with Kelsey's.

"Hey, beautiful, how's things?"

"I'm knocked up and it's yours, asshole. What do you want?"

Kane's eyes shot way, way open, and he very slowly took his feet off the trash can so he could hide better.

"I offered to pay for the—"

"Please don't say it. I'm pretending it's Dex's, 'cause he gives a shit and I don't want to think about how low my standards got. What do you want?"

"I need you to check the schedule. I sent John an e-mail, and I want to make sure he set me up for suicide boy's last spot."

"Chance is doing fine, by the way. In case you gave a shit."

Scott gave a disgusted sniff. "God. All he had to do was keep his mouth shut—he could have had them both on a fucking string."

Kelsey's deep, even breath rattled through the suddenly silent room. "Martin—"

"I told you not to call me that!" Scott snapped, and Kane wanted to cheer.

"Martin Eugene Sampson, you are on the schedule in two weeks for Chase's last scheduled shoot with…." Kelsey's voice suddenly lost the chutzpah she'd infused it with and cracked. "How in the fuck did you manage that?"

Scott preened. "By telling John I'd quit if I couldn't. Good. Let's see how his new Jethro likes him after he slobbers all over my cock and begs me like a fuckin' girl."

Kelsey took another one of those deep, even breaths, and Kane heard her work the phone. "Dex? Yeah. Get out here. You need to talk to Scott about a scheduling problem."

And *that* was when Kane made the connection between the guy Scott was talking about and Dex, and by the time he'd surged to his feet and around the file cabinet, Scott had already pushed through the glass doors at a dead run.

"*I'll kill him!*" Kane roared, and Dex got out in time to grab *him* this time, and Kane was pissed, because he might have caught up to the guy if Dex hadn't done that.

"What in the *fuck*?"

"I'll kill him!" Kane broke away and turned toward him, furious. "Do you know what he did, Dexter? Do you know what that fucker did? You can't do it. You quit first. You tell John you *quit* before that fucker touches you again, do you hear me?"

"He can't quit!" Kelsey interjected. "He runs the fuckin' company!"

Kane looked at her sharply, because for some reason, as much as Dex had done, Kane had never really thought of it that way. Dex had always been John's second banana, and that had been plenty smart for Kane. He hadn't ever really thought of how Dex was the one who made everything go.

And Dex, who'd put eight years of his life into the place, took a step back and caught his breath. "He did what?"

"He made John schedule you for a scene with him," Kane said, and he found most of his original anger surging back. "He… he just wants to fuck with you… God, he did it to Kelsey, he wants to do it to you! I don't get it! It's like Hector! Man, Hector wants to hit on girls and Scott just wants to fuck with people. Why do people *get* like that! It's like those stupid fuckers who spend all day on the Internet and talk trash about anyone else on the fuckin' Internet—I don't understand!"

Dex was breathing hard too, and his face looked like Kane's face felt—hurt and puzzled and desperately unhappy. "You're right," he said quietly. "I won't do it. Let me go talk to John. We've got to be able to switch this." Dex looked up at Kane and shook his head. "Today was hard enough, baby. I don't want to be on the other side of the camera again. I'm… I don't think I'm that person anymore."

Kane shook his head—he was agreeing with Dex, but it felt better to say no. "You can't. You can't. I don't like doing it anymore, but I can do it because I have to. You can't. You promised. It's the only thing keeping me together."

Dex nodded and turned, a surprising resolution on his face. "I'll take care of it," he said, walking away with some serious purpose.

He disappeared into the hallway, and Kane swallowed. God, he wanted to be in there.

"Kane," Kelsey said, something secretive about her voice. "Kane, you want to be a fly on the wall?"

For a moment Kane thought she could really do that, and he was almost shocked out of his rage. Then he saw the intercom headphones and realized that she meant listening in on their conversation, and that was almost as good.

He walked over to the desk, and she held up one of the earbuds for him while she took the other, and then, very slowly, she hit the button on the phone intercom.

They heard the door to John's office fly open and Dex's irritated voice smack into the room.

"John, seriously, man. What in the fuck were you thinking?"

John's voice sounded—well, wired. Suddenly Kane asked himself when was the last time he'd really *seen* John, and he came up with maybe a week after Chase had proved he was tough *and* stupid. God. Dex had told him John was getting wired, but Kane hadn't thought it was *this* bad.

"Dex… man, what's got you so… hey, did you see this? This bit with Kane? God, lucky you! He's so fuckin' hot! I'd like to get me some! And that Bobby kid—so hung. No, hey, don't shut that off! Wait, what did you want to talk about?"

"Scott," Dex snapped. "And me. Do you remember, John? Do you remember the fucking texts? The weirdo stalking? Did you completely fucking forget what I told you about Kelsey? Any of it? *Any* of it ringing a bell?"

"Man, get off my fucking back! I can't be remembering all your fucking drama! All you guys, with the who's screwing who and the I don't wanna fuck that! Who do you think you—"

"I'm the guy who's written the schedule for three years," Dex said, and he sounded… flat. Patient, but flat, like he'd been doing this for a while. "I'm the guy who told you when I wanted off of it. You're the guy who said I'd paid my dues. I filled in for Tommy a while back—it was a one-time thing, and I hired two more guys to fill in the ranks. Now I'm your go-to guy, and as far as I know, Scott hasn't done you jack shit in the way of favors and the only reason he's doing this is to fuck with me. I'm flat-out not doing it."

"Uhm…." John trailed off, and there was the sound of someone blowing his nose nervously. "Uhm… you know. About favors…."

There was a beat. And another. Kane desperately tried to figure out what Dex might be understanding that he couldn't.

Dex's "Oh fuck—are you shitting me?" was more sad than surprised. "You let him sell to you? *John!* Jesus! What in the fuck!"

John couldn't seem to stop talking. "It's just that I was in for a lot, Davy—I was. I was in for a lot. Scott… he… he just gave me some shit and then he gave it to me on loan and then he just asked this one fucking favor, right? And I was like, well, Dex gets it, and I thought it would be okay, because I know you *love* this company, and if I had to pay Scott all off at once, it would break us. I mean, you know, just fucking *break* us—"

"How much?" Dex asked, and Kane and Kelsey looked at each other breathlessly. Oh shit. This was their *livelihoods.* This was their *jobs* and their *families* and the thing that was keeping them the fuck together. Apparently it had been *Dex* keeping them the fuck together all this time, and John who had been falling apart.

John hadn't answered yet.

"*How much?*" Dex demanded again, his voice as loud and as angry as Kane had ever heard it.

"Forty K," John said lowly. "Scott's parents have the money. Scott'll forgive the whole fucking thing if he gets one crack at you in bed."

Kane heard the capitulation in Dex's sigh, ripped out the earbud, and took off down the hall.

He wasn't sure what they'd been saying as he threw open the door or how much he'd missed, but it didn't matter. He ran into the room and snarled, "I'll do it!" as Dex and John turned to him in surprise.

Dex shook his head, looking—well, devastated. Disappointed and frightened and just… well, wrecked. "I don't think your ass is for sale, baby" is what he said. "I'm pretty sure it's mine."

Kane shook his head. "What's he on for? Top or bottom?"

John looked at him, furrowing his brows like it was hard to remember. "Bottom? I think he said it wouldn't matter, but I figured bottom." For a moment John seemed to get his shit together. "I *figured* it wouldn't be that big a deal!" he said accusingly, and Kane snorted.

"It's everything, asshole! It's the difference between Dex being a whore and me being a balls-out pussyfucker. You better make sure you make that trade!"

"Wait!" Dex said, looking at Kane unhappily. Dex had to see that this worked, didn't he? That if Kane did it, Kane would control it. Kane would do a damned sight more than control it—Kane would make sure Scott never fucked with the two of them again is what he'd do. Kane might not have been that smart, but he knew a whole lot more than he used to about sex and power and pride.

"I have to," Kane said implacably. If they were alone, or if he could even trust himself to be gentle, he would have put his hand on the back of Dex's neck and given him a hard shake, just to get him to realize what he needed to do. "Sweetheart, it can't be you. Don't you see that?"

Dex blinked and smiled greenly. "Yeah. Yeah. I see. If you call him that in bed, I'll rip your balls off."

Kane nodded and shuddered, abruptly queasy. "God, yes! Fuckin' shoot me while you're at it!" Oh Jesus—talk about confusing the difference between fucking and love!

"So, okay," Dex conceded. "Maybe. But before you even call him and ask him—and don't tell him we talked, dammit, I don't care *how* stoned you are—we've got a couple things to ask for."

"Anything," John said, nodding. "I'll pay Kane extra—"

"You're not paying me a fucking dime," Kane snarled. "That would make it fucking worse!"

Dex nodded and without warning reached out and grabbed Kane's hand. Dex's hand was icy to the point of discomfort, and it was shaking. "You're going to rehab," Dex said quietly.

"Oh Dex—"

"I mean it, John. I fucking mean it. Before we walk out of here tonight, you will have signed up for a twenty-eight-day stint in rehab. I'll drive you myself, or I'm calling the cops and Kane and I are walking."

Suddenly John's mouth crumpled, and he ran a hand through his stringy red hair. It *was* stringy, Kane realized, and John's normally freckled face had broken out completely. He'd originally been thin, but now? Now he was skin and bone. God, he was strung out.

"You walk and this place folds," John said, and his hand was shaking almost as much as Dex's.

"I know it," Dex said without vanity. "I know it. And I need something that says that."

John looked at him oddly. "What?"

"I need a stake in the company, John. Don't worry. I'm not going to buy you out. But I'm going for the rest of my degree this semester, and the last thing I need for that pretty piece of paper? It's an internship. I have my name as a partial owner on this title, I don't have to do that shit, and the next time you feel like risking this place for a key of coke, I have a way to keep the company going and you can go to hell."

"*Dex*!"

"One hundred and sixty employees, asshole. One hundred and sixty people who depend on you for food, rent, and health insurance. If Kane hadn't been working this last year, his niece? She wouldn't have made it. Kelsey's staying here because she thinks this place has her back. I'm not gonna let you fuck those people over, John. The first thing you told me was that this was just people having sex, and that didn't make it bad. Well, they're good people, and you almost fucked them. You give me twenty-five percent of the place and we can make sure that doesn't happen."

John gaped at the two of them, but Kane just looked at Dex. God, he was worth looking at. He was a good person—*such* a good person. He took care of his family.

"This is blackmail," John said, faintly shocked, and Kane sneered at him in disgust.

"And selling Dex's ass to Scott for drugs *wasn't*?"

And of all things, *that* seemed to break through. "I didn't—" he muttered. "I mean, I didn't—that's not what I meant—I mean, I—"

"You bought drugs from Scott, John. You bought them from *Scott.* I've been trying to get the guy fired, and you went and bought drugs from him, and why?"

Apparently John wasn't arguing anymore. "It was personal."

Dex nodded. "Yeah. One hundred and sixty employees, and you almost flushed their lives down the toilet, and why? It's almost like a personal 'fuck you' to me! I don't get it! You need to go to rehab and get your shit straight!"

"Friends don't make friends go to rehab!" John whined.

Dex let go of Kane's hand and walked very close to John. Close enough for John's bloodshot eyes to have nowhere to look but Dex's. "You go to rehab, John, and I'll still consider us friends."

John blinked, and his eyes flooded, and he sat down abruptly on the couch behind him. Dex sank to a crouch next to him, and John clutched his hand.

"Friends?" he said, his voice still bleary but coming down. "Yeah. Of course. Friends. Dex—I've been in love with you for years. We gotta be friends?"

Dex closed his eyes. "I didn't know," he said softly. "I'm sorry, John, I didn't know."

John grunted like he'd been hit in the stomach and looked up at Kane. "I don't get it," he said, and Kane could tell he wasn't trying to be cruel. "I was just waiting, right? First you figured out you weren't straight, and then I waited for you and Scott to be over, and then you were, and… I was waiting. And while I waited, you fell in love with Kane? In a million years I didn't see it coming. How was I supposed to deal with that?"

Dex sighed. "I'm sorry. It sort of hit us by surprise too."

John's laugh was fractured and not really a laugh at all. "Yeah, well, surprise! Scott went into the drug-dealing business as an F-U to his old man, and I took him up on it."

"Figures," Kane muttered, almost to himself. It was common knowledge that telling his parents "fuck you" was why the douchefucker had gone into porn. That and the fact that his girlfriend liked it too.

"Rehab, John," Dex said quietly. "You call Scott and make the deal. I'll book you a room and call the lawyers." Kane hadn't even known that John *had* lawyers, but he guessed that must be the case.

John sighed. "I'm crashing, Davy," he said, his voice lost. "You'd better get me the phone, 'cause if I don't bump now, I'm gonna sleep for a week."

"One more thing," Kane said, and he moved behind Dex as he was sitting on the couch and put that hand on the back of his neck.

John looked up with a faintly ironic "hit me!" on his face. "Yeah?"

"Don't call him Davy," Kane said, knowing he sounded like a kid and not caring. "His name is mine too."

John grimaced and looked at Dex. "He's sort of a keeper, isn't he?"

Dex looked up at Kane and grimaced too. "If we can make it through that thing next week, I'm thinking so."

JOHN and Dex eventually picked up the phones and started dialing. Kane didn't hear John's conversation with Scott—he figured it would probably make him want to kill someone, so he left the office and walked Kelsey out to her car. Then he went back to John's office, where he pulled out his book again and read quietly while the two of them finished up their business. After a little bit, and after Dex had Kane flush the little row of lines on the mirror down the toilet, John fell asleep in the editing chair. Eventually even Kane fell asleep on the couch, the book against his chest.

Dex shook him awake gently, and together they got John up and into his Lexus. Dex drove them to a place with really nice grounds in a crappy part of town, and together (Kane was there mostly to hold John up) they managed to check John into the private rehab clinic.

John whimpered as the nurse came with the wheelchair to bring him to detox, and Dex turned to him with slumped shoulders and eyes that squinted with exhaustion.

"You're just gonna leave me here?" he begged, and Dex grimaced and sank to his haunches so he could take John's hand.

"You're gonna have to wait until this thing with Kane and Scott is over," he said quietly. "Otherwise I'm probably too fucking pissed to be much of a friend, okay?"

John nodded and looked away. "After that?" he begged, and Kane had to give it to him. The guy wasn't proud.

"Yeah," Dex said softly. "Probably. I'll be here. Maybe not Kane so much. He's a stand-up guy, but with what we're making him do, I don't know if he can forgive us."

John didn't have an answer to that, so they let the nurse take him away.

When they got back in the car, Dex got back behind the wheel. Kane didn't blame him—it was a nice car. They'd figured that they'd bring the car back to John's garage the next day and check on his house plants and make arrangements with his cleaning lady to come a little more often to tend them and the fish and… God. Kane was always surprised at the size of the hole a man left when he was yanked out of the world.

"I may be pissed at John," Kane said into the silent and cold dark, "but I'm not pissed at you."

That was the thing about Dex. He just kept going like he understood exactly what you were talking about. "I'd be pissed at me. You're doing the thing—"

"Yeah, but I'm doing it ugly, Dexter. Don't think I don't got a plan for doing something dirty with this douchefucker. Don't think that he's not going to walk away from this without feeling like he's going to need a shower for a week."

Dex looked sideways at him, his eyes colorless in the shifting lights from outside the car. "It's nothing illegal, right?"

Kane snorted. "As if. No. You… I mean, I never wanted you to see me this way, right? I wanted to be a good guy. But I'm still the same guy who fucked guys' girlfriends behind the portable buildings in high school. I still got that dirty in me. I don't want you to see it. I'll show it to Scott, 'cause he deserves it, but…." He trailed off. He had a plan. It was a simple plan, and it involved sex and humiliation, and those were two things he could dish out.

Maybe his sister was right about the porn. Maybe he *was* a whore. Maybe he *was* unclean. Well, if he was, the least he could do was keep Dex safe from other fuckers just like him. "I don't want you to see it," he said at last.

It was late, and the streets were almost empty. Still, Kane was surprised when the car swerved right there on Stockton Boulevard and Dex came to a halt dead square in the deserted parking lot of a Subway sandwich place. He threw the car into park and pushed the parking brake, then grabbed Kane by the front of the shirt and jumped on Kane for a punishing, bruising kiss that left Kane plastered to the passenger window and Dex draped across the shifting console and mostly in Kane's lap.

His mouth tasted… wonderful, and he was warm, and as the kiss faded and Dex fell limp into his arms, Kane realized he was exhausted. He wrapped his arms around Dex's shoulders and hugged him until Dex mumbled something into his chest.

Kane let him up and looked into his shadowed, squinty eyes.

"I'll look at you any way I want, Carlos," Dex said, his voice soft and passionless. "I'll see you dirty and I'll take you home and clean you. I'll be a part of your dirty if I have to, because I'm not letting you be dirty alone."

Kane's eyes stung, and he hauled Dex up to a final mauling, breathless kiss. "Thanks, David," he said when the kiss was done. "Take us home now. I need to sleep with you next to me. It's how I know we're good."

Dex let out a sad, tired little sound and sat up to start the car. "Kane?" he said once they were under way again.

"Yeah?"

"Nothing we've said or done today has made me want to give back the ring."

With a faint shock, Kane realized it was still the same day he'd told Dex to keep his. And the same day Dex had given it back.

"Good," he said, leaning his head against the car window. "That's real good, Davy. I told you, bring it on."

Dex

THEY started school three days later. Their classes were on Mondays and Wednesdays, and Dex turned off his phone for his three lectures, but in between? He spent his breaks texting to Kelsey to answer her questions, which she very nicely saved up for him. He got back to the house exhausted and ready to start his homework only to find Kane there at the kitchen table with *his* homework, reading alone under the one light in the dining room.

Kane didn't look much happier with his head bent over his book and his eyes dark and shadowed, but suddenly home looked a whole lot brighter.

Dex walked up to him, put his hand on the back of his neck and bent down and kissed his cheek. "Where's Ethan?" he asked, because usually Ethan was in his room playing video games or reading if he wasn't out with Kane.

"He's at the pet store," Kane said, looking perplexed. "There's some guy there that works for Tommy—I guess Ethan just goes there to say hi. It's… it's weird. It's like he's… stalking the guy, but not in a creepy way."

"Courting," Dex said, because Ethan had told him this too. "It's called courting. It's when you try to get to know someone before you get them to commit to anything serious."

Kane stretched and wrinkled his nose. "Well, that's stupid, because it has nothin' to do with fuckin' lawyers, and I think he's pretty damned serious as it is! He hasn't hooked up with *anyone* since before Christmas, and you *know* how that guy needs to be pet!"

Dex laughed and dropped his stuff in the corner. "Yeah, I hear ya. I think it's sweet." Before Kane could give his opinion on the sweetness *or* the idiocy of Ethan's approach, Dex asked, "Have you eaten yet?" and Kane looked up from his book and gave sort of a dreamy smile.

"No," he murmured. "I haven't. But just the fact that you'd ask that makes me a very happy person."

Dex laughed a little and turned on the kitchen light and then the living room light just for comfort. He started pulling out stuff from the refrigerator for basic pasta and salad. "How was your day?" he asked, and Kane started to tell him—and suddenly Dex's day seemed better.

"So I walked into these classrooms, right, and I kept scoping out the place in the back, but you know what? There I am in the back, and suddenly I realize, I actually wanna ask a fuckin' question, and I'm thinking that maybe next time? Next time I sit in the front so I don't feel stupid flagging the teacher down like you're directing an airplane, whattya think?"

Dex laughed a little. "I like that trick too," he said, because he'd staked out the places in the front right away. But then, he'd had more experience at this. "So, reading?"

Kane stood up and started clearing his books from the table. "Reading's not as bad as I thought. For one thing, I did what you said and went and talked to my professors after class. The two profs *not* running the reading class were real good—they gave me handouts and shit and told me that if I take notes during the lectures, the reading would be easier. The reading class was pretty awesome, really," Kane said, thunking his books down in a pile by his backpack in the corner next to Dex's. Hell, there wasn't anything *else* in that corner, right? "It was like… I dunno. I felt like I was *learning* something, 'cause I'm already better at reading that book on primates than I was when I started. I dunno, Dexter. I might not be as stupid as I was thinking."

Dex turned away from adding spices to the sauce from the jar and grinned. "God. It was seriously worth all this fucking hassle just to hear you say that. You have no idea."

Kane's smile back made his dimples pop, and then he thought of something and his smile dimmed. "I, uhm…." He walked back into the kitchen and leaned against the counter—out of Dex's way, but close enough to make the conversation easier. "I, uhm, called my sister and told her that I was in school."

Dex turned from getting some prepackaged ravioli out of the refrigerator. He and Kane had been shopping together a lot and had started buying the stuff they *really* liked, because it meant they'd eat out less. He set the package down on the counter while the water boiled, and turned to give Kane his full attention.

"Yeah?" God. Kane's sister. It was different, maybe, being exiled from a sister and a niece instead of a whole family. A sister and a niece maybe felt more personal.

"Yeah," Kane said, looking down at his feet. "She… she said that I'm still gay, so it doesn't count."

Dex sighed. "What the hell kind of logic is that? You're gay so it doesn't count? Is that like, your money doesn't count as support 'cause you got it from porn? I'm not buying this shit, dammit! You're a good fucking person!"

Suddenly Kane lit up. "And I'm a good person fucking, right?"

Dex snickered, because he knew it would make Kane feel better, and turned to lower the heat on the sauce. "C'mere," he said gently, and Kane did, stepping between his knees as he leaned back against the counter. Dex reached around and squeezed that delicious bubble butt with both hands and closed his eyes to touch Kane's parted lips.

Mmm. God. How had he walked the planet for twenty-eight years and *not* known that was what he wanted to come home to?

"Your birthday's in what? February?" he asked, and Kane nodded.

"Yeah. The eighteenth."

"We should go out and celebrate. You won't be embarrassingly young anymore, and I won't feel like a pervert."

Kane smiled, and it was still sad, but it was a good try. "You're still a pervert," he said softly.

"Yeah? What makes me more perverted than you?"

"You like my squishy ass!"

Dex laughed low, massaged it some more, and kissed him a little harder this time. "Yeah?" he asked. "Maybe tonight I'll make your squishy ass mine, you think?"

Kane's body went limp into his, and he knew that had been the right thing, right there. Sometimes a guy just wanted to be taken care of, didn't he?

They did normal things. They ate, and Dex had brought wine because sometimes when you were eating a dinner you fixed at home, wine tasted good and made you feel like the effort not to eat over the sink was worth it. They rinsed off the dishes and left a covered bowl for Ethan in the fridge, then went to the couch to watch television. Kane got Tomas out, and the snake coiled around his arm while Kane leaned on Dex's chest. Together they watched *Dancing With the Stars*, and Kane called in for his favorite couple. When they won, Dex could tell Kane was proud, like his vote counted.

That night, after the snake was safely in his new enclosure and Kane had washed up, they crawled into bed with the lights off, and Dex found Kane's mouth in the dark. Every touch seemed to whisper then; the pad of a questing finger on the plane of Dex's hip was as delicate and shimmering and magical as any of the raw erotic things either of them had done on screen. Dex kissed a line from between Kane's pectorals down to his belly button, pausing often to nip the soft skin of his stomach. Every gasp Kane made rang as loudly in Dex's ears as the requisite "Fuck me!" they tended to scream on the set, and when he engulfed Kane's cock in his mouth, keeping his lips loose so he could tease the underside of the head with his tongue, Kane traced the whorl of his ear with a teasing thumb, and it made Dex shiver.

When the time came and Kane could either come in his mouth or wait for Dex to come in his delectable, squishy bubble butt, Kane did a surprising thing and pulled Dex up by the armpits and kissed him. Dex kissed him back, and the kiss went on and on while the two of them ground up against each other's thighs like kids who'd never had sex before and didn't know what went where.

That's how they came, Kane first, when he thrust in the crease of Dex's thigh. His come felt good, so good, spattering between them, hot and thick. Dex's cock slid in it, and the contrast and the touch and Kane's teeth nibbling at his ear and his fingers pinching gently at his nipples all felt so good that Dex gasped and came. He came slowly, convulsing on top of Kane in painful waves while Kane wrapped his arms around Dex's shoulders and they shivered together in time.

When they were done, Dex made a move to go get the washcloth, and Kane stopped him.

"No," he said, and his voice shook a little, so Dex stayed. They'd be glued together the next morning, Kane with his nose buried in Dex's throat, Dex with his arm around Kane's shoulders, and both of them stiff from not moving at all, because even in the dark, when their bodies should have been limp and seeking comfort, they sought out each other instead.

The next day was the start of the three-day abstinence before Kane's scene with Scott, and Dex would have worn Kane's come on his skin for the whole three days if he could have found a way to do it.

"I TOLD you," Dex said patiently—and sotto voce—to Kane, "I'm going to see you. This is both of us."

Kane looked behind them to where Scott was staring at Dex, his hand down his pants, an evil smile on his face.

"God," Dex said without waiting for an answer, "I can't believe I thought I loved him. Are you sure you want to stay with me? I'm obviously too stupid to be worth it!"

Kane scowled at him. "Yeah, I say something like that, I get a fucking pillow to the head!"

Dex narrowed his eyes back. "That's because you're not stupid."

"Neither are you." Kane glowered right back at him, and for a minute, they almost had that little bubble, the one where they were the only two people in it, and the only two people who got each other, and the only two people who mattered. Then Scott spoke up and popped the damned thing and left Dex with nothing but the raw urge to beat his face in.

"You're both stupid!" Scott said, smirking. "Jesus, you guys. It's sex. We're whores, it's sex, and Dex, you'd better get over it, because in about ten minutes, your boyfriend is gonna be pounding the snot out of me!"

Kane looked at him levelly. "Jerkoff, you know what? That part about it just being sex? That could be the only smart thing you've said in your entire life." He turned back toward Dex and whispered, "And I'm gonna make him regret every fucking word."

Dex shook his head again and ignored Scott for a moment, his attention completely on Kane. "Don't do anything you'll regret—I mean it. For that matter, you can still back out."

Kane looked over his shoulder at Scott again and smiled so unpleasantly that Scott actually stopped stroking himself. "We're sorta committed, Dexter. Don't…." He swallowed and didn't finish the "don't worry" that was probably about to come out of his mouth. "Don't forget to give me my ring back," he said instead, and Dex held out his hand for it. Kane pressed it into his palm, and then Dex grabbed him by the back of the neck and pulled him and for a kiss before he rested their foreheads together.

"What'd I tell you about the ring," he said quietly.

"You'll tell me if you want me not to wear it."

"I promise I'll give it back."

Kane nodded. "Okay. Now I want you to start rolling when he sits on the bed, right?"

Dex nodded. "Will do. It's your show."

It was a basic bedroom—sturdy wooden bed, easy-wash plain cotton comforter in beige, white walls, blue carpet, a window with mock shutters and a view into the courtyard, a dresser, and a closet door with a vanity mirror on the inside. The door was kept open so the models could watch themselves having sex if they wanted to, and there was a spot on the floor that Dex had marked with tape so the cameraman could stand right on that spot and not get caught in the mirror if they were filming that.

But that was a sort of playful thing, something guys did when they were having fun. As Dex had started bulking up for his shots, he'd enjoyed preening in front of the mirror, and so had Kane. (Kane was, in fact, known for being a bit vain. Dex had to ask him to stop fixing his hair when he was hammering some guy in front of the mirror once, and Kane hadn't been the least bit repentant.)

Dex hadn't thought the mirror was going to get any use today—but he was wrong.

Kane walked into the camera's range and looked at him and gave the nod. Dex said, "Scott, we're filming in five, four, three—" and as he was pointing his fingers for two and one, Scott had just enough time to get his hand out of his pants and look at Kane with appreciation.

Kane stood up and without preamble took off his clothes. He stood for a moment right in front of the camera, semierect and magnificent, his arms and chest massive with muscle, every group defined and sleek, and his porn face on. He didn't smile a lot during sex on camera, didn't laugh, didn't look tender or vulnerable. In fact—and Dex had almost forgotten this—he tended to scowl and look like a guy you didn't want to meet in a dark alley unless you wanted your ass fucked raw.

So he stood there, imposing and scowling and beautiful, and he turned that sexual dominator's face at Scott.

"Strip," he said, and Scott's eyes widened. He had a grin—sort of a trademark smirk on his oval face—and he tried it on Kane now.

"That's it? No foreplay, no—"

"Strip," Kane repeated, not flinching, and Dex saw it. He watched Scott capitulate. That easily, Scott gave his power to Kane and stood and stripped off his pants and his shirt.

"Anything you say," he shot back flirtatiously, and Kane nodded, then looked directly at the camera.

"You heard that, right? This is his choice. Whatever we do here, he's chosen to do this."

Scott rolled his eyes at the camera behind Kane, and then Kane strode to him and planted his hand in the middle of Scott's much narrower chest and pushed back. Scott went flat on the bed and lay there, dreamy eyed, and looked up at Kane like he was expecting the scene to begin.

Dex felt something cold start in the pit of his stomach. Yeah, this was the scene, and it was beginning, but probably not the way Scott had envisioned it when he'd come up with this.

"Grab it," Kane said without passion. "Grab it and stroke it."

Scott had artistically long-fingered hands. When they'd been dating, Dex had thought of them as sensitive and had always used to marvel at how good they looked on a wineglass or curled around Dex's cock. Now they just seemed spidery and creepy, and when Scott wrapped them around his long, slender cock, Dex realized with a shock that Scott's own touch had always been the only touch Scott had ever craved.

His head tilted back and his long neck was exposed as he closed his eyes and started making nummy-nummy porn sex noises, and in that moment, Dex had a sucker-punch of dislike both for this business and for himself that he'd never, not in almost nine years, felt before. Oh God… Kane couldn't. Kane couldn't touch him, Kane just—

"Good," Kane said, looking down at Scott with contempt on his face. "Good little ass-slut. Awesome. Now spread your legs."

Scott reached behind his ass and spread his cheeks, exposing his hole, puckered and pink and bare of any sort of hair at all. Kane dumped some lube on his fingers and, without massaging or teasing, simply thrust his first finger in.

Scott groaned and started to beg. "God, kiss me! Kiss me! Jesus, Kane, touch my cock! Please, please, Jesus, won't you fuck me?"

In response, Kane dumped lubricant on the other finger and slowly thrust it in. "Keep stroking," he commanded, and Scott's noises got deeper, more frantic and more desperate, his body thrashing around as he begged the guy with two fingers in his asshole to do more than just stimulate the nerves in his hole.

Dex shivered, watching him. Kane's face was cold, remote, and hard. He had one hand at his side and the other one was thrusting slowly back and forth into Scott's ass.

Four months Dex and Kane had been having sex. They'd had hot and dirty sex and hot and kinky sex. They'd had it slow and sensual and they'd had it magical, where every touch was bigger than every breath somehow, where it felt like the stars chimed with perfection.

Not once had Kane touched Dex with this much contempt and this little intention, and half of Dex was appalled, just like Kane said he would be.

The other half was thrilled.

God, he was magnificent.

And on top of everything, on top of Scott's increasingly frantic begging, his hard self-stimulation, and Kane's brutally cold finger-fucking, Kane had an enormous, thick purple erection.

And Dex suddenly wanted it. In that moment, he craved everything Scott was craving, but the difference—the one pure difference—was that Dex knew that he would get it.

He'd set the tripod up behind him, thinking he'd set the camera down and go for some secondary shots with the other camera set up over there. Without interrupting the shoot, he pulled the tripod up and put it right where he was. Then he grabbed the other camera and set it up on the dresser, coming in from another angle, pretty sure he knew where it was pointing.

While Kane was engaged, stone-faced, in finger-fucking Scott, Dex tucked both rings in the pocket of his jeans and started taking off his clothes.

Scott suddenly yelped, then yelped again, and when Dex looked, Kane had three fingers in Scott's ass and was flexing them.

"Keep beating off," he growled, and Scott yelped again while Kane just kept hitting his prostate. Finally, after maybe five minutes of stroking, Scott's hand started to fly on his cock, and Kane watched dispassionately as he came all over his stomach.

Kane pulled his fingers out of Scott's ass and wiped them on the towel that was near the lube on top of the bed. He turned toward Dex then and stopped, mouth open. For the first time since the scene started, his face registered emotion.

Dex was naked on his knees not three feet from where Kane was standing. He was looking up at Kane imploringly.

"Please," he said softly, and Kane closed his eyes.

"Yeah," he conceded. He took two steps and stood proudly while Dex put his mouth on Kane's cock.

He tasted like Kane, and Dex didn't mind at all. This was his Kane, the man who cried over lizards and who sounded out words so he could study snakes and bugs. This was Kane, who watched *Dancing With the Stars*, and Kane who played Scrabble with Ethan, and Kane who gave Dex a shoulder rub when Dex got home in the not so forlorn hope that Dex would put out.

This was Kane, whom Dex loved more than he could possibly fathom and whom Dex was not going to leave to do the dirty things all by himself.

"Oh God," Kane groaned, his fingers tangling in Dex's hair. "Oh God, Dexter. I'm… I'm there… I'm there… I'm fuckin' coming, I'm so there…."

And he was coming, and Dex swallowed the first spurt and then pulled out and closed his eyes and let the camera capture the classic porn come shot, all over his face and chest, while he jerked Kane's cock to completion. Kane convulsed and groaned, and Dex sat up completely and wrapped his arms around Kane's hips and rested his come-covered face against Kane's ripple-muscled, soft-skinned tummy. Kane held him there, just held him, until their breathing evened out and they could say the scene was done.

Kane held out a hand and helped Dex to his feet, and kissed him, come and all, and then he wiped Dex's cheeks off with a thumb. "Why'd you do that, Dexter?" he breathed softly.

"'Cause I couldn't stand to let you do it alone," Dex said back.

Kane grabbed his hand—empty of a ring—and squeezed.

On the bed behind them, Scott grunted and rolled over to his stomach and glared at the both of them with unmasked hatred. "What in the hell—"

Kane jerked his chin in Scott's direction. "What's the matter, dickhead? You said it yourself—it was just sex. You got your sex with your ex-boyfriend's boyfriend. What are you complaining about?"

"But—" Scott floundered for words, and Kane's smile was so damned evil that if Dex didn't love him, it would have made him flinch.

"You said it was consensual, asshole. You said it was consensual, and we've got you begging for the world to see."

And *that* brought Scott surging to his feet. "You can't show that video!" he squeaked, and Dex reached for a towel and used it to wipe of his face, then wrapped it around his hips on the way to the shower.

"Why not?" Dex asked. "It's what you said it would be. I saw the contract, Scott. You wanted a sex scene with Kane or me—hell, you got me in there for a two-fer."

"But—but that was *humiliating*!" Scott snarled, and Dex didn't have any pity for him.

"So was being sold for coke, but I'm not whining about it now, asshole, because it's done."

Scott glowered at Kane and then looked back at Dex. "C'mon, Dav—"

Kane was suddenly right there and in his face. "Call him Dex or get your nose broke," he snarled, and Scott blinked.

"Fine," he said, his breath shaky. "Come on, Dex, just… throw me a bone here!"

Dex and Kane looked at each other, and Dex said, "Quit. Quit and go find another house. You don't work for *Johnnies* anymore."

"But what about your precious schedule!" Scott asked, outraged, and Dex shrugged.

"I do the accounts, Scott. If John isn't trying to shove the company up his nose, we'll be fine. That's my deal. You quit, we fill your spots, and you move on to another outfit. I've even got some places I can—"

"I'll find my own goddamned porn, thank you very much!" Scott snarled. "Jesus, Dex! It was just sex! What in the hell was so wrong about that?"

"Nothing," Dex said, not caring enough about him to be angry. "Until you start thinking you deserve more. Kane and I are going to go shower. You're going to use the come towel and go."

"Fine!" Scott snapped and turned toward the bed to start getting dressed, and Dex, who had made sure that he'd be the only cameraman for this one and that not even the gaffer was on set, breathed out a sigh of relief. He gathered his clothes and one of the cameras, and Kane gathered his clothes and the other, and together they headed for the showers. Dex couldn't wait to be clean.

Kane

IN THE showers, Kane couldn't stop scrubbing at his hands. He could have been there all day, but Dex grabbed them and then grabbed *him* and held him in the spray.

"You were awesome," Dex murmured in his ear. "You were great. You're clean now. It's okay."

Kane rested his head on Dex's shoulder, knowing that the wet hair would itch but not able to keep from doing it. "I was gonna do worse," he mumbled, because that had been his plan.

"Yeah?" Dex's arms felt so good around his shoulders that Kane didn't even care that he'd turned the water off.

"I was gonna fuck him," Kane confessed, because if Dex didn't know his heart, the shower wouldn't take. He'd be left feeling like his soul was covered in shit for the rest of his life.

"I thought you were going to," Dex told him softly. "What you did was better."

"I was gonna. I was." He had to know. He *had* to know. If Kane didn't tell Dex, it wasn't real anymore.

"Why didn't you?" Dex grabbed his hand, and dragged him to the lockers. Then, like he had before, Dex started pulling stuff out for Kane. If Dex didn't take care of him when his own head was up in his shit, did that mean Kane would end up wandering around naked?

"I…." Kane was sitting, dripping wet, staring at his hands. There was a big fluffy white towel around his shoulders and one being rubbed on his hair and thrust into his lap, and suddenly he stopped that thought. "You take real good care of me, David."

"Yeah," Dex said, looking pleased. "It's the only thing I'm successful at most of the time. I can live with that."

Kane smiled up into his angel-blue eyes and suddenly found words. "Ms. Darcy—"

"The iguana?"

"No, the real Ms. Darcy, the teacher the iguana was named for. Don't fuck with details, Dexter, I gotta get this out."

Dex had a clean towel around his own waist, and he sat down next to Kane, still and listening. "Shoot."

"So she told me that if I wanted sex to mean something, I had to put a higher price on it, you know? That's why I went into porn."

Dex didn't make a noise, but his entire face froze up like he was processing something really hard. That was okay. It had taken Kane a while too.

"And… and this thing we're doing, the thing with the house and the rings—you were right. It's not a joke. It's serious. And this thing we do with our bodies—when it's just you and me, it's… it's *precious*, man. It's not cheap. It's not easy. It *hurts* sometimes, how much I love you when we're together. And I just couldn't do that with him. I mean, it sucks to do it for money now. Now that I know what it's *really* for, it sucks to do it, even though it means keeping Frances and Lola safe, it sucks."

Kane's voice was rising, and he couldn't sit still. He wanted to hit something or kick something or just do pull-ups until this ache in his chest went away. He stood up and started pacing. "It sucks," he said again, his voice dropping because if he kept saying it, he'd just cry. "But… that thing… that thing I just did… I couldn't take that thing we do and make it dirty. I thought I could. I had plans, man. I thought I could just fuckin' humiliate him, and I couldn't. He got off easy 'cause if I had to do worse, it would have fuckin' broken me, and I finally have this part saved for you, just for you, and it's the best part of me, and I didn't want to—"

Dex all but tackled him, stopping him midpace in the locker room and holding him until he wept like he couldn't remember weeping even when his sister kicked him out and it was just him and a garbage bag full of clothes on Dexter's couch, grateful that he had a friend.

He finished and was down to the baby stage of hiccups and feeling fucking stupid when Dex made his night.

"You know what?" Dex asked, his voice sort of happy and skippy.

"What?" Kane wasn't letting go of his waist. They were getting sweaty and sticky, but Kane wasn't letting go.

"We take cooking class in three days."

Kane had actually been looking forward to that. "Yeah?"

"Yeah. The first thing on the agenda is chocolate-chip cookies."

Kane pulled back, absolutely entranced. "I *love* those!"

"I know, right? And we're bringing ingredients, so I know we're making them and not just getting a lecture. You want to take some afterwards to Frances?"

The world as Kane knew it was suddenly a better place. "I'd love that! She likes you, you know!"

It was true. They'd gone there two days ago, and while Kane and Lola had argued about having to duck Hector again while Lola was living in *Kane's house*, Dex had taken Frances on a heavily insulated walk around the block. She'd come back with flushed cheeks and a big smile, talking about Unca Dex and how she wanted a bunny. She'd been so excited about the bunny that Dex and Kane had taken her to buy a stuffed one, and she'd clutched it to her chest for the rest of the visit. The kid didn't seem that interested in snakes and bugs, but that was okay. Dex could be her uncle with the furry things.

Dex's smile was unforced. "The feeling's mutual. But maybe you and Lola could not argue the whole time. It makes her sad."

Kane shook his head. "Hector—"

Dex interrupted him then, which was probably good, because there was nothing either of them could do. "Hector's an asshole, and we're working on it," he said practically. "You wanna know something else good?"

Oh wow—there was more good?

"Hit me!"

Dex swallowed, suddenly way too serious for something good. “That was your last scene. Ever. No more porn for you, Carlos. You’re fucking retired.”

Kane had to make himself breathe, and by then Dex was talking again.

“I own a quarter of this company. I did the fucking books this morning, and you know something? We need another employee. You can draw a paycheck here being a gaffer or filling in for Kelsey or moving shit around or painting the fucking building. You don’t need to do that thing. Not for anybody but me, if you don’t want to.”

Kane remembered that feeling as a kid when he hated school—that summer vacation feeling. He had that feeling now, but better. Way the hell better. There was probably something wrong with it. “I should probably have some pride about not taking that,” he said after a moment, trying hard to make himself say it.

Dex shook his head. “You want outta porn, Carlos?”

Kane looked at him soberly. “God, yeah, David. I don’t want to fuck another person that’s not you.”

Dex nodded. “Then we’re going to forget your pride, and you’re going to work for a paycheck instead of per film, and we’re going to go home and watch that episode of killer snakes that I DVR’d tonight.”

Oh God. Was it really that simple? It had to be, because Kane couldn’t do much more complicated than this day. “Can we get pizza?” he asked hopefully, and Dex nodded.

“Let’s get dressed and we’ll have Ethan call it in.”

And oddly enough, even knowing that Ethan was there, a friend on the couch to talk to them about anything but the stuff that hurt the most, that was a cherry on the sundae.

“I really love you,” Kane said, and Dex pulled him in and kissed him on the top of his wet hair.

“I do too. Now let’s get dressed. You’re so fuckin’ vain, if your hair dries like that, we’ll be here for another hour while you try to fix it.”

"OKAY," Kane said, standing over the mixing bowl, "so more chocolate."

"No," Dex said. He was squinting at the recipe when he suddenly seemed to notice what Kane was doing and looked in the bowl. "*No!* Don't *add* more, we're still… oh fuck. Kane, you fucking psycho, now we have to double the recipe!"

Visions of tray after tray of cookies danced in front of Kane's eyes. "That's bad?" he asked, confused. "We *like* cookies!"

"Yeah!" Dex wailed. He grabbed a pencil to make notes on the recipe card, which was lying in a puddle of flour on the counter space. "But we like *good* cookies, and if I fuck up this recipe, they'll be shitty cookies. Acres and acres of shitty cookies, and we *promised* Frances on the phone!"

Kane looked at the recipe, then looked inside the overflowing bowl. He got out another bowl from under their counter and dumped half the chocolate-chip soup into it and started adding flour.

Dex made a sound like one of the mice before Tomas ate it, and Kane kept adding flour to one of the bowls until the mixture of butter, eggs, vanilla, chocolate chips, and sugar wasn't soupy anymore. In fact…. Kane grabbed a spoon and popped a spoonful the size of a small apple into his mouth, then closed his eyes and mashed the chocolate chips between his teeth.

"Oh geez… Dex, are you sure you won't hate me if I'm fat? 'Cause I could get fat on this. I'll just stay at home and—"

Dex snatched the spoon from him and scooped up a much smaller bite. "Now you're just bragging. Here, let me…." Dex chewed for a minute. "Oh God. Carlos, I think you've got a talent for this!"

"See?" Kane started pouring flour into the other bowl and turned on the mixer. Dex took another bite of cookie dough—this one decidedly bigger—and then rinsed off the spoon so he could scoop up little lumps of dough and put them on the cookie sheets.

"Did you remember cooking spray?" Kane asked, and Dex grunted, because it was *Dex*, and he didn't forget shit like that.

"Yeah, I remembered cooking spray," he said and then kept doing the little scoop thing until the cookies were all ready to pop into their preheated oven.

He'd just slid the pan in and set the timer when the teacher came over, and Kane, who was finally done mixing the second bowl, thought that maybe it was going to be to compliment the two of them because they got it all done themselves.

"Did you even *follow* the recipe?" The teacher was a plump woman with frizzy dark hair. She was in her early fifties, probably, and had spent twenty years teaching high school students home ec. Kane figured that was where she got her unhealthy quantities of sarcasm.

"No," Dex said frankly, "but seriously. Taste 'em. I think he's got talent!"

Dex gave the teacher the spatula, and she took her own bite. "Mmmf…."

"Good, right?" Kane wanted to know, and Mrs. Frampton took the spoon out of her mouth and looked at him sort of puzzled-like.

"Did you put more than vanilla in there?"

Dex said, "No," at the same time Kane said, "Yeah, why not? I mean, if vanilla was good, vanilla, some almond, some lemon, it's gonna be pretty damned good too, right?"

"Seriously?" Dex asked, and he sounded kind of admiring. "I wouldn't have thought of that."

"That's because it should have tasted like crap!" Mrs. Frampton said, appalled. "I have no idea why these aren't the worst cookies in the history of history!"

"It's because Kane made them," Dex said, sounding confident. "Anyone else, those cookies would have bit them on the ass. Kane? The cookies are his bitches. Just like anything else he cooks."

Kane flushed. "He's just saying that to be nice."

Mrs. Frampton blinked at them. "Sure. That's why he said it. Well, I dare you to remember how to make them again, but for now?

You're going to have to work out for another hour just to work off half of these, and that brings me great joy."

"You know," Dex said, looking at her through narrowed eyes, "sarcasm isn't a real plus in an educator."

Mrs. Frampton smiled thinly. "Sarcasm can be bribed away with a plate of cookies," she said, and Kane smiled happily.

"You like 'em, right? See that, Dex, she likes 'em!"

The teacher smiled some more, then took another bite of cookie dough. "He's pretty," she mused. "Is he taken?"

"Yeah, by me!" Dex snapped, and the woman raised her penciled eyebrows.

"Well, ten years ago, I would have arm wrestled you for him, but I'm wiser now. He's all yours. Gonna hand over that plate of cookies when it's done?"

"If you'd like them," Kane said, undismayed by the byplay. She thought he was pretty and she liked his cookies. Hell, he'd spent the last three years getting paid for exactly those reasons—the fact that next week she was teaching them how to make pasta made that sort of thing not dirty.

Suddenly the sarcasm dropped from Mrs. Frampton's smile, and she looked like one of those maternal women who should have taught third grade. "You *are* a nice kid, you know that? You take care of your boyfriend here—he's looking out for you."

Kane grinned at her. "Yup. Will do!"

Mrs. Frampton walked away, and Kane turned his grin on Dex, who leaned forward and licked some of the cookie dough off his lips.

"None of that!" the teacher called over her shoulder. "It's unsanitary."

Dex pulled back and giggled, and Kane giggled too, and Kane reflected that this could be the most fun he'd had in school, ever. He got serious for a moment and searched Dex's eyes to make sure Dex was as happy as he was. Oh God, it looked like he was. Kane felt his stomach do strange shit just at that thought alone.

Suddenly Dex jerked and swore and wiped his hands on his apron. “Shit. Phone.” He pulled the phone out and checked his texts, and just that quickly, the happy night, Kane’s reward, all of it went to shit.

“God. Oh God. Kane, Scott’s over at Kelsey’s. She just called the fucking cops. He’s raising hell.”

Dex looked blankly around the little kitchen thing and did some quick calculations in his head. Kane tried to do them too, because he could see they had a definite scheduling conflict. They’d driven separate cars because Kane had been coming from home and Dex had been coming from school, and Kane waited for Dex to come up with a plan.

“Okay,” Dex said. “So I’m going to run over there and see what’s up. You finish up with the cookies and take them over—but call me before you go in, okay? I don’t want you there if Hector’s there, Carlos. Any guy that would beat your sister isn’t gonna fight fair with you, okay?”

Kane nodded. “Yeah, I hear ya,” he said. Dex was right. Hector was a real motherfucker, and the last six months of Lola living somewhere else had only made him meaner.

Dex ignored Mrs. Frampton’s meaningful eyebrows from across the room and leaned forward to kiss Kane thoroughly. “Save me some cookies, ’kay?”

“Yeah, sweetheart,” Kane said, helpless against his smell and his pretty blue eyes and the hardness of his legs and the way the grooves at his mouth deepened when he smiled.

“Good. Love you! Like I said, give me a call.”

Dex was running away then, past the other students at their stations, taking off his worn white apron as he walked and pitching it in the hamper and grabbing his leather coat from the long pegboard by the door.

Kane watched him go with a sigh, thinking that he really did need to save the guy some cookies. Dealing with the cops would make anyone need some of those.

ROOMMATES

Dex

KELSEY lived in Carmichael, which was a nice suburb and all, but when traffic was bad, it was a bitch to get to, because most of it wasn't really near any freeways. Traffic was clearing up down J Street and Fair Oaks, but it still took for fucking ever, and Dex was irritated because he just didn't want that girl alone.

Dammit! Why was it any plan he made, anything he worried about, turned to shit? God*dammit*! He'd wanted a good place, a safe place—he'd wanted it to be like any other fucking job: you did it, you were proud, you got paid. Why'd Scott have to be such a fucking psychopath? Man, the guy wasn't even in the porn for the money! He had everything he wanted—a sweet trust fund, a girlfriend who liked the gay thing as a kink, parents to piss off. That last was probably how he was able to front John the coke for his petty little blackmail scheme, but Dex just couldn't figure out why he'd *want* to be that much of a shitacular human being.

Stuck in traffic, Dex was forced to remember that trip to Florida where they'd hooked up. He'd watched Tommy and Chase talking from across the patio and wished he'd gotten there before they became so close, because he'd been feeling lonely. He didn't want to cockblock Tommy, though—he figured he'd just hang back. And then Scott, who had that bitter sarcasm, had started talking to him.

"God, could they be any more *Sweet Valley High*?" he'd asked, swigging his beer. "So glad you know better!"

Dex looked at him—dark hair, dark eyes, perpetual smirk—and felt some pride at being jaded, which was soothing because he'd just had to have "the talk" with Chase (and Ethan too, if he remembered right) about not getting attached. It made him feel particularly shitty, like the guy who told folks there was no Santa Claus.

"Yeah," Dex said, and he waggled his eyebrows to make it a joke. "All sorts of things you know better in this business."

Scott took the initiative then, and oh God, Dex hadn't realized it until Kane first seized the back of his neck and told him to stay put, but that really turned his key. With Scott, he just knew that it made him more receptive, suggestible. When Scott stepped up into Dex's space and brushed his lips against Dex's temple, Dex's mouth went dry and suddenly he wanted to know about someone else's plans, and not just his own, because his own seemed to end so very badly.

"How about you and me, we just cut the shit and do the thing?" Scott purred, and a year and a half ago, Dex had thought that had been clever. He'd had eight years in porn by then. He should have known better.

God, all the shit he hadn't known about love then.

That invading his space thing, the "cutting the shit and do the thing"—that was what porn was all about.

The forcing a spot in your schedule to watch your boyfriend make five hundred pounds of cookie dough? *That* was what *love* was all about.

All those porn videos, all of those girlfriends he'd felt bad about not connecting with, and the one thing he really wished he could go back and change was that one bad decision about Scott. He'd been so lost, he'd thought that had been love.

He had to park four houses down from Kelsey just to get past the cop cars, and then he had to push past some cops who wanted to know what the hell he was doing there.

"I'm her boss!" he snapped. "She called me because she doesn't have family here. What the fuck happened?"

There were some snickers then, and Dex wrinkled his nose at them.

"Boss? What are you the boss of?" one cop asked, and Dex took a deep breath and wished Kane was there.

"Where is she?" he asked flatly. "She's scared, and I need to know what happened." *Ass. Hole.*

"She's in there."

Dex blew past the other lingering cops and found Kelsey sitting at her kitchen table, clutching her wrapper tight around her body to protect her from the draft coming in from the shattered window. When she saw Dex, she stood up, and he took three quick steps so he could pick her up and hug her—mostly because she was barefoot and he wanted to get her feet off the ground.

Dex didn't have Kane's bulk, but he still worked out for an hour and a half a day. He flipped her up, thickening stomach and all, into his arms and was comforted himself when she wrapped her arms around his neck. He remembered this from his "Yeah, I'm straight" days—it was still reassuring to know he could protect someone from pain.

He looked at the cop who had been sitting by the table, and found his inner Kane surfacing.

"She's barefoot and in her nightgown, and you're keeping her in a room with no window full of broken glass. Really?"

The officer was young, with dark hair and a face that looked like it had been scrubbed red, and now he seemed uncomfortable. "We're sorry about that. We were just trying to get her story straight. Who was this guy to her?"

Dex hugged her tight and kissed her cheek and then walked to the hallway. "I'm gonna put you down so you can go get dressed. I want you to call Ethan and tell him to get that plywood from my garage and get his ass down here so we can board up that window. Then I want you to pack a bag—do you mind sharing with Ethan? He might hug you to death, but I swear, Kelsey, your virtue has never been in better hands."

Kelsey hiccupped. "Yeah, baby. I know. Three gay porn stars—it should be the name of a security outfit." She rested her head on Dex's chest. "Thank you."

"Can you tell me what happened before I go out and talk to the cops?"

She was shivering, and Dex held her tighter. Dammit, this girl was his friend!

"He came knocking on my door—haven't seen him in *weeks* when we haven't been at the office, and suddenly there he is, drunk as hell, yelling that he loves me. I… I knew it was bullshit. I called you, I called the cops, and locked myself in my bathroom. When the cops got here, he was bashing in my front window with crowbar." Kelsey shivered. "Omigod, Dex—he was so coked up, he had to be hauled off in an ambulance!"

Dex shuddered. "Shit. Shit. Well… fuck." It made sense. Dex hadn't known he was using, but if he'd dealt to John, it was only likely.

"I just don't know what made him go off like that," Kelsey said glumly.

Dex got her to her bedroom and set her down on her feet, and she burrowed in against his chest like Frances—or Kane.

"He kept screaming your name. I mean, he's beating *my* window in and he's screaming your name!"

"Oh God," he muttered, feeling a little sick. "I do. Fuck. Fuck. It's all my fault—oh God, Kelsey, I didn't know." Scott had his pride. Dex and Kane had shit all over it. They should have seen this coming. "I'm sorry," he muttered. He leaned back against the hallway wall, trying to breathe.

"For what?" Kelsey snapped. "For not letting him fuck you over? Kane and I both were listening, Dex. I know what Kane signed on to do, I know why, and I know that video never went out. I don't even want to know what's on it—all I hoped for was that you two would still be good."

Dex nodded. "Fuck," he muttered again. "'Kay, what did you tell the cops?"

Kelsey shrugged. "I told 'em that he knocked me up and I kicked him to the curb, and he came back for booty call. It's the truth, right?"

"It makes sense, yeah," he said, but he still felt sick. "God, Kelsey… God. I should have known. He… he's a predator. He got me when I was weak, he got you when you were sad. We shit on his pride and he had to get us back. I'm sorry. I'm so fuckin' sorry."

He wanted Kane. *He wanted Kane*. Kane would find something to say that would make this feel okay. Not let him off the hook, just not make him feel like shit.

"Should we tell them the whole thing?" he asked, feeling lost, and was surprised when Kelsey shook her head.

"Fuck no. What's that going to get us, Dex? Gonna get *Johnnies* in the papers, gonna get John in trouble. John's in *rehab.* He gave you part of his business 'cause he almost lost it. No. You said it, hon—we've got people on the payroll trying to feed their families. Scott's not going to talk about this—not when he's down from his high, he's not. He'll take the slap on the wrist and go on his fuckin' way."

But Dex was not convinced. "Restraining order," he said, keeping his jaw tight. "First thing tomorrow. Restraining order on him for you, for *Johnnies,* for me and Kane. And you're not staying here tonight." He looked around the little house—it was tidy but not really decorated. The furniture was plain, there was maybe one poster in the place—Kelsey was a sweet kid, but it was clear she did most of her living at school and at *Johnnies.* "Let's even get you a new place, okay? I'll help. We'll move you somewhere else. I don't want him to know where you are."

"He knows where you live," she said softly, and Dex shrugged.

"Yeah, but I drew blood and Kane humiliated his cowardly ass. No. He's gonna go for you, because he's an asshole and he thinks you're weak."

Kelsey laughed humorlessly. "Yeah, well, I'm pressing charges and we're going to throw his weak ass in jail."

Dex nodded. "Good. And Kelsey? If it comes down to blowing us all out of the water or letting Scott off the hook? You tell the cops everything, okay? Kane and me, we got into porn 'cause we didn't mind having our privates on display. If we gotta do that for a little while longer, we can do that. I want Scott out of your life."

Kelsey shrugged and hugged him. "God, I wish you were straight," she muttered. "Don't worry, Dex, we'll do what we have to."

"Good. Go get dressed and call Ethan. I'll deal with Smiley the Cop."

Smiley the Cop was exceptionally dense. "So Ms. Belnap was dating…." The officer squinted at his notes. "Scott? She kept calling him Scott, but his ID read—"

"Martin Eugene Sampson, yeah. Scott was a nickname."

The police officer was not convinced.

Dex was still talking when Ethan got there with his own truck, the back full of boards and brooms and gloves and shit, and the cop was still getting it muddled. Ethan had started picking up the bigger pieces of glass and throwing them in a big box when the cop suddenly looked at him and then looked at Dex.

"Wait. Independent film studio? Independent film studio my *ass*, you guys are *porn stars*."

Dex smiled humorlessly and reevaluated the guy's intelligence. "Yeah."

"So when that guy was screaming your name, he was—"

Dex flushed. "I'm his boss. I fired him. It was ugly. He moved in on Kelsey, the receptionist, who never hurt a fly and who had her first office love affair with the guy who just broke the window. Look—you can do this big or you can do this right. *She* is innocent in all this. *She* never had any sex she wanted the world to know about. The rest of us, we put our name on a contract to have our bare asses on the Internet, but she didn't. Can we just keep this about a coked-up asshole breaking her window quiet?"

The cop nodded and watched the muscles in Ethan's arms flex as he swept up the rest of the glass. Ethan wouldn't hurt a fly, but he looked dangerous, and Dex laughed a little as the cop got intimidated just by watching a guy sweep a floor.

"Yeah," the cop said, turning back to Dex. "Yeah. We can do that. But…." The cop's voice dropped, and he darted his eyes both ways. "You guys got to sleep with some fine women, didn't you?" he asked, his voice throbbing with hope.

Dex hated to burst his bubble. "Yeah, but mostly off set. *Johnnies* is gay-for-pay."

Dex's best moment in the whole affair was watching the guy almost swallow his tongue.

And there, for a bare moment, he thought maybe they would make it out of the whole night okay, when the phone in his pocket buzzed again and Kane's picture came up.

Sitting outside Lola's. Hector's here.

Oh shit. Dex's nightmare was complete.

Don't go inside. I'm coming right over.

He's yelling at her. I can't let him hit her!

Call the cops! NOW! Don't go inside yet!

Dex looked up at Ethan and tried to hold his shit together. "Dude!" he called while the cop scribbled his statement. "Dude—you gotta take her back to our place. Kane's brother-in-law is about to start beating on his sister—man, I gotta fuckin' *go*!"

The cop looked up at him, actual concern on his broad red face. "You are having a *night*, aren't you?"

Dex looked at his phone, willing Kane to buzz him back. "I'm sayin'," he muttered. "C'mon, Carlos, don't fucking do this."

"Gimme the address," the cop said. "I'll call for a drive-by, how's that?"

The phone didn't buzz, and Dex looked up at him, almost in tears. "Yeah. Yeah, you do that. Ethan!" he called. "Give this guy Kane's sister's place!" And then he couldn't stand there and plan any longer. "I'm gonna go see for myself."

OH GOD. Oh God, oh God, oh God, oh God—twenty minutes. Down Fair Oaks, then onto I-80, then onto I-5, then off at Truxel, then… fuck. Fuck. Dex wasn't sure he could have gone any faster without plowing over someone, but he almost found out.

When he swung off of Truxel and into the little suburb with the big houses, his heart rolled over at the sight of the cop cars. Not car. *Cars.* And not just cop cars, an ambulance.

Oh fuck. *Two.*

And Kane's sister standing at the door much like Kelsey had, in a bathrobe, clutching Frances to her chest. Lola was screaming, and Dex stopped the truck so short on the curb he'd have a bruise on his clavicle for a week. He didn't notice and he didn't care. He came sprinting out of the truck toward the whole debacle, spotting Kane sitting in the back of an ambulance, holding an absorbent ice pack up to the side of his face, streaming blood. He was swatting at the poor girl in the paramedic's outfit and looking around for something that Dex couldn't fathom.

Dex got to him and elbowed the paramedic out of the way, stooping down and holding his hand to Kane's face before Kane even knew he was there.

"Jesus, asshole! I told you not to go in there!"

Kane beamed woozily up at him. "Yeah, I know. But he came out to his car and got a crowbar, Dexter. And he opened the door and I could hear the baby cry. I don't know… did he hit her? I don't know. I got out of the car to stop him with the crowbar and… I think I got a punch in…." Kane looked at his knuckles, which were split and bloody on both hands, and Dex figured he had.

"Yeah," Dex said, his stomach ten times worse than it had been when he'd seen Kelsey. "I think you got two in. And I think you got a crowbar to the head." Oh Jesus. *Jesus.* Fuck. "What were you thinking?" Dex's eyes burned, and he thought about the helpful cop at Kelsey's and how maybe if that guy hadn't gotten there, Kane would be bleeding on the lawn while Hector….

Oh God. More cops. Another statement. All Dex wanted to do was wrap his body around Kane's and never fucking let him go.

"You heard the part about the crowbar, right?" And Kane, being Kane, was not being sarcastic. He honestly thought Dex hadn't heard.

"Yeah, Carlos. I heard the part about you being brave and fucking awesome and fighting a dragon with a crowbar." Dex grabbed his hand and stood up, looking at the paramedic. Kane's face was bleeding a lot into the towel, and his cheekbone was swelling up. It looked bad. Really bad. And then Dex noticed that it wasn't just Kane's face but that he had a gash on his left shoulder and his left bicep and forearm. He'd obviously blocked with his left and led with his right, and his left arm just lay in his lap, limp and bleeding. Dex fought hard to hold himself together. He looked at the paramedic, who was quietly and competently working around him, and said, "You're going to need to take him in, aren't you?"

The girl—she was pretty, blonde, and maybe Dex's age—looked up and nodded. "We're thinking concussion, and his face is going to need stitching. We're not sure if his cheekbone is broken or not, and he might have a crack in his skull. He's going to need a whole mess of tests and stuff before they let him go."

Dex nodded and seriously considered going fetal on the lawn, but that wouldn't help anyone, would it. He just stood for a moment and stroked the uninjured side of Kane's face, pushing the hair back from his forehead and thinking that it was like that fucking deer in the road. Nobody saw it coming.

"I'm so glad you came," Kane said into his stomach after a moment. "I mean, I'm gonna be okay and all, but I was scared. I was scared for a minute. I mean, if I get taken out by some asshole like Hector, who's going to take care of you?"

"I'm sayin'," Dex muttered, closing his eyes. "I can't even make cookies without you. I can't look myself in the mirror without you. I can't look forward to my day. Jesus, Carlos. You gotta take better care of yourself, okay?"

Kane nodded against his middle. "Yeah. Tonight was a… an accident. We won't do this again."

Dex looked up to Lola highlighted at the porch and yelling in Spanish at the cop who was trying to get her statement. "What's her problem?" he asked, mostly to change the subject before he started bawling there and scared the shit out of Kane.

Kane listened for a minute. "She wants to know where they took Hector. I mean, I woke up on the ground and the cops were putting him in a car and taking him away. The ambulance guy helped me over here, but I never got to talk to her. I guess she's saying she wants to know how she can bail him out of jail."

Dex's skin washed cold and his vision went white. "She what?" he asked faintly, and at that moment, the paramedic tapped him on the arm.

"Sir? We're going to help him up into the bus and take off now. We're going to Kaiser, off of Cottage and Arden, do you know where it is?"

Dex nodded and bent down and kissed Kane's temple. "Baby, I'm gonna go get Frances, okay? I'm going to be mean to your sister, though. Can you forgive me for that?"

Kane looked at him with one eye covered and one eye needy as hell. "Make sure the baby didn't get hit, okay? It sounded like he was hitting her."

Dex clenched his jaw and nodded. "I'm going to be a few hours. Don't worry, Kane. I may fuck up in almost every other way on the fucking planet, but I'm not going to let you down with this one."

Kane squinted at him. "Don't go talking bullshit when my head hurts, Dexter. You ain't never let no one down." Kane closed his eyes then and groaned. "God, can we get to the part with the drugs? I hate to sound like a pussy, but this shit fucking *hurts!*"

The paramedic laughed a little and said, "We can start an IV once you're in the back, okay, sweetheart?"

"Don't call me sweetheart," Kane grumbled. "That's his name."

Dex got under one shoulder and helped him up, thinking that Kane was cold and probably going into shock. Dex was fighting not to just howl and push himself into the ambulance with him. *Oh God. Kane*. They got him lying down on the stretcher, and Dex bent down over him and kissed him on the side of his mouth that wasn't swollen (crap, it was all swelling!) and nuzzled his cheek.

"I love you, Carlos. You do me a favor and don't give us any surprises while they're running tests and shit, okay?"

Kane nodded foggily, and Dex jumped out of the back of the ambulance, and it was like jumping back into the world after being in a bubble in time. There were lights and people talking and even a news crew in the distance, and Dex wondered how they didn't make it to Kelsey's house and thought maybe Kelsey had just been lucky. This time the cops cleared for him as he made his way up to Fabiola, who was standing, angry and resentful, as two cops talked to each other next to her. The baby was doing that shudder cry thing, and Dex put his arms out for her so imperiously that Lola handed the little girl over without a qualm.

"Why'd he do that?" she demanded as Dex checked her over.

"She's got a bruise over half her face!" Dex snapped. "Did you see it?"

"Hector hit her," Fabiola said, that resentment still there. "We were fighting and she wouldn't stop crying! And Carlos had to go try and stop him, and now Hector's going to jail! He needs me to go bail him out!"

Dex looked at her, completely without words. All he could think of was business, so he went with that. "If you go down to get Hector out of jail, you're leaving the baby with me, and I'm not giving her back. If you leave the baby with me, Kane is kicking you out. In two days, we'll have all your shit on the lawn, and the baby's shit will be at my place, and since you didn't bother to forward his fucking mail, I'll wager you don't know where it is."

For a moment, Fabiola just gaped at him. "You can't *do* that!" she said, reaching out her arms, and Dex pulled back automatically.

"I'm taking her to the hospital," he said, making sure the officers heard him. They had suddenly become very interested in what Fabiola was doing, and Dex thought he'd make that work for him.

"They're not going to let you keep a baby!" Fabiola said, her voice rising. "You're nasty! You and my brother and those movies—"

"We're not in the movies anymore, Lola. Kane's out of that life, so am I. And I own part of a business, and Carlos is in school. And he owns this house, and if you go down and bail Hector out, you can't live here anymore. And we're taking the baby."

Lola turned her back. "Whatever!" she snapped. "You take her—you go make sure she's healthy." She ran into the house and came out with the car seat and a diaper bag full of clothes. "Here. You have her car seat, and her stuff—"

"You got a porta-crib?" Dex asked, and Lola ran inside to get that too. He wasn't sure she realized the situation yet. He was taking her child, and he was going to make it legal. Kane actually had a copy of her insurance card in his pocket, and Dex knew a really good frickin' lawyer. This baby wasn't going anywhere with the guy who'd tried to cave Kane's skull in, Dex was making damned sure of it.

While Lola was getting the porta-crib, Dex turned to the two officers. "Did you call the social worker?" he asked, and they looked at the baby and shook their heads.

"We didn't even know he'd had a crack at the kid—we just saw your boyfriend there on the lawn." The officer very gently looked at Frances, who was huddling into Dex's arms, and Dex turned her face to the light. The guy nodded then. "Yeah, you're right. It doesn't look hard, but she caught one in the face. Poor kid." The cop looked up and said, "We can call the social worker—it'll take one about an hour to get here. Do you want them to meet you at the hospital?"

Dex nodded. "Would you be willing to put it somewhere official? That she was ready to leave the baby with me while she bailed that abusive fucker out of jail?"

The cop nodded and then said almost confidentially, "She can't, you know. Once the social worker establishes that the baby was hit, those charges *have* to be pressed. And we *saw* the guy whaling on your boyfriend—he's going to have to have a hearing before he gets released, and bail is going to be pretty high."

Dex shook his head. "She's not going back into that home," he said fervently. "Kane paid too goddamned much for her to have to live with that."

The cop nodded. He even helped Dex put the car seat in the truck while his partner called for the social worker, and then he and his partner carried the diaper bag and the porta-crib and loaded them in the extended cab.

Frances was asleep in the back of the cab before he pulled up in front of the hospital, and he knew enough to bring the diaper bag and the blanket to wrap over her in her little pink footy pajamas.

First there was the nightmare of the ER—but he told the doc what had happened, and after Frances got a brief examination, the doctor said she'd be fine as long as she got some rest and some calm in the next few weeks. Dex told him that there was a social worker on the way to make sure that happened, and told the doc he'd be in Kane's room once he got directions.

He finally found the room and his breath caught. Kane was wearing one of those old cloth gowns, and it clung to all of his hard muscles, but that didn't stop him from looking young and helpless when Kane had never looked young and helpless. He had a bandage over his eye and his cheek, and some of the blood was still seeping through. His shoulder was bandaged, and his forearm, and there was even a patch over his eye, because it had probably been bruised too. He was sleeping, and Dex pulled up the chair next to him and sat down in it with the baby on his chest, suddenly so weary he could barely move. He had to move, he reminded himself. He had to.

There weren't any cell phone prohibitions anymore, which was a good thing because Dex had to pull the phone out and leave like six messages before he could rest. First there was the lawyer he'd recommended to Chase and Tommy, and it was a good thing Dex had his personal number because that guy was important. Then there was Kelsey and Ethan to make sure they were okay, and then there was Chase and Tommy, to see if they could help move Lola's stuff out the next day and box it up. Then there was social services, to see if they could forward him custody papers in the morning, and then, finally, there was quiet.

He turned the phone off and sighed. He'd had just enough battery to make it through all that. He checked on Frances, who was breathing softly against his chest with her fat little mouth open. God, she was tiny. She should be bigger at three, but she wasn't. That's why Kane probably still thought of her as a baby. Dex, though, had seen kids grow, had seen his niece and nephew and his little sister and little brother. He knew she wasn't a baby anymore. She needed a home that didn't scare her, and she needed preschool, and she needed people who would listen to her, and she needed…

She needed what he needed. She needed Kane.

Dex adjusted her in his arms and moved the chair so the back was to the wall by Kane's head and they would be the first thing Kane could see out of his good eye.

"'Kay, Frances," he murmured. "Maybe a rest for all of us, what do you think?"

She woke up as he moved her, and sighed. "Unca Carlos?"

"Him too," Dex said and made sure the blanket was wrapped around her shoulders and her head. "How 'bout you, ladybug? You want to come over to your Unca Carlos's house and live with us?"

"Pets?" she asked hopefully, and Dex laughed.

"Yeah," he said. "Maybe we'll even get us a bunny."

Around them was the whir of the hospital, but here, now that he was in the same room with Kane again, that curious bubble, the one that had covered them in the ambulance, that happened again. It felt like they'd worked really hard to make that bubble of peace, but damn, after this night? Dex felt like he and Frances and Kane really fucking needed that benefit. In fact, he was just going to close his eyes and listen to Kane's breathing and have a little faith that the bubble would last.

The social worker woke him up gently, a sweet-faced young man in jeans and a sweatshirt who looked like he might want to help. Since Kane was still asleep, Dex stood up and put Frances down on the empty bed next to him, making sure her blanket was tucked around her shoulders and the stuffed bunny he'd bought her the week before—he'd found it in the diaper bag—was cuddled up under her chin.

They got outside the room and started to talk about the time Brent Cavanaugh, the lawyer, walked up. Brent was a solid looking Mid-Westerner with a long face and a reassuring smile, and together, Dex, the social worker and the lawyer, they had themselves a little powwow.

The social worker was looking a little bit hesitant by the time Dex was done, but Brent was looking fierce and excited. "She's down at the jail now, right? Trying to bail him out?"

Dex shrugged, unutterably tired. "Yeah. As far as I know. Can you believe that?" he asked bitterly, because he still couldn't. "She left me the baby. I was just wondering how I was going to persuade her, and suddenly she's throwing shit out the front door and saying she'd get the baby back after she got Hector." Dex remembered his own father backhanding him in the kitchen and telling him to get out. "How do you just do that to your kid? Do you think you get second chances?" Dex Williams hadn't. They'd thought they'd have other chances to get it right, but they hadn't. They'd only had the one, and it had been a good one, they'd made it count, but how many of those had they missed out on because they'd been afraid to make a move? How many perfect things did God give you in a lifetime? Dex had seen the fucked-up ones—he'd *slept with* the fucked-up chances. How many perfect ones did you really fucking get?

Gerry, the social worker, was still a little green. "Porn stars? Two gay porn stars?"

"Not anymore," Dex said seriously. "We're not shooting videos anymore. We still work for the company, but not like that."

Gerry backed off and started mumbling, then looked up. "How do I make that look good for a judge?" he asked a little desperately, and Dex kept his temper.

"Tell the judge that Kane paid for the baby's medical expenses with that job. Tell the judge that he supported his sister for the last six months with that job. Tell the judge that Kane moved *out of his own house* so Fabiola could have a safe place to live with the baby, and that Lola fucked it up by seeing Hector again. Tell the judge that Kane just got his ass beat with a crowbar to keep Hector from going inside and hurting the baby. You tell him what you got to, but you make the guy see that Kane and me, we got a home. That boy can take care of iguanas and snakes and shit you ain't never thought of loving, and he can make them human. He can give that baby more love and more joy than she's had in her entire life. He's already paid his dues for her. Did you see the fucking bandages? Did you?"

Dex scrubbed at his face with both hands and wished Kane was awake and in there with him. Kane might not have said anything real important to the lawyer and the social worker, but he would have put his hand on the back of Dex's neck and shaken him a little and said, "Take it easy. We'll make this work."

"Don't you see?" he said into the sudden silence. "I know it's hard, because his muscles are the size of a fucking building, but hasn't he done enough good to look into his heart?"

Brent nodded. "I'm going to go try and find the sister. If she can sign the baby's custody over, there isn't going to be a hearing, and this will be moot. Can we do that, Gerry?"

Gerry looked troubled, but he nodded. "Do you two have commitment papers signed?" he asked suddenly, and Dex blinked.

"Like a wedding?"

"Just the papers. They make it legal. If you've got that, it will look better."

Dex floundered for a minute, and Brent looked at him and smiled. "I can draw them up for you if you want, Dex. Were you two heading that way?"

"Heading that way?" Dex asked, touching his ring with his thumb. "We were there! We just… Carlos and me, we don't do anything like the rule books, you know?"

Brent nodded like he'd figured this out. "I'll draw those up, then. You can sign them when you sign the custody agreement, and that way, if anyone challenges it, you're solid. Think Kane will go for that?"

Dex thought of Kane breaking that old cot at his parents' house. "I think Kane would be perfectly fine with that," he said seriously, and that seemed to be that. Dex shook their hands and went back into the room with Kane. It was two in the morning. He just wanted to put his head down for a minute. Just a minute. The space on the bed next to Kane's body looked bright and shining, the grail from a quest, and he sank down into the chair next to the bed and folded his arms there to rest his head and felt like maybe, just maybe, all of his planning and his details and his ways to make the world right had finally, *finally* succeeded.

Kane

THE nurses kept waking him up, which sucked, but they were real considerate of Dex sleeping next to him. Being able to put his hand on the back of Dex's neck and just hold him there was the one thing that let him feel comfortable in the hospital.

"Hey," Dex said, turning his head in his arms but looking too tired and out of it to straighten up. "How you feeling?"

"Like I got hit with a fucking crowbar," Kane grunted. "What in the fuck did they give me?"

Dex shrugged. "I have no idea, but you were out." Suddenly he smiled—just a quick lip twitch, but it made Kane feel better to see it. "Maybe it was just a sugar crash from all that cookie dough."

Kane smiled at him, thinking he was cute when he was funny. "Those were some awesome cookies. Hey—they're still in the car; do you think they're good?"

Dex kept his smile. "They're still in front of your house. I don't think we'll find out."

Kane wrinkled his nose. "Naw, you can go get 'em. Bring 'em back to the house for when I get out."

"When *are* you getting out?"

Oh God, shaking his head hurt. "I don't know. The nurse said they were going to wake me up every hour for the night—you didn't even wake up the first three times she came by."

That made Dex sit up and rub his eyes. "Oh God," he mumbled. "So much to do."

Kane reached out and grabbed his neck again. "Don't go running off now, Dexter. Please?"

Dex's attempt to go all busy seemed to melt, and he nodded and relaxed into Kane's grip. Good. Dex knew how to make Kane feel in control. "Just trying to make sure our home's in order, is that okay?"

"What's to put in order?"

"Well, we're moving Frances into it, for one thing, and I think that means that Ethan and Kelsey are gonna start paying rent on your place, because my place is too small and Scott knows where Kelsey lives, which means she's gotta move."

Kane squinted for a minute. "What about Lola?" he asked, and Dex sighed.

"I wish I could build a big old glass cage for your heart," he said, and Kane opened and closed his eyes again and tried to wrap his head around that.

Dex took pity on him and explained it. "I don't want you to get hurt, baby. This is gonna hurt. She was trying to bail Hector out. She can't live there anymore. And Hector hit his own kid, and she let him. She doesn't get Frances either. I'm sorry, Carlos. I called the lawyer and the social worker and everybody. If we can, we're taking her home with us, and we'll keep her. We can do that, right? I'm almost out of school, and we can get day care and shit. Something. She'll be ours."

Kane swallowed and nodded. Oh wow. Lola. His sister. He didn't want to think about that pain yet. But Frances? Frances could come live with them? She could be safe, and Kane could see her every day? That part was good. That part was *great.* He felt an overwhelming gratitude then, because Dex didn't have to do any of that, but he'd gone the extra mile again, just like when he'd made that special room for Tomas and the lizards.

"Yeah. 'Kay. Why are you doing this again?"

"Because I love you."

Kane closed his eyes. He hated words. They were never enough. "I love you back."

"Good, 'cause we're having a commitment ceremony in a week."

Kane's eyes shot open. "As in the loony bin? Which one of us is going?"

Dex's laugh sounded off somehow, but his grip on Kane's hand was firm. "Me, if you ever pull that hero shit again. But no, this is like, the closest thing gay men get to married. We have a commitment ceremony and sign papers. I think we can have the ceremony at, like, a justice of the peace or something. Anyway, we'll have legal papers signed and maybe have a big cake made, and people can come eat it at our house, and you know. Make a big deal out of it."

Kane was trying to look really perplexed, in spite of the bandages and shit. "Why we doing that?"

One side of Dex's mouth curled up. "You don't want to do that?"

Kane thought about it. "No, that's fine. I got no problems with that. Can we dress up? You'd look pretty sharp in a suit, Dexter. I ain't never banged a guy wearing a suit." The thought sent a tingle through his groin that he thought maybe he'd explore when he wasn't covered in bandages and doped up on painkillers. Bending Dex over in a suit would be *sweet.*

"I'll wear one if you wear one."

"Yeah, but we do that, we gotta wait more'n a week. I don't wanna be wearin' these bandages in that fancy picture everyone puts in their living room."

Now both corners of Dex's sweet Kewpie bow mouth were tucked up. "Okay, so, maybe a month, then. We can do it right. Buy Frances a pretty dress. Have it catered. Do the big cake. Find someone who wants to do a ceremony in the living room or something. Whatever. God, you make shit complicated."

"Yeah, fine, you're the one who suggested it. Why we doing it again?"

Dex's voice went funny places, and Kane made an effort to keep his eyes open so he could see that face—that long, almost girlishly pretty face, with the strong chin to keep it all boy. "You could have died," Dex said softly, and before Kane could protest, he kept talking, and Kane let him. "You could have died, and maybe three people in the world would have known who you were to me. You could have died, and I would have had to fight my way in here to have a funeral. I never would have seen Frances again, and I would have spent my whole life wondering how she was. I would have had to give your house and your car to your worthless sister, who, by the way, is not ever fucking welcome in our home or your house again, in case you were fucking wondering. I don't give a shit what people think about our porn, or our past, or two gay guys raising a kid—but they had better know that we're together, Carlos. Forget the porn and the business degree and anything else I try to do with my life, if people know me, they've got to know who you are."

Aw, fuck. Kane hated being stoned. It made him all weepy, and that was no fun at all. "Man, if one of us goes first, it's gotta be me. You're the only one of us who could survive shit like that."

"You know, that could be *the* stupidest thing I've ever heard you say," Dex told him, and it wasn't Kane's imagination, there were tears in his voice. "I think we need to have a ceremony because if you ever pull that shit again and I just drop dead, everyone'll be able to put a reason to it. 'Yeah, didja hear Dex got his heart ripped out of his body and died?' 'Sucks, dude! At least they'll be rooming together in the cemetery.'"

Kane squinted at him. "Great. So we have a commitment ceremony, both of us drop dead, and we'll still be what we started out as. Roommates. Fucking awesome. At this point, I'm going the long way around to bang a guy in a suit."

Dex's chest started shaking, which made Kane happy, because for once he was being funny on purpose. "Yeah, well, let's hope there's a heaven, because knowing you, you'd probably try to bang me in our coffins, you perverted bastard."

"Coffin. If we're going out together, we're sharing the same space."

Dex wiped under his eyes and took Kane's hand to his lips, careful of the bandages. "Great. So we're getting married. We're getting custody of a kid. We're gonna be roommates forever. Who knew quitting porn could change your life?"

Kane looked at him, serious again. "You knew. You're smart like that."

Dex shook his head and for once didn't say anything. He just sat there, cradling Kane's hand like a precious thing, shaking his head.

Kane felt himself falling asleep and blinked at him. "You should go home," he said muzzily. "You can't really sleep here."

"No," Dex said, settling back in the chair and closing his eyes. "Anything that makes us sleep apart is a bad thing."

Kane couldn't argue with that. He didn't even try.

THREE months later Kane woke up early, which almost never happened. He thought maybe it was the sunshine streaming into his window in the morning, which was great because it meant that Tomas and Ms. Darcy would be out basking. Frances was all set up in their room now, with a real little girl's bed, the Barbie kind, and she loved looking at the reptiles when they were awake. She also liked looking at the mice when they were busy. As of yet Kane hadn't told her *why* they had all those little fancy mice, but there was a reason he kept the bunny in her room and the mice in his. So far the bunny didn't seem to be able to spot the two reptiles in the room, which was good, because he was a tiny little brown dwarf bunny, and Kane didn't think he'd be so cute if he worried himself bald.

But they'd taken Frances to the zoo the day before, and she was tired out and, with any luck, would sleep for a long time, which was good, because Dex was warm and pliant with sleep, and Kane thought they might have some time to get busy. He liked having Frances and all, but he missed all the extra sex. It was okay. He figured he and Dex would still be pretty young when she went away for college—there'd be time.

Dex was snugged up against Kane's front the way he needed to be every morning, and Kane stroked the smooth skin of his stomach, liking the way Dex sighed when he stretched. Kane thrust his morning wood against Dex's ass insistently and knew he had the guy's attention when he grunted.

"Yeah?" he asked.

"Yeah. Absolutely. Here, roll over."

God, this guy really would do anything for him. Without protest, Dex rolled over onto his stomach and let Kane strip his boxers off. He pulled the lube from under the pillow, where they'd left it last night, and without a lot of fuss had Dex greased up and ready to go. Sliding into his body was sweet and easy, and Kane spent a lot of time kissing his shoulders while pushing into his satiny heat and pulling silkenly out. Dex started making nom-nom sounds, soft ones, not loud porny ones, and Kane realized that now that they were married and daddies and everything, the soft nom-nom sounds turned him on even more than the loud porny ones.

Oh God… that sweet space at the back of Dex's neck—it still smelled all sweaty from the night before, and Kane buried his nose into it and behind Dex's ear and then grabbed his chin and kissed him over his shoulder, not caring about the morning breath. Everything. Just everything.

Dex was flush against the mattress, and Kane could tell he was humping up against it, so he backed off and let Dex control the tempo, suspending himself above, still embedded in Dex's body and enjoying the glide of his tight clench around Kane's cock even more. Suddenly Dex scrabbled for the pillow and shoved it in his mouth, muffling his groan as he came, and all Kane needed was a hard thrust, and then another, and then he was biting that smooth, freckleless gold shoulder and shoving his hips forward to come inside him.

Being naked inside him when that happened was a feeling that was *not* getting old.

Kane collapsed on top of Dex and moaned in a good way, resting his nontender cheek on Dex's back. He didn't think about it much, but it still hurt, and the puckered scar was a surprise in the morning. On their wedding day, Dex had told him it made him look rakish. Kane had needed to look that shit up and was still all puffed up and proud about that word.

The wedding had been… well, easy. They got an old *Johnnies* graduate who was a Unitarian minister and a librarian now, and he performed the ceremony—with his wife and kids in attendance too. Kane was still blinking over that. Apparently some of the guys in gay-for-pay really *were* straight. Who knew?

Anyway, they'd had their friends in their home and had stood up, holding Frances in her sweet little dress with the red velveteen bodice and floaty white skirt, and pledged to be a family. Kane, who still hadn't heard from his parents or his sister, had gotten a little teary then. He'd made his own family when he really hadn't believed he could effectively take his own dump without help. But then, Dex helped him do shit better.

Dex had looked *so* beautiful. Kane hadn't really thought seeing his groom standing across from him would make his chest tight like he'd always imagined his *bride* there, but God. It was Dex. How could you look at Dex and not think he was the most beautiful thing in the world?

And now they were partners officially, but the best and funniest thing was that it felt like they had always been like this, and they would always *be* like this, and that the world would ebb and flow around them, and they would be fine.

It made waking up and making love in the sunshine from their window almost like church.

"You comfortable up there, Carlos?" Dex's voice was sounding a bit smushed.

"Yup." Kane hmmed and thrust again, because his cock wasn't quite soft.

Dex groaned a little. "I could probably do this all day, but I got plans, remember?"

Kane grunted and rolled off of him. "On the weekend?"

Dex rolled over to his side and Kane busied himself tracing the lines of come on his softening erection. It was a lazy, stupid, dirty thing to do, and it made him insanely happy. It must have made Dex happy, because his erection wasn't soft anymore, and he groaned comically into his pillow.

"Oh my God, Carlos! Really?"

Kane grinned. "Heh heh heh heh heh."

"Jesus—I got a meeting today, remember? It's important."

Fuck. "Yeah, why are you seeing him again?"

"Because we're still trying to be friends."

Yeah, well, friends showed up to your wedding. Kane didn't say that, though, because John's wedding present had been 15 percent more of the company for a total of 40 percent. Now that Dex was in charge, the place was doing great—thriving, in fact. And Dex wanted to go public. Kane had no idea what that meant, because the shit he'd done when he'd been filming at *Johnnies* had been as public as anything he could imagine, but Dex seemed to think it would make them a lot of money. So that's what the meeting with John was about today, and Kane was not particularly happy about it.

"So why do we need all that money?" he asked, and it was the first time he'd asked that, but now, faced with Dex letting him put his mouth on that beauty of a boner or rolling out of bed, extra money was not a necessity.

He was not prepared for Dex to get all serious, and suddenly he was on his side and close, so that their chests were only inches apart. "What?" Kane asked. "What are you thinking?"

Dex flushed. "Okay, I got this plan, and you can't laugh."

"Why would I laugh?" They laughed a lot, but always together.

"Because the only plans I've ever made that didn't include you went to shit."

Kane didn't really see that, but Dex kept saying it, so he nodded. "So run it by me, and it'll be all good."

"'Kay. So, you know how Tommy's PetSmart is going out of business, and he's going to have to transfer to one farther away in a couple of months?"

Kane nodded. There were PetSmarts everywhere, but still, it was a hassle. "Yeah?"

"I want to buy it."

"You want to *what*?" The thought of owning… just all those animals… it made Kane dizzy.

"Well, see—I figure this. We get the company to go public, and we'll make some money. I make some money from *Johnnies* and suddenly I can buy this other company, and Tommy can be the manager there, right?"

"Yeah. Like the guy who runs it, like you run *Johnnies.* Gotcha."

Dex smiled a little like he was gaining confidence. "Right. So Tommy runs it, and we revamp the reptile department in a year, and guess who runs that?"

Kane's smile felt like it was going to spread and crack the room in two. "Oh my God, *really*?"

"Don't get too excited!" Dex said, looking panicked. "If I can't do it, I'll feel like shit!"

"Don't piss on my high, Dexter. Tell me more! You got all this shit planned—I want to hear!"

"Well, we can put Kelsey in charge of sales, right?"

And Kane nodded, because Kelsey kept working at *Johnnies* just because her friends were still working there, but she was due in a couple of months, and Kane was getting antsy to get her out of there. "Yeah, can we do that right away?"

"As soon as she's back from maternity leave, if this thing goes the way I want." Dex looked concerned too. "And you know how Ethan's been watching Frances, right?"

"Yeah?" Because Ethan had been doing that for them, and they cut him a break on rent. He was great with her, and it gave him a chance to be loved for just being Ethan, which was something they figured he needed. Kane's old house had four bedrooms—they set up two for Frances to sleep and play in, but it was a whole lot of room. Ethan and Kelsey had been rooming together pretty successfully, actually, and the idea of Ethan watching her baby too made Kelsey really happy. Of course, they all knew that only people who had been in the business with Ethan would be able to understand why he was such a good choice to leave around children. For Ethan, life was all about being hugged. When Frances hugged him at the end of the day, he looked completely at peace, and there wasn't anything dirty or scary about that.

He still worked the occasional video, but that thing with the kid in the pet store seemed to be progressing beyond friendship, and Kane could see that Ethan's porn days might be over too—and Kane and Dex were pretty damned relieved.

And the entire idea made him excited. "So, like, Ethan could watch the babies—you know he's taking units, right?"

Dex nodded. "Yeah, right! So he can be a day care person and start helping Frances with her numbers and letters and shit. So Chase and Tommy'll have day care after their baby's born too, and Ethan can make a business doing that, right?"

Kane looked at him with big eyes. "Dexter, you… you got us all a way out! You buy that business and we can, like, give people a start after *Johnnies*, right? I mean, there wasn't anything bad being there when it was time, but… you don't realize it, but you're trapped there for options if you're not careful." Kane hadn't realized how hard it would be until he'd only wanted to be with Dex *ever*. "That's… that's a real fuckin' good plan, there, Dex!"

Dex smiled shyly, obviously pleased. "Yeah?"

"Yeah! I mean, you'll get your diploma and shit, but I'm thinkin' you already fuckin' graduated!"

Dex's shy smile popped his dimples, and his face went blotchy and red and so did his chest. Kane had a sudden realization of how much his good opinion mattered, and although he already knew it in a way, seeing it now, patterning Dex's skin and making him smile like that shy angel, it gave Kane the same chills he'd had when they were speaking their vows. Suddenly he smothered Dex in a massive all-encompassing hug.

"You done good," he said, his throat thick with pride and sheer, balls-out joy.

"I haven't done it yet," Dex warned in a small voice. "Remember, it's taken me nearly ten years to get my damned degree."

"Yeah, but you became a whole other person in that time, and he's awesome."

Dex started kissing his neck then, and his chest, his lips soft and reverent on Kane's skin and they just might have had themselves another round before Dex went off to conquer the universe, but they heard Frances's usual morning knock at the door.

Suddenly they were all about sliding on the boxers and finding their T-shirts and their sleep shorts and making themselves respectable so they could go be the daddies. That part they'd just had—the part when they were in bed, skin to skin—that would always be waiting for them. It was just private, that was all.

Kane got to the door first and opened it, and Frances was standing there in her pink floaty nightgown, holding her stuffed bunny, not the real one, and looking disgruntled.

"I'm hungry," she said, and Kane smiled because that appetite meant she was healthy, about as healthy as she could possibly be.

"What do you want?" he asked, scooping her up and kissing her cheek. She kissed him back and rode in his arms like royalty rode one of those chair things held up by peasants.

"Pancakes. Unca Dex makes the whipped cream."

"Yeah? Why not me?"

"You made it yellow."

Oh yeah. Last time Kane had used the wrong beater attachments and had ended up with butter. It had tasted real good on toast, but it wasn't whipped cream.

"Yeah, okay. Uncle Dex has to go do business—"

"After breakfast," Dex said mildly, coming around to Kane's other side and kissing Frances's other cheek.

She turned her head and kissed him too. "Cartoons?" she said hopefully, and Kane was going to say, "Yeah, why not?" but Dex said, "Want to help me make whipped cream and pancakes instead?"

She lit up visibly and decided to do that, so Kane set the table and listened to Dex give her directions. He did a really good job of that, and she listened attentively—and then sat and ate an outstanding-sized spoonful of whipped cream while Dex made the pancake batter and cooked them some pancakes. Sometimes when she smiled, Kane saw Lola in her, the Lola who'd loved him and protected him and made him feel like he was a good kid in spite of being chubby and slow, and it was getting so that didn't make him sad anymore. It was getting so he wanted to see that, because there was hope that maybe someday Lola could find her second chance too.

But Kane wasn't giving her Frances back—not without a fight or a compromise or something. Frances smiled with him, and he thought maybe he got to raise her as some sort of reward.

Breakfast was finally served, and they sat down at the table, Frances on her little yellow chair and Dex and Kane on either side of her, and ate pancakes. Dex made them with blueberries inside and strawberries outside, and Kane thought he could probably eat a thousand of them, but he only got through about five when the phone rang. Dex got up to answer it, and suddenly his whole long body zapped up straight like he'd touched a wire.

"Ohmygod, really? She did? Already? Isn't she like, early? Two weeks, yeah, that's not bad. Oh geez, really? The baby? It's okay, right? That's awesome! So when do you take the baby home? Two days? Yeah—yeah, we'll be able to help. Wait—what'd you have?" Dex rolled his eyes and grimaced at Kane, who was sitting on the edge of his seat. It could only be Chase and Tommy, because Kelsey wasn't due for another two months, and Tommy had been helping the mom with the Lamaze and everything.

Dex laughed then and said, "Awesome, I'll tell Kane!"

Kane bounded up, excited. "So, they had a baby? What was it? Girl or boy? C'mon!" Tommy and Chase had specifically not asked what it was when Mercy was pregnant. Kane thought this was stupid as hell and not something he could have done at all, and now he was losing his goddamned mind.

"You want to know?" Dex asked, laughing, because Dex had been able to deal with the uncertainty. "You really want to know?"

Kane stopped and glared. "Dexter, you really need to frickin' tell me, okay? I need to—"

Dex stopped him with a kiss, and then whispered in his ear.

Kane gasped excitedly, and about the time he realized that it wouldn't have mattered if it was a girl or a boy, Frances said, "What kind of baby is it?"

Kane went over to her and rubbed their noses together. "It's a healthy baby," he said softly. "The best kind."

Frances giggled, and Kane and Dex winked at each other. When Dex was done making plans for their future, the two of them would have to go shopping. Frances would come with them, and they would keep practicing this family thing, because so far, it felt like they were getting it right.

AMY LANE is a mother of four and a compulsive knitter who writes because she can't silence the voices in her head. She adores cats, knitting socks, and hawt menz, and she dislikes moths, cat boxes, and knuckle-headed macspazzmatrons. She is rarely found cooking, cleaning, or doing domestic chores, but she has been known to knit up an emergency hat/blanket/pair of socks for any occasion whatsoever or sometimes for no reason at all. She writes in the shower, while commuting, while taxiing children to soccer/dance/karate/oh my! and has learned from necessity to type like the wind. She lives in a spider-infested, crumbling house in a shoddy suburb and counts on her beloved Mate, Mack, to keep her tethered to reality—which he does while keeping her cell phone charged as a bonus. She's been married for twenty-plus years and still believes in Twu Wuv, with a capital Twu and a capital Wuv, and she doesn't see any reason at all for that to change.

Visit Amy's website at http://www.greenshill.com. You can e-mail her at amylane@greenshill.com.

Romance from AMY LANE

http://www.dreamspinnerpress.com

KEEPING PROMISE ROCK

GREEN'S HILL

LITHA'S
CONSTANT
WHIM
AMY LANE

GUARDING
THE
VAMPIRE'S GHOST
AMY LANE

I LOVE YOU,
ASSHOLE!
AMY LANE

Romance from AMY LANE

http://www.dreamspinnerpress.com

Romance from AMY LANE

http://www.dreamspinnerpress.com

Dreamspinner Press
For more of the
best M/M romance,
visit
Dreamspinner Press
www.dreamspinnerpress.com

Made in the USA
San Bernardino, CA
28 August 2019